Also by Jenna Hartley

Love in LA Series
Inevitable
Unexpected
Irresistible
Undeniable
Unpredictable
Irreplaceable

Alondra Valley Series
Feels Like Love
Love Like No Other
A Love Like That

Tempt Series
Temptation
Reputation

For the most current list of Jenna's titles, please visit her website www.authorjennahartley.com.

Or scan the QR code on the following page to be taken to her author page on Amazon.com

Reputation

usa today bestselling author

jenna hartley

ISBN: 9798870304892

Editing: Lisa A. Hollett
Cover: Qamber Designs

There is grace in
letting go.
Trust yourself.
Be fearless.

jenna hartley

Content Warnings

This story contains explicit sexual content, profanity, and topics that may be sensitive to some readers.

For more detailed information, visit the QR code below.

Playlist

"Shake It Off" by Taylor Swift
"We Are Never Ever Getting Back Together" by Taylor Swift
"22" by Taylor Swift
"I Knew You Were trouble" (Taylor's Version) by Taylor Swift
"You Belong With Me" by Taylor Swift
"Cruel Summer" by Taylor Swift
"Don't Blame Me" by Taylor Swift
"I Did Something Bad" by Taylor Swift
"Karma" by Taylor Swift
"What Are We" by Virginia to Vegas
"End Game" by Taylor Swift, Ed Sheeran, Future
"You're On Your Own, Kid" by Taylor Swift
"The Man" by Taylor Swift
"Paper Rings" by Minnz Piano
"Champagne Problems" by Minnz Piano
"Snow On The Beach" by Minnz Piano

You can find this playlist and more at
https://www.authorjennahartley.com/playlists

CHAPTER ONE

Emerson

Y ou've got to be fucking kidding me.
   I stared down at my phone, reading the email a second time.

> To: EmersonThorne@TheHartwellAgency.com
> From: NateCrawford@RainShadowProductions.com
>
> Dear Ms. Thorne,
>
> We need to discuss your social media accounts, especially regarding your latest posts. As Brooklyn's nanny, you must realize that your online presence has an impact on my reputation as well. Please confirm receipt of this email and affirm that you will post more appropriate content in the future.
>
> Best,
> Nate Crawford

"MORE APPROPRIATE CONTENT." I BIT OUT THE WORDS.

I'd dealt with my fair share of entitled and eccentric celebrities and pain-in-the-ass parents, but none of them compared to Nate Crawford. He was unbelievable.

I sighed and turned my phone on silent before returning it to my bag along with my foam roller. I'd been putting up with Nate's bullshit for months, and I was over it.

I didn't care that he was my boss or a billionaire. I didn't even care that he'd been my celebrity crush once upon a time or that his eleven-year-old daughter was quite possibly my favorite human ever. He'd gone too far this time. He'd pushed me too hard for too long, and I was done.

More appropriate content.

What exactly had bothered him about my content? Was it the fact that I was wearing a bikini in some of my photos, or was he objecting to my hurdle challenges and technique demonstrations? I mean, really. It wasn't as if I was posting naked photos of myself or hateful speech or anything but encouragement and empowerment.

"Hey, Em," Dad said, setting his bag down on the bench. "I noticed you didn't log your calories for breakfast. Everything okay?"

"It's fine." I ignored the tension building behind my temples and smothered my feelings about Nate—for now.

If I told my dad, he'd only reiterate *yet again* his disapproval of my nannying job. Of my boss. He didn't like how Nate treated me. But more than that, he didn't like anything that distracted from my training.

It was pointless to argue otherwise, even if the job was great. Brooklyn was a delight; the house was incredible. The gym especially was fucking amazing—it had a sauna, a yoga room with walls covered in live plants, a cold plunge tub, and all the equipment a heptathlete like me could ever need.

There was just one problem: Nate.

A man who was both insanely attractive and intensely irritating.

It was as if my body had yet to get the signal that we didn't like him. It didn't matter that Nate seemed intent on making my life miserable. That he was off-limits. I'd been watching the man act for years, and while I knew he wasn't the same person as the characters he portrayed on-screen, in a way, I felt like I'd known him longer than I had.

I'd catch glimpses of Tate from *Home Along the Bay* or Ryder from *Prairie Canyon*—brave, heroic, kind, men. But most of the time, as my boss, Nate was guarded, aloof. I got the feeling it was just another façade. Another role to play. I felt as if I only saw the real Nate when he was interacting with his daughter.

I stood and dusted off my hands. The only thing stopping me from ripping Nate a new one right this second was the fact that he was out of town. And despite his insistence on communicating via email—rule number one—this was a conversation we were going to have face-to-face.

Fuck the rules.

Hell, the moment I'd seen Nate's "house rules," I should've known he'd be a pain in the ass. Most parents I'd worked for had some guidelines regarding expectations for living in their houses or caring for their kids. That wasn't unusual.

But Nate's rules...well, they'd certainly taken the cake.

Rule Number One: I was to communicate with Nate solely via email, despite the fact that I was *living* in his house.

Rule Number Two: Nate's bedroom was off-limits. *Okay. Fine.*

Rule Number Three: When I was off, I was expected to stay out of sight.

There were a few others, but those were the ones I found most offensive.

He was coming home from Canada tomorrow. He'd

flown there earlier in the week to put out the latest fire with an action movie his production company was making. He wasn't acting in it this time, but as the executive producer and studio head, he sometimes traveled to visit a set. Especially when problems arose. And lately, it seemed there had been a lot of problems.

I tightened my ponytail as I stared out at the University of California, Los Angeles training field. I set up my tripod so it would be ready to film snippets of my workout that I could later splice into a short video.

"I should've known you'd already have your camera set up." Dad chuckled. "Did you at least finish your warm-up and stretches before posting on Instagram?"

"Yes." I mean, seriously? I knew my dad was likely teasing, but why did the men in my life think I was so incompetent? And why did they care so much about my social media?

Nate was my boss, and he paid me to do a job. That didn't give him the right to dictate my personal life. And had Dad forgotten that my Instagram selfies were a big reason I'd attracted so many sponsors?

If only I could get Hermès to sponsor me. I sighed. Then I wouldn't constantly have to scan resale sites for the off chance someone would list the Birkin bag I'd been coveting in Rouge. It was damn near impossible to buy one from a trusted reseller, let alone directly from the Hermès boutique.

I tried to focus on that instead of my frustration. The big picture instead of my current situation.

Dad explained the drills, and I worked through them. All the while, my head was stuck on Nate. God, he was such an ass.

For months, I'd tried to adhere to his rules. I'd tried to be polite and professional, but the man seemed determined to drive me over the edge. He hadn't fired me—yet. How could he? I'd done everything he'd asked and then some. And his daughter loved me.

But if he didn't pull his head out of his ass, and soon, I was tempted to ask the Hartwell Agency for a different placement. Sometimes I wondered if that was Nate's goal. Though I had no idea why. What could I have possibly done to make him dislike me with such intensity?

Because even now, three months in, Nate continued to act as if he was personally offended by my presence. We were polite to each other in front of Brooklyn. Otherwise, we did our best to avoid each other. I made myself scarce on my days off—rule number three. But it was difficult, if not impossible, to avoid him completely when my room was just down the hall and I was caring for his daughter.

And his emails...those fucking emails. My hands shook just thinking of them. It was as if he was trying to micromanage me to failure. I'd never had a parent who was so *involved*...for lack of a better word. And that was putting it nicely.

He was so different from the charming man on-screen. Nothing like the man rumored to have women dropping their panties faster than you could say "Golden Globes."

Hell, once upon a time, I'd wanted to play with *his* Golden Globes. But ever since I'd been hired as his nanny, his demeanor was so chilly, it was as if I'd submerged myself in an ice bath like I sometimes did during recovery.

Painfully cold, harsh, and unrelenting.

It made me wonder how an asshole like Nate had ended up with such an awesome kid. Brooklyn was funny, sassy, confident, but also kind. Just thinking of her made me smile.

"Focus, Emmy," Dad called as I headed around the track again.

Tap-tap. Tap-tap. Inhale. Tap-tap. Exhale.

I was so sick and tired of Nate's fucking emails. I

clenched my fists. Why couldn't he just talk to me? Was I truly that repulsive?

That was how he made me feel. Like I was nothing more than a piece of gum stuck to his shoe. At first, I'd thought maybe it was a "staff" thing. He wasn't the first rich client I'd worked for. And I got that he was under a lot of pressure.

But I also saw the way he treated his chef Andre and his house manager Belinda and the others in his employ. He was polite, grateful, warm. Even when he didn't like what Jackson or his team from Hudson Security had to say, Nate was still professional.

But with me, he was distant and cold. Sometimes condescending, and I was over it.

"Visualize the competition."

Instead, I imagined pounding Nate's face into the track every time one of my feet struck the ground.

"Lighter steps," Dad called. "You want to fly down the track, not stomp it to death."

Right. I took a deep breath. *Okay, Emmy. You've got this.*

If I didn't, Dad would just tell me to do it again. And again. *And again.* The sooner I got it right, the sooner I could be done.

I tried to focus on the rhythm of my shoes as they connected with the track. Inhale slowly. Let it out slowly. Inhale. Exhale.

I made another lap around the training field as the sun poured down on me. Sweat dripped down my back, and I made another, my body moving on autopilot after years of doing these exercises.

I visualized running in a competition. Women on either side of me. I imagined a crowd in the stands. I blocked them out. I shut out everything and tried to focus on the race. I made it a few meters, but then the crowd started laughing.

Their taunts growing louder and louder as they chanted, "Loser. Loser. Loser."

I squeezed my eyes shut briefly and tried to center myself. *Focus on your body. Block out your thoughts.*

But my pulse charged ahead, my heart climbing into my throat until I thought I was going to be sick.

"Now is not the time to back off," Dad said, and I got the feeling he was referring to more than my speed on the track. "Keep going. Keep pushing."

I tried. I really did. But finally, I stopped, doubling over and placing my hands on my thighs. Spots danced in my vision, and I nearly collapsed to the ground.

It's not real. It's not…real.

Maybe if I repeated it often enough, my brain would believe it. But I'd been trying for months, and I still couldn't seem to get it through my head.

When I glanced up, Dad was frowning from the sideline. I took my time, walking around the track to cool down. To give myself a moment.

"What happened?" Dad asked when I finally approached for some water.

"Just…" I lifted a shoulder. "Got in my head."

"Mm." He glanced down at his tablet, making notes. "You mean you let other people's opinions get in your head."

I huffed, drying my face and neck with a towel. Sometimes having my dad as my coach was a blessing and a curse. Like now—when he saw too much and knew me too well.

My dads had always encouraged my twin Astrid and me in anything we'd wanted to pursue. But they'd invested a lot of time, money, and energy into my career. Dad especially had devoted himself to it, to me. It was our thing.

But lately, I couldn't shake the feeling that I was a disappointment. Or worse, a failure.

"Come on, Emmy." He lifted his baseball hat with a hawk

embroidered on the front—a reminder of the years he'd spent playing pro hockey for the Hollywood Hawks—and scratched his head. "We've talked about this. It was one race. You weren't ready then, but you are now."

Was I?

I'd torn my plantar fascia nearly a year ago. Since then, I'd rehabbed my body. Improved my technique. I should've been at the top of my game, yet I wasn't.

The ironic part was that it wasn't even the fear of pain or reinjury holding me back. No, my mental game was trashed because the first time I'd tried competing after my injury, I'd had the worst showing in my entire career. I hadn't competed since.

"Don't let that one race define you. Define your career." Perhaps sensing I remained unconvinced, he added, "What would Taylor say?"

I smiled, thinking of my idol Taylor Swift. "Shake it off," I muttered, shaking out my wrists as if to loosen the bad mojo that seemed to haunt me since that race.

"What was that?" Dad held a hand up to his ear, a smile teasing his lips.

"I said…" I dragged out the word. "Shake it off."

"You can give me more than that," he taunted.

I belted out some of the lyrics, complete with a few dance moves. Dad joined my dance party, and I instantly felt better. Taylor's music might not solve all my problems, but her songs helped me forget. Even if only for a moment.

"That's right." He nodded as a passerby whistled their appreciation. "You can do this. You can shake off that experience and dominate. I know you can."

I appreciated his faith in me, but I wasn't sure I even wanted to compete anymore. I'd accomplished all my goals and then some—four-time All-American, two Olympic gold medals, and enough trophies to fill an entire room. I'd hinted at wanting to retire before but never outright said it.

"I made you an appointment with another sports psychologist," he said.

I moved into my stretching routine so I wouldn't have to face him. *This.* He'd spent years training me, molding me into a successful athlete. But every day, this felt more like his dream and less like mine.

I was honestly happier not competing than I had been in years. Traveling for competitions was exhausting. I had other things I wanted to pursue, like designing an inclusive and adaptive athleisure line. And so many other opportunities I'd had to put on the back burner because they'd take too much time away from my training—Dad's words, not mine.

Not to mention just living life. I wanted to stay up late every so often. Go to parties. Drink alcohol. Normal things I'd missed out on in my late teens and early twenties because I'd been training for the Olympics.

"I'm done," I said in a quiet voice. Hesitant despite how freeing it felt to admit those words aloud.

"You've said that before," he said, brushing off my comment.

He was right, but I shook my head. "It's different. I mean it this time."

He stilled, perhaps sensing my sincerity. "Look, Em. I know you're nervous, but we've got this. You will be ready for the USATF Indoor Championships by the time February rolls around. I promise. You just need to stay focused."

I appreciated his confidence, but I wasn't sure I had it in me.

"I'm just…so tired." I slumped.

He narrowed his eyes, crossing his arms over his chest. "Yeah, because that boss of yours works you too hard."

"Dad," I chided. "We've talked about this."

I didn't want to quit. I couldn't quit. My sponsorships brought in some money, but they didn't give me that sense of fulfillment that nannying did.

Besides, even if Nate was an ass, I couldn't do that to Brooklyn. But something had to give. He gave me a pointed look, so I said, "I'm not quitting my job."

"But you'll quit on your goals?" *Ouch.* I tried not to wince.

"I'm not. I'm...ready to transition to something new."

"That's just it. You don't have to. Not yet. There will still be time for your clothing line and whatever else you want to do later."

"I'm tired of waiting," I said. He'd been telling me the same thing for years.

I'd put off dreams of traveling, starting other projects, just...not being so regimented about every fucking thing.

"We've worked so hard for this. Are you really willing to throw it all away? And for what?" He threw his hands in the air, his tone growing agitated. "Something you aren't even sure will work out?"

His words stung. And while I knew he'd only said them because he was upset, that didn't lessen the hurt. Deep down, I suspected he was just trying to motivate me, but I hated when he got like this. It had happened more often lately, and it was only making things worse—both for my mental state and our relationship.

"Face it, Dad. You want this more than I do."

He sighed and stared at the sky, the clouds blowing past as the silence descended between us. His frustration was palpable, and while I hated disappointing him, I couldn't keep doing this.

Finally, he met my eyes. "Let's get through the Indoor Championships. One more competition. Then, if you still want to quit, I'll respect your decision."

Right. Only because he secretly hoped I'd change my

mind. Pinning his hopes on the fact that I'd do as well as I had in the past and that another taste of victory would make me eager to return to competition. But I already knew that even if I won, it wouldn't make a damn difference.

"You're twenty-eight," he continued. "Almost twenty-nine. You won't be able to do this for much longer. Hell, if I'd had the chance you do…"

I sighed, guilt mingling with frustration. My dad's pro hockey career had been cut short by an injury. And while I certainly sympathized, I often felt as if he were pinning his hopes and dreams on me.

What about my goals? What about what *I* wanted?

"Look, I know you think you're ready to retire, but this is what we've worked toward for years. This was always your goal." He rubbed the back of his neck. "And if you don't compete soon, you're going to lose your chance."

You're going to lose everything, was the unspoken threat hanging in the air.

He wasn't just my dad and my coach; he was also my manager. He knew the stakes better than anyone.

Maybe I'd lose my chance to compete at the level I once had. And if it weren't for the popularity of my tutorial videos and online hurdle challenges, I would've been more concerned with losing sponsors we'd spent years cultivating relationships with. Heptathletes weren't as well-known or popular as other athletes, like Olympic gymnasts or professional tennis players. I'd had to work harder just to get their attention and keep it.

But ever since my injury, I'd realized there was so much more to life than competing and winning medals. Watching my best friend Kendall take care of her mom through cancer had been another powerful reminder. As had seeing her fall in love.

I couldn't be happier for her, but sometimes it made my

chest ache to see the way Knox looked at her—besotted. Or to know how much he loved her. Enough to fly home early from his pro soccer team's game, even if his mysterious abrupt departure had sent the media into a stir.

I wanted that for myself. I wanted a man who never made me doubt what we were or how much I meant to him, like my ex had. A man who actually listened to me and supported my goals without feeling threatened by my ambition or success. A man who acknowledged me as his equal; a partner who made me feel both protected and empowered.

More than that, I wanted a family. Nannying had given me a sense of fulfillment unlike any I'd ever known. It had made me realize that I wanted to fall in love, get married, and definitely have children.

But I'd barely had time to date with my rigorous training schedule and the other demands on my time. And I had yet to find someone who seemed worth the effort. Most guys my age weren't ready to settle down, and I was done wasting time on relationships that didn't go anywhere.

So while my dad was worried about time running out on my athletic career, I was more concerned with the count-down of another clock entirely.

CHAPTER TWO

Nate

"Can I get you a refill, Mr. Crawford?" the flight attendant asked.

I shook my head without meeting her eyes. She'd already tried hitting on me once, and I was going to have to ask the employment agency for a replacement. The Hartwell Agency was a bespoke recruitment service that placed nannies, jet crew, and other household staff with high-net-worth clients around the globe.

Emerson and Andre had been placed by the Hartwell Agency. As had many of my brother Knox's household and yacht staff, and the jet crew for the small fleet of private planes we shared with our three cousins—Graham, Jasper, and Sloan.

I rested my ankle on my knee, wondering where Tabitha was. She was one of our newer hires, and I liked her. She was respectful. Quiet. She left me alone.

"No. Thank you."

"Can I get you anything else?" she asked, her voice breathy with desire.

"No," I said in a firm tone. I was fucking exhausted. It had been one hell of a week, and I didn't want her to get the wrong idea.

I just wanted to be at home. Spending time with my daughter. And sleeping in my own bed—alone.

So I turned my attention back to my inbox, relieved when she disappeared to the galley. Most of the emails were back-and-forth conversations about the Meghan Hart movie—a love story. At this point, it was a fucking disaster, and I worried the film was going to burn through money like none other. Plus, the lead actor was threatening to back out at the last minute.

When we'd acquired the rights to the project, I'd been so optimistic. It was a solid story. There was a rabid fan base, which was good and bad. The built-in revenue source would be nice, but everyone had an opinion on the casting, especially for the character of Brock Ransom.

My phone buzzed, and my agent's name flashed across the screen. "Pierce," I answered.

Technically, he was my agent. But he was more of a "fixer." He helped with general PR and strategy, as well as smoothing things over when necessary. And though he no longer practiced law, he knew the ins and outs well enough to work it to our advantage. Apart from my brother and cousins, he was one of the few people I trusted implicitly.

"I got wind of a project you might be interested in," Pierce said. "In fact, it's one you're already familiar with."

"Oh yeah?" I asked, skimming an email from my brother Knox. He wanted to know what Brooklyn wanted for her birthday, even though it was still months away. I chuckled to myself. Gifts were definitely his love language.

"It's last minute, but I think it's right up your alley."

"Just what I love to hear," I deadpanned.

I had a million emails to respond to, school forms to review and sign for Brooklyn, and a script to read over. And

I was determined to make a dent in it before we landed. I'd already spent the last week away from my daughter, and I hated being apart for so long. I refused to spend any more of our precious time together working than I had to.

"Director and casting want you to take the lead role for Brock Ransom."

"The fuck?" I sat back in my chair. "I figured he was bluffing," I said, referring to the lead actor. Excuse me, *former* lead actor.

"Well, someone finally called his bluff. He's gone, and the team wants you."

I barked out a laugh. After how much I'd chewed out their asses this past week, I highly doubted that was the case. But they also knew how passionate I was about the project. And the fact that they'd ask me to star in it spoke to their confidence in my ability to carry the film to fruition. Their trust that I would bring the role to life.

As flattered as I was, I didn't know if I could commit. "I'm not sure."

"Because you need more time to prepare?"

"That's definitely part of it."

Pierce knew how selective I was about the parts I agreed to. And how much time I typically liked to have to prepare, especially in a case like this one where there wouldn't be as much flexibility with the script.

The author, Meghan Hart, had been intimately involved in the entire process, even if it had all been done via email. She was very reclusive, but I'd figured she'd want to come on set for some of it. So far, she'd had her assistant send her videos. I wasn't sure whether to be relieved or disappointed.

"What are your other objections?" he asked. "Because I think you'd be perfect for this role."

Of course he did. Though Pierce wasn't the type to say shit he didn't mean.

"Brooklyn," I said, voicing my main hesitation.

"As you know, most of it will be filmed in LA. And the Abu Dhabi filming portion will only last for three weeks. Hell, part of it's over winter break. You could take her with you."

I wasn't sure I had the time, let alone the desire, to take on another project. I was already stretched thin, and I knew it was affecting my daughter. So to ask her to give up part of her vacation to join me in Abu Dhabi for work… I scrunched up my face.

"Is it a hard no?" he asked.

"No," I sighed, knowing he was right. It was an elegant solution for the studio, and the part was a good fit for me.

Hell, when I'd first read the script, I'd had the same thought. And even though casting had contacted me about it, I'd turned it down. Despite being a solo parent with a frequently unpredictable work schedule, I'd always tried to prioritize stability and routine in my daughter's life.

Looking back now, I almost wished I'd said yes from the jump. It might have saved us all a lot of heartache.

"Anything else?" I asked after a beat of silence. Pierce was usually more efficient.

"There is one thing, actually."

I frowned. "What's that?"

"I heard about a book that might be released."

"Okay," I said, dragging out the word and wishing he'd get to the point.

"Supposedly, Annalise Windsor is going to release a memoir. A tell-all…" He waited a beat, then added, "A few early excerpts were leaked. And they don't paint you in a very favorable light."

"Fuck," I said, leaning back in my chair. "How bad?"

I held my breath, hoping it wouldn't be as terrible as I expected. Publicity—good or bad—was an occupational hazard and a fact of life. I was even more of a target since I was one of the billionaire heirs to the Huxley Hotel fortune.

My grandparents had started the company decades ago with one hotel and their entire savings. Today, the Huxley Hotels empire spanned the globe, ranging from budget-friendly extended stays to high-end luxury resorts. I might not have a hand in the day-to-day operations of the family business anymore like my cousins did, but my time there had taught me some valuable lessons that carried over into my role as an executive producer and studio head.

"Bad. I'm sending them over now."

As soon as the email arrived, I opened it and scanned the contents. Supposed lurid details of our relationship. Allegations of wild parties, alcohol, illicit sexual acts. Not all lies. But not all truth either.

Still, her greedy, attention-seeking behavior reminded me so much of my ex-wife Trinity that I couldn't see straight. I gripped the armrests, wishing I could toss my computer across the cabin. I should've known better. To most people—most women, especially—I was nothing more than a meal ticket, a conquest, or a fast-track to the Hollywood career of their dreams. Annalise was no different. Though she must be really hard up for money if she was trying to cash in on our failed relationship even now, years after it had ended.

"Unbelievable," I seethed.

How the hell was I supposed to model healthy love and romantic relationships for my daughter when my exes kept pulling shit like this?

Fortunately, I had a great kid. And while I'd once dreamed of having more children, I couldn't imagine putting myself in a position to give someone that much power over me ever again.

"We'll take care of it. I've been in touch with your legal

team, and I've already started working on some PR strategy as well. We don't want this to impact awards season."

"Agreed. Let's have a meeting later this week to discuss it more in-depth," I said, hoping we could quash this quickly and with little drama or expense.

"Oh, and um—" He cleared his throat. "We might also need to have a chat with your nanny."

Pierce and I had spoken earlier in the week about Emerson's social media now that she'd been featured in some tabloids as Brooklyn's "hot new nanny." It didn't help that most of Emerson's social media posts featured her in the tiniest running shorts or barely there bikinis. She had a great body, and she liked showing it off. Hell, I liked looking at it. Not that I was going to admit that. I could *never* admit that.

So instead, I'd sent her an email at Pierce's insistence. Asked her to post more "appropriate content," even though I'd been hesitant to do so. I understood where Pierce was coming from, but Emerson hadn't posted any pictures of my daughter.

And while, yes, Emerson was my employee and a reflection of me and my values, she should be free to post what she wanted. Her social media was as much a part of her brand as mine. Even if I hated the thought of so many eyes on her gorgeous, scantily clad body.

"I already emailed her," I said, and I hadn't given it much thought since. Though, come to think of it, I hadn't seen a reply from her.

"Good." There was a muffled sound in the background. Then he added, "Recently?"

"A few days ago. Why?"

"Because her latest posts aren't going to help your image. Especially since we need to lean into the family man narrative and away from the billionaire bad boy one. At least until this tell-all thing blows over."

I nodded, wondering what the hell Emerson had posted that had riled up Pierce. I typically avoided her socials, but only because I already found it difficult enough to hide my attraction to her when she was in my home. I didn't need to add more fuel to the fire.

"How long do you think *that* will take?" I asked.

"Not a fucking clue. Rumor has it Annalise plans to release it before the holidays."

I nodded. That didn't give us much time. "Is that why you're pushing me so hard to take the Brock Ransom role?"

"It could help refocus attention, especially if we aren't successful in stopping publication."

I nodded, considering. "I'll give you an answer tomorrow."

After we ended the call, I navigated to Emerson's social media feed despite my better sense. She'd posted several new images—a video of her doing a hurdle challenge, an image of her stretching. No big deal.

That last one, though—it almost felt as if she was sending me a big fuck-you instead of replying to my email. The post featured Emerson in a red bikini, kicking up her heels by the pool. Not *my* pool. I frowned at the screen and zoomed in, recognizing some of the tile—Knox's.

She'd probably been hanging out with Kendall. Hell, when she wasn't at my house, she was often at Knox's, especially now that Knox and Kendall were no longer hiding their relationship.

I still couldn't believe it—my older brother was in love. With his son's ex.

I couldn't judge him, though. Not when I'd been lusting after my daughter's nanny for months.

Emerson was hot. I mean, fuck. She was all lean muscles and long legs. Wavy blond hair and full lips that curled into the most beautiful smile. Though, more often than not, a scowl was directed at me.

But even that was sexy. Honestly, I almost liked it more when she was fired up and fighting with me. She wasn't just another simpering Hollywood hanger-on. I scrolled through some of her other recent posts, my cock hardening.

Jesus. Fuck. How were these photos legal?

And why was I even torturing myself by staring at pictures of my twenty-eight-year-old nanny?

This was exactly why I shouldn't have come on here.

I was forty-three. *Forty-three.* I should know better. *Do* better, especially since my daughter loved Emerson. And the feeling was clearly mutual.

I couldn't imagine a better fit for Brooklyn. And that was quite the feat, considering the fact that our previous nanny, Amalia, had been with us since Brooklyn's birth. When Amalia had retired, it had been a struggle to find a suitable replacement.

And so, knowing how much Brooklyn liked Emerson and how difficult it would be to replace her, I refused to do anything to jeopardize Emerson's position. I'd had a somewhat tumultuous childhood myself, and I craved stability for my daughter. Even if it came in the form of a fiery blonde bombshell who was a pain in my ass.

I exited the app, hating my body's reaction to her. Willing my dick to calm down. That was one of the biggest reasons why I'd been opposed to her from the start. I needed calm and order in my home. And being around Emerson made me feel neither of those things.

Still, I knew better than to sleep with the nanny. I'd seen that story in the tabloids one too many times. It was such a cliché, it was laughable. Not to mention foolish. The past few months—and now Annalise's stunt—had me rattled. NDAs or not, people just didn't seem to care when money or fame was involved.

I closed my eyes and tried to recenter myself. But as I listened to the hum of the jet engine, my mind drifted to Trinity, Brooklyn's mother, if you could even call her that.

My ex was a piece of work. I'd been foolish to marry her, but I'd been young and in love. It was only later that I realized I'd been using her to try to fill the hole that my parents' death had created. That I'd been desperate for family and security and ignored all the red flags.

Marrying Trinity had been a mistake. And even now, years after the divorce, I was still pissed about what she'd done. How she'd tried to use Brooklyn... *Fuck.* I clenched my fists.

You trusted someone. Loved someone. And to have them treat you like she had Brooklyn and me... I let out a heavy sigh. Never again.

It was a big reason why I rarely dated. And when I did, I didn't let myself get attached.

I clenched my fists at the thought of Annalise fucking Windsor. A supermodel, a one-time relationship, and the current bane of my existence. I'd once thought that title would only ever belong to Trinity, but apparently I'd been wrong.

My divorce had been nasty, public, and expensive, despite the prenup. And my breakup with Annalise—long ago though it was—was turning out to be a big headache of its own.

CHAPTER THREE

Emerson

The security alarm chimed twice, indicating that the front gate had opened, and I braced myself. After I'd picked Brooklyn up from school, I'd taken her to a therapy appointment, and then we'd come home and finished her homework. Eaten a snack. She'd been distracted and fidgety, eager for her dad to return. Hell, I was eager for his return myself, albeit for different reasons. We had some important things to discuss.

The house alarm chimed once, alerting us that a door had been opened. The front door, judging from the direction of Brooklyn's gaze and the huge smile on her face.

"Daddy!" she yelled, popping up from her seat and running toward Nate.

His megawatt smile was blinding, and for a second, I forgot my anger over his email and saw a father who absolutely adored his daughter and was happy to be home. The way he looked at her…it always made my ovaries quiver.

He's your boss, I repeated in my head. He's just a dad boss. Definitely not a dad bod, though.

Great. This was *so* not the time for my brain to short-circuit and focus on the fact that Nate had been my celebrity crush for a decade, while ignoring the way he'd treated me the past few months.

Even so, I couldn't help but appreciate his physique. I mean, *damn* he looked good. I'd always been a sucker for a man in a suit. And this one was no exception, despite my personal feelings toward him.

The subtle pattern of his gray suit drew the eye from his broad shoulders to his tapered waist and down to his designer loafers. The top few buttons of his white shirt were undone, revealing skin that was even darker after a summer by the pool with Brooklyn. Scruff lined his jaw, the rich brown color slightly darker than his wavy hair that looked as if it had been highlighted by the gods themselves.

"Dad!" Brooklyn yelled, launching herself into his arms and breaking me out of whatever trance I'd been in. "I missed you so much."

He buried his face in her neck, and I hung back, giving them a minute. The way he doted on her was…gah. Sometimes, it made it easy to forget how infuriating he could be.

Fortunately, between Nate's busy work schedule and my training, we were rarely ever home alone together.

"I missed you too, Queen B." He lifted his chin in greeting. "Thorne."

He always addressed me as if I were a thorn in his side. And with that one word, all my anger came rushing back. But the second Nate walked in the door was not the time to ambush him about his email, even if the idea was tempting.

I forced his name past my lips. "Nate."

Brooklyn chattered nonstop about school and her guitar lessons, and I quickly excused myself. I had plans—a workout and hanging out with Kendall—and if I stayed, I was likely to blow up on my boss. I'd had a few days to calm down, but I wasn't willing to let this go.

So, for the moment, I made myself scarce. *Rule number three.*

I didn't return to the house until after dinner. And then I waited until long after Brooklyn had gone to bed to approach Nate. I padded down the hall to his office.

I was sick of the men in my life telling me what to do. Thinking they knew what was best for me. First, my dad and his insistence that I wasn't ready to retire. And Nate and… everything.

I rapped my knuckles on the door, and he barked, "What?"

I stepped inside, barely passing over the threshold. A stack of books was piled on the desk. If I wasn't mistaken, they all looked like romance novels. *Huh.*

"Is Brooklyn okay?" he asked, immediately glancing toward the door, his brow etched in concern.

"Brooklyn's fine," I said, and his shoulders relaxed. "But we need to talk."

He rubbed a hand over his face, and I wasn't sure I'd ever seen him so distressed. He was usually unflappable. "Unless it's an emergency, please email me. And while you're at it, you can provide an explanation for why you never responded to my last email or complied with my request."

Oh. Was it a request? Because it had sounded more like a demand.

I could feel a headache building.

I'd come here, prepared to be reasonable. And then he had the *audacity* to demand this? To treat me like this?

"No."

Because it was stupid. And, of course, I wasn't going to email him about why I hadn't responded to his email. He was being ridiculous.

He finally met my eyes, his simmering with irritation. "Did you forget the password to your email account?"

"No," I said, feeling my power surge with every "no." I was taking back control.

"Is there some other technical error I should be aware of?" he asked.

"No." Damn, that felt good—defying him. I wasn't being rude. But I was done taking his shit. It was almost difficult *not* to smile at this point.

"I expect you to respond to all emails in a timely fashion." I simmered with pent-up rage, with unspoken comments and snide remarks. "And yet, you haven't replied to my email from—" He glanced at his computer screen. "Three days ago. Would you care to explain?"

I crossed my arms over my chest. "No."

I absolutely did not care to explain.

He arched his brow, a haughty expression overtaking his face. "Should I remind you that a violation of house rules can result in immediate termination?"

"I'm well aware," I said in a calm tone.

"And yet you choose to stand here and defy me."

"I choose to stand here and have an actual conversation with you. And frankly, you're lucky I'm doing that instead of just quitting."

He leaned back in his chair, resting his ankle on his knee. "You're not happy about the social media thing. I get it. But my PR team thinks it's necessary. So, what do you want in return?" he asked in a bored tone. "A raise? More time off?"

Termination, my ass. The man wasn't going to fire me. Brooklyn adored me, and Nate needed me. Hell, he was offering me a raise on the heels of threatening to enforce the house rules.

He gestured to the chair across from him, but I remained

standing. He tilted his head to the side, eyebrow raised. If he was trying to intimidate me, it wasn't going to work.

There was no way in hell I was going to let him dictate what I could and couldn't post. It was my profile, and it was my body. But that wasn't even the real issue.

"Some respect would be nice. I adore your daughter. I take care of her and love her, and yet you treat me with nothing but contempt."

"What will it take?" he asked, as if it was a foregone conclusion. "Five hundred extra a week? A thousand?"

"No!" I clenched my fists. Hell, maybe I'd come here looking for a fight. "This isn't about money."

"What is it about, then?" he asked, clearly exasperated. As if that was the only thing I could possibly want. Did he really think so little of me?

"It's about having some fucking *decency*. You've made it very clear that you don't want me here and that I'm not valued. If I didn't adore Brooklyn, I would've already left."

Something passed through his eyes, and it looked a lot like respect. In reality, it was probably just shock. I didn't get the feeling Nate was used to anyone contradicting him.

He rubbed his jaw. Part of me was convinced he was going to tell me to fuck off, but then he said, "Contrary to what you might think of me, I don't allow many people into my life. Let alone into my home." He shifted. "And the fact that I've let you anywhere near my daughter…" He shook his head. "Well, I wouldn't if I didn't trust you."

"You say you trust me, but you micromanage me. More than Andre or Belinda or anyone else. And while I get that you're entrusting me with your daughter, that doesn't mean you get to dictate aspects of my life that are private."

"Is it 'private' when you post about it on the internet?"

I narrowed my eyes at him, prepared to call him out for being a hypocrite. But he had the decency to look chagrined.

"You're right. I—" He hesitated then said, "Overstepped. But this is...new." He seemed to have difficulty with the word. "You have to understand that for the past eleven, almost twelve, years—since Brooklyn was born—we've had the same nanny. A woman who was also one of my nannies as a child."

I nodded. I understood how difficult change could be, but that didn't excuse his behavior toward me. At least he was finally opening up. Finally acting more human.

"I'm all Brooklyn has," he said, tapping his chest. "*Me*. Her mother..." He sighed and seemed to think better of whatever he'd been going to say. "My daughter means more to me than life itself."

I softened at his words—and the vulnerable look on his face. "I know." I shifted on my feet, my voice suddenly quiet. "I see how much you love her. But you're wrong."

He furrowed his brow.

"You're not the only person in her life," I said. "She has her aunt and uncles. She has her cousin. She has Sophia and her family. And she has me."

"But for how long?" he asked.

"That depends on you." This was it. I was putting it all on the table. He could fire me for all I cared. "I adore Brooklyn, but I can't live like this anymore. If things don't change, I will request a new placement."

He jerked his head back, clearly shocked. "What would it take for you to stay?" he finally asked. "Since I know it's not more money."

"You're not going to like my answer."

"Perhaps, but Brooklyn likes you. She trusts you." He paused, turning more contemplative before he added, "And I need you now more than ever." I wasn't sure what that meant, but it definitely piqued my interest.

"I didn't think you needed anyone," I said. Least of all me.

"I appreciate you. I probably don't tell you that enough."

Enough? I wanted to laugh. He'd *never* told me that. And the timing felt a little too convenient, except for the fact that he seemed sincere.

"I do," he said, perhaps sensing my surprise at his words. "And I know Brooklyn does too, especially when I can't be here. Which brings me to something I'd like to discuss." He shifted in his chair. "I'm considering a role in a film, but I can't accept unless I know you're on board."

I frowned, shocked he'd even seek my approval. "Is it a long filming schedule or something?"

He shook his head. "Quite the opposite. But it could be disruptive, considering the location and the fact that I want to take her with me."

"When?" I asked.

"Late December, after Christmas. We'd be gone for a few weeks."

"Where?"

"Abu Dhabi."

My eyes went wide. Oh my god. Was he going to—

"Yes. The role is in the Meghan Hart adaptation." *Ahh. So that explained the books.* "And since I don't want to make Brooklyn's life any more chaotic than necessary, I'd need you to come too."

For a minute, my mind got stuck on the words "need you to come," spoken in Nate's rich voice. A myriad of fantasies threatened to play out in my head, but I quickly shut them down. Sleeping with my boss was out of the question.

Not that he was even remotely interested, at least if his disdain for me the past few months was anything to go on. Besides, the Hartwell Agency had a firm nonfraternization policy. Breaking that rule would have serious repercussions —at least for me. For Nate, it would probably only add to his allure.

I might love to push the boundaries, but even I had some lines I wouldn't cross.

I didn't want to be known as the girl who'd had sex with her famous boss. I wanted to be remembered for my accomplishments. My athletic career and...well...whatever the future might hold.

"Thorne?" he asked, using my last name as he often did.

"What?" I shook my head to clear it.

More like what the hell was wrong with me? Nate had been kicked off my celebrity fuck-it list months ago.

"Abu Dhabi?"

It was months away, but I knew it would be here sooner than I realized. This was my chance to establish new boundaries. To figure out a path forward with Nate. If that was what *I* wanted.

Part of me wanted to tell him to go fuck himself. But a bigger part of me wanted to stay for Brooklyn. Oh, who was I kidding? I couldn't leave her, no matter how deplorable Nate's behavior had been.

"First," I said, ticking off a finger, "I'm not changing my social media."

He huffed. "You don't have to stop posting. Can you please just...tone it down some? Less..." He cleared his throat. "Sexualized."

My eyebrows rose so high I could only assume they'd disappeared into my forehead. Was he serious? The man who had shirtless photos in his boxers on his own feed was telling me to post less sexualized content? *What a hypocrite!*

"No," I said, standing my ground. He could take it or leave it, but this was nonnegotiable. "I shouldn't have to explain to you that my social media is tied to my career. My livelihood."

"You're right," he sighed, and I was shocked he'd caved so quickly. "I'll talk to my team. What else?"

I blinked a few times. He really must be desperate.

"I'll need time to train while we're in Abu Dhabi. I have a competition in late February, and I need to be prepared."

"We'll make it work. I'll have some free time. And if it's too much, we can arrange for an additional nanny from Hartwell."

I nodded. I had faith he'd make that happen. Nate was a man of his word.

"No more emails, unless it's about Brooklyn's schedule. If you have something you want to discuss, you talk to me. Face-to-face."

He dragged a hand down his face. "Yeah. I know that was a little ridiculous, but I didn't have the best experience with the two nannies I tried before you."

Wait. What? I couldn't believe he'd actually admitted that. What the hell was going on?

Instead of questioning it, I decided to question him. "Were they irresponsible or something?"

"That would've almost been preferable."

I waited for him to elaborate, surprised when he finally said, "One was so starstruck, she couldn't seem to speak in my presence. Definitely not something you struggle with."

I barked out a laugh, still trying to grapple with the fact that I'd come here pissed. And now Nate was revealing things about himself. Putting me at ease. "No." In fact, I seemed to have the opposite problem. I said too much. I was too honest. It got me into trouble most of the time.

"And the second tried to seduce me and sell my underwear on the internet."

I started laughing, but when Nate didn't join in, my eyes went wide. "You're serious?"

"Oh yeah." He rubbed a hand over his jaw.

"That's horrible."

He lifted a shoulder, as if that type of thing was a regular occurrence. "Welcome to my life."

I seethed, a fire burning inside me. "No one deserves that."

He rubbed a hand over his jaw, evaluating me. "Most people think it comes with the territory. If you're famous, you're fair game. They feel entitled to a piece of you."

"Well, I think that's bullshit," I said, feeling as if I understood him better now. As if I...sympathized with him. "And I would never violate your trust like that, even if I hadn't signed an NDA. I'm sorry that happened to you."

"Thanks." He blew out a breath. "So, will you stay?" There was hesitancy in his tone, vulnerability too.

I considered it a moment before answering. "Only if you'll agree to my terms. You'll stop with the emails and the micromanaging," I said, leaving no room for confusion. "You'll treat me with respect. You won't pretend I don't exist." He opened his mouth, presumably to protest, and I held up a finger to silence him. "If you can do all that, then yes. I'll stay."

I adored Brooklyn. And the fact that Nate had heard my concerns and acknowledged them made me more hopeful than I'd been in a long time.

So when he said, "I will try," with a solemn expression, I was willing to give him a chance.

"And Abu Dhabi?" he asked. "I need time to prepare for the role, and there will be studio parties and other events I need to attend before then. So you'd have to miss Christmas with your family."

I waved a hand through the air. "It's fine."

Better than fine, actually. It would give me a break from my dad and all the tension simmering between us. I couldn't imagine spending a week with him scrutinizing my every move—if I was getting enough calories, the *right calories.* Debating if I was building muscle fast enough. Resting adequately. It was all too much.

My dad wasn't happy that I wanted to retire. And it was impacting my relationship with Papa J and Astrid. It was affecting everything from my day-to-day life to my holiday plans.

Holiday plans that now included spending Christmas with my boss. *What have I gotten myself into now?*

CHAPTER FOUR

Nate

Emerson strode into the kitchen, her hips swaying to the beat of the music streaming through her headphones. It had been a week since our conversation—our "truce," if you could call it that. And I was trying to be more…accommodating. More friendly.

Brooklyn was still at school, and Emerson must have just finished a workout. She headed for the fridge without noticing me. It was a good distraction. A dangerous distraction.

A necessary one, especially after my latest conversation with Pierce. Not only was Annalise Windsor's tell-all still moving forward, but Trinity's lawyers had been in touch. My ex-wife was contemplating filing for a change in our custody agreement.

It was bullshit. But I had faith that it would blow over; it always did.

With Emerson's back turned to me, she moved her ass, sinking low to the floor in a move that had my blood thumping and my cock standing up to take notice.

Holy...

I felt bad for watching, but what the hell was I supposed to do now? I couldn't look away. Didn't want her to stop.

Her body was beautiful. Powerful. But she was also lithe. Graceful.

She yanked out her earbuds and grabbed some protein powder from the pantry.

"How was your workout?" I asked, knowing I shouldn't let this go on any longer than I already had.

She jolted, her back still to me. She seemed frozen for a minute then asked, "How long have you been standing there?" in a tight voice.

"Long enough," I said.

Long enough to get a hard-on.

Long enough that I should've said something sooner.

Walked away sooner.

She took a deep breath, straightening before she faced me. "My workout was…fine." Her smile was forced. Her voice too bright.

I coughed into my fist to stifle a laugh.

She tilted her head.

"What?" I asked.

"You've never once asked me about my workout before. Are you feeling okay?" she teased.

I rolled my eyes and shut the door to the fridge. I was trying this new thing called talking to her. Because even now, nearly a week later, Emerson's words still rang in my head.

You don't want me here.

I'm not valued.

If I didn't adore Brooklyn, I would've already left.

She couldn't have been more wrong.

And I hadn't realized how close I'd been to losing her.

I was still worried she'd decide to leave. And while I'd been determined to keep her at arm's length in the past, that strategy wasn't going to work anymore. I respected her for speaking her mind. Even more so for sticking it out for Brooklyn when she was clearly miserable.

I made her miserable.

"I'm fine," I said. "And you're deflecting."

"I—" Her jaw dropped. "What?"

"You're joking to avoid having to answer the question."

"Yes. I know what deflecting means."

"I should think so." I leaned my hip against the counter. "You're practically a master."

She glared at me.

"Hey." I held up my hands. "You're the one who wanted me to stop with the emails."

"Yeah." She tilted her head. "I'm seriously reconsidering that now."

"Mm." I crossed my arms over my chest, gratified by the way her eyes darted to my biceps.

"Don't 'mm' me." She wagged her finger at me. *Damn, this was fun. She* was fun when I allowed myself to let my guard down around her. "You're a master at deflecting yourself."

"Am I?"

She pointed at me. "See. That's exactly what I'm talking about. You answered a question with a question."

"Is that a problem?"

"And again." She threw her hands in the air.

"Fine," I said, amused by her irritation. "Tell me how your workout was, and I'll answer a question of yours."

She arched an eyebrow. "You'll answer it without answering in a question."

"If that will make you happy."

She rolled her eyes then said, "My workout was fine."

I pressed my hands to the counter. "You already said that. I'm going to need something more. Why was it just 'fine'?"

She huffed. "My legs felt like lead when I started."

I barked out a laugh. "That wasn't what I expected you to say. So what'd you do?"

"Decided that maybe one hundred percent doesn't look the same every day, but I'd give the hundred percent I could today."

I nodded. "That's very...astute."

Lately, it felt as if my one hundred percent wasn't good enough. That there wasn't enough time or energy to do everything that needed to be done. From running the studio to parenting Brooklyn to learning the lines for my new role and working out to maintain my physique. I often dropped into bed exhausted and feeling like I'd fallen short in at least one area, if not more. If not for my team, if not for Emerson, I didn't know how I'd accomplish anything.

And I'd done a terrible job of showing her just how much I valued her. Which was why I'd made a stop on the way home.

"I have something for you."

"You do?" She eyed me suspiciously, leaning her hip against the counter.

I grabbed the orange gift box from the floor and set it on the counter. "Happy birthday," I said, quickly adding, "From Brooklyn and me." I'd wanted to do something nice, something to show my appreciation for everything she did for us. For me, really. And her birthday had given me a convenient excuse.

For a minute, she stared at the box with the Hermès logo on it, unblinking. *Oh no. Did I screw up?* Kendall had assured me that this was the one Emerson would want. And the hoops Jay and Sloan had jumped through to make this happen...

Emerson lifted the lid, gasping when she saw the brand-new Hermès Birkin in Rouge. The bag cost almost twenty grand, which wasn't a big deal. But the waiting list often stretched for months. Even my celebrity status and offer to pay above the asking price weren't enough to secure the bag in such a short time frame. At least, not until I'd called in reinforcements.

Sloan—an Hermès collector herself—and Jay, my stylist, had been able to pull some strings. Though their assistance had come at the cost of revealing *who* I wanted the bag for. Magically, two days later, the bag was mine despite the popularity of the color.

"Wow." She looked at the purse but didn't remove it from the wrapping. "It's beautiful." She blinked a few times then shook her head. "Thanks, but I can't—" She pushed it toward me. "I can't accept it."

"Why the hell not?" I barked before I could stop myself.

She let out a heavy sigh. "It's too much."

"If you ask me," I said, pushing it back to her, "it's not enough."

Her eyes lingered on it, the longing clear even as she looked as if she was going to refuse again. Before she could say anything, I said, "Take it, Thorne. You know you want to."

"I—" She dropped her head. "Yeah. But I can't."

I stepped closer, ducking to meet her gaze. "You can, and you will. Now say thank you and enjoy carrying it."

"So bossy." She smiled despite herself. After a pause, she seemed to give up the fight. "Thank you. I absolutely love it."

"Good." That filled me with more satisfaction than it should've.

"I'm surprised you're home so early. I thought you had a meeting at the studio today."

"I did, but I left early so I could be home in time to get Brooklyn."

"Is everything okay?"

"Everything is more than okay. I'm giving you the rest of the day off as well as tomorrow."

"Really?"

I nodded. "Yes. Really. Happy birthday."

"But how'd you—" She glanced toward the garage then back at me. "Traffic is awful this time of day. Well, it's LA, so it's pretty much always terrible."

"I took the helicopter."

"Oh, right." She scoffed, affecting a blasé expression. "The helicopter."

"What?"

"Sometimes I still can't wrap my head around your life. Around the fact that you take a helicopter regularly, just to avoid traffic."

"It's not *that* unusual."

She barked out a laugh. "Maybe not in your world."

"What are you talking about? *You're* part of my world."

She scrunched up her face. "Um. No. I'm not. Not really."

She'd never outright said it, but I knew her family was well-off. One of her dads, Declan Cross, used to play pro hockey for the Hollywood Hawks. And her other dad, James Thorne, was one of the most sought-after plastic surgeons in LA. They'd had twins—Emerson and Astrid—via surrogacy, an expensive process. And their Aspen vacation home had been featured in a prestigious design magazine.

"So you've never taken a helicopter to avoid LA traffic?" I asked.

She shook her head. "No. I've never taken a helicopter, period."

"Are you scared?"

"No." She scoffed. "I've just never had the opportunity."

"Would you want it?"

"I don't know. I guess. Maybe."

Interesting. Most people I knew would've jumped at the chance to avoid LA traffic. To take the easy way. The VVIP way.

"Did Brooklyn tell you about her school play?" she asked, and I was grateful for the excuse to continue talking.

"Only that she's excited to play Rumpelstiltskin."

Emerson grinned. "I love that she went for that part."

I busied myself with filling my water bottle. "I love that she's taken an interest in acting, but I hope she doesn't make a career of it."

"Why?" Emerson asked.

"This industry can be brutal. And it can really fuck with your head. She's already going to face enough media and scrutiny for being my kid. Even if she's talented, people will always say she didn't earn it."

"People could say that regardless of who her dad was or what industry she works in."

I inclined my head. "True."

"And she *is* talented. We were practicing her lines last night, and she's a natural."

I nodded. "You don't think her classmates will find it odd that she's performing a traditionally male role?"

Emerson's expression darkened. "Are you referring to that little shit Randy?"

I sighed. "Is he causing trouble again?"

"Is he ever not?" Emerson asked.

Touché. "Has he done something specific to Brooklyn? Do I need to get involved?"

"It's handled—for now." She let out a sigh, her eyes flicking briefly toward the ceiling.

I wondered what that meant, but I trusted Emerson to take care of it. She was just as protective of Brooklyn as I was. I'd never doubted that—not for a moment. But now that I'd stopped avoiding her so much, I'd seen the full extent of just how devoted she was to my daughter.

"Speaking of Brooklyn," I said, thinking it was the perfect segue. "I have a huge favor to ask."

"Besides going to Abu Dhabi?" she teased.

"Yeah." I rubbed the back of my neck. "Besides that. In fact, this might be an even bigger ask."

"Ah. So that's why you gave me the Birkin," she joked, eyeing the purse.

"No." I butted her shoulder with mine. "I gave you the Birkin because you deserve it."

"But you're still hoping I'll keep the gift in mind when you tell me the favor." She smirked.

"I wouldn't object if you did."

"Hmm." She arched an eyebrow then tapped a finger to her lips. Soft. Pink. Kissable. "You want me to run lines with you like I am for Brooklyn."

I shifted. Just thinking of some of the scenes we'd be filming, well, it would definitely be *crossing* a line to prepare for them with Emerson. I didn't usually act in films that involved sex scenes, so this one would be a new challenge for me. Some nudity, even, though nothing more than my ass and the appearance of sex. Still, I'd have to get up close and personal with my costar, Mila. And we'd have to make it look real.

But god, the idea of "practicing" with Emerson was tempting. Hearing her moan my name. Watching her pupils dilate as I leaned in to kiss her...

"Nate?" she asked, snapping me out of my fantasy where she played a starring role.

"No. That's not it."

"You want to work out with me?"

"Um." I furrowed my brow, my body immediately reacting to her statement, my imagination running wild with all sorts of ideas about our "workout." God, that wasn't helping. "No."

Her expression remained nonchalant even as her eyes sparkled with challenge. "I get it. You're scared you can't keep up."

"Thorne," I scoffed. "I can keep up."

The corner of her mouth lifted. She was much more playful now that I'd lightened up a little. I liked it, even if I was still struggling to maintain those boundaries. She might live in my home, but I was still her boss.

She eyed me with a fair bit of skepticism. "I'm not so sure about that."

I leaned forward, pressing my palms to the counter. "I'd be more than happy to prove you wrong."

"Mm. Maybe someday you can *try*. Now, back to this favor," she said. "You want me to drive the McLaren."

I barked out a laugh. "Also no." Though I wondered if she wanted to drive it. Hell, who wouldn't? It was a gorgeous car, and imagining her long legs behind the steering wheel had me hardening.

Fuck. What is wrong with me?

This blonde bombshell, that was what. This was exactly why I'd avoided her in the past. Not because I'd wanted to be rude, but because I was trying to be professional.

"Okay," she sighed. "Tell me."

"Brooklyn wants to have a slumber party at the Huxley Grand for her birthday. There will be about six girls, including Brooklyn and Sophia. I know Brooklyn would love if you came, and I'm sure the other parents would feel more comfortable if a female adult was there. I'll pay overtime—"

She rolled her eyes. "Brooklyn already mentioned it. Of course I'll be there. And no, you're not paying me overtime."

"Yes. I am." I was adamant. I valued her time, and I'd never want her to feel like I'd taken advantage of the situation, especially in light of her recent comments.

You don't want me here.

I'm not valued.

But she'd turned down my offer to pay her more—both then and now. Clearly, I needed to get more creative with showing Emerson my appreciation. The Birkin was a start, as was the additional time off, but I didn't intend to stop there.

"No." She crossed her arms over her chest. "I won't accept the money. I want to be there."

When I opened my mouth to protest again, she held up a hand. "Consider it part of Brooklyn's birthday gift."

"What about your training schedule? I don't want the lack of sleep to interfere with your recovery." I knew from experience how important rest could be to recovery. Some of my roles in the past had required me to pack on muscle. And it was exhausting.

"One night won't make or break me."

"You're sure?" I asked.

"It'll be fun."

A night at a luxury hotel with Emerson did sound like fun. Only, in my head, it didn't include six preteen girls. I sighed and stared at the ceiling. I hoped I wouldn't regret this.

Even before I opened the front door, I could hear the music playing. I rounded the corner to the living room and spied Brooklyn and Emerson. They didn't see me, so I hung back and watched as Brooklyn handed the microphone to Emerson.

Emerson hopped up on the couch and started belting out the lyrics, something about staying out too late. And then when it came to the chorus, she jumped down and started dancing around the room, shaking her hips in the most hypnotic way.

Our old nanny, Amalia, would've never done something like this. Something so fun and completely unrestrained.

And for all my fears of a new nanny disrupting Brooklyn's stability, I'd been wrong. I'd seen a positive change in Brooklyn since Emerson had moved in. She seemed more confident, empowered even.

Emerson shimmied, her bedazzled leotard leaving little to the imagination. The neckline scooping low on her chest. Her nipples hard beneath the material.

A memory flitted through my mind—the first time I'd met her. It was long before she'd ever come to the house to interview to be Brooklyn's nanny. Before I'd ever known she was a nanny.

Knox had been hosting a party on his yacht. Jude and some of his friends were there, including Emerson. And everyone had been drawn to her. Probably because she was confident as hell and didn't seem to give a fuck what anyone thought.

That night, I'd discovered her and a few others playing a game of strip poker on the upper deck. I should've left, but I was entranced by her. Amused by the way she trash-talked and impressed by her poker skills.

She hadn't known I was watching. And I shouldn't have been. But I couldn't look away—then or now.

At the time, I'd blamed it on the alcohol. On the ever-present loneliness I felt, despite often being surrounded by others. She seemed like a genuine person in a sea of fake.

And every time after that when our paths crossed, I'd been so damn tempted to flirt with her. Sleep with her. I knew she was interested—it was clear in the way she watched me. Hungrily.

But I'd always stopped myself. She was friends with my nephew. Her best friend was Knox's personal assistant—and now his girlfriend as well. Everyone was too connected. I didn't need to invite even more drama into my life.

It was more than that, though. As fun and flirtatious as Emerson was, she didn't strike me as the type of woman who was into one-night stands. And I couldn't bring myself to treat her like some meaningless fuck.

Brooklyn danced around Emerson, singing along at the top of her lungs. She had on the fluffiest dress I'd ever seen, the layers of tulle floating around her.

Now that Emerson was Brooklyn's nanny, I was even more grateful I'd never acted on my impulses. Especially with how attached my daughter was to her. But despite knowing all that, it was fucking torture to see Emerson day in and day out and know that nothing more could ever come of this. Of my attraction to her. Of the way she made me feel.

Emerson spun to face me and stilled. Her eyes went wide, but she quickly recovered, singing as if nothing had happened.

"Dad!" Brooklyn called. "You're home!" She frowned at my suit. "Go get changed."

"I can't believe you started without me."

She gnawed on her lip. "It was Emerson's idea."

Emerson lifted a shoulder. "Sometimes a girl's just gotta take matters into her own hands."

I wasn't sure if she'd intended for it to sound sexual, but that was where my head immediately went.

Was it really a surprise? The past few months since Emerson had started working for me, it felt as if she was everywhere I turned. Brooklyn was always gushing about Emerson. Or her scent lingered in the air. I couldn't fucking escape her, not even in my sleep.

She haunted my dreams, my dirtiest fantasies come to life in lurid detail. And then I'd wake up, hard as fucking steel and completely unsatisfied. It had to stop.

And yet I found myself saying in a low voice so that only Emerson could hear, "I can be okay with that, as long as we finish together."

Her cheeks flushed with color, though maybe that was from the dancing. I smirked and turned for my bedroom, but then the song changed and "22" came on.

Brooklyn grabbed my wrist. "Dad! It's your song."

I could feel Emerson's curious gaze burning into the side of my head. I closed my eyes and wished I could go back in time. Wished I could tell myself to say no to a dance party. Because then I wouldn't be accepting the microphone from Brooklyn and preparing to make a fool of myself in front of my daughter's nanny. In front of Emerson, of all people.

Brooklyn gave me two thumbs up, and I started tentatively singing the lyrics.

During the chorus break, I turned to Emerson. "This better not end up on the internet," I grumbled.

She held up her hands, biting her lip as if to fend off a smile. "I wouldn't dream of it." And somehow, I believed her.

In all the months she'd been with us, I'd never once felt as if she was going to betray my privacy. In fact, she'd been determined to protect Brooklyn and me, going above and beyond on multiple occasions.

At the moment, she honestly seemed too amazed I'd played along to say much at all. Or too amused, if the smile playing at her lips was anything to go by. I liked that smile. I liked those lips even more.

And I wanted to see if I could make her grin, so I leaned into the lyrics. Going all out with my performance. Showing off. Which was completely ridiculous since she was the nanny and I was her boss. I wasn't supposed to try to impress her, yet I couldn't seem to stop myself.

I spun Brooklyn around the room, and she laughed and laughed. It was times like this I wondered how Trinity could just turn her back on her daughter. And how she could justify using Brooklyn to get more money. I'd give up my entire fortune, I'd make a fool of myself, for even a moment with my daughter.

When the song finished, Emerson was in awe. "Is there anything you can't do?"

I leaned in and rasped, "Wouldn't you love to know."

For that brief beat between songs, we were frozen in time. Our eyes were locked, and everything else ceased to exist. She drew in a jagged breath, and my eyes darted to her lips.

God, I want to kiss you.

So. Fucking. Bad.

But then "I Knew You Were Trouble" blared through the speakers, and it felt like a reminder. A warning.

My reputation was already hanging on by a thread. And I'd seen way too many careers derailed by sex scandals to let mine follow that path. Not to mention the effect it would have on my daughter. I shuddered.

Nothing had happened. And nothing was going to happen. If I was smart, I'd stay far, far away from my daughter's nanny.

CHAPTER FIVE

Emerson

"**Y**ou weren't kidding. This is like a Broadway production," Kendall said, zooming in on the image of Brooklyn's Rumpelstiltskin costume on my phone.

"Right?" I laughed.

Brooklyn's school play was tonight. Kendall had given me a ride home after yoga. A few paparazzi had been hanging around outside the yoga studio, but I'd ignored them as I had most of the rumors swirling about Nate. Though today had definitely been more intense—more paparazzi. More insistent with their questions.

"One of the parents is a costume designer," I said. "And she volunteered to make them for the school."

"I guess I shouldn't be surprised, but damn." She handed back my phone, and it was reassuring to know that I wasn't the only one who felt out of place in this world of wealth and privilege.

"I know." I went over to my closet, digging through the options. "I mean, what am I even supposed to wear to something like this? This school is…" I blew a raspberry. "Next level."

And typically, the only time I was at the elite private school was for pickup or drop-off. But tonight, I'd be streaming into the auditorium along with the other parents.

"Well, yeah, I mean, most of the parents are celebrities or business moguls, right?"

"Yeah."

"What's got you so nervous?" Kendall asked.

"I just want Brooklyn to do well." I was both nervous and excited to watch her perform onstage. She'd worked really hard to memorize the lines over the past month, and I knew she could do it.

"Is that all?" she asked.

"I'll probably be one of the few nannies in attendance. I just—" I chewed on the inside of my cheek. "I'm worried it's going to spark even more rumors." There'd already been enough gossip about Nate's "hot new nanny." Hell, Kendall had heard the paparazzi shouting questions at me about my relationship with Nate after yoga. Perhaps Nate had been right to ask me to tone down my social media.

"Who cares?" she asked. "You know the truth. And people are going to talk, regardless."

"I know, but what if it gets back to Brooklyn?" I grabbed a dress from the rack and held it up.

She pulled a face at my outfit suggestion. "Boring."

That was what I'd been afraid of.

Kendall rested her palms on the mattress. But when I held up another outfit choice then cast it aside with a huff, she appraised me with keen interest.

"What's that look about?" I asked.

"You really like her."

"Of course I do. She's a good kid. I like all the kids I care for."

"No." She shook her head. "Brooklyn's different."

"What can I say?" I asked, returning yet another dress to the closet. "She's special."

"And her dad?" Kendall asked, knowing we'd had a tumultuous past.

"Doesn't annoy me as much as he used to," I conceded, my back still to her.

"I'm sure this helped," she teased, picking up the Birkin from my dresser and admiring it.

"It definitely didn't hurt," I said, still shocked that Nate had known it was my birthday, let alone... The magnitude of the gift was staggering.

I mean, it was the *exact* bag I'd coveted. In the *exact* color I'd wanted. I'd been saving up for it. Waiting for it.

And this one had come straight from the Hermès store. It wasn't resale. It was brand-new. And *Nate* had given it to me.

But as nice as the gesture was, the shift in our relationship was due to more than a designer bag. After Nate had told me about the naked nanny, I'd had more compassion and understanding toward him. And he had followed through on his promises—forgoing emails unless it was about Brooklyn's schedule.

He no longer mentioned his asinine house rules; it was almost as if they ceased to exist. Though, I never went in his bedroom—that was still a rule I adhered to. And while he respected my time off, I was no longer relegated to the guest room like a piece of furniture. He'd invited me to join him and Brooklyn for homemade pizza nights—just the three of us. And we'd had a dance party—or two.

Kendall stood, going over to the closet. "What about this?" She held up a dress, clearly avoiding my question. "It'll look great with your Birkin."

"Everything looks great with my Birkin," I said, studying the dress. "But that definitely has potential." I held it up to me.

"You're going to look hot. You always do."

"Thanks, but I wasn't going for hot."

"I know, but…" She rolled her lips between her teeth. "I just figured with all the sexy single dads…"

I rolled my eyes. "Nah. Not interested."

"When was the last time you even went on a date?"

"My life is too hectic right now."

She narrowed her eyes at me. "You always say that."

"Maybe things will be different after my next competition." I hadn't told her it would likely be my last. I didn't have the energy to get into the drama with my dad. And even if I did, I didn't want to burden Kendall with it. She already had enough going on.

"Mm-hmm." She crossed her arms over her chest. "I've heard that before. Anyway—" She stood. "I should get going. I'm sure you need to get ready."

A glance at the time had my pulse quickening. "Yikes! Nate will be home soon." Sooner than I'd realized.

I walked her to the front door, giving her a big hug. I ran back up the stairs and showered, quickly styling my hair and doing my makeup. Finally, I slid into the dress Kendall had suggested, pairing it with my Birkin bag. Evaluating my reflection, I was pleased with the result.

When I went downstairs, Nate was waiting in the kitchen, sipping a beer. He glanced up when I approached, his eyes lingering on my legs.

"Hey." I set my bag on the counter.

"Hey." He grinned, clearly pleased by my choice of accessory. "You look nice."

"Thanks." I tried not to preen. "Are you ready?"

"Whenever you are." He gestured toward the door to the garage. "Jackson's outside."

He downed the rest of his beer then tossed it in the recycling bin in the garage. Nate drank sometimes, usually in social situations. So for him to come home and open a beer right away was...unusual, to say the least.

Jackson held the car door open for me. I slid into the back seat, and Nate followed. He leaned his head back against the seat cushion and closed his eyes.

"Long day?" I asked, while Jackson pulled out of the garage.

"Yes." His lips parted on an exhale, and I couldn't look away. Couldn't imagine doing anything but kissing them. *Him.*

I really needed to stop. *This* had to stop. It was distracting and wildly unrealistic.

"Problems at the studio again?" I asked.

He shook his head. "My ex."

I jerked my head back. "Trinity?" He rarely mentioned her, and Brooklyn never did. "Does it have something to do with Brooklyn's birthday?"

The family celebration was next weekend, and then we'd have the slumber party with Brooklyn's friends the weekend after that. I couldn't believe it was already almost Thanksgiving.

"If only it were that simple," Nate said, dragging a hand down his face. "She's threatening to file for increased custody."

My heart gave a painful lurch. "Can she do that?"

"She can." He stared out the window. "And she often says she will, but rarely follows through."

"Why bother, then?"

When he turned to me, his eyes were flat as if he were devoid of emotion. "Because she likes to fuck with me. Because she wants more money. You name it."

Wow. I didn't know what to say. I'd never heard Nate speak with so much vehemence. They'd been rumored to have had a nasty custody battle, but that had been...what? Eight years ago?

It was the first time I'd heard him speak badly of Trinity. Though from the sounds of it, he had every right to.

And maybe I was overstepping, but I said, "I don't think that's what Brooklyn would want." Brooklyn never mentioned her mom. Never talked to her on the phone. It was almost as if Trinity didn't exist.

"Exactly." He pinched his lips together. "But Trinity doesn't give a fuck about what anyone else wants. Least of all her daughter."

My body tensed. The idea that Trinity or anyone would try to use Brooklyn...especially, her mom... It made me so incredibly angry.

"Sorry." Nate scrubbed a hand over his face and then stared out the window. "I shouldn't be telling you all this."

Shouldn't. The word fell like a hammer, cleaving me apart. Did he not trust me?

And could I really blame him if he didn't? I knew it wasn't personal—at least, I hoped it wasn't. Nate had been burned countless times. By his ex-wife. By former nannies and staff. And I was positive I didn't know the half of it.

"Nate." I reached out as if to place my hand over his but then retracted it. "I care about Brooklyn. And if Trinity decides to pursue this, I'd be happy to testify or help in any way I can to make sure she stays with you."

He turned to me slowly. "You mean that?"

I nodded. "Yes. Of course. Brooklyn adores you. And from what I've seen, I don't think she'd want to live with her mom any more than you want her to."

"You're right," he said. "But unfortunately, the state of California won't let Brooklyn tell the court what she wants until she's fourteen. And even if they would, I wouldn't want to put that kind of pressure on her."

I could respect that.

"When was the last time Brooklyn spent time with Trinity?"

"Two years ago. And if I have my way, that will be the last."

"That long ago?" I asked.

He nodded. "And while it pains me that Brooklyn doesn't have a mom who realizes how amazing she is, it's also my job to keep her safe."

"I know," I said, feeling that same obligation, nay desire, to watch out for Brooklyn. I felt this fierce need to protect her as if she were my own.

He blew out a breath. "I fucking hate that she still has so much control over our life."

"You had a prenup, though, right?"

He nodded. "Yes, but she tried to use Brooklyn as leverage to get more money out of me. She knew I didn't give a shit about the cash, but I would give anything for more time with my daughter."

Unbelievable. I didn't even know what to say other than, "I'm here. Whatever you need."

"Thank you, Emerson," he said, his expression solemn. "Lately, it feels like everyone's out to get me. And it's nice to know that someone's on my side."

"Anytime," I said, and I meant it.

Not because he was my one-time celebrity crush. Nor because he was my boss. But because I knew how much he loved his daughter. And he'd always do the right thing for her.

"Is there something else going on?" I asked, as if the potential custody battle wasn't enough.

He scoffed. "You've probably seen the rumors about Annalise Windsor and her tell-all?"

I nodded. I'd seen ads for the book, but I'd ignored them.

"I haven't paid them much attention." Though the paparazzi stationed outside the yoga studio today had asked for a comment about Nate's wild ways.

"If her book gets published as planned, it could give Trinity more ammunition if she decides to file for a change in custody."

"Can't you file a suit against Annalise for defamation or libel or whatever?" I asked.

"My legal team is doing everything they can. Ideally, the book will never be released. But if it is…well, people are going to form their own opinions. And it could potentially sway a judge's feelings about my ability to parent Brooklyn."

Fuck.

I wondered how long this had been going on. How he'd been dealing with all of this on top of all the other stressors he juggled. Running a studio. Preparing to star in a film. Solo parenting.

Jackson slowed as we neared Brooklyn's campus. We were almost there. I felt the need to say something, anything, to reassure Nate. I just didn't know what.

So, of course, I blurted the first thing that came to mind. "You really know how to pick 'em." I immediately cringed, wishing I'd just kept my mouth shut.

Nate chuckled, and I was relieved he didn't seem offended by my comment. "Don't I know it."

Jackson pulled onto the school grounds, driving through the gated entrance and then up to the theater building. Nate took a deep breath, his face transforming into the mask I saw him don anytime we were in public. It was fascinating, really. To peek behind the curtain. To know he felt comfortable enough with me to let his guard down.

He exited the car then held out his hand, waiting for me to take it. Other parents were filing in, but all I could focus on was his warm hand clasped around mine.

Feeling off-kilter from our conversation and his touch, I waved to his cousins Jasper and Graham when I saw them waiting on the steps. We stood outside, chatting while other parents arrived. Someone tapped me on the shoulder, and I turned to find Sophia's dad, Preston, smiling at me. Brooklyn and Sophia had been best friends since kindergarten, so I saw their family quite a bit.

I grinned. "Preston, hey. Good to see you. And you—" I smiled at Blair with her pigtails. "Hey, Blair bear." I glanced around. "Where's Alexis?"

"Inside," he said, shaking hands with Nate and his family. "She helped with some of the sets."

"Oh, that's right."

Alexis owned and ran a residential real estate firm. But she developed some residential projects on the side. She and her construction team had volunteered their time and skills for the sets.

"Want to sit together?" he asked.

"I'd love to."

We followed him inside, Preston and I chatting about the girls and their latest schoolwork and developmental stages. He was a pediatric oncology counselor. But before that, he'd been a nanny. Sophia's nanny, in fact.

People whispered Nate's name as we passed, and I tried to ignore them. Sometimes, I didn't know how Nate dealt with it. I'd had some experience with fame—my dad had played for the Hollywood Hawks, and I occasionally got recognized for my own athletic achievements. Now that I was Nate's nanny and had been featured in the tabloids several times, I definitely felt the curious stares, trying to ignore them and the jealous glances at my purse.

Maybe I shouldn't have brought the Birkin.

Preston leaned in. "Ignore them."

"I'm trying." I smiled. "But it's hard sometimes."

"You can't even imagine the uproar when people discovered I was dating Alexis."

"Oh yeah?" I asked, turning into a row and taking a seat between Preston and Nate.

"Yeah." He laughed. "Male nanny and the single mom. Not to mention the fact that I was younger." He shook his head with a rueful grin. "But eventually, everyone moved on. There's always a new scandal."

"That's a relief," I said while we waited for the curtain to rise.

It was only when the lights dimmed and the curtain rose that Nate finally seemed to relax a little. The constant attention and scrutiny had to be exhausting.

Sophia came onstage, acting the role of the miller's daughter. I smiled to myself, loving that Brooklyn and her best friend had taken the lead roles in the play. Preston beamed as Sophia delivered her lines with confidence, playing the part perfectly.

Finally, it was time for Brooklyn to make her entrance. And she did in a puff of smoke. I gripped Nate's arm without thinking, pride and excitement and nerves coursing through me.

For a minute, she didn't speak. Didn't blink, as far as I could tell. I started mouthing her lines, praying all our practice would kick in. Nate placed his hand over mine, his touch oddly reassuring.

Come on. Come on.

And then she started speaking, and Nate gave my hand a pat. I realized I was still gripping his arm, and I released him and mouthed, "Sorry."

He shook his head as if to wave away my concern, and any awkwardness I felt faded.

Brooklyn seemed to embrace her role fully, and I relaxed.

When she got to a section that she'd struggled with, I

silently mouthed her lines, sending her all my encouragement. She'd only just finished delivering them when Nate nudged me with a smile.

"What?" I mouthed, fighting a smile of my own.

He shook his head, his eyes lingering on my lips as he said a silent, "Nothing."

I narrowed my eyes at him, grateful for the dim lighting.

He leaned in, his breath brushing the shell of my ear when he whispered, "You're cute."

I tried not to shiver. Tried and failed. So much for banning him from my celebrity fuck-it list.

CHAPTER SIX

Nate

"I t's not too late to back out," I teased, nudging Emerson.

The limo was parked out front, and most of the girls had started to arrive. We'd already celebrated Brooklyn's birthday with family, and now it was time for her slumber party with friends at the Huxley Grand.

"Are you kidding?" Emerson said, grinning up at me. "I wouldn't miss this for the world."

I shook my head with a smile. But then my mood darkened. If only Brooklyn's own mother felt that way. Trinity had sent a card and a present—shocking. But the gift was something Brooklyn would've liked three years ago. Which only proved just how out of touch Trinity was with her own daughter.

Despite Trinity's meager effort, she hadn't even called to wish Brooklyn a happy birthday. Nor had she asked about attending Brooklyn's party, not that I'd want her there. The woman had a way of poisoning everything, making it about her.

Like now. On the eve of the release of Annalise's tell-all.

Fucking hell.

When Trinity's lawyer had contacted mine a few weeks ago to see if we needed to revise our custody agreement because of some of the leaked excerpts, I'd balked. But now, I was feeling less confident. This time, she might have some actual ammunition against me.

I sighed. Lately, it felt as if all my time and energy went to fighting legal battles against the women of my past. The judge had refused to issue a temporary restraining order or block the publication of Annalise's book.

Fortunately, Pierce and I had been working on my image in anticipation of such an event. Emerson had posted fewer bikini photos—thank fuck. If for no other reason than my sanity.

My new film was certainly generating a lot of positive buzz. Unfortunately, it also seemed to be prompting increased presales of Annalise's tell-all. And once the book released—assuming we couldn't stop it—my legal team would continue to try to get it removed from the market. Regardless, people were going to form an opinion of me from the leaked excerpts alone.

But for now, I had to trust that my team was handling it. And focus on spending time with my daughter and shielding her from all of it as best as I could.

"I appreciate it," I said to Emerson. "I'm sure you have many other fun things you could be doing on a Friday night."

She scoffed. "Um. I've been living with you for how long?"

"Five months." *Five months and four days.*

"Right. And in that time, how often have you seen me go out?"

I had to think about it. Thanks to the security system, I was aware of anyone who entered or exited the house. I had monitors in my office, and I would've known if she'd left the property. "Not very often."

"Exactly."

"I guess I'm just surprised someone like you is single," I said, immediately regretting it. "I mean," I backtracked, "I shouldn't have assumed that."

"I'm single by choice," she said with a hint of defiance. "Because I have yet to find a man worth my time."

"Oof," I joked. "On behalf of all men, I apologize."

"I'm sorry." She shook her head. "I didn't mean to sound so..." She waved a hand through the air. "Whatever."

"Bad breakup?" I asked.

"Just...disappointing, I guess. We were both very driven." She chewed on her bottom lip. "And after I got injured, he decided I was no longer useful to his social media presence. So he dumped me."

"And since then?"

She lifted a shoulder. "There seem to be a lack of worthy candidates."

I nodded, wondering what Emerson would consider a worthy candidate. Would I make the cut?

I pushed away the thought. I shouldn't care.

"I just figured you might have plans with Kendall," I said, knowing they often hung out. Especially since Knox and Kendall had broken up, though I didn't mention their split. I didn't want to get in the middle of *that*.

"We'll probably go to yoga this weekend before she..." Emerson trailed off, quickly closing her mouth as if to swallow back whatever she was going to say.

"Before she...?"

She shook her head. "Nothing. I shouldn't have said anything."

"Ah, but now I'm curious. Tell me." I narrowed my eyes at her.

She sighed, seeming to relent. "Before she moves to Paris."

"What?" I nearly choked on my tongue.

Did Knox know?

Even if they were no longer together, I couldn't imagine he'd be okay with it. I'd seen the way he'd looked at her. I knew how much he loved her, likely still loved her.

"It's a new assignment from the Hartwell Agency. I'm actually pretty jealous."

"Would you want to move to Paris?" I asked, desperately trying to quell the panic that arose at the idea of losing Emerson.

"I mean, maybe." She gave a little shrug. "But what I want is something money can't buy," she said with a wistful sigh.

What did that mean?

Before I could ask, the doorbell rang. Emerson went to answer the front door, welcoming Preston and Sophia in.

It wasn't long before all the girls had arrived, and we loaded into the limo and headed over to the Huxley Grand. After that, it was a blur of manicures and pedicures, silly games, pizza, and more. My event planner—Juliana Wright—had done a great job, as always. She'd transformed the living room of the Presidential Suite into a cozy-looking sleep space for all the girls. And Brooklyn was loving her party, which was all I really cared about.

There was a knock at the door. "Room service."

Emerson went to answer it. The man rolled in the cart, and I returned my attention to the girls.

"What are you doing?" Emerson asked, drawing my attention. She was frowning at the hotel employee. "Are you taking pictures?"

I stood and straightened. Rage flowing through my blood. But before I could confront him, the man turned and ran. Emerson took off, and I followed them out into the hall, my hand still on the door to the suite.

"Hey!" she shouted.

Jackson opened the door of the suite next to ours and

peered into the hall, while I stared on in shock. Jackson and the team from Hudson had set up a temporary command center next door, but we'd decided not to post anyone outside the girls' room since we didn't want to draw unnecessary attention. Besides, we'd rented out the entire floor, and it could only be accessed by a key card.

The guy was fast, but Emerson was faster. And I watched as she quickly caught up and tackled him. *Holy shit.*

"Did Emerson just tackle that guy?" Jackson asked from beside me.

"Yeah. She did." I tried not to laugh.

I was both in awe of her and...just wow.

Jackson jogged over to them while I texted my cousin Graham, who ran the hotel. It wasn't long before Graham exited the elevator along with hotel security. The intruder was escorted away.

"What happened?" Graham asked, his scowl even deeper than usual.

"Fucking paparazzi," I said, dragging a hand down my face. I'd just wanted Brooklyn to enjoy a normal birthday party. *Was that too much to ask?*

"But everyone's okay?" Graham asked.

"Yes. At least—" I glanced at Emerson. "I think so. Are you okay?"

Her cheeks were flushed, but she was barely winded. *Damn.* "I'm livid, but yes. I'm fine."

"If you ever want a career change, I'd hire you in a heartbeat," Jackson said, appraising her with a keen interest I didn't appreciate.

Emerson laughed. "Not sure I'm cut out for executive protection. I do better with kids."

"Many of our clients act like children," Jackson said, then his attention went to me as if remembering that I was standing there. "Present company excluded, of course." He straightened.

"Of course," I mused in a wry tone. Jackson and I had always gotten on just fine. Mostly because he didn't try to tell me what to do too often, and I let him do his job.

"Speaking of children—" Emerson hooked her thumb toward the hotel suite. "I should check on the girls."

"Thank you," I said, grabbing her hand and giving it a squeeze.

She nodded but seemed distracted. I watched her go, but I wasn't the only one. I didn't like the way Jackson's eyes lingered on her ass. If he weren't so damn good at his job, I would've fired him on the spot.

As soon as the door to the suite closed, Jackson apologized and assured me that his team would redouble their efforts.

Graham spoke up. "I'll find out if the photographer was an employee or if he bribed someone to pose as one." He placed a hand on my shoulder. "I'll make him pay."

"Thanks," I said, confident he would. Graham valued loyalty above anything else.

Graham turned for the elevator but then stopped. "Did Emerson actually tackle him?"

I laughed. "Yeah. She did."

His brow rose, but he said nothing more. Even so, I could tell he was impressed. Hell, so was I.

When I returned to the suite, the girls were making friendship bracelets and watching a movie as if nothing had happened. That was a relief, at least.

I went to the kitchen, where I found Emerson pacing, and kept my voice low. "Hey. You okay?"

"No. I'm not okay. That man snuck in and tried to take pictures of Brooklyn's party. How are you not more upset?"

My shoulders relaxed. I understood her frustration, but it

was a fact of my life. I was just glad the girls hadn't noticed, and Emerson was otherwise okay.

"I'm pissed, but it happens." Besides, the guy hadn't gotten the pictures he'd wanted.

"No." Her voice was stern. "It's bullshit."

I wasn't sure I'd ever seen her so angry.

"Hey." I wrapped my arm around her. "It doesn't matter. Don't let an asshole like him ruin a great evening."

Finally, she sighed, her shoulders seeming to relax. "You're right. I should know better by now. And I'm sorry if I made things worse by chasing after him."

"Nah. It was pretty awesome. I thought you were a heptathlete, not a football player," I teased.

She elbowed me, and I let out an "oomph."

"You better be nice, or I'll go work for Hudson Security."

"You wouldn't dare." I pinched her side. It was the second time in one evening she'd mentioned a career change, even if in jest. I didn't like it. Didn't want to imagine my life—or Brooklyn's—without her.

Emerson cocked her hip. "Jackson said he'd hire me in a heartbeat."

"Well, I'm not letting you go," I said, draping my arm over her shoulder.

She blinked up at me, her lips parting in surprise. I was so damn tempted to kiss her. But I couldn't. Wouldn't.

"Come on." I ushered her back toward the living room, even though all I wanted was a few more minutes alone with her.

When we returned, the girls were on a sugar high. Emerson laughed, taking it all in stride. She got them playing games until it burned off their energy and then turned on another movie. A few hours later, most of them were passed out in front of the TV.

"I'm going to owe you big-time for this," I said to Emerson as she yawned.

"Nah." She smiled. "It's fun. Reminds me of when Kendall and I were younger."

"You guys have been friends a long time, huh?"

She nodded. "Since middle school. I can remember making prank calls at slumber parties and staying up late playing truth or dare."

"Truth or dare, huh?"

"It's a classic. God, I love that game." Her smile was full of mischief and delight, and I wanted more.

"Let's play."

What am I doing?

"What? Truth or dare?" She laughed.

I lifted a shoulder. "Why not?"

Her smile faded, her expression turning more serious. I expected her to say no, but then she said, "Okay. You first. Truth or dare?"

"Dare."

She laughed. "I knew it." She glanced around, tapping her finger to her lips. "I dare you to call someone as yourself."

I chuckled. "Okay." I picked up my phone and held my finger over the button to indicate Sloan's number.

"No." She yanked it away from me. "Someone you don't know." She pulled up a random number on her phone. "Here. Use the hotel phone."

"You have to be more specific."

"I *am* being specific. Now, are you going to do it or not?" She gave me a look as if to say, "I doubt you'll ever go through with this."

Ha! I couldn't wait to see her face when I proved her wrong.

One glance at the girls told me they were out. I went to

the primary bedroom, feeling like a kid myself. Emerson plopped down on the bed, sitting cross-legged.

I picked up the phone and dialed the number. A woman answered, and when I told her my name, she thought I was joking. I tried to convince her it was me, but she hung up soon after. Emerson and I burst out laughing. It was ridiculous and childish, but I couldn't remember the last time I'd had so much fun.

"Your turn. Truth or dare?" I asked.

"Dare," she said, clutching her knees to her chest, her expression eager.

I chuckled. "Should've known you'd pick dare."

She scowled at me. "What's that supposed to mean?"

"Nothing." I glanced around the room, ignoring her glare. "I dare you to blindfold yourself and drink a beverage of my choice."

Her eyebrows climbed so high on her forehead, they nearly disappeared into her hair. "Blindfold myself."

"Mm-hmm." I glanced around, searching for a blindfold. I found one of the sleep masks from the girls' goody bags and handed it to her.

"And drink…" I watched her throat bob. I could think of something else I'd like to see her swallow down. And then the innuendo behind my words hit me. "Nope." She shook her head, her eyes no longer hooded. "Too vague. I'm going to need more details."

Had she been imagining the same thing I'd been? My cock between her lips. My come…

Jesus. What the hell is wrong with me? Emerson was my daughter's nanny. And my daughter and six of her friends were sleeping down the hall.

"No alcohol, right?" she asked.

"Promise," I said. Emerson was training. And even if she

weren't, I knew she'd never drink when she was responsible for Brooklyn and her friends.

"Fine," she huffed. "I'm willing to take a sip."

"This is truth or dare. Not truth or negotiation," I teased, though I would never push her to do anything she didn't want to.

"Fine," she huffed. "You're right." She slid the blindfold over her eyes. "Okay. Give it to me."

For once, I let myself admire the view. Emerson sitting on a plush hotel bed, her hands gripping the edge of the mattress. Her legs long and toned and...

"Nate?"

I jerked my attention to her face, grateful she was blindfolded. "Yes?"

"Are you coming?"

Oh god, how I wanted to.

"Yes. Yes." I moved over to the mini bar. "Just a sec."

I grabbed a clean glass and a few of the non-alcoholic beverages and mixed them together, along with some maple syrup and other items. I glanced over my shoulder. "No peeking."

"I'm not," Emerson said.

The beverage fizzed and the colors mingled. I was positive it would taste awful, and I tried not to laugh.

I strode over to her, gently placing the cup in her hand and wrapping my hands around hers to make sure it was secure. "Got it?" I had to force the words out, too focused on the feel of her skin on mine to think of much else.

She nodded, my attention snagging on her lips. "Got it."

She lifted the cup to her mouth. Her nose wrinkled, and she took a deep breath then swallowed some down. Her cheeks bulged, and for a minute, I thought she was going to spit it out.

"Swallow," I commanded, trying not to laugh at her expression.

She gulped loudly and then stuck out her tongue. "That was disgusting." She lifted her blindfold and glared down at the cup. "What was in that?"

I stifled a laugh. "It's probably better if I don't tell you."

She shuddered and handed me the cup. "Bleh. Take it away."

"Okay." I chuckled, dumping the contents into the bathroom sink.

"Your turn." She bounced on the bed, and her glee made me even more wary. "Truth or dare?"

"Truth," I said, hoping I wouldn't regret it. But currently, it seemed safer than opting for a dare.

"What was it like living in a hotel as a kid? Because my mind always goes to the movie *Eloise at the Plaza*."

I laughed. "I'm not sure I've ever seen it."

"It's a classic. It's got Julie Andrews and this six-year-old who lives in a hotel and has a knack for going on adventures with her nanny." When I said nothing more, she gave me an expectant look. "So…"

"So…" I leaned forward, resting my forearms on my thighs.

"Are you going to answer the question?" She leaned on her side, propping her head on her hand.

I considered giving her my standard answer, the one I gave in interviews. But the way she looked at me—with such trust and vulnerability—I found myself wanting to tell her more.

"It wasn't as glamorous as you'd think. It felt as if we were constantly moving from one hotel to another with no real place to call home."

She frowned. "That sounds…lonely."

"It was lonely at times, even though I had my cousins and my brother."

"I'm sorry."

"What are you apologizing for?" I asked. "It wasn't your fault. And it's not like I wasn't living a life most people can only dream of. I certainly wasn't lacking for anything." Implying otherwise made me feel guilty for complaining when it could've been a lot worse.

"Except a home. Parents," she said, her expression more solemn. She shook her head. "I'm sorry. I shouldn't have said anything."

"It's okay. They've been gone a long time." I took a shaky breath, not wanting to dwell on it. After my parents had died in a plane crash with my aunt and uncle, my grandparents had taken care of Knox, Graham, Sloan, Jasper, and me. "Truth or dare?"

"Truth."

"What do you want that money can't buy?"

"World peace."

I leaned closer, needing to be near her. "Liar."

"I'm not lying. I *do* want world peace."

"Yes, but there's something else. Something you were referencing earlier, and I don't think it was world peace. What was it?"

She groaned. "Seriously, Nate?"

I narrowed my eyes at her. "Yes. Seriously. You did choose truth after all."

She sighed. "Fine. Since you're forcing me to answer." She wouldn't meet my eyes. "I want to get married. I want to be a mom."

I nodded. That didn't surprise me. What surprised me was the fact that she was reluctant to talk about it. Almost as if she felt she didn't deserve it.

"You would make an amazing mom," I finally said, knowing it with certainty.

She smiled. "Thank you."

We played a few more rounds, continuing to flirt and push the boundaries. We were both getting tired, even if neither of us seemed willing to admit it. This was the most uninterrupted alone time I'd had with Emerson maybe ever, and I didn't want it to end. Was it wishful thinking to believe that she didn't want it to be over either?

"Since you made me drink something without seeing it…" She glanced around and grinned, settling on her next dare. "You have to eat something without using your hands."

My mind immediately went to eating her out without using my hands. My cock hardened, but then she left for the living room. *Get it together, man.*

She soon returned with a plate topped with several vanilla cupcakes with pink frosting. Disappointing but definitely more appropriate. I joined her at the table, taking a seat, our knees brushing.

She set it on the table, removing all but one from the plate. I started to take off the wrapper, and she tsked. "Nope. No hands."

I sighed and leaned forward and used my teeth to separate the pink paper from the cupcake. I was getting frosting all over my face. The cupcake kept falling over. It was a mess. *I* was a mess. Emerson covered her mouth with her hand, laughter bubbling out of her.

I glared at her and refocused my efforts. "Oh, you think this is funny, do you?"

She rolled her lips between her teeth. "Nope. Not at all."

"I don't mind getting dirty. Especially if it involves something sweet." I flicked my tongue over the icing like I wanted to flick her clit. "And pink. And perfect."

Her breath hitched. She knew exactly what I was doing.

I got a mouthful of cake and a face full of frosting. I kept my eyes on her as I devoured that cupcake, our gazes locked. Her breathing grew erratic, her lips parted. I imagined licking her pussy. I would bet it was even sweeter.

"Mm." I licked my lips, and she shifted, pressing her thighs together.

She stared at me, finally closing her jaw. "Your face is covered in frosting."

"I dare you to lick it off," I blurted before I could stop myself. But instead of trying to take it back, I held steady, wondering if she'd actually go through with it.

"What if I was going to choose truth?" she asked. Taunted. God, this was torture.

"Were you?"

She shook her head slowly, her eyes darting between my eyes and my lips. The air was charged with…something. It felt dangerous. Like we were teetering on the edge of a precipice.

She slid her finger across my cheek, swiping some of the pink frosting. She held her finger to her mouth then sucked it between her lips. "Mm."

God, how I wished that were my finger in her mouth. My cock. It took everything in me not to reach out for her.

I swallowed hard, wondering if she was intentionally trying to torture me. And then she leaned forward, her breath coasting over my cheek. Her lips mere inches from my skin.

The tension stretched between us, pulled taut like a bowstring. Her tongue flicked against my skin, and I shuddered. *Oh god.*

She inched back and swiped some icing from my cheek before painting it on her neck. "Your turn."

Fuck yes.

This was a bad idea for so many reasons, yet I couldn't

seem to stop myself. I leaned forward, pausing to inhale her scent. To soak in this moment. And then I swiped my tongue over the frosting, thoroughly cleaning her skin.

She let out the most erotic sigh. Goose bumps rose along her skin, and I wanted to explore every inch of her with my tongue.

"I think you missed some." I pointed to my face, knowing full well it was covered in sugar.

"Mm." She leaned forward. "You're right. There is a little —" She licked the skin near the corner of my mouth. "Here."

I dabbed my finger in the frosting of the other cupcake. "What about here?" I asked, painting my lips.

Her eyes darkened, and I waited for her to kiss me. She had to be the one to make the first move. And she looked as if she was going to do it, her entire body angling toward mine. Her gaze on my mouth.

She closed her eyes and leaned forward, but then there was a knock at the door. "Emmy?"

Emerson darted out of the chair like her ass was on fire. "Yeah." She swiped at her skin as if to hide any evidence of what we'd been doing.

Sophia peeked her head around the door. She clutched her stomach, her face a grimace. "My stomach hurts."

"Okay, sweetie. I'm coming." Emerson guided Sophia out of the room without a backward glance at me. I slumped in the chair.

What the fuck were you thinking?

I stood and locked the door before heading to the bathroom. I needed to cool the fuck down. I needed a shower to rinse the stickiness from my face and the dirty thoughts from my mind.

I switched on the water then climbed in, not even caring that it was still cold. Hell, it was probably a good thing, though nothing seemed to cool my desire for Emerson.

I pressed my palm to the tile and squeezed my eyes shut. I couldn't stop thinking about the feel of her lips on my skin and how they might feel...other places.

I swallowed hard, my cock lengthening. I gave it a tug, but then I remembered where I was and who I was thinking about. And how inappropriate it all was. I willed away those thoughts and scrubbed myself clean.

Emerson was the only woman I wanted, and the one I absolutely could not have.

CHAPTER SEVEN

Emerson

"Do you want me to call your dad?" I asked Sophia. We'd been sitting together for a while, talking while she sipped some water.

She shook her head. "I don't want to go home. I don't want to miss the rest of Brooklyn's birthday party."

"I know." I smoothed my hand down her back. "But she wouldn't want you to be miserable."

"I'll be fine," she said, straightening.

"If you're sure," I said, following her to the door that led to the living room where the rest of the girls were sleeping.

She nodded and tiptoed out to her pallet.

The door to Nate's bedroom opened, and he leaned against the doorframe. His face was clean, his hair wet as if he'd showered. As if our icing kisses had never happened. "Is she okay?"

I wasn't going to tell him that Sophia had gotten her period. "She's okay. I'm going to—" I hooked my thumb over my shoulder. "I should probably get some sleep."

He nodded. "Good idea. See you in the morning."

"Yeah." I headed into the other bedroom, my mind and body still abuzz after our game of truth or dare.

I washed my face and changed before climbing into bed. *Did that really just happen?* Had Nate licked frosting from my skin and then dared me to kiss him?

Our relationship had changed a lot in the past few months, but still…to kiss Nate? He wanted that? Wanted *me?*

I pushed away the thought, forcing myself to fall asleep. It didn't matter. It was a momentary lapse of judgment, and it wouldn't happen again.

I stared at the ceiling of my room at Nate's. It was Christmas. *Christmas!*

Weeks had passed as if in the blink of an eye. The night of Brooklyn's slumber party and my almost-kiss with Nate was never far from my mind. But I'd been so busy, I'd barely had time to think about it or what it meant.

Okay, that wasn't entirely true. But nothing like it had happened since.

And I'd filled my time with other activities so I wouldn't dwell on it. So I wouldn't put myself in another situation where I'd be tempted.

Oh, who was I kidding? I was always tempted by Nate.

But my time had been spent training. Researching materials for my athleisure line. Developing designs. Caring for Brooklyn. Celebrating Thanksgiving. Arguing with my dad about Abu Dhabi. Watching Nate prepare to take on this role. More training.

This was the first time in years I'd missed my family's annual ski trip to Aspen. Astrid and Papa J had been disappointed, but Dad had been livid. We'd argued about it, and he'd accused me of purposely going to Abu Dhabi just to avoid training.

I'd been so tempted to tell him that maybe I was avoiding *him*. But I didn't. I was angry, but I didn't want to hurt him.

Even so, his words continued to haunt me, our conversation going around and around in my head like my feet on the track.

And now, it was Christmas. And while part of me missed my family and our traditions, the other part was fucking excited for my upcoming all-expenses-paid trip to stay in a palace. Well, a hotel that used to be a palace anyway. And yes, technically, I was going to be working over the holiday. But spending time with Brooklyn never felt like a job.

I stretched, glancing at the time on my phone. I'd chatted with family last night on a video call. Dad hadn't pushed about training, and we'd had a nice conversation. Mostly thanks to Brooklyn. After a Christmas Eve dinner and a movie with Nate and Brooklyn, she'd joined me for part of the call. My family had been so sweet to her.

It was still early. Maybe I could go for a run. I'd been keeping up with my workouts—logging them online, so Dad knew I was holding up my end of the bargain. But considering the increased scrutiny from the paparazzi, I'd likely have to do it in the home gym.

The media attention had been relentless in the wake of the release of Annalise Windsor's tell-all. Parked outside the gate. Following our every move—even mine, though to a lesser extent. I'd never been more grateful for Jackson and his team. They kept us safe, provided a bubble of protection anytime we went out.

Nate seemed calm, and I didn't know how he was coping with all of it. I supposed it wasn't the first time he'd dealt with this level of frenzy. And it likely wouldn't be the last.

But I was furious. Enraged that Annalise had tried to capitalize on her relationship with him and succeeded. She may have been required to remove Nate's name from parts of her book, but everyone knew who she was referring to. And in several instances, the judge had let her keep the references to Nate, agreeing with her ridiculous argument that since there were so many people at a few of the parties referenced, it fell within the scope of "public knowledge."

I almost wished we'd gone to his cabin in Bear Creek as planned. It was about five hours north of LA by car, but the weather had been treacherous, and power was out in the surrounding area. Still, it sounded so cozy and Christmassy. So far away from Hollywood and all the bullshit currently swirling around Nate.

It was probably for the best, considering what had happened at Brooklyn's slumber party. I definitely didn't need a repeat, even if I wanted one. I closed my eyes and relived that memory, as I often did. But instead of being interrupted, I let it play out.

I imagined licking the frosting from Nate's lips, until he lost control and claimed my mouth. I dragged my fingers down my lips, down my throat, imagining they were his. *His* hands sliding over my breasts and tweaking my nipples. His mouth exploring my body, insistent to touch me through my underwear. To devour me like he had that cupcake.

I shuddered, slipping my hand beneath my underwear to glide over my clit. But in my mind, it was Nate's hand getting me off. Nate's rich voice in my ear. Telling me how badly he wanted me and exactly what he was going to do to me.

I let out a shaky breath, increasing the pressure until my toes curled. *Yes,* I hissed. *Yes.*

I could feel the pleasure building. My orgasm was so close. I was on the cusp. I quickened my pace. *That's it. That's...*

There was a knock at my door. "Emerson?"

Nate?

My eyes went wide. *Oh shit!*

"Just a minute!" I called in a high-pitched voice.

Had he heard that? Heard me?

There was whispering in the hall, and I realized Brooklyn must be with him. *Double shit!*

I grabbed some hand sanitizer from my nightstand, cleaning my hands before frantically smoothing down my hair. I threw on a robe then called, "Come in!"

Brooklyn peeked inside my room, still dressed in her PJs. They were navy with gingerbread men and candy canes all over them. "Merry Christmas!"

I smiled brightly. "Merry Christmas, B!"

I heard some whispering outside the door. "Oh, right. Can I come in? I have something for you." She held up a gift.

"Of course." I sat on the edge of my bed, grateful Nate had stayed in the hall. I'd always loved surprises, but having my boss catch me mid-orgasm when I was fantasizing about him wasn't my idea of fun.

"Here you go." She grinned. "Open it!"

I tore at the wrapping, grateful for the distraction, and smiled as soon as I saw what was inside. I held up my own pair of Christmas PJs. The pattern matched Brooklyn's, but they had shorts instead of pants. "Thank you. I love them!"

"Put them on quick! Breakfast is ready." Brooklyn ran off, pushing the door wide open as she went.

I hadn't expected to be included in Nate's celebration with Brooklyn. And I didn't want to intrude.

I glanced up at the doorway to find Nate standing there in his own pair of matching pajamas. "Oh, um—" *Shit.*

Nate smirked and lifted his mug of coffee to those decadent lips. Lips I'd been fantasizing about only minutes before. "Morning. Merry Christmas."

His deep morning voice rumbled through me, lighting up my nerves like a Christmas tree. I wasn't sure what surprised me more. The fact that he was standing in the doorway to my bedroom wishing me a merry Christmas or that he'd agreed to wear matching pajamas. A small part of me wanted to geek out that I was spending Christmas with the man who'd once been my celebrity crush. Was this real life?

"Merry Christmas," I said, still feeling off-kilter. And horny. God, I was so horny.

I must've stared too long because he tilted his head. "You feeling okay, Em? You look a little flushed."

Em? I wasn't sure he'd ever called me anything but Thorne or Emerson. And I was still trying to process that when Brooklyn called out, "Come on, guys! What's taking so long?"

"I hope you'll join us," Nate said, pushing off the door and putting his back to me.

How could I say no to that?

"Just give me a sec to change."

I headed to the bathroom and freshened up, combing my fingers through my hair before changing into my new pajamas. They were incredibly soft. And I was touched that Brooklyn and Nate had invited me to join them in their family tradition.

When I padded out to the dining room, my jaw fell to the floor. The Christmas tree had appeared in the living room weeks ago, but now gifts were piled beneath it. They were beautifully wrapped, as if Santa had just delivered them. And the table was set with gold plates and crystal goblets, covered silver trays lining the center.

"Wow."

"Do you like it?" Brooklyn asked, practically bouncing on her toes.

"I *love* it."

"Told you, Daddy," she said, elbowing Nate.

I smiled, loving the way they teased each other. "You did a great job, B."

"Oh no," Brooklyn said. "This was all Dad. He always goes all out for the holidays."

I met his eyes and smiled, thinking back to the night of Brooklyn's slumber party. Remembering Nate's admission that he loved the holidays. He'd always felt displaced as a child; he'd always wanted a home. So, ever since Brooklyn was born, he'd insisted they spend Christmas at home or his cabin in Bear Creek.

But when he'd talked about "going all out," as Brooklyn put it, I'd figured he'd have his staff do most of the work. And yes, they'd definitely done their fair share. But Nate had decorated his own tree—with Brooklyn's and my help. And I got the feeling he'd wrapped every single present himself.

"Well then, thank you, Nate."

He smiled and pulled out a chair for me, leaning down until his mouth was next to my ear. "Hungry?"

I shivered from his words and his proximity. "You have no idea."

"I wouldn't be so sure about that," he said, his hand skimming my shoulder. Or at least, that's what I thought I heard before he moved away and lifted the first dome.

My mouth watered. "Breakfast tacos? Are you serious?"

"Dad's idea," Brooklyn said, and I found him watching me with eager anticipation.

I'd once mentioned my love for tacos in passing—not just breakfast tacos, but any tacos, any time of day. They were so versatile. So delicious. I'd had no idea he was paying such close attention. And the idea that he wanted to please me made my skin heat for an entirely different reason.

"I thought Andre had the day off," I said, glancing around for Nate's private chef.

"He does. Brooklyn and I made them."

Nate had cooked me breakfast? My favorite breakfast, no less. I was so touched I nearly started crying.

Instead, I turned to him. "Thank you. This…" I cleared my throat. "It means a lot to me."

"BRB," Brooklyn said, seemingly unable to sit still. But her absence meant that Nate and I were completely alone.

"I appreciate you," Nate said, sincerity ringing through his voice. "And I'm really glad you're here."

What? I nearly choked on my tongue. *Am I dreaming?*

Boss. He's your boss, Em.

He's paying you to be here. And what he *means* is that he appreciates that you take care of his daughter. When it came time to open gifts, I worried that what I'd gotten Nate seemed silly, but it was incredibly difficult to find something that was both appropriate for my boss and a billionaire. I mean, what was I supposed to get a man who could buy literally anything?

Brooklyn went first, gushing over the waterproof camera and temporary tattoo pens I'd given her. Then it was Nate's turn. I chewed on my lip while I waited for him to open his gift from me. It was a daily calendar, each day with a different picture of Brooklyn.

He flipped through it and smiled before glancing up at me. "Thank you, Emerson."

I'd never had the full force of one of his smiles directed at me, and it was…wow. It was like being bathed in sunlight. I felt like I must be glowing in return.

Off-limits, I reminded myself even as I fought to deny the attraction I'd always felt toward him. Attraction that had only grown since the night of Brooklyn's slumber party. It was no longer a silly crush based on an idea I'd built of a man I didn't know. It was powerful and potent and real. And perhaps even reciprocated, judging by Nate's behavior that night.

I held my breath as he unwrapped the next box from me, hoping he'd like it as much as the last one.

"Is this a scrapbook?" Nate asked, while Brooklyn hopped up from the couch and darted toward the door. She and I shared a conspiratorial smile.

I refocused my attention on Nate. "I, uh—" I tucked my hair behind my ear, feeling shy all of a sudden. "I know how much you hate being apart from Brooklyn, so I filled it with pictures from when you were away. So maybe then you could feel like you were still part of everything."

He finally met my eyes, and when he spoke, his voice was clogged with emotion. "Thank you. That's…the nicest thing anyone's ever done for me."

I dipped my head, unable to handle the intensity of his stare. "Of course."

I shouldn't have worried he'd think the gift was silly or cheap. He turned the pages slowly, lingering on the images with a loving gaze.

When Brooklyn returned, she was wearing the costume I'd designed for this song. For the one she wanted to perform for her dad. And her guitar was slung around her neck.

"I wrote you a song." She beamed.

"You did?" He grinned, then teased, "Nice to know that your guitar lessons are paying off."

She focused on her guitar and took a deep breath, and I started recording on my phone. Then she launched into the song. It was upbeat yet slow, hopeful without being trite. And the lyrics. My god.

I'd heard her practice. And yet, seeing her perform it for Nate and watching him react to the words she said about him and their relationship… Well, it had me swiping away a tear.

He really was an amazing man and a wonderful father. Even if it had taken me some time to realize it. To peel past his controlling bullshit and get to the real Nate. Because that's who it felt like I got to see when it was just the three of us.

I wasn't falling for Nate Crawford, celebrity billionaire. I was falling for Nate, a man who happened to be famous and rich.

Falling for... My eyes widened. No. No. Not happening.

Brooklyn finished playing the last chord and looked to Nate. His expression was full of awe and adoration.

He stood and pulled her in for a hug while I was still processing my bombshell. "That was amazing."

"I can't take all the credit," Brooklyn said. "Emmy helped with some of the lyrics and made my costume. She said it was good practice for her athleisure line."

"Those lyrics were all you, B."

"You want to design a clothing line?" he asked, while Brooklyn returned her guitar to her room.

"Someday, yes." It felt like such a pipe dream at this point, it was laughable.

He hesitated then said, "I know someone who could help you with that."

I appreciated the offer more than he could know. It was nice to know that he saw potential in my idea. "Thanks, but I want to do this on my own."

He lifted his chin, and I got the impression my answer surprised him. Before he could say more, Brooklyn skipped back into the room.

"I loved your song," Nate said, hugging her close. "Thank you."

Brooklyn busted out her new temporary tattoo markers now that we'd finished opening presents. "Okay. We're doing matching tattoos."

"Awesome!" I held out my arm. They'd given me so much, and I couldn't believe how thoughtful and personal all the gifts were. "Me first."

Brooklyn grinned. "Okay, but no peeking." She started drawing on my arm, and it tickled. "Stay still." She held my arm more firmly, and I tried not to laugh—both at her expression and the way the marker felt on my skin.

"Come on, Dad." She waved him over. "Help me."

"You're doing just fine," he said, and I was both relieved and disappointed.

"Please?" Brooklyn added, turning up the charm.

It was so predictable, I nearly laughed. As expected, Nate sighed and stood, coming over to where we were sitting. "What do you want me to do?"

"Can you color this in?" she asked him just as her phone rang. The design was a surprise since I'd told her to do whatever she wanted. I figured it'd wash off in a few days anyway. "Oh! Sophia's calling."

"Go. Go," he said, and she ran toward the stairs that led to her room.

Nate took her place, picking up where she'd left off. The marker tickled my skin, and I tried not to focus on how close he was sitting to me. Or how amazing he smelled.

"Thank you for the gifts," he said, setting down the first marker and picking up another. What was he doing? Whatever it was, I didn't want him to stop. Especially not when his thumb caressed the inside of my forearm, swiping back and forth over the sensitive skin. "I hope you're not missing your family too much."

I smiled, appreciating his concern. Trying to focus on his words instead of the way his proximity made me feel. "I chatted with them a bit last night. But honestly, I think this time apart was a good thing."

"Yeah?"

"I love my family, but my dad has been pushing me hard about my next competition."

"Is that unusual?" he asked, lifting his head to meet my gaze.

"Yes and no. It's just…" I tucked my hair behind my ear. "It will probably be my last." It felt strange to admit that aloud to someone other than my dad. Strange and liberating.

"Oh." Nate frowned. "Is everything okay?"

"Yeah." I sliced a hand through the air, unwilling to mention my performance anxiety. Because, really, that wasn't the main reason behind my desire to retire. It had merely accelerated my decision. "I'm just ready to shift directions, and he isn't. So we made a deal that I would do one last competition and then decide."

"If you could quit competing now, would you?"

"Yes." Even though part of me knew my dad was right.

Our time apart had given me some perspective, and I knew I didn't want to end my career on such a low note. But that didn't make me any more excited about competing.

"Wow." He jerked his head back. "That was definitive."

I smiled. "Yeah. It's been a long time coming."

"Yet you're still planning to compete in February," he said, an unspoken question in his words.

"Fulfilling a promise."

"To yourself?" he asked.

"And my dad." Mostly my dad, even if he was the one helping me keep my promises to myself.

A muscle in Nate's neck twitched. "So he's pushing you to do it." It wasn't a question. Not really.

"It's not that simple."

"I can appreciate that, but are you sure it's worth it?"

"I—" I wasn't sure how to answer that. I wasn't sure I had enough distance from the situation to know. "I don't know. But you probably don't want to hear about all my drama.

Especially when it's Christmas, and you already have enough of your own."

I'd hoped that everything had died down with Trinity and her threats to battle Nate for custody. He hadn't said anything about it, and I'd been too afraid to ask.

He returned his attention to my arm. To my temporary tattoo. "Understatement of the century."

I followed his gaze to my skin. Brooklyn had drawn a butterfly. But Nate had added a red rose, complete with thorns. It was beautiful. I wondered why he'd chosen it, though I was impressed by his artistic ability.

"Well, at least you know your nanny drama is a thing of the past." I smiled, hoping to reassure him that I was on his side. "No more naked nannies."

"Yep," he said in a clipped voice. "No more naked nannies."

Only in my dreams. My cheeks heated.

CHAPTER EIGHT

Nate

"Dad."

"Hm?" I said absent-mindedly. My focus was on the scrapbook Emerson had given me, lingering on a rare image of the two of them. Most of the others were of just Brooklyn—ice-skating, hanging out with Sophia, laughing. All the things I'd missed.

A drop in the bucket compared to the ones I'd miss if Trinity got her way. I gripped the edge of the book tighter, wishing there was something I could do to put an end to her threats once and for all.

Pierce had been hounding me to post more images of my family. To show that I was a family man, a loving dad. But I didn't want to share my private moments with the world. I resented the mere suggestion. It was an invasion of my privacy and Brooklyn's privacy, and I wouldn't do it.

"*Dad*," Brooklyn said again, this time more insistent.

"What's that?" I asked, finally lifting my head.

"Auntie Sloan wants to know if now's a good time to video chat."

Graham and Jasper had gone to spend the holiday with

Sloan in London. She'd received a series of threatening letters in the past few weeks, and we were concerned. Well, everyone except Sloan was concerned. She thought Graham and Jasper were being overprotective and ridiculous, but Knox and I had agreed they should go.

Knox was in Paris. And Jude was off with friends in Turks and Caicos. Our family was spread out across the globe this year, but unlike years in the past, it didn't bother me as much.

Because of Emerson.

I stood and pushed away the thought.

"Yeah. Of course," I said, giving Brooklyn's shoulder a squeeze as I passed the bed. She was sprawled out on my mattress, her feet in the air as she peered down at her phone. "You can ask her to call on my tablet if you want since the screen's bigger." I tossed it on the bed.

"Good idea!" Brooklyn said, grabbing the device. But when my phone rang a second later, Brooklyn answered it instead. "Auntie Sloan! Hi! Merry Christmas!"

I could hear my cousin's warm voice through the phone, and I leaned over behind Brooklyn and waved. "Hey, Sloan." It was always nice to connect with my family, even if only virtually.

"Hey, Nate." Her smile was warm but tired. I wondered if Graham and Jasper's bickering was wearing her out.

"How's London?" I asked.

"Jolly good!" Jasper popped into view behind her, a paper crown on his head and a fake British accent in full force.

I laughed despite myself. "I see *someone's* having fun."

"Oh yes." He grinned wickedly. "Now if only we could get Graham to loosen up." He panned the camera over to Graham, who scowled. *What's new?*

Brooklyn narrowed her eyes at him. "Uncle Graham, it's Christmas. Don't be a Scrooge!"

"Bah humbug," Graham said, but everyone else laughed.

"Oh, Uncle Graham," Brooklyn sighed. "Are you grumpy because that travel blogger's picking on you again?"

I raised my brow, surprised that Brooklyn paid that much attention—not just to our previous conversations but to a travel blog. I watched Graham for his reaction. Apparently, I wasn't the only one. I could see Sloan and Jasper just as anxious to see how he'd respond. Nothing got Graham as fired up as an attack on the hotel empire, especially one from Gilded Lily, a popular luxury-travel blogger.

"When is she *not* picking on me?" Graham muttered.

Brooklyn's expression was sympathetic. "You just have to do what Emmy always tells me."

"Hack her site and make it crash?"

I glared at him, but it was unnecessary. Brooklyn's chiding tone was likely punishment enough. Graham might be a grumpy bastard, but he'd always had a soft spot for my daughter.

"No, silly," she said. "You need to shake it off," she sang the words. "Shake it off."

He rolled his eyes but grudgingly complied, dancing along with Brooklyn briefly.

"Where's Prince Albert," Brooklyn asked. "And V?"

Jasper angled the camera so it was pointed at Graham's dogs, who were—predictably—resting at his feet. He spoiled them rotten. One of the Irish Wolfhounds—I never remembered which was which—lifted its head at the sound of Brooklyn's voice saying their names.

"So," I said. "How are things otherwise?"

"It's fu—" I glared at Jasper. And he said, "Flipping cold here," angling the camera so we could see the snow falling on the London skyline.

"How pretty!" Brooklyn said. "Now *that* looks like Christmas. We might go swimming later."

"That sounds fun," Sloan said. "What else have you been up to?"

"We had tacos for breakfast and tried out my new karaoke machine. Thank you for my present. I love it!"

Sloan smiled. "I'm so glad. Hopefully, your dad is enjoying it too." She smirked.

"Oh yeah." Brooklyn laughed. "Especially when Dad and Emmy sang a duet."

I scowled, wishing she hadn't decided to share that tidbit. My family's interest was definitely piqued.

"Duet, huh?" Sloan asked, brow arched in question. She'd been needling me almost nonstop about Emerson since I'd asked for her help acquiring the damn Hermès.

Fortunately, Brooklyn didn't leave anyone time to respond, saying, "We're going to watch Christmas movies after this." She turned to me. "Right, Dad?"

"Yep." I nodded. It was tradition.

"Will Emmy be joining you for that, too?" Graham asked with a sardonic twist to his lips.

"Of course!" Brooklyn said. "Want to say hi?"

"Of course," Jasper said, mimicking Brooklyn's tone. *Fucker.*

Brooklyn carried my phone to the living room, and I trailed behind. I could hear Emerson talking with my family, jumping into the conversation and teasing as if she was one of us. I was certainly coming to view her as family and not an employee, though I knew it was dangerous to blur those lines.

The night of Brooklyn's slumber party was proof of that. Emerson and I hadn't spoken of it since, and everything had gone back to normal. And that was part of the problem.

Since our almost-kiss, I found it harder to act like everything was "normal." I didn't want to hide my feelings for her. I was sick of putting on an act when I was at home. When she was around. Pretending I felt nothing for her beyond her role as my employee.

So when Jasper flirted with Emerson—again—I had to clench my fists to keep from smashing the device. He was an incorrigible flirt. A playboy. And he thought she was hot.

Hell, so did I. But she was my daughter's nanny. And I kept telling myself that kind of thing never ended well.

I could think of only one instance in which it had—Alexis and Preston. Preston had been Alexis's nanny, and when they'd first started hooking up, I'd figured he was only interested in Alexis's money. And she only wanted him for sex. How wrong I'd been on all accounts.

But that was how jaded I'd become since my divorce. My fame didn't help. *Before*, women had been after me for my money. But now that I was an actor and executive producer, they wanted even more from me. A role in a movie. An *in* with the studio. Whatever.

Emerson placed her hand on my arm, and my eyes were glued to the spot where our skin touched. "Nate?"

"Yes?"

"Graham had a couple questions for you about the Huxley Grand Abu Dhabi."

"Oh." I blinked a few times and turned my attention back to the screen, where my cousins were studying me with keen interest. *Fuck.* "Sure."

"Oh, come on." Jasper slugged Graham's arm. "It's Christmas. Do you ever stop working?"

"Someone has to keep the family business running," he shot back.

Sloan rolled her eyes. And Jasper scoffed. "Of course."

Emerson jumped in, perhaps wishing to dispel the growing tension. "Is it true that the Huxley Grand Abu Dhabi is larger than Buckingham Palace?"

Graham nodded, a spark of appreciation in his eyes. "The

Queen of England was once a guest in the suite where you'll be staying."

Great. And now, thanks to Emerson's interest in the Huxley empire, Graham would likely be interested in her too.

The thought was laughable. I hadn't seen Graham date someone in years. Not since he was in college. So I had no idea what his type was or if he even had one. But I had a feeling that as much as he might appreciate Emerson's protectiveness, loyalty, and interest in the Huxley Hotel empire, her energy would be overwhelming for someone as grumpy and brooding as him.

"Holy...wow." Emerson said, bringing my attention back to the conversation.

"There are more than 6,000 square meters of 22-karat gold leaf," Graham continued, always happy to talk about the Huxley empire he oversaw. "And the wallpaper is pure silk. Imported from India."

"I'm sure it's beautiful," she said, her voice full of admiration. "And hopefully we won't have any more issues with paparazzi posing as staff."

A muscle twitched in Graham's neck. "We better not. I've taken additional measures to prevent it."

"And so has Jackson," I said.

"Good."

Emerson returned to asking questions about the Huxley Grand Abu Dhabi. Graham was more than happy to drone on about the history of the building until another call came in. I stilled when Trinity's name flashed across the screen. *What the...*

Emerson turned to me, eyes questioning. She'd never had to interact with my ex before, and I could tell she was surprised Trinity was calling. Hell, so was I.

Brooklyn glanced up at me, her brow furrowed. "Dad, why's *she* calling?"

I schooled my face into a neutral expression as I tried to push aside my personal feelings about my ex. I reminded myself that Trinity was Brooklyn's mother, even if she didn't act like it most of the time. I mean, hell, Trinity couldn't even find the time to call and wish her daughter a happy birthday, but she could try to fight me for custody?

I smiled, hoping it came off as reassuring instead of deranged. "I'm sure she just wants to wish you a merry Christmas."

Brooklyn dipped her head then asked, "Do I have to talk to her?"

My heart cracked a little.

I wanted to say no, but I knew Trinity would try to twist it to accuse me of parental alienation—that I was intentionally trying to keep her away from her daughter or poison their relationship. I never said anything negative about Trinity in front of Brooklyn. I rarely even talked about her because, for the most part, she didn't exist in our world. Except when it was convenient for Trinity or benefited her.

"Who is it?" Sloan asked.

"Trinity."

Sloan was fuming. Jasper opened his mouth to say something—likely negative. And Graham took over. "Merry Christmas. Talk to you later." He ended the call abruptly.

I knew he was only trying to protect Brooklyn, but I nearly laughed at the gruff way in which he'd done it.

"I'll just answer, and if you want to say hi, you can," I said to Brooklyn.

Emerson excused herself, standing just as I'd tapped the button to connect the call. I took a deep breath as Trinity's face filled the screen. The sight of my ex immediately set me on

93

edge. But I was an actor. I could act pleasant for five minutes or however long it took Trinity to grow bored and end the call. To prove whatever point she was currently trying to make.

"Brooklyn, darling," she crooned, and I clamped my mouth shut. "Merry Christmas."

"Merry Christmas," Brooklyn muttered, becoming a shell of her usual bubbly self.

I clenched my fists and then released them, placing my hand on Brooklyn's back and rubbing circles in silent support.

Trinity blabbered on for a few minutes before finally saying, "Hey, sweetie. Can I talk to your dad alone for a sec?"

As much as I despised Trinity for abandoning our daughter, a selfish part of me was grateful I'd never had to deal with the logistics of sharing custody. I got all Brooklyn's birthdays. All her Christmases. And I was determined not to let that change just because Trinity had suddenly decided to act like she cared.

If she genuinely wanted a relationship with our daughter, then I was all for it. But she'd always viewed Brooklyn as a pawn, and I refused to play her games.

"Yep." Brooklyn handed me the device and then darted toward Emerson's room without even saying goodbye. And definitely not "I love you."

I stood and carried the phone to my office, closing the door behind me. I was grateful Brooklyn had someone like Emerson to turn to. Someone she could trust and confide in in addition to me.

"What do you want?" I snapped, unable to control myself after seeing how Trinity's call had impacted Brooklyn.

"Merry Christmas to you too," Trinity said in an upbeat tone.

"If there's a point, you better get to it."

She sighed and studied her perfectly manicured fingernails. "Oh, Nate. Always in such a rush. If only you could've slowed down and stopped being so controlling, maybe we would've had a chance."

I tried not to let her see how her words affected me. Even if there was a kernel of truth to them, they didn't tell the entire story. We would've never had a chance because she'd never been authentic about who she was. And by the time I'd realized it, it was too late.

That said, I knew my ex well enough to know she was baiting me. But I refused to stoop to her level. It wasn't worth my time.

"Fine," Trinity said in a snarky tone. "Be that way."

I gripped the device so hard I was surprised I didn't crack the screen. She could be so immature sometimes. I honestly wasn't sure what I'd ever seen in her.

"I just thought it would be nice for us to talk," she continued. "You know, without involving all the suits. Because this doesn't need to be that complicated."

If only I'd talked her into relinquishing her parental rights when we'd divorced. Then I wouldn't have had the threat of another custody battle hanging over my head all these years. But at the time, I'd just wanted to be done.

And initially—naively—I'd thought maybe Trinity would want to have a relationship with her daughter. Besides, I couldn't do that to Brooklyn. If Trinity didn't want to be involved, that was her choice. But I wasn't going to be the one to cut Brooklyn's mother out of her life.

"You're right. It doesn't," I said, cutting her off. "Why don't you just tell me what you really want since we both know it isn't more time with Brooklyn?"

"Of course I want more time with my daughter," she said in an indignant tone. As if I'd somehow offended her, when I could count the number of years she'd sent birthday gifts to our daughter on one hand.

"You have a funny way of showing it," I said, growing more and more agitated.

We both knew she wanted more money, not more time with Brooklyn. But she wasn't going to come right out and say it. She was too cunning. Hell, she probably suspected that I was recording this conversation. And maybe I should've been.

"Ooh. Someone's testy. Having trouble learning your lines again?"

I seethed. I wanted to remind her that that had happened *once.* But her comment was unnerving because I was used to taking on roles that allowed for more improvisation. Since my new part stayed faithful to the text of the novel, I wouldn't have as much freedom with my lines.

"Maybe you should have your nanny help you run them," she said, her voice dripping with honey.

Emerson had offered to help months ago, though I knew it was in jest. But I couldn't impose on her more than I already had. Even if I could use the practice, running lines with Emerson would be too risky, considering the subject matter.

"I'm sure she'd be happy to help you with all sorts of things," Trinity added in a suggestive tone. "If she isn't already."

I clenched my fists. Trinity had some nerve. She'd upset Brooklyn, on Christmas, no less. And now she was insulting Emerson. I was done.

"Get to the point, Trinity. Or I'm hanging up."

"I want Marie Antoinette's diamond and pearl necklace."

No. I scoffed. "No fucking way. I'd rather see you in court."

I ended the call without giving her a chance to respond. I would never give her that necklace—or any other piece of jewelry that had been part of my mother's collection.

I threw my phone across the room, and it collided with the wall with a satisfying crunch. I'd probably regret that later, but at the moment, I couldn't find it in me to care.

Trinity didn't matter. Her bullshit didn't matter. My time with Brooklyn was precious, and I wasn't going to let Trinity —or anyone else—ruin it.

CHAPTER NINE

Nate

I lifted the champagne glass to my lips, surveying the room as I counted the minutes until I could leave. It was the annual end-of-year party for the studio, and it was a star-studded event. I wondered what Brooklyn and Emerson were up to. I wished I were watching movies on the couch with them, instead of parading around in a tux and pretending to be remotely interested in any of these banal conversations.

I peered out at the LA skyline, my mind elsewhere. Preoccupied with our upcoming trip to Abu Dhabi.

Jackson had already sent part of his team there to prepare. In a few days, he and another one of his team would fly out with Emerson, Brooklyn, and me. I was wound tight with anticipation. About the filming. About…everything.

Annalise's tell-all had released. Trinity had filed her custody challenge. I was trying to hold it together while running a studio and raising Brooklyn. And in the center of it all was Emerson, the true calm in the chaos, grounding both Brooklyn and me whether she realized it or not.

The past few months, I'd come to rely on her, trust her.

And not just with things that pertained to my daughter. I'd ask Emerson for fashion advice. Business advice. Her thoughts on my workout. I'd make excuses to spend time with her. I couldn't stop thinking about her.

It was a problem.

My phone buzzed, and I removed it from my pocket to see Brooklyn's name flashing on the screen. I furrowed my brow. She wouldn't have called during a work event unless it was important. Maybe she'd called by accident?

I stepped into the hallway. Before I could even say hello, Brooklyn was talking at full speed. Something about Emmy and an ambulance. Panic zipped through me. I wasn't sure whether her words were garbled with tears or my ears were full of blood. The stuff whooshed through my head, and my heart was racing.

"Brooklyn," I said, heading straight for the parking garage. Since I'd only planned to attend the party and then go home, I'd asked Jackson to stay at the house. "Take a breath, sweetie." I waited a beat then asked, "Are you okay?"

"Yes, but Emmy—" She started crying harder, and I fought to stay calm despite my rising panic.

"Something happened to Emmy," I said, trying to understand. Trying not to freak the fuck out. Losing my cool wouldn't help.

I heard some noise in the background, and then Andre, our chef, said, "Emmy had some kind of allergic reaction and was taken to the hospital. Brooklyn did the right thing—calling 9-1-1."

I was so proud of my daughter—staying calm. Calling for help.

"How's Emerson?" I climbed into my car, yanking off my tie and unbuttoning the top two buttons of my shirt. I'd hoped that would help me breathe easier, but it hadn't made a damn difference.

"She was conscious when they took her," Andre said. "I think." His voice wavered, though I could tell he was trying not to scare Brooklyn. "I don't know. There was so much going on."

"Daddy. I'm scared," Brooklyn whispered, and it damn near broke me.

"Where was she taken?" My only thought was of getting to Emerson. Of making sure she was okay.

Andre was too upset to relay the details, so Belinda took over, filling me in and assuring me she would take care of Brooklyn. I promised to call Brooklyn as soon as I had an update. We ended the call, and I punched the gas, speeding toward the hospital.

I kept picturing Emerson in the back of the ambulance. Her body limp and lifeless. Her warmth and personality just…gone.

Fuck. I slammed my hand against the steering wheel, filled with regrets for how I'd treated her in the past. For all the things I'd left unsaid.

I can't stop thinking about you.

I don't know what I'd do without you and not just because of Brooklyn.

When I pulled up to the hospital, I grabbed the baseball hat I kept in my glove box and climbed out of the car. The valet's eyes went wide when he saw my McLaren, and I was grateful he seemed more interested in my vehicle than its owner.

I jogged inside, stopping at the nurses station despite my every instinct telling me to keep moving.

Don't make eye contact.

Don't let them recognize you.

"I'm here for Emerson Thorne," I said in a rush, careful to keep my head ducked and my hat pulled low.

"Unless you're family, you'll have to wait," the nurse said

without giving me a second glance. So far, I'd been successful at concealing my identity.

"I, um, I—" I glanced around, desperate to see Emerson. To know she was okay. I cleared my throat and slid a Benjamin across the top of the counter.

Her eyebrows nearly rose to her hairline, but otherwise, she didn't react. "I'm going to pretend I didn't see that."

I debated slipping her more money, but I got the feeling she wasn't going to budge. *Fuck. Maybe I would've had more luck offering her a selfie.*

I walked away from the desk and stood in front of the vending machines, feigning interest in their contents while debating my options. Brooklyn had already texted me a handful of times, and I knew she was freaking out. I didn't know what to tell her. I didn't know anything.

I could feel the curious stares of several people in the waiting area. There was a whispered hush of interest, and I heard my name uttered once or twice. They talked about me as if I weren't even there. As if I weren't a real person. I had about ten seconds before someone approached for an autograph.

Fuck. Fucking. Fuck.

What had I even been thinking? Coming to the hospital. Hoping I could go unnoticed.

I *hadn't* been thinking. That was the problem. When I'd heard that Emerson was hurt, my first thought was to comfort her.

Now I was at risk of causing an incident, and I was still no closer to seeing Emerson.

My blood pressure skyrocketed, even as I ducked my head, trying to hide behind the bill of my hat. It didn't matter what I did; I was running out of time.

I sighed and pinched the bridge of my nose. If only she'd been taken to Cedars. I had some pull there since I'd donated enough money to have an entire pediatric wing with my name on it. *Fuck.*

The first nurse left, and another one—a more friendly looking one—took her place. I sidled up to the counter once more.

"I'm here to see Emerson Thorne."

"Your relation?" Her monotone voice did not inspire much confidence.

"I'm her fiancé," I blurted, immediately kicking myself. Why couldn't I have said I was her brother? Her cousin? *Anything* but her fiancé.

She lifted her head, and when her eyes met my face, I saw them light up with recognition. *Fuck.*

Should've gone the selfie route.

"Is that so?" She stood and planted her hand on her hip, skepticism written across her face.

"Yes," I said, knowing I was stuck now. I couldn't back down; all I could do was sell it.

"I know who you are," she said, wagging her finger at me. "And I haven't heard *anything* about you being engaged."

I could've laughed at that. Most of the stuff printed about me was bullshit. But that wasn't the point. Not right now. I was lying, but I needed her to believe it.

"Also—" She peered down at her computer. "You weren't listed as her emergency contact."

"It only happened recently," I said, assuming her dad was her emergency contact. But Declan was still in Aspen with the rest of her family. "I doubt she thought to change it. Besides—" I leaned in, and I could see that eager look in her eye. She was just waiting for me to share something juicy. "We wanted to keep it private as long as possible. Just enjoy being engaged a little while longer without the world knowing."

What the fuck is wrong with you?

The lies just kept spilling out of me.

The nurse held my gaze, her eyes narrowing. Sweat trickled down my back, and I tried not to tug on the collar of my shirt. If this didn't work, I didn't know what I was going to do.

Emerson wasn't answering her phone, and I needed to see her. I *would* see her, even if I had to donate enough to have a wing named after me at this hospital to make it happen. Hell, maybe if my star status or my money wouldn't do the trick, I'd have Graham hack the patient database and add me as her emergency contact.

The nurse finally relented, jerking her head in the direction of the door that led to the patients' rooms. "Room 412."

"Thank you," I breathed.

I rushed down the hall and entered room 412 without knocking. Emerson was lying in the bed with her eyes closed. She had on a hospital gown, an IV pole connected by a tube and some wires strapped to her.

"Emerson." I nearly choked on her name. Her skin was so red. So puffy. Her lips and cheeks and eyes swollen to the point that it looked painful.

I reached out as if to touch her but then stopped myself, my fingers curling into a fist instead.

Her eyes fluttered open—well, open as much as they could in her current state—and she blinked a few times. For a minute, I worried she'd forgotten my name, but then she said, "Well, hello, Mr. Crawford," in a sultry tone that went straight to my cock.

I cleared my throat. "Emerson?"

"That's my name. Don't wear it out."

I had whiplash from her quick change of tone and my body's reactions. "Are you okay?"

"Oh yeah." She shifted, wiggling her feet under the blanket. "Never better."

I furrowed my brow. "That's...good." I was pleased that she was awake and talking, but I remained cautious. "Brooklyn will be happy to hear that."

I was just relieved to know my daughter was safe at home. Even if I hated that I couldn't be there to comfort her.

"Oh." Her expression was one of pure adoration. "I just love her. Don't you?"

"Well, yeah." I smiled, leaning my hip against the hospital bed. "She is my daughter."

"That she is." She grinned. "You're a good dad. I should tell you that more often. Because you are."

I smiled, touched by her comment and relieved that she seemed relatively okay. "Thank you."

She crooked her finger, and I was lured to her despite my better judgment. "What are we doing here?" she whispered, spinning her finger around.

"At the hospital?" I asked.

"Yes," she hissed, gripping my lapels, pulling me closer. "Don't talk so loud, or they'll hear you."

"Who?" I wondered aloud. *The paparazzi?*

"You know who," she said with a meaningful look and an ominous tone. I wasn't sure I did.

By this point, our noses were practically touching. Our breath mingling. And despite her swollen face, she was captivating.

Her expression changed again, just as suddenly as her mood. "Hi." She giggled.

"Hi," I said, amused despite my concern. I had no idea what they'd given her, but it was clearly having an effect.

"You're cute." She bopped me on the nose.

"Cute?" I shuddered playfully, enjoying this unrestricted, unfiltered access to her thoughts. "So *that's* what you really think of me?"

"You want to know what I really think of you?"

I nodded, completely captivated by this woman. I rarely allowed myself to get this close to her, and her eyes were striking. Denim blue but with these white lines that went out from the center, like when Brooklyn had touched a Van de Graaff generator at a science museum. Her hair had gone out in all directions, and she'd laughed and laughed. I imagined Emerson having a similar reaction and smiled.

"That smile." She shook her head.

"What about it?" I asked.

"Devastating."

"Devastating, huh?" I smirked.

"You always have been."

I knew I shouldn't take advantage of her current state, but I couldn't seem to stop myself. "I thought you couldn't stand me."

"Maybe in the beginning." She'd loosened her grip on my lapels, but she'd pinned me in place with her stare.

"And now."

"Meh. You're okay."

"Okay?" My tone darkened, and I took a step back. "*Just* okay?"

"Yeah. Well, you can be aggressive and overbearing at times."

"Is that so?"

"But then you're surprisingly present, especially in your interactions with Brooklyn. And you are hot, which helps."

"How so?" I crossed my arms over my chest.

"It helps to counteract the assholeness. You know, like those companies that offset their carbon footprint by planting trees. You do that with your face and—" She scanned my body, and it sparked something deep within me. This desire to take her and claim her. And show her just how controlling I could be. "Yeah." She shivered.

Before I could respond, she said, "Brooklyn. Is she okay?"

The fact that Emerson was thinking about my daughter's well-being when she was the one in the hospital only endeared her to me. Over and over again, I'd seen just how much Emerson adored Brooklyn. She went above and beyond, and I wondered if she did that for every family or if we were special. I wanted to think it was the latter.

"Brooklyn was really worried about you." *So was I.*

I nearly took her hand in mine but stopped myself, instead asking, "Do you remember what happened?"

My phone buzzed in my pocket, but I ignored it.

"Do you need to get that?" Emerson asked, furrowing her brow.

My phone buzzed again, and it didn't stop this time. I removed my phone from my pocket. Ten missed calls and countless unread texts. Several were from Pierce; none of them from my daughter.

"Shit," I muttered as I swiped through the texts, including a link to an article with the headline, "Hollywood's Billionaire Bachelor Nate Crawford is engaged to America's Sweetheart Emerson Thorne."

Fucking hell. This was quickly turning into even more of a disaster.

"What's wrong?" she asked.

"Nothing." I shoved my phone into my pocket, not wanting to add to Emerson's distress.

I knew I'd taken a risk, referring to Emerson as my fiancée. But I'd expected more discretion from a fucking hospital. That said, I had mentioned it in front of an entire waiting room, even if I'd been careful to keep my voice low. I'd sort it out later. What mattered right now was that she was okay.

There was a knock at the door, and a nurse bustled in. "Hello, Emerson. How are you?"

"I've been better," Emerson said.

The nurse—a woman with silver hair and hot-pink scrubs —smiled brightly at me, blinking a few times as if she couldn't quite believe her eyes. She mouthed the word "Holy…" before seeming to regain her composure.

I would've been irritated by her lack of attention to Emerson if I weren't terrified about what was going to come out of the nurse's—or Emerson's—mouth next.

Fortunately, the nurse busied herself with taking Emerson's vitals and asking some questions. Then she peered down at her tablet and made some notes.

"Can I get you anything?" she asked Emerson.

Emerson shook her head.

"Okay. Well, I'll—" She glanced at me again, scanning me head to toe. Likely comparing me to the characters I'd played. Deciding whether I matched up to her expectations. Who the fuck knew. "Be back in a while to check on you."

I followed the nurse out to the hall, closing the door softly behind me. "How's she doing?"

She gaped at me but then seemed to collect herself. "It sounds like she had an anaphylactic reaction to something. The EMTs gave her two Benadryl, as is the usual protocol. And we later found out that she'd already taken a Benadryl at home before their arrival."

I nodded. "Has she been given anything else?"

She shook her head. "No, but we're monitoring her. The Benadryl may have contributed further to the swelling."

"She's, um—" I didn't know how to say it, so I rocked on my feet. "She's not acting like herself."

The nurse's smile was sympathetic. "It happens sometimes. Three Benadryl can be a lot. And for some people— like your fiancée—it makes them a little loopy. Confused and silly. A bit like when someone has woken up from anesthesia."

"Mm." I rubbed my chin.

"Don't worry," she said. "The effects will wear off. Usually in four to six hours."

"Four to six—" I swallowed hard. *Four to six hours?*

"I have to check in with my other patients, but I'll be back in a little while. In the meantime, did you need anything else?"

I shook my head. "No. Thank you. I appreciate you taking such good care of her."

"Of course. She's lucky to have such a caring fiancé," the nurse said with a look that could only be described as adoration.

Down the hall, someone had her back to us, but I could see exactly what she was doing. Taking a selfie with me in the background. I tried not to outwardly react even though I was anxious to duck back into the room. To hide.

"I should return to Emerson."

"Of course." She smiled.

I darted into Emerson's room before anyone else could spot me. I leaned against the door, feeling like a hunted animal, when I wanted to focus on what the nurse had told me. This wasn't about me. Or at least, it shouldn't be.

The news about Emerson was both encouraging and frustrating. But I didn't have long to dwell on it because I was distracted by the sound of Emerson's voice. She was singing "You Belong With Me."

I tried to ignore my phone, silencing any notifications except those that came from Brooklyn or my household staff. I sent Brooklyn another quick update to let her know Emerson was okay. But there was one call I couldn't continue to ignore.

"You good?" I asked Emerson.

"Yeah, but I have to pee." She winced.

I pinched the bridge of my nose. I would've carried her if she'd let me, but I knew she'd throw a fit. "Come on." I held out my arm. When she hesitated, I bit out her name. "Emerson."

She rolled her eyes. "And here we go again. Just when you were being so nice."

"I *am* nice," I growled.

She had no idea how nice I was. How hard it had been—how hard *I'd* been—these past few months. How much restraint it had taken to keep her at a distance. To keep myself in check.

And now…everything was spiraling out of control.

I was worried about Emerson. I knew Brooklyn was concerned despite my attempts to reassure her. And my phone was blowing up with news of our engagement.

"It's a good thing you have carbon offsets." Emerson wagged her finger. "Maybe you should smile again."

I pulled a face and smiled. She immediately started laughing. Laughing so hard she plopped back down on the bed with a snort. It was quite adorable.

"Did you just snort?" I offered her my arm, concerned she'd fall.

"No!"

"You so did," I said, gently guiding her toward the bathroom.

"After today, we shall never speak of this again."

I wanted to agree, but judging from all the texts rolling in, that might be difficult.

I stood just outside the bathroom, scanning the messages from Pierce and promising to call soon. She'd just flushed the toilet when I heard a shriek. I nearly dropped my device.

"Are you okay?" I called.

"No. Yes!" What the hell was going on in there?

I placed my hand on the knob. "You have two seconds to tell me what's wrong, or I'm coming in."

"I, uh—"

"One," I said, my impatience growing along with my concern. I pulled open the door, not even bothering to wait. "Two."

"Oh my god." She covered her face with her hands. "Oh my god. You can't be here. You need to go. *Now!*"

"What?" I jerked my head back. "Why?"

"Because I look like Shrek's bride, and you're you, and please just…" She groaned from behind her hands. "Haven't I endured enough embarrassment for one lifetime?"

"Emerson." I stepped closer, my tone gentle. She kept her face covered, and I hated that she was embarrassed. "Emerson," I said in a more commanding tone.

"What?"

"It's not *that* bad."

"Not that bad?" she scoffed, finally removing her hands. "Not *that* bad? I look like a freaking puffer fish." She glanced at her reflection and cringed. "If puffers could sunburn."

I wanted to tell her that she'd always be beautiful to me, but instead, I said, "What matters is that you're okay. The swelling will go down."

She nodded, but it was clear she remained unconvinced.

"Wash your hands," I said. "So I can get you back to bed."

"Get me back to…" Her eyes widened. "Bed?"

Now that she'd mentioned it, I couldn't stop thinking about it. Her. Us. *Ugh!*

"Why do you always look so pissed off around me?" she asked.

I didn't respond. What could I possibly say? *Because I want you. And it's distracting and infuriating and inappropriate. I can't have you, and yet, I can't stop thinking about you.* So yeah…

She sighed. "Fine. Don't answer. It's not like I expected you to anyway."

She leaned on me as we walked back to bed, and then I got her settled once more. "You good?"

"I'm great. You're great. We're all great." *Oh boy.* She was all over the place, but at least physically, she seemed fine.

I excused myself to the bathroom and called Pierce. He didn't even say hello. Merely launched into a tirade of, "What the fuck were you thinking? Engaged? You can't drop a bomb like that without running it by me."

"I know." I dragged a hand down my face, the fluorescent light and the square beige tiles setting me on edge. "I know. It was sort of spur of the moment."

And it was probably only going to make matters worse regarding the situation with Trinity. God, what if *this* gave Trinity even more ammunition against me? What if…

"I wish you would've at least given me a heads-up. Something. But fuck, I can't say I blame you. She's gorgeous, and the media is lapping this shit up. Calling it a modern-day fairy tale."

"Seriously?" I jerked my head back. I hadn't expected that.

"Yeah, seriously. A billionaire playboy falling for the all-American girl. An Olympic athlete, no less. 'Nemmy' is trending big-time, my friend."

"Nemmy?" I frowned at my reflection.

"You know—" I heard shuffling in the background. "Nate and Emmy. Only the hottest celebrity couples get a moniker. Damn. I wish I'd thought of it myself."

"I—" I cleared my throat, hesitating. "That would be great, but we're not engaged."

He was quiet a moment, but when he spoke again, his tone was lethal. "Explain."

I explained what had happened. Pierce listened quietly on the other end then finally said, "What's the big deal? We can work with this. Fake engagement. Publicity stunt. It's brilliant, and people do it all the time."

He was right, but I'd never dated someone for a publicity stunt. It had always seemed distasteful, plus I hadn't cared that much about my reputation. My films spoke for themselves. My stature was solid as a billionaire Hollywood star. Or at least it had been until fucking Annalise Windsor.

Besides, I wasn't sure if Emerson would go along with this. Even if Pierce was all for it.

"I never thought I'd say this," Pierce continued, "but your nanny could be just what you needed to finally quiet the rumors surrounding Annalise's tell-all and show the public and any judge that you really are a family man. Plus, it's going to be great publicity going into awards season."

I should've said no. I should've shut it down. The risks were too high. I was too attracted to Emerson. Brooklyn was too attached to her. But instead, I found myself thinking of the possibilities.

I found myself thinking back to the night of Brooklyn's slumber party and the way it had felt to touch Emerson. To almost kiss her. And all the stolen moments, the promises of intimacy, since.

"Yeah. Maybe," I said, then added in a hushed whisper, "But you forget that I have to get her to agree first."

He scoffed. "Everyone has their price."

I wanted to tell him that he was wrong. That Emerson was different. But time and time again, I'd seen it play out the same way. Anyone could be bought for enough money, fame, or whatever.

I wondered what Emerson's price would be. I wondered if I really wanted to know.

"I should go," I said, praying she hadn't overheard any of my conversation.

"Go. *Go.* We'll talk more soon. We need to discuss what interviews and photo shoots you guys want to do. My phone's been ringing nonstop with requests for exclusive engagement photos."

"Oh, um—" I swallowed hard. This lie was so much bigger

than I'd even anticipated. It was on the tip of my tongue to tell him to put a stop to it, but instead, I found myself saying, "I'll have to get back to you on that."

We hung up, and I slumped against the wall. How the hell was I going to get Emerson to agree to this? And did I even want her to?

CHAPTER TEN

Emerson

I stretched beneath the sheets and frowned. They were rough. And my room was freezing.

I opened my eyes and glanced around. A heart rate monitor beeped beside me, and a man slept in a chair beside the window where the sun was rising over the city. I did a double take. Nate? Surely I was hallucinating.

His cheek rested in his hand, his eyelashes dark against his tanned skin. His white shirt was unbuttoned at the collar, the jacket of his tux thrown over the back of the chair. His brown waves were messy, as if he'd been tugging on them nonstop.

This wasn't real, was it?

I squeezed my eyes shut and then opened them again, but he was still there. Still dozing peacefully in his tux. What the hell?

How long had he been there? All night, judging from his clothes.

He'd spent the night at the hospital with me?

Wait…had he left the studio end-of-year party for me?

I reached up and started checking my head for signs of an injury. Did I have a concussion? Amnesia?

No. I couldn't have amnesia. I remembered his name. I remembered my name. The only thing I didn't remember was much of what had happened after coming to the hospital.

I took a calming breath and squeezed my eyes shut, trying to reconstruct what had happened. I'd been itchy. *So* itchy. And my tongue had started swelling. I'd taken a Benadryl.

More swelling. Panic. Brooklyn… Riding in the back of an ambulance. And then…the hospital?

Nate stirred and then straightened, rubbing a hand down his face. When his eyes met mine, he said, "You're awake," in a gravelly voice that went straight to my core.

I nodded, fighting the urge to squeeze my thighs together. "And you're…here."

"I am."

I wanted to ask him why, but instead, I said, "What about Brooklyn?"

"She's with Andre and Belinda. I'm sure they're feeding her donuts and letting her watch whatever she wants." He smiled, and I knew he was joking. Or if he wasn't, it didn't bother him.

"She called 9-1-1."

He nodded. "I know."

I covered my face with my hands. "I'm so sorry."

"You have nothing to apologize for," he said, gently peeling them away. "How are you feeling?"

"I'm—" I slid my hand down my throat, assessing. "I'm okay. I hope Brooklyn wasn't too traumatized. I can't thank her enough for what she did."

He smiled, pride infusing his words when he said, "I'm glad she did."

A whisper of a memory floated through my mind. Something about Nate telling me how worried she'd been—but there'd been a look in his eyes. Something that made me think he was actually talking about himself. Surely I'd imagined it.

I glanced around for my phone, but there was no sign of it anywhere. I had no idea how long I'd been asleep. "I don't even know what time it is."

He glanced at his watch. "Almost seven."

I sighed, though I supposed the phone was the least of my worries. My dad was going to freak out when he heard about this. And I didn't even want to think of how much this little overnight stay was going to cost.

"I…" I opened my mouth then closed it.

"What?" he asked.

"I guess I'm just surprised you're here." Of all the people I would've expected to see sleeping in the hospital chair at my bedside, Nate wouldn't have been one of them. My dad, yes. But he was still in Aspen with the rest of my family.

At least, I assumed he was. I hadn't called him yet, and the hospital probably hadn't either. Thanks to Kendall's experience with her mom, I knew they only called the emergency contact if it was "serious." While the definition of "serious" often varied from hospital to hospital, I had to assume my dad's absence meant my case wasn't considered "serious."

"Brooklyn was worried," Nate said as if that explained his presence.

"Right, but, um—" I chewed on my lower lip. "What if someone recognizes you?"

I knew how hard Nate tried to live a normal life. To fly under the radar. I saw what it cost him at times, going out in public. Which begged the question—what had he been thinking coming here?

Before he could answer, there was a knock at the door, and a doctor and nurse bustled in and introduced themselves and asked some general questions. I waited for Nate to excuse himself, but he seemed intent to stay by my side. Was he worried I wouldn't be able to take care of Brooklyn?

"Have you ever had a reaction like this before?" the doctor asked.

I frowned. "No."

"It could be an undetected food allergy, though nothing showed up on our tests. Or it could be related to stress. Have you been more stressed than usual?"

"Me?" I shrugged, my laughter sounding nervous to my own ears. "No more than usual."

It was a lie. Everything about my life was stressful. I'd almost kissed my boss last month, and I couldn't stop thinking about it, even if we both pretended otherwise. My training was intense. I was often at odds with my dad, all while trying to prepare for my upcoming competition. I was worried about Brooklyn and Nate and Trinity's potential custody challenge. And, oh yeah, the upcoming trip to Abu Dhabi in the midst of everything; I was spread thin.

The doctor nodded, seeming satisfied, even while Nate glowered. *What's his deal?*

"We're going to discharge you," the doctor said.

Nate crossed his arms over his chest. "But you still don't know what caused her to react like this."

"Unfortunately, we don't. She should check in with her primary care doctor and an allergist after she's released. For the next few days, drink lots of water and take it easy."

Why were they talking to Nate like that—like he was my caregiver or something? And why was Nate…

"So, that's it?" he asked, exasperation bleeding into his tone. "You're just going to kick her out? Her body is still reacting to whatever freaked it out in the first place."

Someone was clearly grumpy after spending the night in the hospital chair.

"We're going to send you home with an EpiPen in case it happens again," the doctor said to me before addressing both of us. "You should switch to Xyzal and avoid Benadryl. And your skin already shows improvement. It should return to normal soon."

"Should?" Nate asked, raising his voice. "*Should?*"

And then he took a breath, as if seeming to realize that we were watching him. That *I* was watching him.

I wasn't sure I'd ever seen him so worked up about anything that wasn't related to Brooklyn. And definitely not in public. He was always very controlled, his public persona firmly in place.

So to see him upset on my behalf, to realize he cared so much—about me—was quite the shock. And it was the only excuse I had for my continued silence.

"We've already kept her longer than we would've ordinarily," the doctor said, giving Nate a pointed look. What was that about? "We wouldn't discharge her if we had concerns. As it is, we have limited beds, and your fiancée's case isn't life-threatening."

Fiancée? I opened my mouth then shut it just as quickly. Surely I'd misheard.

"Fine." Nate pinched the bridge of his nose. Had he— I whipped my head between the doctor and Nate. Had he not heard that? Had I imagined it? I glanced down at my ring finger, but it was bare like always. "I'll arrange for someone to pick us up. Can we use the helipad?"

The nurse gaped at him, but the doctor merely shook his head. "Emergencies only."

Hell, I would've gaped at him too, were I not still stuck on the fiancée comment.

"Then I assume you have a private entrance," he said in a curt tone.

"Yes, sir," the nurse said as the doctor wrote something down.

"We're supposed to leave for Abu Dhabi in a few days," Nate said. "Will we need to postpone?"

"What?" I jerked my head back, distracted from the fiancée comment—at least for right now. "Nate, we can't postpone the trip."

He ignored me, his attention fully on the doctor who said, "It should be fine, but I'd have the number of a local doctor just in case."

"The hotel has one on call. I've already been in contact with them."

He had?

My head was spinning. I could barely keep up with this conversation.

"Good," the doctor said.

"But what about flying?" Nate asked, clearly unwilling to let it go. At this point, all I could do was stare.

"Just keep an eye on her. No alcohol. Minimize stress. Take a doctor on the plane with you if you're concerned."

Nate nodded.

The nurse said, "I'll be back to escort you in a bit." And then the two of them left.

As soon as the door closed, I expected Nate to say something. *Anything.* But after a minute, I couldn't take it anymore. "Funny thing."

"What's that?"

"I think I'm hallucinating because the doctor just referred to me as your fiancée."

I expected Nate to laugh it off. To tell me I was crazy, but instead, he started pacing. Stopped and pinched the bridge of his nose. Started again. I wasn't sure I'd ever seen Nate so... flustered.

"Nate?" I asked, concern creeping into my voice. "Why do they think I'm your fiancée?"

"Because…" He blew out a breath. "Because I may have told them we were engaged so they'd let me see you."

My eyes went wide. "You did *what* now?" My voice rose with every word until the last one came out as more of a shriek.

"And now everyone thinks we're engaged."

"What do you mean by 'everyone'? Who thinks we're engaged?" My tone was low. Lethal. "Just the hospital staff, right?"

"Um." He glanced around, looking anywhere but at me.

"Nate?"

He dragged a hand down his face. "It sort of spiraled out of control."

Oh. Holy. Shit.

"Explain," I said and stood from the bed, gathering my hospital gown around me. "Explain to me exactly what that means." I glanced around, wishing I had my phone. If the world truly believed we were engaged, it would be buzzing nonstop. "And where the fuck is my phone?"

"Emerson," he said in a commanding tone as I continued searching. It was a small room. There were only so many places it could be. "Look at me."

My heart rate was skyrocketing. I couldn't focus. Couldn't breathe.

"Emerson." He grabbed my arms and forced me to still. "Hey. Take a breath. Breathe. Calm down." His calm tone did anything but put me at ease. And his touch—I shook my head. His touch felt like being struck by lightning. Electric. Consuming.

"Calm down," I said. "Calm down?"

My family was probably freaking out. And Kendall, she had to be worried sick about me being in the hospital.

"It was a mistake, and I will make it up to you."

"Yes, you will. And you can start by telling everyone the truth. I can release a statement or whatever. And we can coordinate our response. It was a silly joke. A misunder-standing—" I sliced a hand through the air dismissively. "Blah. Blah. I mean—" I started laughing, practically doubling over at the prospect. "Could you even imagine? The two of us engaged?"

"Why not?"

My eyes went wide.

"Think about it," he said. "We get along great. And anyone can see how much you adore Brooklyn."

"Yeah, but there's a difference between 'getting along' and trying to convince people we're in love."

"I can pull it off," he said, undeterred. "Can you?"

"Oh no. I know what you're trying to do." I wagged my finger at him. "And it's not going to work."

"What am I trying to do?" He wore an expression of innocence.

"You're trying to goad me into agreeing to this ridiculous charade. What I don't understand is why."

He rubbed the back of his neck. "As you may have noticed, I haven't had the most favorable press lately."

"Maybe not, but it will blow over eventually."

He shook his head. "This time, I'm not so sure."

I'd never experienced this level of...intensity from the press, and I knew I wasn't the only one feeling suffocated. I mean, damn, they were relentless. Harassing. I couldn't even imagine how Nate felt.

Even so, it was his life. Not mine.

"Mm." I crossed my arms over my chest. "And that's my problem, how?"

"It's not, but I think you understand how frustrating it is

to have people focus on your shortcomings or meaningless drama instead of your accomplishments."

He was right. I did. And it sucked. But agreeing to be his fake fiancée would have people doing just that—focusing on my romantic status instead of my achievements. Thinking I'd been secretly dating my boss for god knew how long.

"Oh my god. The Hartwell Agency is going to fire me." And if I'd had any idea where my freaking phone was, I had a feeling they'd probably already called to do just that. And my dad...the competition.

"I'll pay you," Nate said as I turned my back on him and pulled on my pants. "A million dollars." His voice came out strangled.

"Ten," I blurted, just so he'd realize how completely ridiculous this entire conversation was.

I finished dressing and turned back to face him. He considered it a moment then shrugged. "Fine. Ten."

"What?" I sputtered. He couldn't possibly be serious. "I was joking." *Not negotiating.*

"You heard me," he said, his voice gravelly.

I blinked a few times. It wasn't every day I was offered ten million dollars to be fake-engaged to a famous actor. To Nate Crawford, of all people. The seventeen-year-old girl inside me was freaking out. But the twenty-nine-year-old knew better.

For the first few months I'd worked for him, Nate had seemed to despise me. He'd barely tolerated me, and it was mostly for the sake of his daughter. Yes, our relationship was a million times better now. And we definitely had chemistry. But still...

"You vowed never to marry again."

He arched an eyebrow, cocky smirk lifting the corner of his mouth. "Someone's been reading up on me."

I rolled my eyes. "Everyone knows that."

"True. After what my ex did, I don't want to get married again. But the way you love and care for Brooklyn, well, that would go a long way to making everyone believe I'd changed my mind. Obviously, we'd both know this is a business arrangement. Nothing more."

"One hell of a business arrangement," I muttered, thinking he might be better off getting engaged for real.

"It'd be cheaper than giving Trinity what she really wants." I was still processing that statement when he said, "You can still help out with Brooklyn, if you want. Or I'll hire a new nanny so you can focus on your training or your clothing line or whatever. And—" His eyes were wild yet calculating. It was exhilarating and terrifying all at once. "I'll cover any expenses that arise in the course of being my fiancée. A stylist. Designer gowns. Personal…care."

What he was offering was staggering. A real-life Cinderella story. But I shook my head. *No.* I was done entertaining this idea. "It feels…wrong." Especially when I thought of what it would mean to Brooklyn.

"People do it all the time."

"Right," I scoffed. "So that makes it okay? Where's my damn phone?" I muttered, stomping back to the bathroom.

"You can have it back after we finish discussing this."

I turned slowly, my jaw dropping as anger rippled through me. "Wait. You knew where it was all along?"

He had the decency to look chagrined.

I stepped closer, and to his credit, he held firm. "You knew, and you didn't say anything?" I seethed.

"Yes, but—"

I narrowed my eyes at him. "I want my phone. *Now.*"

He rubbed the back of his neck. "I'll give it back." When I glared at him, he added, "I will. I just wanted to be able to talk to you first. To explain."

I held out my hand expectantly. "Give it."

"*After* you've made your decision. I don't want other people's opinions clouding your judgment."

Oof. Had he been talking to my dad? Or was I truly that transparent?

"Nate." My voice was deadly. "Give. Me. The. Phone."

"Trust me, you're better off not looking."

"I swear to god—" I marched over to him. "If you don't give me my phone in the next ten seconds, I'm going to march out front and tell all the paparazzi likely camped there the truth."

He crossed his arms over his chest. "You wouldn't dare."

"Watch me." I turned for the door, but he grabbed my wrist before I got very far. My skin burned from the contact, the heat of his touch singeing me despite my ire.

When I turned back to look at him, his eyes were full of an emotion I couldn't name. "Sit down. We're not done discussing this."

I yanked my arm out of his grasp, my earlier sympathy forgotten. "If you want my help, you better start treating me with more respect. I'm not a child. And you can't just take my phone away."

"I'll treat you like an adult when you stop throwing a tantrum."

Unbelievable. "And you think we could make people believe we're in love?" I scoffed. "No one would buy it."

"You're wrong." He rocked on his heels. "They already are."

"Who?" I asked, throwing up my hands in frustration. "Strangers on the internet?" I scoffed. "People who don't know us? What about our friends? Our families?" I swallowed hard at that thought.

"I can be convincing," he said, his voice a low rumble of dark promise. "Trust me." He inched closer, but I refused to budge. Despite my bravado, my heart started pounding faster and then faster still.

He wrapped my hair around his finger then tucked it behind my ear. He leaned in, our breath mingling, and I forgot about everything else. Everything but him. "Can you?"

CHAPTER ELEVEN

Emerson

"Can I?" I whispered, feeling as if I'd been sucked into a vortex where only Nate existed. "What?"

He held my gaze, grazing my cheek with his nose. It didn't matter that I was wearing yesterday's clothes or that my face was still swollen. Nate looked at me as if I was the most beautiful woman in the world. He looked at me as if…

Oh my god. Nate Crawford is going to kiss me.

His lips brushed my cheek, and I shivered. Holy fuck. Holy—

But then he backed away. Everything else came rushing into focus once more, but my body was still buzzing from his touch. From the reminder of what we'd started the night of Brooklyn's slumber party and what I'd spent weeks trying to forget. What we could finish now that people thought we were engaged.

"Not bad," he said in a haughty tone. It felt as if he'd doused me with a bucket of ice water. "We can work on it."

I crossed my arms over my chest. I wasn't sure what bothered me more. The fact that he could be so convincing and I'd fallen for it. Or that he seemed completely unfazed, when I was a combination of annoyed and turned on. "Work on what exactly?"

"Being convincing. Think of this as an acting job. You'd be playing the part of my fiancée," he said, ignoring the fact that I lacked acting experience.

"And how long would this 'acting job' last?" I asked, complete with air quotes. I wasn't seriously considering this, was I?

He contemplated it a moment then said, "One year."

My eyes went comically wide. At least, that was how they felt. As if they might actually pop out of my skull. After the events of this morning, it didn't seem as unrealistic as one might think.

"One—" I coughed. Sputtered. "Year?" I croaked.

That was a long time to pretend to be in love with someone, no matter how much money was on the table.

"Five million up front. Five million at the end of the year. Hell, consider it an investment in your athleisure line."

"Why a year?" I asked, thinking of the life-span of most Hollywood relationships. A housefly had better longevity.

He lifted a shoulder, the picture of nonchalance. As if this weren't the most bizarre conversation we'd ever had. "It would give me enough time to campaign for the Meghan Hart adaptation, and the breakup would give me a publicity boost right before awards season. Plus, by that point, no one would suspect it was fabricated."

"And so as not to steal your spotlight," I said, needing to lighten the mood. Ten million dollars was no joke, but the idea of accepting it felt wrong.

His cocky grin was sexy, even though I didn't want it to be. "It's like you know me."

I honestly wasn't sure I did. The more time I spent with Nate, the more I learned about him. But then he went and did something like this, and it felt as if I didn't know him at all.

I mean…a fake engagement? I still couldn't believe he'd be in favor of this, let alone advocating for it.

"And having me on your arm would help you how?" I asked.

"It would distract from all the other bullshit, while reframing me as the family man I really am. Everyone loves a wedding. Look at the royal family. A negative story crops up in the press. What better way to squash it than with a wedding?"

"Right, but this time, there would be no wedding. I mean, how do you suppose we'd explain that?"

"When the time comes, we'd release a joint statement that we decided to part ways. Mutual decision. Nothing but the utmost love and respect for each other. The usual."

Yeah. The usual bullshit. "Mm-hmm."

"You don't like it."

"No," I said. "Because first of all, I'm your nanny." Well, former nanny now since the Hartwell Agency was going to fire me if they hadn't already. "So I'm not sure that lends itself to respectability. And, secondly, everyone will know you dumped me."

"Yes, it would be better if we'd met a different way. But this makes the story more believable. We spent so much time together. I saw how wonderful you were with my daughter. And it only made me fall harder."

For a minute, even *I* believed him. And then I remembered who he was and what he did for a living.

"As to the breakup—" He waved a hand through the air. "That's how everyone does it. Gwyneth Paltrow and Chris Martin. Reese Witherspoon and Jim Toth." When he saw I wasn't budging, he said, "Look, we have plenty of time to figure that part out."

"And Brooklyn?" I asked, voicing one of my biggest concerns.

"Yeah." He sank down in the chair and cradled his head in his hands. "I don't like the idea of lying to my daughter, but if we do this, *everyone* has to believe it's real. Especially her."

"And how's she going to feel about the engagement?"

He chuckled. "Are you kidding? She'll be ecstatic." I didn't doubt that.

I adored Brooklyn, and the last thing I wanted was to hurt her.

"And when we inevitably break up?"

"I'm sure she'll be upset," he said. "Even in the time you've been with us, she's grown very attached to you."

"I don't like it," I hedged, thinking about the impact on Brooklyn more than anything.

"I appreciate how much you care about my daughter. It would only make our fake engagement seem more believable."

Wow. He had an answer for everything. It almost made me wonder if he'd planned this. Surely...

"I'm just saying," he continued. "I think we could turn this into an opportunity. A mutually beneficial way to improve both our careers."

I nodded slowly, even though I didn't want to admit it. Still, that didn't mean that I should pretend to be engaged to Nate Crawford. I mean...was he out of his mind?

"No," he said, making me realize I'd said the last part aloud. "Look—" He moved closer, his expression softening. "I know it sounds crazy, but I think this could work."

"Right," I scoffed, clinging to my humor. My armor. He'd gotten too close earlier. I'd nearly fallen for his act. "Because I love media attention, and I want everyone to think I screwed my boss."

"That's not—"

"Oh, come on." I flung my hands in the air. "We both know that's *exactly* what people will say. Hell, I'm sure they already are. Saying I'm a gold digger and worse."

I thought of the parents at Brooklyn's elite private school. I remembered the curious whispers and the barely concealed interest the night of her school play. That had been uncomfortable enough, and pretending to be Nate's fiancée would magnify that by a thousand.

"Maybe, but they don't matter," he said. "And it's not like you need this job anyway."

I jerked my head back. "What's that supposed to mean?"

"Nothing," he said.

"No." I moved closer. "If you have something to say, say it."

He sure as hell hadn't held back earlier.

"You're so fucking talented. And not just as an athlete. You could do anything—design your athleisure line. Coach. Whatever. But I get the feeling you're using your job as a nanny as a crutch. As an excuse so you don't have to face your fears and find out what you're really capable of."

"Oh yeah?" I asked, feeling his words as if they were a slap to the face. Probably because they'd hit a little too close to home. "And what about you? First, you're a bad boy. Now a family man. You seem to care a lot about your image for someone who acts like he doesn't give a shit what anyone else thinks."

"I don't."

"Then why do this?" I asked, hung up on the fact that Nate would be willing to lie to Brooklyn. Especially when I knew their relationship meant everything to him.

"You know why," he said more softly.

I gnashed my teeth as the answer came to me. "Trinity."

He nodded. "She filed an order asking the judge to reevaluate our custody agreement. The lawyers are working on setting a court date."

"What?" I gasped. How had I not seen anything about this in the news? And why the hell hadn't he told me sooner? "When did this happen?"

"Yesterday. I'm doing my best to keep it out of the press for Brooklyn's sake. But I'm running out of time."

"Fuck." I sighed. "I thought she was going to back down."

He shook his head, his expression downright murderous. "Not this time. You know—" He huffed. "The most infuriating part is that she doesn't actually want more time with Brooklyn. She wants something that's almost as priceless to me as my daughter. So, you're right. I don't care about most people's opinions, but I do care when it could affect my relationship with my daughter."

"That's…" I clenched my fists, my nails digging into my palms. I didn't even have words for how wrong that was. How angry Trinity's behavior made me—mostly on behalf of Brooklyn.

"We're not going to let that happen, right?" I asked. Nate looked at me with such surprise that I said, "What?"

"*We?*"

"Well, yeah. I told you I'd do what it took to keep Brooklyn where she belongs—with you. I know I'm not her parent, but I love her. And it's obvious that sharing custody with Trinity wouldn't be good for Brooklyn."

"Obvious to us, but perhaps not a judge. But I appreciate you saying that. And I will do everything in my power to prevent it." He clenched his fists. "Which is why the engagement would need to be believable. Trinity's legal team even cited several sections of Annalise's tell-all to show why I'm an unfit parent."

I clenched my fists. "What does Trinity really want?"

"Did you know my mother collected rare gems and jewelry?"

I blinked a few times, thrown by his question. "Um. Maybe?"

"My mom loved jewelry. To her, it was both beautiful and practical. It was sentimental but also an investment. A way to create a legacy. I can remember watching her pore over auction catalogs when I was little. Or she'd drag me along to a private showing. She had exquisite taste, and her jewels are one of the few things I have left of her."

I frowned. "And Trinity knows this?"

"Yes. And she wants a piece my mom owned."

Rage burned through me, flaring even hotter. *How dare she.*

"Why not offer to give her the item's estimated value instead?" I asked, even though the mere idea pissed me off beyond measure.

"Because the last time it was estimated for insurance purposes, it was worth over thirty-six million dollars. And that doesn't factor in how high it could go for at auction."

I coughed and sputtered. "Thirty-six million dollars? What the hell is it?"

"A necklace that once belonged to Marie Antoinette."

My jaw dropped. "You're kidding me." He had to be joking. Right?

He shook his head. "And even if I gave her the item or the equivalent dollar amount, it would only be a temporary fix. Trinity will just keep doing this again and again." He gnashed his teeth, and I hated her for putting him in this position. "I don't want that threat hanging over me for the next six years until Brooklyn turns eighteen. And I don't want that toxic drama for my daughter either."

I understood his reasoning, but, "Would this be any better? Lying about our relationship?"

"At least it's something we'd agree to. And we wouldn't be hurting anyone."

"Except Brooklyn." That was a huge sticking point for me.

"Except Brooklyn." He hung his head. "But we'd be doing this for her."

That was what had me nearly agreeing. But instead, I tried to think through everything. To understand every angle.

"Because you're worried Trinity could win this time?"

He nodded slowly, and I'd never seen him look so defeated. "But maybe you're right. This is…" He dragged a hand through his hair. "I'll call my PR team. See what alternate solutions they can come up with. Hell, Graham knows a guy. Maybe he can have the video scrubbed from the internet."

"Video?" I asked, the word catching in my throat.

"Someone posted a grainy video of me telling the nurse you were my fiancée."

Fuck. It seemed a little late to try to retract it. And while I didn't want to lie to Brooklyn, the story was already out there. There was no going back now.

"Backtracking is only going to look even worse," I said. "Numerous people heard you say I was your fiancée. It's not like this is coming from 'a source close to the couple.' We can't deny it now, or it'll make you look bad."

"You don't think I know that?"

"Okay," I sighed. "Let's just…hypothetically speaking, say I agree. Walk me through what this would look like."

"Okay. Hypothetically speaking, we would only have to act like a couple when we're in public. When we're at home, nothing has to change."

"What about Jackson and the guys from Hudson? What about Belinda and Andre?" I asked, thinking of how it would feel to lie to them. They weren't just my coworkers;

they were my friends. What were they going to think about me?

"True," he conceded. "We would need to act like a couple around them as well."

I scoffed. "So pretty much everything would change."

"Only when we have an audience," he said.

I threw my hands in the air. "Which is all the fucking time."

"Not *all* the time," he said. "Besides, if they believe we've been hiding our relationship from them all along, then it's not like we'd suddenly switch to a ton of PDA. Especially not when Brooklyn's around."

"Okay. True," I admitted. Maybe we could work with that. "But what about your private life?" When he continued to stare at me, I said, "Other women? You can't be seen with them."

He lifted his chin, peering down his nose at me. "First of all, when was the last time you saw me with someone?"

Well. Never. At least not at the house. That didn't mean he hadn't slept with someone at a hotel or their home.

"You shouldn't believe everything printed about me," he said. "And I would never cheat on my fiancée, even if this is a fake relationship."

"So, no flings. No one-night stands. No…"

"Sex?" he asked with an amused curl to his lips.

"Exactly," I said on an exhale. I wasn't usually this much of a prude when talking about sex, but this conversation had hit me square between the eyes. And as much as I didn't want to admit it, Nate Crawford still had an effect on me. He always had.

"A small price to pay for what we'd gain."

Was he serious? I gawked at him.

"What?" he asked.

"You're a notorious playboy. You don't do relationships."

"Am I?"

"That's what…" I trailed off. I didn't want to make him uncomfortable by mentioning the tabloids and celebrity blogs. I didn't read them—I hadn't in nearly a decade—but you'd have to live under a rock not to know of Nate's reputation.

Yet his expression was so open. So…earnest. I realized maybe I'd put too much stock in what other people had said about him. It wasn't fair of me, but still…the man oozed sex appeal.

Even so, now that I'd been living with him, now that I'd seen the behind-the-scenes, day-to-day of his life, I had no idea when he'd have time for sex. Between solo parenting, running a successful Hollywood studio, acting, his family, he was busy. Not that there weren't opportunities. It just… I was beginning to realize that maybe everyone had gotten it wrong about Nate. Maybe I had too.

"Still…" I hedged, not wanting to delve deeper into that topic. "A vow of celibacy for a year?"

I liked sex. A lot. Sure, I'd been in a bit of a dry spell, but I wasn't keen for it to continue. Definitely not for *another* year.

He chuckled, shoving his hands into his pockets. "Who said anything about a vow of celibacy?"

My eyes went wide. Surely he wasn't saying… He wasn't thinking *we'd…*

"Would you like to make that part of our deal?" he teased. At least, I thought he was teasing. The fact that I didn't know was infuriating.

I rolled my eyes, unwilling to show my body's traitorous reaction to his suggestion—real or otherwise. "Dream on, Crawford."

Our situation was already complicated enough as it was. I was *not* adding sex to the mix.

That was the way it had to be. That was the only way I'd

survive this. I couldn't get my feelings mixed up in a fake relationship with my celebrity crush.

He smirked, and it was both sexy and exasperating. The man was going to drive me nuts. Was I crazy to consider pretending I was in love with him? Could I even pull it off?

"So, do we have a deal?" he finally asked.

I knew Nate would do anything for his daughter. Apparently, that now included pretending to be in love with me.

"I-I need to think about it."

He seemed surprised. Though, I supposed a man like Nate was used to getting what he wanted, when he wanted it.

"Is there anything else I can do or say to convince you?" he asked, and I imagined him in a boardroom, closing a deal on one of his films. It was the type of soft-sell tactic someone made when they were confident they were going to get their way. Or when they were scared they were going to lose everything and knew better than to push.

"You can give back my phone," I said.

"Trust me. It's better this way."

I scowled at him. "I need to update my family."

He shook his head. "I already took care of it. Besides, you heard the doctor. We need to limit your stress."

I crossed my arms over my chest. "Too bad you're the cause of all my stress."

"Now, sweetheart," he chided. "I could also be the answer to all your prayers."

"If you're trying to convince me to agree to your plan, you're going about it all wrong."

"Okay." The corner of his mouth twitched as if he was holding back a smile. "Then tell me what you want."

Something you can't give me.

I thought of my desire to get married—for real. To have children. This would only set me back even further. And yet,

I knew I couldn't say no, not if it would help Brooklyn. Help Nate.

So instead, I said, "I told you," in an exasperated tone. "My phone."

"Something else," he said, standing firm. Hell, part of me was afraid he could read my thoughts.

"Fine. Answer one question."

"What is it?"

"Why did you sleep in that chair last night?" I hooked my thumb in the chair's direction.

He rubbed the back of his neck, his earlier bravado evaporating in the face of surprise. Then he finally said, "What kind of fiancé would I be if I left you while you were in the hospital? Talk about bad publicity." He tsked.

Talk about deflecting.

His nonanswer was infuriating. We both knew he was lying. But why? And why had he lied about our being engaged in the first place?

I wanted to ask him, but I was afraid to know the answer. This situation was already complicated enough. Before I could open my mouth to push him on it, someone knocked on the door.

God, how I wished Kendall were here. I needed her to tell me this was a bad idea. The worst.

Twelve months.

Ten million dollars.

And one big, fat, fake engagement.

Was I actually going to say yes? Did I really have another choice?

CHAPTER TWELVE

Nate

The nurse peeked her head in. "We're just finishing up the discharge papers."

"Great," I said, my eyes on my phone. My team had reached out to a few physicians about Emerson's case. I'd already spoken to the hospital billing department and taken care of all charges. And Jackson was in place and ready to pick us up. "Our driver is waiting by the service entrance."

My phone buzzed, a text from Pierce with a link to some of the latest coverage of my surprise engagement. He was right—there was a hum of excitement. A flood of positive stories.

This was good, wasn't it?

Then why did I feel so bad?

Maybe because I knew it was all a lie. I tried to console myself with the idea that it wouldn't be the first time a celeb had pretended to date someone for publicity. And it wouldn't be the last. I'd just never thought it would be me.

Pierce had wanted us to make a big splash. Come out the front entrance and be photographed, but I'd insisted on a private exit. Emerson needed time to adjust to the idea of our engagement. But more importantly, she'd just gotten out of the hospital, for chrissakes.

"Give me just a few," the nurse said to Emerson with a wink. "And then we'll get you out of here."

"Thank you." Emerson smiled, but it was tinged with fatigue and anxiety.

Hell, I was exhausted, and it had little to do with sleeping in an uncomfortable hospital chair. My family was blowing up my phone. Jasper was surprised but happy for me, perhaps begrudgingly so. He had questions. As did Sloan and Graham, who were both incredulous.

Knox had promised to call soon, and I needed to get my shit together before then. My brother knew me better than anyone. So if anyone was going to catch me in this lie, it would be him.

I couldn't imagine how Emerson was feeling at the moment. Shock? Dismay? Disgust? Pity?

I still couldn't quite explain what had possessed me to tell the nurse we were engaged. I mean, seriously? Emerson and I had developed such a good rhythm; she made my life run smoothly. She was important to Brooklyn.

She was important to me, and not just because of her role as my daughter's nanny. Whether I wanted to admit it or not, I liked Emerson. Trusted Emerson. And while I didn't have to fake my attraction to her, I knew this was a recipe for disaster.

She was nearly fifteen years younger than me.

She was my daughter's nanny.

Well, at least, she had been until about twenty-four hours ago when I'd imploded her career without her knowledge. Without her consent.

And now she was my fake fiancée.

I mean...how did she even really feel about me? About this engagement?

I kept thinking back to that night at Brooklyn's slumber party and our game of truth or dare that had almost gone too far. Then there was last night and what she'd said to me. How she'd looked at me when she'd told me my smile was devastating.

But then I remembered that she'd been loopy from the Benadryl, and she probably hadn't meant a word of it. Hell, I wasn't even sure she remembered it. Part of me was dying to ask, and the other part was afraid to know. An even bigger part of me worried she'd resent me forever.

The door shut behind the nurse with an audible click, leaving us alone once more. I stood and faced Emerson. This was it. The moment of truth.

"Before we step out of this room, we need to know how we're going to handle this," I said. "So, you tell me. What do you want?"

It was her choice. Did I want to have to retract my announcement? No. But would I if that was what Emerson asked of me? Yes.

I just really hoped she didn't.

We both knew I could give Trinity what she wanted—the jewelry or the money. But it was the principle of it. That necklace had belonged to my mother. And my daughter belonged with me.

Emerson glared at me, but the dark circles beneath her eyes spoke of exhaustion. I felt as if I might burst out of my skin while I awaited her answer. Even so, I remained silent. She had to agree on her terms.

Finally, she sighed. "How would this work as far as Brooklyn's concerned?"

We discussed our options. I offered to hire a full-time or part-time nanny, but Emerson refused. She wanted to keep that continuity and routine for Brooklyn. Something I appreciated more than she could ever know.

Instead, she suggested we hire a nanny as needed, for additional support when she had a competition or I had work events that she'd need to attend. But otherwise, life would continue much as before. To the outside world, we were engaged. But at home, everything would remain the same.

I apologized for roping her into this mess, and I meant it.

Finally, perhaps sensing that our time was growing short, she held out her hand. "Okay. You have a deal."

I should've been fucking relieved. And I was. But a bigger part of me was consumed by guilt. Overwhelmed with the enormity of what I'd asked and what we'd both just agreed to.

But it was too late to back out now.

"So formal for a fiancée," I teased. "Maybe we should seal the deal with a kiss instead." I wasn't kidding, not entirely.

"Ha-ha." She wasn't amused.

"What?" I lifted a shoulder. "Don't couples usually kiss when they get engaged?" I joked, desperate to wipe the weary look from her face. Eager to see her skin flush with color like it had earlier when I'd mentioned sex.

"Yeah. They usually *ask* their partner to marry them before announcing it to the world too."

I bit back a laugh, trying not to antagonize her further. Even if it was a relief to see her back to her usual, spirited self.

Instead, I took her proffered hand and shook. We locked gazes and then dropped our hands just as quickly. Did her skin tingle like mine? Did she feel it too? I couldn't help but clench my hand as if to hold on to the feeling of her skin against mine.

The door swung open once more. "Ready, lovebirds?" the nurse chirped, backing in with a wheelchair.

Emerson scrunched up her face in disgust, but she smiled

and leaned into my side as soon as the nurse turned to face us. "Yep. Thank you for everything."

I wrapped my arm around her. Maybe she was a better actress than I'd given her credit for. Already, she was off to a great start.

"Of course," the nurse said. "Hop in, my lady." She gestured to the wheelchair. "And we'll get you out of here without anyone knowing."

I highly doubted that, but I appreciated the nurse's determination, nevertheless. Shockingly, Emerson didn't put up a fight about the wheelchair. But she did ask, "Don't I need to sign some discharge paperwork and pay my bill?"

"It's been taken care of already," she said.

Emerson frowned, but then she whipped her attention to me, her eyes narrowing in recognition. I said nothing, following them through the maze of hallways until we exited the hospital into a corridor where a black Escalade with dark tinted windows was waiting.

Jackson was standing next to it, and he stepped forward when he spotted us. "Mr. Crawford. Emerson."

"Thank you, Jackson," I said as he held open the door for us. I waited for Emerson to climb in, and then I followed her.

The discharge process had been surprisingly quick. I got the feeling the hospital wanted to expedite our exit. Sure, I'd been a dick at times, but we were talking about Emerson's well-being. I didn't think I was being completely unreasonable.

Though, considering the way she'd looked at me this morning when I'd berated the doctor, maybe I *had* gone overboard. I told myself I was just leaning into this new role —fake fiancé. But I knew that wasn't the truth. I'd been worried about her. I still was.

I ground my molars so hard I thought they might crack, frustrated by the lack of answers. How did they have no idea what had happened? How could we prevent it from happening again?

Reduce her stress, maybe. I sure as hell wasn't helping with that.

I hated myself for putting her in this position. I knew she was under a lot of pressure with her competition coming up. And I didn't want to add to that, especially not after what the doctor had said about stress potentially causing the reaction that had landed her in the hospital.

And while the doctor seemed satisfied with her answer, I wasn't convinced. I lived with Emerson, and I'd noticed that she'd seemed tense lately. She sang less, smiled less.

"Congratulations," Jackson said, once he was settled in the driver's seat.

"Thanks," I said, appreciating his support. If he had his doubts about the true nature of my relationship with Emerson, I trusted him to be smart enough to keep them to himself.

It would be relatively simple to make Brooklyn believe this was real. I had a feeling she was going to be too excited to question it. But Emerson was right—the rest of my household staff might take more convincing. More *proof* of our love. Emerson and I had some work to do.

I studied her from the back seat of the Escalade. She'd given no hint as to her thoughts, even if she'd agreed to go along with the charade. Instead, she peered out the tinted windows, her silence putting me even more on edge.

We needed to talk about Brooklyn and so many other things, but I sensed Emerson needed a moment to collect herself. I'd thrown a lot at her in a short amount of time. Hell, it had been my idea, and I was still reeling from the shock of it all. From how quickly my life had spiraled out of control.

"Holy shit," she whispered as the front of the hospital

came into view. Her attention snagged on the army of paparazzi flanking the front entrance. "Please tell me they aren't waiting for us."

I didn't want to lie or sugarcoat it. "They are."

"So, this is my life now." She didn't sound happy about it, and I felt even worse for dragging her into this.

She hadn't asked for the media attention. She didn't even seem to want it, unlike other women I'd been with.

I placed my hand over hers. "Hey. You okay?"

She shook her head slowly, her attention focused on the frenzy outside the window. "You're sure they can't see us?"

"Yes." I didn't mention that they would've already swarmed the car if they'd known we were in here. I didn't want to give her even more cause for alarm.

Hell, I'd offered her ten million dollars to play the role of a lifetime—my fake fiancée. Ten million dollars to pretend to be engaged to me for a year. Any other woman would've leaped at the prospect, even without the additional offer of a princely sum of money.

But Emerson wasn't just any other woman.

When I'd given her the chance to ask for anything she'd wanted, she hadn't. Then, when I'd accepted her offer of ten million dollars, she'd told me she was joking.

For a split second, I'd wondered if she was playing hard-ball. If she was trying to squeeze me for more, like my ex would've done. But I knew Emerson, and I didn't think that was true. In fact, the more we'd talked at the hospital, the more concerns she'd listed—especially regarding my daughter—the more I was certain that wasn't the case.

We drove in silence, and I didn't move my hand. I told myself to, but I didn't want to. I liked the feel of her hand in mine. I needed the reassurance that she was okay.

I was grateful I didn't have to focus on the road, because all I could concentrate on was the woman beside me. I stared down at the hospital bracelet with contempt. I should've been grateful she was okay—and I was. But all I kept thinking was how terrified I'd been when I'd heard that Emerson had been taken to the hospital.

How had I let this happen?

I'd vowed never to let another woman have control over me, yet here I found myself wrapped up in Emerson. Concerned about her well-being. And not just as an employee or a friend, but as someone I cared about.

She was magnetic and funny. Smart and fucking gorgeous. And the way she interacted with my daughter made me think she was the missing piece from our lives.

When Jackson exited the highway, I finally found my voice. "We're almost home." I liked the sound of that more than I had any right to.

Home. As if it were our home and not just the place she was currently living because I paid her.

Emerson's shoulders slumped. "I know." She was quiet a minute, her eyes darting to Jackson and then back to me as she weighed her words. "Should I let you talk to Brooklyn alone first? So she doesn't feel pressured to react a certain way."

I gave her hand a squeeze then released it. She was always thinking of Brooklyn, and that only endeared her to me more. Hell, she'd agreed to turn her life upside down just to help my daughter. It wasn't the money that had convinced her; it was her desire to protect Brooklyn.

"I think we should tell her together," I said with a confidence I didn't feel. Because the closer we got to home, the more nervous I grew.

I'd only introduced one other woman to Brooklyn, and that had been years ago. Now Emerson and I were going to drop the bomb that we were engaged?

"We'll be casual about it." I smiled. "But excited."

"Excited. Right." She looked like she was going to be sick, but I couldn't let her falter. Not when Jackson could overhear us. I trusted the man, but this secret was too explosive to risk anything slipping out.

I leaned in, grazing her cheek with my nose. Seizing any excuse to touch her under the guise of portraying a couple in love and newly engaged. "Just remember why we're doing this," I whispered, trying to ignore my own anxiety as I pulled away.

She nodded and turned to me, our eyes meeting with a sense of solidarity. She didn't have to say my daughter's name to know we were both thinking the same thing—for Brooklyn.

More paparazzi surrounded the entrance to the house. Emerson's shoulders coiled tighter, only relaxing slightly after the gate had closed behind us. Shutting them out.

The door to the house opened as Jackson pulled into the garage. Brooklyn immediately ran over. I didn't dare glance back at Emerson, afraid of what I'd see on her face. So when Jackson opened the door for us, I took a deep breath and climbed out, ready to put on the performance of a lifetime.

"Dad!" Brooklyn called, running over. Her smile widened when she said, "Emmy!" She bypassed me and ran straight to Emerson, throwing her arms around her. "I'm so glad you're okay!"

"I am," Emerson said, locking eyes with Brooklyn. "Thanks to you. You were very brave."

She shrugged, her eyes on the floor. "No biggie."

"Well, it's a big deal to me," Emerson said, placing her hand on Brooklyn's shoulder and giving it a squeeze.

"Don't I get a hug?" I teased. I would've been offended if I didn't love the fact that Brooklyn adored Emerson so much.

It hadn't been like that with her previous nanny, Amalia.

Brooklyn had loved her, of course, but Amalia was stern. And she'd never been very affectionate.

Since Emerson had moved in, Brooklyn had blossomed. She was happier. More confident.

"Oh. Yeah." Brooklyn laughed. "Of course."

I pulled her into my side, breathing in her scent. "I'm so proud of you for what you did yesterday."

She put on a brave front, but I could tell the incident had scared her. "I'm just glad Emmy's okay."

"Me too." I smiled, thanking Jackson before guiding Brooklyn into the house. I knew he and his team would have their hands full with fending off the paparazzi. "How about some lunch? Are you hungry?"

She shook her head, but I hoped by the time the food was ready, she'd want to eat. I asked Andre to prepare lunch. Emerson, Brooklyn, and I caught up on what we'd missed, and Emerson answered all of Brooklyn's questions about the hospital. Through it all, Brooklyn never left her side.

While Brooklyn was telling us a story about breakfast, I caught Emerson's eye over the top of her head and mouthed, "You ready?"

She'd picked at her food, and she looked as if she might be sick, but still, she nodded. We both knew we were running out of time. Soon, Brooklyn would hear the news from one of her friends or someone else, and I wanted it to come from us.

"Well, it's been quite the exciting weekend," I said, hoping this went over well. "Emerson and I have some news for you."

Brooklyn squirmed on the couch. "Good news or bad?"

"Hopefully good." I smiled at Emerson, knowing it was showtime. "We think it's a good thing, and we hope you will too."

Ideally, I would've had this conversation with my

147

daughter *before* proposing to someone. But since this was fake, and I'd opened my big mouth, well...here we were.

I took a deep breath and said, "I asked Emerson to marry me, and she said yes."

"What?" Brooklyn looked from me to Emerson and then back again. I slid my hand into Emerson's, needing her touch to ground me. There was no going back now.

I held my breath, waiting for Brooklyn's reaction. I could feel the tension leach from Emerson, even as she held her smile. So far, this was the hardest part—lying to my daughter. I wasn't proud of myself, but I tried to tell myself the end goal was worth it.

"Seriously?" Brooklyn asked, glancing between the two of us with a hopeful expression. "You're getting married? Emerson's going to be my mom?"

I was relieved she was excited, but also...*oh shit.*

Before I could formulate a response, Emerson said, "I love you, and I will always be there for you."

"So..." Brooklyn scrunched up her face. "Wait. So, if you're marrying Dad, who's going to be my nanny?"

"Me," Emerson said. "Well...sort of. I'll still take you to school and help with your homework."

There was a long pause, and I realized I was holding my breath. And then Brooklyn squealed.

"Best. News. Ever!" she shouted before throwing herself into our arms.

We laughed and hugged, and over the top of Brooklyn's head, I mouthed, "Thank you," to Emerson. She shook her head as if it was nothing. But to me, her love for my daughter was *everything*.

Brooklyn sat back, her eyes going to Emerson's hand. "Wait. If you're engaged, where's your ring?"

"I, uh—"

"It's at the jeweler," I said. "They had to size it."

"Oh," Brooklyn said, easily accepting my explanation.

I'd called the jeweler earlier in the day, and he'd been more than happy to size the ring. It would be delivered this evening. It had belonged to my mother, and despite Trinity's bullshit, I couldn't wait to see the look on Emerson's face when she saw it. Because it was perfect, and she was going to fucking love it.

I told myself that I was okay with giving Emerson the ring because it was a loan. Because we both knew she'd give it back at the end of our fake engagement. Even I knew that wasn't entirely true, but I also wasn't going to dwell on it.

Brooklyn sat back, but the questions started flowing faster than the paparazzi shouting comments to get a rise. "When's the wedding? Can I be the flower girl? Are you going to have a baby?"

My head spun, but again, Emerson took it all in stride. She smiled and gave Brooklyn's hand a squeeze.

"We just got engaged," Emerson said with a huge smile. "And we want to enjoy this time together." Excellent answer. "As to the rest, we'll see."

"So, I might have a little brother or sister like Sophia?"

Emerson's eyes looked as if they might bulge out of her head, so I redirected Brooklyn's attention to me. "Sweetheart." I smoothed down her hair. "That's a long way off." As in *never going to happen.* I didn't want to get my daughter's hopes up about yet another thing I'd ultimately disappoint her with. "Besides, Emerson is very focused on her training."

Though, I didn't know if that would still be the case after her upcoming competition. She'd said it would be her last, but I wondered if she'd have a hard time walking away when it came down to it. I knew I would if I were in the same position. I couldn't imagine giving up acting.

Regardless of what she decided, I trusted that Emerson

knew what she wanted. That she knew what was best for her. So why didn't her dad?

I gnashed my teeth. I hated that she felt pressured by him to do something she didn't want. And now, I was doing the same thing. I blew out a breath, hating myself a little more.

Like her questions, Brooklyn's enthusiasm about our engagement seemed endless. She talked all through dinner about what this would mean. Unfortunately, the more she talked, the quieter Emerson grew. As she had at lunch, she pushed her food around her plate even though I'd asked Andre to prepare her favorite—tacos.

After dinner, Brooklyn skipped upstairs to shower and change into her pajamas. It was nice to have some normalcy in what had otherwise been a crazy twenty-four hours. I knew the engagement was a big deal, but I was more thrown by what had happened to Emerson. And I kept watching her for any sign that something was amiss, even though her skin had returned to normal and the swelling was almost completely gone.

Andre talked with Emerson, congratulating her on our engagement and asking if she was okay. He apologized for anything he might have done to cause the reaction, and Emerson reassured him it wasn't his fault.

After he excused himself for the evening, Emerson busied herself in the kitchen, preparing her protein and snacks for the next day as she did every night.

I brushed my shoulder against hers and lowered my voice. "Are you okay?"

"Of course," Emerson said in a chipper voice. She sealed her reusable snack bag and headed to the fridge.

I didn't buy it, but I also wasn't going to push. For now. Emerson had never seemed so…fragile. Breakable. I didn't like it.

Brooklyn bounded downstairs. "Can we watch a movie?"

"Sure," I said, glancing at Emerson. "You'll join us, right?"

"Of course she's joining us," Brooklyn said, taking her hand and staring up at Emerson in adoration. "We're family now."

If someone had asked me to describe the perfect mom for Brooklyn, it would be Emerson. She was playful and creative yet enforced boundaries. Brooklyn trusted her, loved her. And while I wished I could give my daughter the world—including a mom who would love her and be there for her in a way my ex hadn't, I had to remember that this was all just an act. I only hoped Brooklyn wouldn't be too crushed when it inevitably came to an end.

CHAPTER THIRTEEN

Emerson

"Well, that went well," I said, yawning.

We'd just put Brooklyn to bed, and she'd been bubbling over with excitement—and questions—about the engagement. It made me feel both better and worse about the situation, about lying to her. She was clearly overjoyed by the news—a relief. She didn't seem to suspect or question that it had come out of the blue—also a relief. But her enthusiasm only made me feel even worse for perpetuating the lie.

"It did," Nate said. "You must be exhausted."

I nodded. If tonight was any indication, this whole charade was going to be even more difficult than I'd expected.

My shoulders slumped. "I am, but I still need to finish packing for our trip."

He pursed his lips. "Maybe we should push our departure back." When my eyes flashed to his, he added. "Just by a few days."

"You need that time to help combat jet lag before you start filming. And check in with the crew." I couldn't believe he was even considering it. "Plus, Brooklyn's looking forward to spending that time with you."

"Delaying the trip by a few days wouldn't be that big of a deal. It would give us time to talk strategy, and I can spend time with Brooklyn here."

"Where? Cooped up at the house?" There was no way we were going outside. Not with the paparazzi still parked at the gate and helicopters and drones buzzing overhead. "We should just go. I'm fine."

I didn't disagree about the need to discuss our strategy, but I didn't think it was going to take *days.* At least, I hoped not.

He eyed me with no small amount of skepticism. But before he could open his mouth to protest, his phone vibrated. He pulled it from his pocket, and I recognized my bejeweled phone case. I'd been so caught up in telling Brooklyn that I hadn't pushed for Nate to give back my phone. And honestly, it was almost easier to ignore reality if I didn't have to deal with the missed calls and messages that were sure to be piling up.

"It's your dad," he said, arching an eyebrow. "He's called a few times. Do you want me to talk to him?"

I shook my head and held out my hand for the phone. I knew I needed to answer it. I didn't want Dad to worry.

"You're sure?" he asked, clearly hesitant to hand over the device.

I swiped it from him. "Yes."

I headed down to the gym for some privacy before I connected the call. "Hi, Dad."

I closed the door. The large space was soundproof, and the yoga room was one of my favorite places in the house. The walls were covered in a mix of porthos, ferns, and other greenery that added dimension and texture. And there was this amazing skylight that went up to the first floor, flooding the room with natural light during the day.

On the wall next to me was a hidden keypad that led to the panic room. I hadn't used it, and I hoped I'd never need to.

"What the hell, Emmy? I've been worried sick."

I wanted to ask if he'd been worried about me or how this would affect my chance to compete, but I bit my tongue.

"You should've called," he said.

"I'm sorry." I dropped my head. "I would've, but things have been...crazy."

"No shit. You're engaged? To your boss, of all people?" His questions came fast. *Too* fast. Each word laced with judgment and disappointment. "What the hell are you thinking?"

"I didn't ask for your opinion," I said, hating that I felt the need to defend myself to him. All my life, I'd looked up to my dad. I'd sought his approval. His praise. "And I could really use your support." My voice cracked. Why wasn't my best ever good enough?

"Look, kiddo," he sighed. "I get it. You can't control what they print about you. And I'm sorry if I was harsh, but I'm worried about you."

"Really? I wouldn't have guessed that." Despite his words at the beginning of our conversation. "You haven't even asked if I'm okay."

"Are you?" he asked. "Okay?"

I blew out a breath. "Yeah. At least, the doctors seem to think so."

"When do you think you'll be able to return to the track?"

I peered up at the sky through the skylight, the bridge of my nose stinging. *That's* what he cared about? Not what had landed me in the hospital or if it might happen again?

I thought back to the hospital—Nate's anger and frustration with the doctor. He'd been outraged on my behalf. And as much as he tried to pretend it was because he was my fake fiancée, I wasn't buying it. At least, not completely.

"I don't know," I sighed. It didn't matter right now. "Nate arranged for me to practice at an indoor track in Abu Dhabi." At least he had before my hospital stay. "I'll try to go once we're settled in."

Dad groaned, letting out a sound of frustration. "You're still going, then."

"Yes. Nothing's changed."

"*Everything's* changed," he gritted out. "Astrid and I were mobbed on the chairlift. I found out you were engaged from a reporter. A fucking reporter had to tell me that my daughter was marrying her boss. And proceeded to try to question me about your relationship."

I hung my head, trying not to cry. This was everything I'd never wanted. "I'm sorry."

He was quiet a moment, then more softly, he asked, "Why didn't you say anything?"

"I…" I hesitated. What could I say that wouldn't jeopardize the narrative Nate and I were working to create without fabricating an even bigger lie? And then the answer came to me. "You've never liked him. How could I possibly think you'd be supportive of our relationship?"

"You're right. I don't like him. And I don't like this."

I scoffed. "Because you're afraid it will affect my training."

"Damn right, I am. We've talked about needing to focus, and this is a huge fucking distraction. I want you back on the track soon. Back practicing shot put and javelin."

I didn't know when I could commit to that. I didn't know if I'd ever be ready because I was positive the next time I stepped on the track, there would be a lot more eyes on me. Even if it was just practice.

So instead of committing, I said, "It's getting late. I should go."

"You promised you'd give your all at the Indoor Championships before making any decisions."

"And I *will*," I huffed, still regretting that I'd ever made that promise.

"What's the point? If you're not going to give it one hundred percent, you might as well retire now."

I sighed, sick of having this argument. Sick of feeling guilty over a decision that I knew deep down was best for me.

"You know what? Maybe I should." It would make things a lot easier in some ways. Hell, I was half convinced my anxiety over the upcoming competition was to blame for my reaction that had landed me in the hospital.

"I guess it's a good thing you're engaged to a billionaire, huh?"

I disconnected the call before I could say something I'd regret. He had no idea what he was talking about. I couldn't even explain the real reason I'd agreed to Nate's proposal. And even if I could, I wasn't sure my dad would understand or support me.

I sighed and stared down at the screen. There were countless missed calls and texts. Social media notifications that continued to rise. How had so many unknown numbers gotten my contact info?

I couldn't deal with it. I couldn't deal with any of it. So, I switched off my phone and pushed it away. I wrapped my arms around my knees and curled into myself, letting the tears fall.

THE FOLLOWING MORNING, I WOKE UP FEELING EVEN MORE exhausted than when I'd gone to sleep. But as I tossed and turned in my bed, I knew it was futile. So I dressed in my workout clothes and tried to pretend everything was fine.

It was easier said than done.

A quick glance at my phone revealed the truth. Overnight, my life had changed. I was famous now. For no other reason than the fact that I was engaged to Nate Crawford. And everyone had an opinion about it.

I was used to people having an opinion on me, especially my body. The more my social media had grown, the more incendiary the response—both good and bad. Random guys messaging me dick pics. Telling me they jerked off to me. People criticizing my body or my form. But this… I inhaled a shaky breath. *This* was a million times that.

My inbox was flooded with messages. My social media notifications were overwhelming. Comments on older posts —both positive and negative. It was all too much.

Let alone the fact that I didn't even know what to tell my family or Kendall. I was avoiding everyone, and I knew that strategy would only last so long.

We were leaving for Abu Dhabi tomorrow. I sighed and opened the door to the gym, hoping a workout would help me clear my head. But I stopped short when I spotted Nate filling his water bottle. His navy athletic shirt flowed like silk over his sculpted shoulders.

He turned to face me, frowning. "Emerson?"

"Morning," I muttered, heading for the treadmill to warm up.

He stalked over to me. "What the hell are you doing?"

"What does it look like?" I barked back, not appreciating his tone. "Warming up for my workout."

He shook his head, his lips forming a line. "You can't be serious."

"Of course I'm serious." I placed my hands on my hips, annoyed that he thought he knew what I did or didn't need. "I have a training schedule. My coach is expecting me to log my workout."

"Don't you think *your dad* would want you to take the day off, considering you were just in the hospital?"

"Doubtful," I muttered. Nate didn't know my dad.

"We should at least talk to a doctor first," he hedged, concern tingeing his expression.

I was still trying to reconcile Nate's words with his actions, starting with visiting me in the hospital. Maybe it had been partially motivated by Brooklyn's worries, but Nate didn't have to go to the lengths he had. Then staying the night at the hospital with me—sleeping in a chair, no less. And now his continued apprehension.

While part of me was annoyed with him for being over-bearing and pushy, I couldn't deny that another part of me liked it. Liked that he cared.

"I'll be fine. Besides, it'll help flush my system. Purge whatever caused my reaction." *And, hopefully, my desire for you.*

Nate narrowed his eyes and stepped closer, closing the distance between us. "Emerson, you need to—"

"No." I cut him off. I swear to god, if he tried to tell me what to do, I was going to junk-punch him. I'd had enough of that from my dad.

"You were in the hospital less than twenty-four hours ago," he growled, his tone sending a tingle down my spine. "We still don't know what landed you there in the first place."

"I'm just going to do a light workout," I said. "Nothing strenuous."

"I don't like it."

"You don't have to," I seethed. If he'd just keep his mouth shut, this would be so much better. "You aren't *actually* my fiancé. And even if you were, I'd still make my own decisions."

"Like you do with your dad?" he asked, our faces mere inches apart.

"Enough." I placed my hands on his chest and shoved. I'd had enough. "I have a workout to do, and I'm done arguing with you about it."

"Fine." He crossed his arms over his chest.

Fine? I clenched my fists, my annoyance growing with every second. For a fake fiancé, he was awfully overbearing. I scrutinized him, trying to decipher the reasons behind this sudden change of heart.

"You can't stop me."

"You're right." He softened. "I can't stop you, but I would feel better if you'd let me join you. What do you have planned?"

I laughed, but he didn't. "Oh. You're serious."

"Very." He stepped closer, placing his hands on my hips.

"What are you doing?" I asked, again keenly aware of just how close he was standing. The way he was touching me. Looking at me.

God, he smelled good. His scent was layered with richness and complexity, much like the man who wore it. Fresh. Clean. Sensual. But then a hint of something else. Something more. Something mysterious. I wanted to drink it in.

I placed my hands on his chest, and I wasn't sure whether it was to push him away or pull him closer. God, this was so messed up. *I am so messed up.*

He lifted a shoulder. "Kissing and making up. Isn't that what couples do after they fight?"

I barked out a laugh, though nothing about the situation was remotely funny. It wasn't the first time he'd suggested kissing, and since nothing had ever come of our almost-kiss at Brooklyn's slumber party, I figured he was only doing it to mess with me.

"Maybe if we were a real couple."

"To the rest of the world, we are." His eyes danced between my eyes and my mouth. "Which brings me to my next point. We should practice."

My mouth went dry. "Practice...what exactly?"

"Touching. Kissing. At least, if we want this to be believable."

"Right." I nodded slowly, my breathing turning ragged. *Nate Crawford is talking about kissing me. Me!* "Believable."

He slid his hand into my hair. Using his other hand, he gripped my hip and pulled me even closer. With painstaking slowness, he traced my jaw, my chin. I was practically panting when he used his thumb to drag down my lower lip.

My heart raced, beating against my lungs as if I were running a full-out sprint. How many times had I imagined kissing him? And yet none of my fantasies could ever compare to this.

To the intensity with which he looked at me. To the way our breath mingled, the air sparking with electricity. To the feel of his lips as they finally, slowly brushed against mine for the first time.

Soft. Gentle. Sensual.

I melted beneath his touch. His lips. Even as I burned for him.

He slid his hand down my back, cupping my ass. Pulling me into him. And I couldn't help it, I moaned.

I allowed myself to give in to the kiss. To him. Granting his tongue access when he nudged the seam of my lips. Rocking my hips into him just to feel more of that delicious friction.

It was nothing like I'd expected. And yet somehow, everything I could've ever wanted.

I didn't want it to end. I didn't want to face the consequences. I didn't want to have to admit how much I liked kissing him and wanted to keep kissing him. How much I wanted more.

But then he gave my lips one last gentle peck, lingering as if he wasn't ready for it to end either. I took a few steps back and gripped the arm of the treadmill, both to brace myself and so I wouldn't try to jump him for more. If I thought our engagement announcement had rocked my world, it had nothing on that kiss.

I am so screwed.

"I think we can sell that." His words were a powerful reminder that I couldn't take anything Nate said or did at face value. This was fake, and I needed to get that through my head, even if our attraction felt genuine.

I sputtered, insulted by his word choice. I definitely wasn't going to tell him it was the hottest kiss of my life. Fuck no. His ego was big enough; it didn't need any help from me.

"Great," I said, feeling completely out of control. I needed an orgasm. But since that wasn't on the table, a workout would have to do. "Now, if you're done trying to distract me, I'm going to work out."

I couldn't fall behind in my training, and it would help me clear my head. Especially after that kiss. Holy hell. My core was still tingling from it.

He gestured to my tablet. "We should get started, unless you'd rather talk strategy."

"Later." I typed in the code on my tablet where I accessed and logged my workouts. "After Brooklyn goes to Sophia's."

"Agreed," he said. "I already gave Belinda and Andre the day off."

I nodded. "Good idea." This was the type of conversation that required maximum discretion.

He hooked his phone up to the speakers, but when a song by Nickelback started playing, I shook my head. *Oh, hell no.*

I picked up his phone. It was a circuit training day, so I needed something with a good beat. Motivating. But not too fast. I selected a playlist and smiled. Perfect.

"Cruel Summer" started playing through the speakers, and Nate groaned, his back still to me. "This is *not* workout music."

"It is today," I said in a chipper voice. "We're doing circuits, and this is perfect for circuit training."

I was about to set down his phone when a new message came through, and I stilled.

JAMES THORNE: WOULD THE 26TH WORK FOR DINNER?

JAMES THORNE: OUR HOUSE

WHY WAS PAPA J TEXTING NATE? HOW HAD HE EVEN GOTTEN Nate's number?

I scrolled back up, seeing messages between them while I was in the hospital. Nate had given my parents updates. And it hadn't taken long for Papa J to invite Nate and Brooklyn to join us for family dinner.

"Um. When were you going to tell me about this?" I asked, flashing him the screen where the messages were displayed.

"That was part of the strategy I wanted to discuss."

I scoffed. "Discuss? What is there to discuss? You said we'd be there. You didn't even ask me."

"I wasn't aware I needed to."

Was this how our engagement was going to be? Him

steamrolling me every time, expecting me to fall in line because I was his fiancée?

"Let's get one thing straight," I said. "We may be engaged, but you don't get to make decisions for me. Especially not without consulting me first."

"I was only trying to help."

"It's my—" I jabbed my chest "—family." Why wasn't he getting this? "What else did you do on my behalf while I was in the hospital? Did you talk to Hartwell? My sponsors? I mean, fuck, Nate. You had no right to do that. How did you even get my dad's contact info?"

"James was listed as your emergency contact in your paperwork for the Hartwell Agency."

He gently took the device and placed it on the bench. Now Taylor was singing about love making her crazy. I certainly felt crazy, but it had nothing to do with love and everything to do with the man standing before me.

"We should get started if we're going to finish before Brooklyn is up."

"We're not done talking about this," I said, glaring at him.

"I'm sure we're not," he said in a calm tone that only irritated me more.

I spun and forced myself to focus. Focus on the workout. I took a deep breath, inhaling peace, exhaling frustration. Once I'd demolished my goals, I'd deal with my fake fiancé.

I smoothed my hair into a high ponytail, using the rubber band from my wrist to secure it. I headed over to the treadmill, placing my water in the cupholder and draping my towel over the arm.

"Time to warm up," I said in a cheery voice. I mentally rubbed my hands together. This was going to be so much fun.

I went through my usual warm-up sequence, walking Nate through the steps. I started with foam rolling and progressed to a brief run on the treadmill. Then it was on to leg swings.

"You have to hold your core tight," I said, trying to explain the proper technique.

"I am," he grunted.

I dropped my head and shook it before going to stand behind him in the mirror. "May I?" My hands hovered near his waist.

He hesitated then gave the briefest of nods.

"So, you want the movement to come from the legs, not the core or hips." I gripped his hips and tried not to think about how good they felt beneath my hands. How his skin singed me, even through his clothes. How his kiss had made me forget everything else.

"All right." I finally backed away, removing my hands. "Normally, I would do A-walks, A-skips, and some other stuff, but let's get back on the treadmill since we're not at a track."

"A-walks? Is that like Ewoks?" he joked then mimicked the voice and mannerisms of an Ewok from Star Wars.

I laughed despite myself. Maybe the endorphins were already kicking in. Or maybe it was just that I was in my happy place and nothing was going to bring me down. "No. It's certain types of steps—a cadence, if you will. Like this." I demonstrated a few.

"That takes a lot of coordination."

"You should see me do hurdles." I grinned.

"I have." He cleared his throat. "I mean, I saw a video—once—of you doing hurdles."

"Mm-hmm." Well, wasn't this amusing? I'd been watching him most of my life—he'd starred in some of my favorite movies. And even though I'd gotten used to living in his home, to being around him, it was surreal to think of Nate paying attention to anything I did.

He climbed on the treadmill next to me, and I was curious to see how he'd fare with my workout. I knew he trained with one of the best personal trainers in the industry, but he was trying to build muscle to look a certain way for a specific role. I was trying to win a two-day, seven-event competition. Or at least...I would be if I didn't freak myself out at the thought of it.

"You're scowling at the treadmill."

"Ready?" I asked, finger poised over the start button.

There was a fire in Nate's eyes. A spark of challenge. "Ready."

We'll see about that.

CHAPTER FOURTEEN

Nate

O h. Holy. Jesus.

Emerson was trying to kill me.

I panted, my heart beating so fast it would likely no longer register on a heart rate monitor. Sweat dripped down my temple. I should never have agreed to a workout with an Olympic gold medalist. Let alone one who clearly wanted payback for my sins.

Her workout clothes didn't help. I mean…those shorts were indecent, barely covering her delectable ass. And the way her sports bra pushed up her tits… It was fucking distracting.

I mean…that *kiss*.

I couldn't get that kiss out of my head. Her lips parting in surprise. The feel of her hips beneath my hands. And her mouth… God, her mouth.

Fucking amazing. Even better than I'd ever imagined.

But then the workout had started, and I was so focused on surviving, it didn't leave time for much else. I wondered if that was her intent because there was no way this was a "light workout." None.

I couldn't help but think she was taking her aggression out on me. But damn, she was strong. And even though my energy was flagging, I sure as hell wasn't going to show her any weakness.

She was a beast. She'd barely been discharged from the hospital, and part of me wondered if she attacked all her workouts this hard.

"Time for a water break," she said.

Thank fuck.

I trudged over to my water bottle and sank down on the floor, trying not to flop down pathetically like a fish. Was this what the next year would be like? Painful. Punishing.

"You done?" she asked, cocking her eyebrow.

I scoffed, though my body said otherwise. "Not unless you are."

She smirked, the devil dancing in her eyes. A drop of sweat traveled a path between her breasts. Disappearing beneath her sports bra.

Fuck me, the woman was hot. Even if she was intent on killing me. I'd thought my trainer pushed me hard, but the infamous Dirk Steele had nothing on Emerson.

"Nope!" She hopped up from the bench with renewed vigor, and I tried not to groan at her enthusiasm.

How the hell was she doing all this?

"Come on." She held out a hand, and it drew my eye up her long legs, past her core. That tight stomach. Her pert breasts. Then her face, which was flushed with color and glowing from exertion.

I tried not to groan. If this was taking it "light," what the fuck did intense look like for Emerson?

I placed my hand in hers, electricity dancing along my skin. She pulled me up to a standing position. We were so close, our chests practically brushed. Her soft breasts against my hard chest. Her…

She took a step back, breaking the spell. "All right. You ready to run hills?"

I glanced around. "Hills?"

Emerson hooked her thumb toward the treadmills, and I groaned. "More?"

"You don't have to," she said, but I got the feeling she was testing me. Trying to see what I was made of.

I survived the rest of the workout—though I didn't know how. But then she bent forward and started stretching and... dear god. All the blood fled south. I envisioned the profit and loss statements I'd been working on the other day for the studio. Tried to focus on something, anything but the sight of Emerson's perfect ass as she dove forward in the most graceful—and flexible—of stretches.

"You should stretch," she said.

I opened my mouth, but it was as dry as the Sahara Desert. And how the hell was I supposed to hide the semi in my gym shorts? The flimsy fabric did nothing to disguise my growing desire, even though she had to have felt it earlier during our kiss.

Fuck. Fucking. Fuck.

I seemed to lose all control when it came to this woman.

"Nate?" she asked when I didn't move.

I cleared my throat and slid to the floor, my muscles screaming from the grueling pace she'd set. I moved into child's pose, my cock aching with every brush against the silky material of my shorts.

"Do you always work out at that intensity?" I asked as she joined me on the floor.

She laughed, the sound bright and cheerful. Like wind chimes dancing in the breeze. "Did you think that was intense?"

"Well, yeah," I said. "Kind of made me wonder what I've

been paying Dirk Steele so much money for. His workouts aren't nearly as thorough."

She preened. "Well, thank you. My coach designed it, so I can't take full credit."

"Yeah, but you executed it. And you got me to work harder and sweat more than I have…well, any other time in my life."

Probably because she was punishing me—for roping her into being my fake fiancée. For holding her phone hostage temporarily, even if I'd done it for her own good. For agreeing to family dinner with her parents without consulting her first. But she didn't get it—I'd done those things *for* her.

To shield her from the publicity storm I'd started by telling the world we were engaged. To try to limit her stress when I knew it was already too high. I had decades of experience with living in the public eye; Emerson didn't realize what was coming.

"I love working out. It's my happy place."

I turned and gawked at her. "Seriously?"

"Yeah. Seriously. I love challenging myself. I love pushing past what I think I can do. I love the rush of endorphins. And the high of a job well done. I love seeing my progress."

I nodded.

"How are you feeling?" she asked.

Like it's going to hurt later.

"I feel like that's my line," I teased. "I hope you didn't push yourself too hard after being in the hospital."

She pursed her lips. "It's part of being an athlete—pushing your limits."

She'd certainly pushed mine. Not just with today's workouts, but generally. Whether Emerson realized it or not, ever since she'd started nannying for us, she'd pushed me to lighten up. To have more fun.

"I get that, but—" I didn't know how to broach this subject, so I just went for it. "Do you think maybe you've found that limit? The doctors mentioned that whatever had caused the reaction may have been exacerbated by stress."

"I—" I expected her to tell me to fuck off, but instead, she just let out a heavy sigh. "I don't know. Maybe."

It couldn't be the fake engagement because that hadn't happened until after the attack. But still, I felt responsible.

"Does it have anything to do with your upcoming competition?"

"I…" She swallowed hard. "It'll be fine."

I wasn't convinced.

"Emerson," I growled. "Don't bullshit me. Everything is not fine. You blew up like a balloon. I—" I swallowed, stopped myself. "Brooklyn was terrified." *I* was terrified.

"I know. And I'm sorry, okay?"

"You don't need to apologize. I just—" I ran a hand through my hair. "I'd hate to have something like that happen again."

"So would I," she said. "Hell, I got an annoying fake fiancé out of it. One who takes away my phone and loves to argue with me."

I rested my elbows on my knees and leaned forward. "Our engagement might be fake," I said, "but I do care about you. So, tell me. What's going on?"

She moved to stand. "I'm sure you have better—more important—things to do."

I had many things to do, but none of them seemed important. At least not compared to Emerson.

"Emerson. Sit down," I commanded. She hovered midair, then sat. "Good. Now tell me what's bothering you."

She huffed and crossed her arms over her chest. "You wouldn't understand."

"Try me," I said, hoping I hadn't come across as too

demanding. I knew I could only push her so far, but I wasn't willing to give up easily.

"Do you ever get performance anxiety?" she finally asked.

"On set?"

"Yeah. Like when you know you guys only have a certain amount of time to shoot at a particular location. And you only get one chance, and it has to be perfect."

"Sure," I said. "It's high stakes. Lots of money on the line. Lots of people relying on me."

"Have you ever *not* gotten the shot?"

I screwed up my face, trying to think of an instance. But somehow, we always made it work. And if it didn't work during filming, we fixed it in editing.

"That means no," she said.

"No," I said. "It's just… It's different. There are other ways to make it work, even when everything seems to be going wrong."

She was quiet. Contemplative.

"Do you have anxiety about your race?" I asked. When she nodded, I said, "Isn't that normal to some extent? I mean, I still get nervous about big days on set or premieres, despite having done them countless times."

"Not for me. Not like this," she added in a quieter voice, and I sensed it was difficult for her to open up about it. But I was proud of her for trying. For trusting me.

"Why do you think that is?" I asked.

"My last competition didn't go so well. Granted, it was the first time I'd competed since my injury. But every time I think about stepping back onto the track—" she glanced away "—I start to panic."

I frowned, hating that she was struggling. Wanting to wipe that scared look from her face. Yet relieved she'd told me.

"I'm sorry you're dealing with that. I'm sure it makes it

very...challenging to compete or even mentally prepare for competition."

She nodded, her expression so forlorn that I wanted to wrap her up in my arms and comfort her. "You have no idea."

I wondered if her dad knew. I wondered if he'd even care, or if he'd tell her to suck it up. To push through it. The idea that he might encourage her to ignore what she was feeling made me want to punch him in the face.

But that wasn't helpful to Emerson. Even though my gut reaction was to protect, right now, she needed comfort. Reassurance.

So I decided to tell her something I'd never admitted to anyone else. "You know, when I was filming *Darkness 340*, I had to do this scene in a water tank. In the dark. Fucking terrifying."

"Yeah?" She lifted her head. "I saw that movie. I remember that scene."

"Well, I can tell you that my fear was not an act." I chuckled, leaning back to rest my weight on my hands. Thinking back on it now, I could laugh. But it had been intense.

"I had no idea," she said. "I mean, you always execute whatever scene you're in. That's what I love about your acting—you make everyone believe it's real, even when the scenario is ridiculous."

"Thank you." I wasn't sure accepting my Academy Award could compare to receiving that compliment from Emerson.

"So how did you get through it?"

"Sheer force of will," I said. But then I added, "Honestly, I had to take a step back and look at the big picture. Filming had been great. The crew was pumped. I was proud of this movie, and I wasn't going to let one scene ruin everything."

"Right, but—" She tucked her hair behind her ear. "Most people didn't even know that happened. There was time for editing before the film came out. My events are live. There is no editing. No room for error."

"Is that what scares you most?"

She shook her head. "No." Then she said in a softer voice, "Failure."

I nodded. "Oh. I feel you there. I used to make myself crazy, wanting to micromanage every detail of the film. Make sure every scene was perfect."

"Ahh. It makes sense now why you were micromanaging me," she teased. She quieted then said, "So, what made you stop? How did you move past it?" She seemed genuinely curious.

"I realized that nothing would ever be perfect."

"I don't expect perfection," she said with a touch of defensiveness to her tone.

"You sure about that?" I asked. "You seem to be putting a lot of pressure on yourself."

"Yeah," she scoffed. "And now I'll have even more eyes on me. Even more people waiting to see me fail."

Because of me. My heart squeezed.

"Fuck them," I said. She shook her head. "No, really. All you can expect of yourself is that you do your best."

"And what if my best isn't good enough?" she whispered.

"Your best," I said, "has gotten you this far, hasn't it?"

"Yeah, but that was before. Now I'm not just competing as Emerson Thorne, an Olympic athlete. I'm also 'Nate Crawford's fiancée.'"

Fuck. How the hell was I going to protect her from this?

At the moment, I had zero ideas. And the situation was all my fault.

"I'm not going to lie, being in the public eye is… It's a lot. And I'm sorry my actions added pressure to a situation you were already stressed about."

"That's not—" She shook her head. "I appreciate you

saying that, but I'd still feel this pressure even if we'd never gotten fake-engaged."

I nodded, hoping that was true. But it didn't lessen my guilt.

"I've seen a sports psychologist to try to help me overcome it. My dad wants me to meet with a new one even though the coping strategies didn't make a difference."

At least her dad was aware of the issue, and he seemed to be trying to help.

Hmm. I rubbed a hand over my chin. "Maybe you should create an alter ego."

She furrowed her brow. "An alter ego?"

"Yeah." I grinned. "Channel your inner badass and project that. Be *her* when you compete."

"Huh." She appraised me with newfound interest. "That's not a terrible idea. Is that what you do?"

"Sometimes." I'd never admitted this to anyone, but I found it easy to confide in Emerson. "Sometimes it's easier to don a mask. To never let them see the real you."

She nodded. "So that when they criticize Nate Crawford, they're not attacking you. Because they don't know *you*."

My attention snapped to her. "Yeah. How did you—"

"Know that?" She gave me a sad smile. "Because I've watched you do it, even if I couldn't quite articulate the reasoning behind it until now."

I scoffed, trying to hide my surprise. "Maybe I'm not such a great actor after all."

"Maybe people just aren't paying enough attention," she said. She paid attention. And for a moment, I was sucked into her gaze. Transfixed by this woman and the fact that she cared enough to see *me*.

Not the billionaire. The celebrity. The hotel heir. The dad. Though those were all roles I played. But me, Nate.

I finally shook it off. "Fortunately, I know just the person to help," I said, struck with inspiration. "Jay has created an alter ego of sorts for me, especially for when I have to walk the red carpet."

"Oh my god." Her eyes went wide. "Jay, as in Jay Crowe?"

"You know him?" I asked.

"I know *of* him. He dresses all the biggest celebrities. And Kendall has always gushed about him."

I grinned. "He's my stylist, and now he'll dress you too."

Her smile was so bright, it nearly made me forget everything else. "For the first time since we got engaged, I think I might actually want to kiss you."

"Oh?" I arched an eyebrow. "So when we kissed earlier…"

"You initiated that. Remember?"

"And the next time?" I asked.

Her eyes were homed in on mine like a laser. "There won't be a next time unless it's to maintain this charade."

"You're wrong." I leaned closer, the corners of my lips curling upward. "And I can't wait to see you beg."

"Then you'll be waiting a long time, Crawford." She threw her towel at my face then stood.

I grinned, watching the sway of her ass as she walked away. *We'll see about that.*

CHAPTER FIFTEEN

Emerson

When I emerged from the shower, my phone was buzzing and chiming nonstop. I'd let it charge while I'd tried to cool down from that workout. More like, cool down from Nate.

His words from earlier echoed in my head. *I can't wait to see you beg.*

Something had changed since my hospital stay—and not just the fact that we were engaged. Nate was different. And while I told myself he was leaning into the role of fake fiancé, his protectiveness, flirting, and kissing didn't feel like an act.

Or maybe I just didn't want it to be all for show.

But the longer I thought about it, the more I realized that it hadn't started with my hospital visit. I thought about the night of Brooklyn's slumber party. Of so many other instances where he'd compliment me or I'd catch him looking at me, watching me, a certain way. Like he wanted me. Cared about me as more than an employee or even a friend.

I sank down on my bed, trying to make sense of my thoughts. Of his actions.

Regardless of what I wanted or what Nate was thinking, our arrangement was just business. It had to be.

My phone vibrated again, and I sighed, silencing it completely. As tempting as it was to go online, I knew better. The past few days already had me feeling off-kilter. I didn't need to add to it by reading what strangers on the internet thought of me.

I was still trying to figure out what I thought of myself for doing this. What I thought about Nate.

He'd stayed with me at the hospital when I'd looked... awful. And then there was the way he'd blown up at the doctor. That kiss. Then our workout and my confession about competing. All of it had me feeling extremely vulnerable.

I didn't like that Nate had coaxed so much out of me, more than I'd shared with Kendall in recent months. I blamed my confession to Nate on the craziness of the past few days, and the fact that there weren't many people I could confide in now that I'd been thrust into the spotlight.

But it was more than that. During the months I'd been working with Nate, I'd come to like him. Trust him, despite our rocky start. And now that we were fake-engaged, it felt like it was us against the world. This was our secret. And only the two of us would understand our motivations.

I forced myself to get dressed and head downstairs, knowing he was waiting for me to discuss our strategy. I reached the kitchen and stilled when I spotted Nate standing at the island, a knife in hand. His forearms flexed and... Why did he always have to look so sexy? He was good at every-thing, and it was annoying.

He glanced up at me and smiled. "Thought this might go better with food."

I laughed. "You're right about that. What can I do to help?"

"Nothing," he said. "It's almost ready."

He carried the plates to the dining room, and I followed. We were leaving for Abu Dhabi tomorrow, and I'd expected the house to be more...chaotic or something. Especially in the wake of our engagement announcement. But it was quiet —almost eerily so.

Jackson had taken Brooklyn to Sophia's. Belinda and Andre were gone. Leaving Nate and me completely and utterly alone.

"I have something for you. Well, two things," he said.

"Oh yeah?" I asked, taking a seat. "What's up?"

He slid a packet across the table. "Contract and updated NDA."

I skimmed the contents of the contract. One year. Ten million dollars. I frowned.

"What?" Nate asked.

"It feels wrong to take your money, especially when I know I'm going to get a shitload of visibility as your fiancée."

He shook his head. "It would be wrong *not* to take it. I trapped you into a situation that ended your nannying career and turned your life upside down. Plus, you're going to be stuck with me for the next year."

I rolled my eyes. "Yeah. Such a hardship." I swept my arm wide to encompass the house.

"Consider it compensation for your trouble."

"Fine," I sighed, sensing that he wasn't going to relent. Besides, he was right. I was technically out of a nannying job now. And I could use the money.

I resumed scanning the contract. The ring was on loan and would be relinquished. Public appearances required. All of it conformed to what we'd agreed to already, and none of it seemed like a big deal. At least until I got to the section on breach of contract.

"In the event of disclosure by either party..." I continued

reading, arching my eyebrow the more I read. "So, if either of us tells anyone, we have to pay the other ten million dollars?"

"Yes."

I scoffed.

"What?" he asked.

"You know what. You have a significant economic advantage over me. This is more to deter me from violating the contract than you because I have more to lose."

He shook his head. "Do you realize what this could cost me if the secret got out?" He shook his head. "Brooklyn."

Okay. Fine. He made a good point. And when I thought about it that way, I realized he had even more at stake than I did.

I continued reading, grateful for all the contracts I'd reviewed in the past for my sponsorships and endorsements. It made it easier to parse through some of the boilerplate language. To feel at least moderately confident about what I was agreeing to, even if this was the most unconventional contract I'd ever signed.

"What's this section about an extension?" I asked.

"Oh." He waved a hand through the air. "It's fairly basic. It merely leaves open the possibility to extend our *arrangement* should we find it advantageous."

"Okay." I skimmed the terms, and they looked reasonable, though I assumed they'd be unnecessary. "And what if we want to end it before the year is over?"

"Is that—" He paused then asked, "Is that something you foresee happening?"

I lifted a shoulder. "I don't know. I just think if you're going to go to the trouble to outline the terms for extension, you should also spell out early termination."

"I believe it's detailed on the next page."

I flipped the page, and sure enough, there it was in black and white. "This agreement shall terminate one year after the date of execution, unless the parties agree otherwise."

Blah. Blah. Blah. Early termination of contract...if all the terms are fulfilled and the parties agree. Then it spelled out any changes to the compensation and terms for material breach of contract.

"Any other questions or concerns?" he asked.

"Nope. I think that about covers it."

He slid a pen to me. I took it and signed my name before I could back out.

"Great." He took the contract and turned it facedown. His shoulders seemed to relax. "Thank you. Now…" He pulled something out of his pocket—a small box. "Catch." He tossed it to me. Red leather. Gold details. It was clearly an engagement ring.

"So romantic," I teased, though my heart was racing at the prospect of what the little red box might contain.

If I remembered correctly, Trinity's engagement ring had been an emerald-cut diamond worth two million dollars. It was beautiful, tasteful, and classic. I wondered what Nate had selected for me.

"That reminds me, we need to come up with a proposal story."

"Uh-huh," I said, still staring at the box. When had he had time to do this? Last night?

I guessed when you were a billionaire, you could have whatever you wanted. Whenever you wanted it. Hell, he now had a fake fiancée at his disposal.

"My agent has already lined up a few interviews for us, and we'll need to start posting about our relationship on social media." His words went in one ear and out the other.

I stared at the box before finally prying it open. *Holy. Shit.*

The man had exquisite taste; I'd give him that. The ring was gorgeous. A large radiant cut stone set on a platinum band. The deep red color and setting looked just like one I'd pinned to my private Pinterest board years ago. But unfortunately, this one wasn't for keeps.

"This is…" I blinked down at the ring in shock. "Wow."

"Only the best for my pookie bear," he teased.

"Oh, hell no." I slid the ring on my finger and held out my hand to admire it. But even his ridiculous pet name couldn't dim the sparkle on my finger. It was a perfect fit.

"Sugar lips?" he asked.

I blew a raspberry and took a seat at the table. "Pretty sure we aren't the type of couple to do pet names. But you did well on the size." I couldn't stop admiring the ring.

He joined me. "It suits you," he said, taking my hand in his to inspect the ring. My breath caught. "It's from my mother's collection."

Considering how important her pieces were to him, well… I glanced at my ring again. No. Not *my* ring. *The* ring.

"You sure you wouldn't rather pick something less… sentimental?" I asked, even though I couldn't take my eyes off it.

"You don't like it?" he asked, and the hesitancy in his tone caught me off guard. "A red diamond seemed like you."

"It's perfect." *Too* perfect—that was the problem. But this was all pretend anyway.

"But…" he prodded.

"But nothing." I shrugged, trying to play off my discomfort. "I guess I'm just surprised you'd give me something from your mother's collection, considering the situation with Trinity." Even if it was merely a loan.

"I wanted you to have it," he said. "Besides, this is the type of ring everyone would expect me to give the woman I'm going to marry."

"I get that," I said, but still. It was his mother's ring! Appearances or not, he could've selected something else.

Something with less personal meaning. "But I don't want to damage it working out." Or washing my hands. Or breathing.

"So take it off for workouts. Or don't." He shrugged. As if it were replaceable.

Replaceable? Ha! What a joke. Red diamonds were incredibly rare. And it was from his mother's collection. Just how vast was this collection? I was dying to know.

"I just—" I stared down at the ring, enjoying all the facets. "Are you sure?"

He took my hand in his, and I met his gaze, feeling as if we'd been sucked into a vortex where only the two of us existed. Nate had a way of making me feel as if I was the only person in the room. The only person who mattered.

"Yes. I'm sure."

I held my breath, feeling as if he was referring to more than just the ring. But then he drew a jagged breath and said, "Let's talk strategy," and it burst whatever ridiculous bubble I'd been living in.

I followed him over to the couch. We discussed some basic logistics—our proposal story, interviews, and things his team wanted us to do. Awards shows coming up. My head was spinning, especially when he mentioned the ones we'd be attending.

"Do we need to talk about your family?" he asked.

"What about them?"

"Are they going to buy our story that we were secretly dating?"

I rolled my lips between my teeth. "Honestly..." I tilted my head. "Papa J is probably so overjoyed that he's not going to look too hard at it. And Astrid is so busy living her life most of the time that she won't either." She was nearing the end of her residency, and she worked nonstop.

"What about that whole twin sixth-sense thing? Aren't you concerned she'll realize you're lying?"

I shook my head. "Even if she did, she wouldn't say anything."

"And your other dad?" he asked. "Declan."

My stomach churned with unease. "Is going to take some convincing."

"About our relationship—or me?"

"Both," I said.

"How did it go when you talked to him last night?" I scrunched up my nose, wishing he hadn't asked. "That bad?" he prodded, and I nodded. "What did he say?"

"He wasn't happy about it. He's afraid it will affect my training."

"Jesus," he spat. "Is that all he cares about?"

Sometimes it certainly felt that way, but I wasn't going to admit that to Nate. "He's right to care. He's invested a lot in me and my career."

"Yeah." He scoffed. "He also has a vested interest in you continuing to compete."

"What?" I furrowed my brow, understanding dawning on me. "No."

"Think about it. As your manager, he gets a percentage of every deal you sign."

"Yeah, but that's industry standard. And he's never taken a salary as my coach."

"True, but what do you think happens if you stop competing? Stop getting endorsements? You told me he hasn't been supportive of your clothing line."

"That's not—" I huffed. "Nate, this is my dad we're talking about. He wouldn't do that." I knew he wouldn't.

Nate leaned back in his chair. "I once thought the exact same thing about Trinity. And Annalise. About countless others. People will exploit you, especially now that we're engaged. Be wary, particularly of those closest to you."

"No. You're wrong."

"If I were your dad, I wouldn't be thinking about your competition. I'd be worried if you were okay."

"He was," I said, but Nate's comment stuck in my mind. The fact that my dad's concern for my well-being felt like an afterthought, not his first priority.

I mean, hell, Nate had offered to postpone our trip to Abu Dhabi out of concern. He'd tried to talk me out of a workout. And when he couldn't, he'd joined me. What had my dad done apart from argue with me and add to my stress?

I pushed away the thought. People showed their concern in different ways.

My phone chimed with an incoming text, and I glanced at the screen.

> Kendall: Is it true?

I clicked on the link to the article she'd sent, one of many announcing Nate's and my engagement.

What was I supposed to say to that? Nate had warned me about the dangers of my phone being hacked. And I didn't want to lie to my best friend.

Instead of typing a reply, I took a quick photo of my ring, holding my hand up in front of Nate's button-down shirt. I ignored his furrowed brow and sent it to her.

> Kendall: 😍 😍 😍
>
> Kendall: OMG. That ring. It's your dream ring.

> I know. Gorgeous, right?

> Sorry I didn't get to tell you before the news broke. Nate's proposal was quite the surprise.

All technically true, though still a lie by omission.

Kendall: I'll say. Sounds like we have a lot of catching up to do. But I'm glad you're feeling better. Are you still going to Abu Dhabi?

We leave tomorrow. When are you back from Paris?

Kendall: Friday. Ugh. I'm so sad that our time in LA won't overlap. I really wanted to celebrate with you because it looks like we'll both be *ringing* in the new year in style. 😜

I wanted to ask what she meant, but before I could, a picture came through. Knox and Kendall were standing on a balcony with the Eiffel Tower in the background, and... I zoomed in. There was a giant diamond resting on the ring finger of her left hand.

Holy...

"What?" Nate asked, scooching closer.

"Did you know about this?" I asked, showing him the picture of his brother and my best friend.

"They're engaged?" he asked, incredulous.

"Looks like it."

OMG. Congratulations. So, so happy for you!

Kendall: I'm sure you're busy with everything going on, but we clearly have a lot to catch up on.

Clearly. LOL

Kendall: Meet up for yoga when you're back?

That sounded like heaven—a chance to stretch. To do something normal with my best friend. To get out of the house. But then I frowned, remembering how impossible something as simple as attending a yoga class would be now that I was engaged to Nate.

> I wish, but I don't see how. The paparazzi are relentless.

> Kendall: I bet. Everyone's abuzz about your engagement. I can't wait to hear all the details.

Fortunately, a new message came in, saving me from responding.

> Kendall: Let's pick a date once you're back. You can come to our house. I hired a private teacher so we could relax in peace.

> You did?

That didn't sound like her. Kendall might be engaged to a billionaire, but she usually eschewed spending money.

> Kendall: Yes. Well, sort of. It was a gift from Knox.

Ah. That was more like it.

> I bet he likes that you're flexible.

I added a winky face emoji then sent it off.

At least I had a few weeks until I had to deal with that mess. I was positive she had a lot of questions since I'd never once mentioned dating Nate. And I had no idea what to tell her.

"What's wrong?" Nate asked.

"Nothing," I sighed, tossing my phone aside. *Everything.*

"Clearly, it's not nothing." He gave me a pointed look. "Are you still upset with me for what I said about your dad?"

"Yes." I gnashed my teeth. "But also, I don't like lying to my best friend."

He furrowed his brow. "You know we can't tell anyone."

Yeah. And I had the contract to prove it.

I understood his reservations, but still… "She's marrying your brother. Surely if there was someone we could trust with this secret, it's Kendall. And Knox."

"No." His lips were drawn in a firm line. "It's too big a risk."

I flopped back on the sofa, knowing he was right even if I didn't like it. It was hard enough to lie to my parents, my twin. But Kendall?

"What am I supposed to do, avoid her for the next year? Even if I wanted to—which I don't—I can't. I'm pretty sure she's going to ask me to be her maid of honor." And I had a feeling Knox was going to ask Nate to be his best man. I sighed.

"It'll get easier," he said. "We'll get more comfortable playing these roles. Especially if we remember why we're doing this."

Right. We were doing this for Brooklyn.

I wasn't sure I'd ever be comfortable lying to the people I cared about, but I didn't say that. Instead, I tried to focus on Brooklyn. I felt a little calmer already.

"Well," he said. "At least we don't have to lie to my parents."

I frowned. "I'm glad I don't have to lie to even more people, but that makes me sad."

"Don't be." He took a sip of his water. "It was so long ago, it feels like a different life."

"Even so," I said, studying him. "I'm sure you still miss them."

He tucked his arm behind his head and stared at the ceiling. "I have some memories of them, especially my mom. But I was still so young when they died. I think…" He sighed. "Sometimes I wonder if it's the idea of them I miss more than who they actually were. Does that make sense?"

"Yeah." It made complete sense. "Like you're mourning the idea of what you missed out on."

"Exactly. Yes." He turned and stared at me, as if he was seeing me for the first time.

"You forget—no mom."

"I'm sorry. I should've…"

"It's fine," I said. "Really. I know how much my dads wanted Astrid and me, but sometimes…"

"You can't help but wonder."

"Yeah," I said on an exhale. It was so nice to talk to someone who got it. I wasn't sure I'd ever admitted that to anyone, even my twin.

"Tell me more about your childhood," he said.

"It was…" I hugged a pillow to my chest. "Well, I always knew my family was unique. It didn't help that people used to ask the rudest, most intrusive and insensitive questions."

"That's shitty. I get it."

"It was, and I bet you do. But it also made us stronger. More of a team. Even if most people were well-meaning, it was still us against the world."

"That's how it was with Knox and me and our cousins. Though the five of us have always thought of ourselves as siblings."

I nodded, considering. Maybe we were more alike than I realized. "Don't you think they'll question our engagement?"

"Nah," he said casually, too casually.

"Mm-hmm." I crossed my arms over my chest.

"I imagine Knox is too blissed out with Kendall to care about anything else. Graham is too much of a workaholic to give a damn unless it concerns the Huxley Hotel empire. Jasper is…" He trailed off.

"Jasper is…" I prompted.

"Lazy. A shameless flirt."

"Agreed." I laughed. "At least to the flirting." But his expression darkened. "And Sloan?" I asked, concerned that Nate's cousin might be a sticking point. I'd only met her a few times since she lived in London, but she and Brooklyn had always been very close.

"Fortunately, we won't have to see her very often."

Be that as it may, I remained unconvinced. "If all the people closest to us are going to buy this," I said, gesturing between us, "we're going to need a good story."

"I know. And I've been thinking about that." He told me his idea, and it wasn't half bad. "Now let's do a quick social media post. Come 'ere."

I scrunched up my face. "But I don't have any makeup on. And I didn't do my hair."

Not to mention the fact that my face was still slightly swollen from my allergic reaction, my eyes puffy from crying myself to sleep last night.

"You look beautiful." I nearly swooned at the sincerity in his voice, but then he had to go and add, "Besides, it feels more authentic this way. Remember, everyone loves that you're the girl next door. We need to continue to lean into that."

This is a job, I reminded myself. He was paying me to play a role, albeit an unorthodox one.

"Fine." I scooched closer to him.

I was irritated from sitting for so long. From spending so much time working on our "image." God, it was exhausting. I was definitely earning my ten million, not that I had big plans for it.

Five million dollars had already been deposited into my

account. My bank had called to ask if there'd been a mistake. I still didn't know what I was going to do with the money or if I was even going to keep it. It felt…wrong.

I was doing this to help Brooklyn, not…take advantage of a shitty situation. I didn't *need* the money to live. Yes, it would've been nice to use toward my athleisure line or travel or whatever. But I was already getting a boost to my career. Wasn't that enough? Even if I could no longer work as a nanny.

Which reminded me… "What'd you tell Hartwell?" I asked.

"What do you mean?"

"I haven't heard a peep from them. I assume you had something to do with that."

"My team smoothed it over. Hartwell has already issued a statement that they are happy for us and wish us the best."

"Ha!" I barked out a laugh.

"What?"

"How much did you have to pay for that?"

"Nothing. They know I'm a valuable client. And that my family and I will continue to refer a lot of business if they handle things well. Perhaps it's not the type of press they desire, but they're getting a lot of attention from our engagement."

"True. And we'll use them to find my replacement."

"Replacement?" He jerked his head back. "What are you talking about?"

"Well…" I twisted my hands together, hating the idea of leaving Brooklyn or Nate. "I figure once the year is up, Brooklyn will need a new nanny for after our 'breakup.' We can use this time to vet potential replacements under the guise of hiring them temporarily for when we have an event or something."

He rubbed a hand over his face. "I—I hadn't considered that."

I had, even though I didn't want to.

"Thank you," he said. "That's very considerate."

I nodded. "You know I'd do anything for Brooklyn."

"I do." His expression was solemn, gratitude written across his features. "And I appreciate it more than you could ever know. Now—" He wrapped his arm around my shoulder and pulled me close. He held out the phone and took a few selfies. He knew how to work the camera, and looking at the two of us on the screen, even I was tempted to believe the lie.

"Hold up your ring," he said, directing me like an actor in one of his films. "Place your hand on my cheek."

I did as he asked, hating how choreographed and orchestrated this felt. It was going to look stiff. Everyone would know it was fake.

But then he turned his head toward me and buried his face in my neck, making me giggle.

He checked the screen again. "Perfect."

He was right; we did look perfect. And I wasn't sure what was more unnerving. The fact that we looked like a real couple. Or that part of me wished we were and not just because it would make my life easier.

CHAPTER SIXTEEN

Nate

"Whoa," Brooklyn gasped as Jackson pulled up to the Huxley Grand Abu Dhabi. "It's like something out of a fairy tale."

Jackson parked beside the VIP entrance, the black-and-white tiles beckoning to us like a giant checkerboard. He'd joined us on the flight, but the rest of his team had arrived several days ago. Everyone at Hudson always did a great job of making sure everything ran smoothly and safely, and this time was no exception. Though I knew it had to be more of a challenge, considering the increased media scrutiny surrounding my engagement.

When Jackson opened the door, I climbed out first, offering my hand to Brooklyn, then Emerson.

"Oh. My. God. This place is...incredible," Emerson said, breathless as she scanned the courtyard. Our hands were still linked, and I didn't move to release her.

Instead, I followed her gaze, lifting my free hand to shade my eyes from the desert sun. The hotel had a huge dome on top and looked as if it were dripping with gold. Majestic palm trees swayed overhead, shading the path between a symphony of fountains.

Best of all, it was blissfully quiet. There wasn't a photog in sight, and I could only hope it stayed that way. Though, with all the drama currently swirling in my life, I knew it was only a matter of time before they found us.

A hotel employee appeared as if by magic, his gilded tail-coat formal and elegant. I was sure even Graham would be pleased. "Welcome to the Huxley Grand Abu Dhabi, Mr. Crawford. My name is Saeed, and I would be happy to serve you during your stay."

"Thank you, Saeed."

"Please, follow me to your room."

Only then did Emerson seem to notice we were still holding hands. She dipped her head as she slid her hand from my palm. I hated the loss of her touch, so I placed my hand on her lower back, unable to resist.

For the first time in my life, I didn't mind having so many staff and other people constantly surrounding me. Giving me an excuse to touch Emerson under the guise of perpetuating the story of our engagement. It was pathetic, and yet I couldn't stop myself.

We passed through shaded courtyards with tranquil fountains where Emerson stopped to smell one of the large, colorful flowers. She was radiant, and I couldn't stop touching her now that we were engaged. She'd always been too tempting, and it was so nice to finally act on my feelings, even if she thought it was only pretend.

Even if it was only short-term.

My relationship with Emerson—much like this peaceful interlude—wouldn't last. One day, our fake engagement would end, and Emerson would leave. That was the last thing I wanted, but I'd all but assured that when I'd set a one-year expiration date on our relationship.

"Welcome to the Palace Suite," Saeed said, opening a large wooden door covered in ornate carvings.

Brooklyn and Emerson continued "oohing" and "aahing" over the accommodations. No expense had been spared for the $15,000-a-night suite and no detail overlooked. Our lodgings were fit for a monarch, from the glittering chandeliers to the mosaic tiles to the large vases of fresh flowers that perfumed the air.

"There is a private pool just outside the living area," Saeed said, and Brooklyn rushed over to the windows.

"Dad, come here! You have to see this."

I joined her at the window, admiring the rooftop pool. It certainly looked inviting. And it was very private, with walls and plants shielding it from view.

"Here is Miss Brooklyn's room," Saeed said, continuing the tour to a large bedroom with a king-sized bed and private bathroom. "And you and Ms. Emerson will be in the room next door."

Wait. What?

Emerson flashed me a panicked look over the top of Brooklyn's head.

I peeked around the corner into the primary suite. There was a bed—*one* large bed. An upholstered bench at the foot of the mattress, a desk, a massive full-length mirror set in a gold frame.

Saeed glanced between the two of us, a worried expression firmly in place. "Is there a problem?"

"No," I said. Because—of course, everyone would expect that we were sharing a room, including my assistant, who'd arranged the travel. Emerson and I were engaged. Madly in love. "No problem."

"Great. Can I get you anything else?" Saeed asked, still wary.

"That will be all," I said, walking over to the balcony. It

boasted uninterrupted views of the Arabian Sea. "Thank you."

"Excellent. Please do not hesitate to call should you need anything. We are available to you anytime—day or night."

I nodded, the staff soon excusing themselves. Brooklyn was still in her room, and Emerson joined me on the balcony. The wind blew her hair around her face, her eyes the color of the Arabian Sea. The scenery was gorgeous, but I couldn't take my eyes off the woman standing next to me.

"You planned this, didn't you?" Emerson hissed.

I barked out a laugh. "Trust me. I'm just as surprised as you are."

And sharing a bed with Emerson was the last thing I needed if I was trying to respect her desire to keep our relationship business only.

Her shoulders slumped, the fight going out of her as the reality of our situation sank in. "What are we going to do?"

"We'll figure it out," I said, turning my eyes to the scenery as I feigned nonchalance.

"Figure what out, Dad?" Brooklyn asked, appearing as if from nowhere. *Shit.* Emerson and I were going to have to be more discreet.

I straightened. Brightened. "What we want to do first."

Brooklyn was bouncing on her toes. "Can we go swimming?"

"That sounds nice," I said, looking to Emerson. "What do you think?"

"I'd love to, but I should probably do a workout."

"Why don't you go get changed," I said to Brooklyn, wanting to speak with Emerson alone. Brooklyn skipped off to her room.

I reached out as if to touch Emerson then stopped myself. "You're supposed to be taking it easy."

"Aww. You do care about me," she teased.

How did she not realize that by now? Or perhaps she did, but she wasn't interested.

She returned her attention to the view, as if dismissing me. She lifted her chin in a way that made her seem regal and had me watching the column of her throat. "I'll be fine," she said. When I said nothing, she added, "I *will*. Just a light workout."

I barked out a laugh. "Based on our workout the other day, I'm not sure you know what a 'light workout' is."

She rolled her eyes. "Okay. So maybe I got a little carried away."

"A little?" I chuckled, but then sobered. "Please just…be careful."

"Nate," she sighed. "I appreciate your concern, but I'm done talking about this."

"Fine," I said, sensing I wouldn't make any more headway at the moment. My only consolation was that she hadn't shown any signs of another reaction, and I had the resort's doctor on call. "But I have something to show you first." I held out my hand. "Something that might take the sting out of having to share a bed with me," I joked, trying to get a read on the situation.

"So much for rule number two, eh?" she teased.

I couldn't help myself, I laughed. "I'm never going to hear the end of those rules, am I?"

"Nope." She placed her hand in mine.

"Quit stalling and close your eyes."

She hesitated then did as I asked. I took a minute to study her—the way her lashes fanned out. The pout of her lips. And then, realizing I'd paused long enough, I took her hand in mine and led her into the bathroom then through to the closet.

"Okay," I said. "Open."

She peered around the space, wide-eyed. "Wh-what is all this?"

"My stylist Jay sent over some clothes for you."

"Holy…shit. Seriously?" Her eyes were wild with excitement. "Is this why you told me to only pack workout clothes?" I nodded. She released my hand and immediately went over to the rack, flipping through the options. "Oh my god. These are incredible."

"They're all yours," I said.

"What?" She turned to me, aghast. "Mine? Not on loan?"

"Anything you want to keep is yours." *Including me.*

Holy. Shit. Wait. What?

Did I want to be Emerson's?

Was I…

"Wow." She shook her head, and I ignored that thought. "Damn. I mean, there are some serious perks to this gig."

Right. This gig. To Emerson, this was still just a job—fake fiancée.

And why would she think otherwise? I'd never given her a reason to believe anything else. I supposed maybe I'd been better at hiding my attraction than I'd suspected.

She lingered on each and every piece. "Gah! I just want to try them all on right now." She was practically vibrating with excitement. Jay had impeccable taste.

I chuckled. "Be my guest."

I imagined Emerson stripping out of her clothes and sliding into the dress she was currently holding. It was backless and had a slit up the thigh. I held back the urge to groan.

"I'll leave you to it." I couldn't get out of there fast enough. I grabbed my swim trunks and raced toward the bathroom.

"Nate," Emerson called. "Wait." I turned back to face her. "Thank you."

"You're welcome." I smiled, genuinely pleased by her reaction.

I spent the rest of the afternoon in the pool with Brooklyn. I'd left my phone inside, and it was nice to get away. Escape LA and all the pressures I faced there.

I so rarely got to spend so much uninterrupted time with my daughter, and I treasured these moments. She was growing up way too fast. And with the threat of the custody battle looming, I felt even more determined to make my already-limited free time with Brooklyn count.

I wouldn't start filming for a few more days, but now that Emerson and I were engaged, my team had lined up some interviews and press ops. I was dreading them, but I told myself it was necessary.

Brooklyn passed out soon after dinner, leaving Emerson and me alone. Neither of us had made a move for the bedroom, opting instead for the living room. It seemed safer somehow, even if I knew that was ridiculous.

I ran a hand over my face. It had been a long day of travel, and swimming with Brooklyn all afternoon had worn me out. I'd been attempting to review my script for the last hour, though my eyes had glazed over long ago. Being in Emerson's proximity was too distracting. Especially with the way she'd draped her long legs over the couch.

She seemed to have more luck concentrating than I had. She'd been busy with something on her computer for a while, but she kept yawning. When I looked over again, her eyelids were drooping.

"You're tired," I said. "You should go to bed. I'll take the couch."

"And what's Brooklyn going to think when she comes out and finds you here? Or the staff when they bustle in in the morning?" She shook her head then paused. "Wait. Maybe I could sleep out here. Blame it on your snoring or something."

I gave her a flat look. "I don't snore, and Brooklyn would know it's a lie."

"Okay, then…" She glanced around as if a solution would magically appear. "What if we say you sleep better alone, and you need your rest while you're filming?"

I chuckled. It was certainly creative, but… "It feels like a stretch. We're supposed to be madly in love. Newly engaged. Everyone probably thinks we're fucking all the time."

Her breath caught, eyes flaring with heat.

"True." She gnawed on her lip, and damn if my cock didn't start to harden. *Fuck.* "Fine. It's fine," she said, as if trying to convince herself. "We're adults. I'm sure we can manage to share a bed. Besides, we're both so exhausted, we'll probably pass out almost immediately." I could only hope she was right. "Do you want to use the bathroom first?"

"Sure." I stood, setting the script aside.

I brushed my teeth and then returned to the bedroom so she could have a turn in the bathroom. While she changed, I tried to ignore the thought of her naked in the next room. Instead, I lay on the bench at the foot of the bed. It was no match for my six-foot-four frame. There was no way I'd be able to sleep on it.

I eyed the tile floor, imagining how hard it would be. How hard *I* was going to be sleeping in the same bed as Emerson all night. I sighed and sat on the edge of the mattress, unwilling to make the first move to get beneath the covers.

The bathroom door opened, and Emerson padded out, a fluffy white robe encasing her. I wondered what—if anything —she wore beneath it. I tried not to think about it. Tried not to think of the curve of her back or the way her ass had looked in the thong she'd been wearing at the hospital the other day.

"What's wrong?" she asked, pausing beside the bed.

I swallowed hard. "Nothing. I'm just tired." Physically, yes. But I was tired of fighting this. Fighting my feelings for her. And now that we were pretending to be engaged, pretending to be in love, it was even more difficult to switch off my desire for her when we were alone.

"You should get in bed, then," she said. "You need your rest."

"So do you," I said, yanking my shirt over my head with a yawn.

"W-wh—" she stuttered. "What are you doing?"

"Getting ready for bed." I folded back the covers and climbed beneath them, gratified by the way her eyes lingered on my bare chest. The room was warm, sure. But I typically slept in boxer briefs and nothing else, so this was a concession. "What are *you* doing?" She joined me, and I gave her robe a pointed look. "Why are you still wearing a robe? Are you cold?" I asked, thinking it impossible.

"I, um—" Her cheeks turned a beautiful pinkish hue. "No. The temperature is fine."

"Then what is it?"

I was exhausted, but the second she joined me in bed, it was as if my brain switched on. She was so close. And she smelled so good. *Fuck.*

I clenched the sheets, fighting the urge to touch her. To pull her into my arms.

"Since you only told me to bring workout clothes, I didn't pack any pajamas."

I clenched the sheets, trying to hide my reaction to her words. "Didn't Jay send any?" I'd asked him to send an entire wardrobe—clothes, shoes, accessories, undergarments, etc. I couldn't imagine him forgetting something. He was always so meticulous.

She laughed, and the throaty sound went straight to my

cock. "They would be perfect for someone newly engaged, but I wouldn't exactly call them pajamas."

I frowned, my curiosity piqued even as my concern overrode it. "I don't want you to be uncomfortable." Especially not around me.

She huffed something that sounded like "Too late for that."

I cast the covers aside and moved to the edge of the bed.

"Where are you going?" she asked.

"It's fine. I'll sleep on the floor."

I was the one who'd gotten us into this mess. And I was the one making her uncomfortable.

"No. I'm sorry. Wait." Emerson grasped my wrist, and I froze at the heat of her touch. The gentle way her delicate fingers wrapped around me. I could imagine her hand wrapped around an entirely different part of me. "I appreciate your offer, but it'll be fine."

I turned to face her, needing to know the truth. "Emerson, do *I* make you uncomfortable?"

I'd never gotten that vibe from her. And she'd always stood up to me, but I had completely changed our circumstances without her consent. Sharing a bed together hadn't been part of the plan; none of this had.

She stared up at the ceiling, saying nothing. I scrutinized her expression for clues, the collar of her white robe peeking out from beneath the covers.

"Emerson," I said, trying to hold back the growl from my voice. "Talk to me."

"I *am* uncomfortable." She swallowed hard. "But probably not in the way that you think."

I arched my eyebrow. "What does that mean?"

"It means—" She inhaled deeply and then let it out slowly, but a flush of color painted her cheeks and neck. "It means nothing. We should get some sleep." She turned and switched off the lamp on her nightstand. Then kept her back to me.

"It's not nothing," I said in the darkness. "Come on," I teased. "You can tell your fiancé anything."

"If you were my real fiancé," she said through gritted teeth, "we wouldn't be having this conversation because I wouldn't be having *this* problem."

"Because you'd let me take care of it," I said, connecting the dots. She wasn't irritated because she was mad about our sleeping arrangements; she was turned on.

She huffed, confirming my suspicions but saying nothing more.

Eventually, I heard some rustling and realized she was removing the robe. I tried to imagine what she was wearing. I squeezed my eyes shut and pushed that thought from my mind. It didn't matter what she was or wasn't wearing because nothing was going to happen. She'd made that abundantly clear, and I was determined to respect her wishes.

I stared at the ceiling, my eyes finally adjusting to the relative darkness. I was tired, yet sleep continued to elude me. Meanwhile, Emerson had been so quiet for so long, I assumed she'd fallen asleep.

"Nate?" she whispered.

"Yeah?"

"Are you nervous?"

"About what?" I tucked my hand behind my head. And then the answer dawned on me. "The interview?" We had our first interview as a couple tomorrow. The first big test of our relationship and how convincing we could be in public.

She blew out a breath. "Yeah."

I stared at the ceiling. Was I nervous? Yes. But I couldn't let it show. "It'll be fine. Just follow our plan. And stick to the truth as much as possible."

"I hope you're right."

After a beat, I asked, "Would it help to practice?"

Her breath hitched, every sound magnified in the dark. "Kissing?"

"The interview." *Though I certainly wouldn't be opposed to kissing.*

"Oh. Right. Of course." I wished I could see her face. She sounded flustered, and I imagined the blush creeping over her skin. "I'm sure you're right. It'll be fine." She turned again, and when I glanced over, her back was to me. In the moonlight, I could see the delicate lacy red straps of her lingerie. I swallowed hard at the sight of so much bare skin. "Good night."

"Good night." I somehow forced the words past my throat, wondering how I'd ever be able to fall asleep now.

Every time I tried to shut off my thoughts, they immediately went to the woman next to me. My every muscle was pulled taut, and I was so keyed up, I was tempted to take a cold shower. But I knew from experience that it wouldn't do a damn thing.

I punched down my pillow and tried to focus on memorizing my lines instead of imagining all the things I wanted to do to Emerson. It was going to be a long, restless night.

Eventually, I must have fallen asleep because when I woke, it was to the feel of a warm body pressed against mine. *Emerson.*

My arm was wrapped around her, and she was nuzzled into my side, one leg intertwined with mine. I squeezed my eyes shut and let out a slow, measured breath. I was *really* trying to respect Emerson's wishes, but she was not making it easy. Not when her body was draped over me, the early morning light only just peeking in. Not when my dick was already hard and aching to be inside her.

And then she pressed her core against my leg, her breath coasting across my chest, a moan on her lips. A plea.

I froze.

For a second, I was positive I'd imagined it, but then she moaned again. "Nate. Yes."

I slid my hand down her back, which was mostly bare. Her skin was warm to the touch and as smooth as silk. I pressed my lips to her forehead, wanting to stay here as long as possible. It was a rare moment of connection and intimacy without an audience. There was no pretending. No arguing.

It was so...freeing. To be myself with her. To not have to put on a mask.

And after all this time of holding myself back, of pretending I felt nothing, I craved this intimacy. I was dying to sink inside her and make her scream my name.

But then her breathing changed, and she jolted. "Am I—" She blinked up at me owlishly, as if only just remembering where she was and who she was with. "What are we doing?"

Oh shit. Had she been asleep the whole time?

Her words echoed in my head—what are we doing?

The hell if I knew. All I knew was that I wanted to keep doing it. I waited for her to push me away, to try to escape. So when she didn't, I said, "Whatever you want." I nuzzled her ear, her thighs warm against my body.

She'd been dreaming of me. *Fuck yes.* My chest puffed with pride, and I wondered if that was a frequent occurrence.

"Tell me about your dream, Em," I whispered, trailing my hand over her shoulder, down her arm. "What were we doing?"

"H-how..."

"You moaned my name." I smoothed my hand down the same path once more. "What did I do to have you moaning my name?"

She hesitated, rolling her bottom lip between her teeth. "You were...kissing me."

"Where?" I asked, brushing my lips against hers. "Here?"

She swallowed hard and nodded. "Yes, and then..." I pulled back, keeping my mouth just out of reach until she added, "Other places."

"Mm," I hummed, kissing her lips, then her cheek. "Like here?"

"I, uh—" She turned away.

I leaned over and grazed the shell of her ear with my teeth.

"Oh god." She shuddered.

"Answer my question, and I'll kiss you anywhere you want."

I continued exploring her body. Teasing her with the lightest of touches—skimming my fingers over her back. I followed the same trail with my lips, taking my time. Drinking her in.

"Here." She smoothed her palm down her throat, then used both hands to cup her breasts and push them together. "And lower still." She slid her hand over her stomach, sliding down to cup her pussy.

Her chest was heaving, and she was on the verge of snapping. It was clear in the way she kept arching her back. Her hips rising as if searching for something to fill her. In the way she parted her lips on a needy sigh, looking so fucking sexy.

God, I want her.

I knelt between her legs. My dick was so hard it was painful. I needed this. Needed *her.*

I need her. The words echoed through my mind, reminding me that I couldn't fuck this up because I needed Emerson's help. And adding sex to our already complicated situation could definitely fuck things up.

So, as difficult as it was, I forced myself to stop. To focus on the bigger picture and ignore my own needs.

Emerson frowned, perhaps sensing the shift in my thoughts.

"I, um—" I released my grip on her thighs. She was going to hate me for this. Hell, I hated myself for it. "I got carried away. I shouldn't have…" I sat up, my back to her as I willed my hard-on to go down.

Part of me knew I'd done the right thing by stopping. But another—bigger—part couldn't help imagining what would've happened if I hadn't.

"What?" She swallowed hard. "You… Unbelievable." She huffed, and I could hear shuffling behind me.

A moment later, the bathroom door closed. I didn't blame her for being upset, even if I'd been trying to do what was best for both of us.

I let out a sigh, burying my head in my hands. *Great. Just fucking great.*

CHAPTER SEVENTEEN

Emerson

I pressed my palms to the bathroom counter, concentrating on the intricate pattern of the tiled floor. What a mess. What a fucking mess.

I wasn't supposed to be sharing a bed with Nate. And we sure as hell weren't supposed to be…well, doing whatever had just happened.

But I'd spent years fantasizing about him. And with the way he was acting, it was difficult to separate truth from fiction.

I lifted my head and stared at my reflection in the bathroom mirror. My skin was flushed with anger and desire. My head was at war with my heart. And my entire world felt as if it had been turned upside down, thanks to him.

Our fake engagement was causing friction with my dad. I was avoiding my best friend. I couldn't train on the track. And I was lying to Brooklyn.

But it wasn't just about the fake engagement, though that was certainly messing with my head. It was about the way Nate treated me, especially in those rare moments when no one was watching and he didn't have to put on an act. Like this morning.

Waking up tangled in his arms. His breath warm on my skin. His desire evident. My own overpowering. Nearly causing me to make a huge mistake.

My phone lit up, blinking at me the entire time as the number of unread messages and social media notifications continued to rise. I hadn't checked it since posting our engagement photo, and...

I pushed the thought from my mind. Checking my phone would be a mistake. Just like sleeping with Nate.

But boy, was it tempting. *He* was tempting.

Mussed hair. Hooded eyes. Bare chest.

For the first few seconds after I'd woken up, I'd been convinced I was still asleep. Convinced this was all just a dream. I'd been so turned on that I was damn near ready to give in. At least until he'd shut it down.

I covered my face with my hands. Talk about mortifying.

This might be worse than when he'd come to the hospital and I looked like a sunburned puffer fish. Did the universe have it in for me? I was seriously beginning to wonder, because now I was going to have to sit with him and pretend we were in love while being interviewed.

My stomach clenched at the idea of facing him, let alone lying to a journalist while she scrutinized our every word. Our every move.

I groaned. Why had I ever agreed to this?

Right. Brooklyn.

My phone screen flashed again, taunting me. Tempting me. Maybe I'd just...I'd just check. See how my post announcing our engagement was doing.

But from the second I opened the first app, my eyes nearly bugged out of my head at the number of new followers. The number of comments on my post. It was nuts.

Most of it was good, but some people were questioning why Nate would want to marry me. Debating whether I was hot enough for him. Others arguing that I was too hot for him. Discussing our relationship. Our future.

It was stupid. *I knew* it was stupid, but I couldn't seem to stop myself. I also couldn't imagine dealing with this level of scrutiny for as long as Nate had.

Sure, there were perks to being a celebrity billionaire. He got invited to the hottest parties. He got the best tickets and free stuff and often rode in a freaking helicopter to avoid traffic. But was it worth it?

Was the invasion of privacy—the attacks on your self-worth—worth the fame?

I was about to respond to one of the comments when Nate snatched the phone from my hand. I hadn't heard him come in until I felt him at my back, peering over my shoulder. His breath tickled my neck, and I could feel the heat radiating off him.

"Um. Excuse me." I planted my hands on my hips, my annoyance flaring hot and hard. "That's *my* phone."

I didn't want to do this whole song and dance again, especially after he'd just rejected me. I held out my hand expectantly, grateful he'd at least put a shirt on.

Instead of returning the device, he switched it off and slid it into his pocket. I frowned.

"Nate," I all but growled. "Phone. Now."

"Just—" He held up a hand, and something in his expression halted me. "You shouldn't read things other people say about us."

"I was reading the comments on *my* post."

"I can hire someone to handle that for you. To manage your social media and your brand."

"I like doing it myself. I want it to feel personal."

"I can understand and respect that, but most celebs hire someone," he said in a placating tone.

"Yeah, but I'm not a celeb."

"You are now." He leaned his hip against the counter. He typed something on his phone. "My social media manager will call later to discuss strategy."

Just like that? Ha! He willed it, so it was done?

"What if I wanted to hire my own person?" I asked.

"Trust me. She's the best in the business. You want her."

"Fine," I sighed and turned my back to him so I could start preparing myself for the interview. "Now, can you please let me get ready?"

I didn't have the energy to argue, especially not if I was going to make it through our interview. Dad had already been hassling me about my splits for yesterday and suggesting ideas for improving my times. I was jet-lagged, and I couldn't deal with any more drama.

Nate sighed and placed my phone on the counter before turning away and heading for the bedroom. The tension between us was so thick, I worried we wouldn't be able to pull this off. But that wasn't an option, so I needed to find a way to shift my thoughts.

Nate was pissing me off, but I wasn't doing this for him; I was doing it for Brooklyn. And like anything in life, the pain would be temporary.

I kept my thoughts on her as I got ready. I focused on Brooklyn and all the reasons we were doing this as the film crew set up in the living room. And when it was finally showtime, I smiled, and it felt genuine.

"Sweetheart?" Nate called loudly, probably for someone else's benefit, as he entered the bathroom. "Em," he said, and I was taken back to this morning in bed. When he'd whispered my name in the darkness and promised me the world, only to take it away from me. To embarrass me. "They're ready for us."

I nodded and smoothed my hands down my pants. "Is this okay?"

"You look perfect." He held out his hand.

I told myself he was only saying that because someone might overhear. Just like he'd called me "sweetheart" earlier. It was all part of the act.

I nodded and allowed him to lead me out to the living room, where the space had been transformed. There were lights and camera equipment, and the furniture had been moved.

"I'm sure Graham would love this," I mused.

Nate chuckled. "Actually, I'm sure he will. He's such a publicity whore when it comes to the Huxley empire."

A woman in a pale-blue suit stood as we entered, smiling at our joined hands. Brooklyn was hanging out with Jackson and his team from Hudson. I was glad she was relaxing and having fun, even if I'd rather be hanging out with her than suffering through this interrogation.

"Emerson," she said. "It's so nice to meet you. I'm Bridget with *Vogue*."

Vogue? Nate hadn't told me that. I mean, holy shit. This was *Vogue* we were talking about. I knew they'd branched out into video, but I'd thought it was limited to their popular *73 Questions* series, where they asked a celebrity seventy-three questions rapid-fire.

"Nice to meet you."

"We'll take a few pictures and then move on to the interview."

The photographer posed Nate and me, telling us to look into each other's eyes. Having us move different ways. It all felt so…stiff. So choreographed, and I couldn't possibly imagine how everyone didn't see right through us.

As if this situation weren't stressful enough, I was embarrassed about what had happened with Nate this morning. He knew I'd wanted him, and he'd gotten me all... My body heated just thinking about it. The buildup. The anticipation. And then...well, it was as if someone had let all the air out of a balloon.

"Smile for the camera," Nate murmured. "Act like you like me."

"Maybe it would be easier," I gritted out. "If you stopped bossing me around." And if I weren't horny as well.

So much for focusing on my reasons for doing this.

We moved into a different pose, his grip tightening on my waist. The lights were hot, and a makeup artist jumped in to touch up our faces. It felt as if we'd been here for hours, but it could've been minutes for all I knew.

In the background, the photographer said something to Bridget. They both shook their heads, and I worried I was fucking it all up.

Get it together! You're staying in a palace. With your childhood celebrity crush. Everyone thinks you're engaged.

Sometimes I still couldn't believe this was my life.

When we returned to our positions, I slid my hand up Nate's chest, and Nate pulled me to him. He grasped my chin, bringing my gaze to his, his lips hovering less than an inch from mine. "Eyes on me, Em," he said under his breath.

I let out a shaky breath, everything and everyone else fading to the background. Nate's attention was wholly on me, and he looked at me as if I was the only person in the world. He smiled, and it put me at ease despite everything that had happened this morning. In this moment, we were united. We were a team.

"That's it!" the photographer shouted. "Yes." And then took a few more for good measure.

After light refreshments and a quick touch-up to our

makeup, we moved to a cluster of chairs where Bridget would conduct the interview. Nate waited for Bridget and me to sit, and then he joined us. He took my hand in his, playing the devoted fiancé to perfection.

"So…" Bridget smiled at me, the lights so hot I was starting to sweat. Or maybe it was the idea of lying about my relationship with Nate while being filmed, even if it wasn't live. "I know we're all dying to hear about the proposal."

I froze. Everything about this was so surreal. And there was so much pressure. But then Nate jumped in, saving me. "It was Christmas Eve—"

"And it was so romantic," I added, placing my left hand on his thigh. He turned to me and smiled, and even I could've believed his feelings for me were genuine.

His desire this morning certainly had been.

The feeling of his body pressed against mine. Waking up to his hard length and his gravelly morning voice.

Oh god. I swallowed hard, and it felt as if all eyes were on me as Nate finished telling the story of our proposal. Brooklyn had gone to bed. He'd knelt beside the Christmas tree, the lights twinkling. Blah, blah.

He was flawless in the role of fake fiancé. I only hoped I was half as convincing.

I peered down at my engagement ring, admiring the facets in the red diamond. It was beautiful, and it was *so* me.

"When did you first *know* it was love?" she asked Nate.

His smile was soft as he turned to me. "Honestly, the night of my daughter's school play."

Bridget leaned in like a vulture looking for a tasty morsel. "Why then?"

Yeah, I wanted to ask. What was special about that night?

"Emerson has always been supportive and encouraging of my daughter. But that night, I realized that she was just as invested in Brooklyn's success as I am. I spent most of the

213

play watching Emerson watch the performance. Silently mouthing the lines. Poised on the edge of her seat."

Bridget's smile was one of delight. "So you were together, even then?" Nate nodded. "How long have you been in a relationship? Because to all of us, your engagement comes as quite the surprise. But it sounds as if you've been together forever."

"Sometimes it certainly feels that way," I muttered.

"What was that?" Bridget asked.

He pinched my side. "Oh—" I jumped, fighting the urge to glare at Nate. *He better watch it.* "I just was saying that I can't imagine my life without Nate." I smiled up at him with what I hoped looked like adoration. When in reality, I wanted to kill him.

He leaned in and kissed my cheek. Another reminder to behave. *Oh, I'd behave all right.*

"What about you, Emerson? When did you know it was love?"

"Oh gosh. Probably…" I smirked, deciding to make him sweat a little. "Probably the night we had our first family dance party, and he sang Taylor Swift."

He narrowed his eyes at me in a playful manner, though he couldn't disguise the flash of concern that accompanied it. "Emerson. You weren't supposed to tell anyone about that."

"Are you a Swiftie?" Bridget asked, latching on.

"Oh yeah," I said, eager to make him squirm. Payback was a bitch, and her name was Emerson. "He knows all the words to all her songs."

"Only because you and Brooklyn listen to her on repeat." He shook his head with a rueful grin. "Taylor is a talented artist, but I only sang the song to impress Emerson."

I wondered if that was true or not. I wondered if anything he said was true. It was becoming too difficult to tell. Which was exactly why having sex with Nate was a terrible idea.

Terribly tempting.

"When did you first realize you were attracted to your daughter's nanny?" Bridget asked, and I tried not to let my surprise at her wording show. That was what she'd wanted after all.

"Now, Bridget," Nate said in a silky voice, charming as ever. "We agreed that all questions would avoid that phrasing."

"I'm sorry." She smiled, and it was clear she wasn't sorry in the least. "It must have been from an old version of my notes. We'll fix it in editing. When did you first realize you were attracted to Emerson?"

"Two years ago."

I jerked my head back. "What?" And then I immediately regretted opening my mouth.

Bridget glanced between us with undisguised glee. "Please tell us more, Nate."

"My brother—"

"Knox Crawford, owner of the LA Leatherbacks," Bridget confirmed.

"Yes. My brother, Knox, hosted a party on his yacht, and Emerson was there."

I couldn't believe he remembered that night. Remembered *me*.

It was a night I'd never forget. The first time I'd met my celebrity crush in person. The first time I'd seen Nate up close.

"Do you remember this party?" Bridget asked me. I nodded, too shocked to speak.

"She was stunning," Nate continued with a wistful smile. "And everyone was drawn to her."

I was? They...were? He *was?*

"Based on Emerson's reaction, I'm guessing nothing happened between the two of you at that party."

I dipped my head, still trying to grapple with Nate's statement. "No. I had no idea he was even attracted to me."

Bridget laughed. "One of America's hottest bachelor billionaires was too timid to make a move? That doesn't sound like you, Nate. At least not if the rumors about your reputation are to be believed."

"Typically, if I see something and I want it, I go after it," Nate said, wisely ignoring the comment about his reputation. "But Emerson was different."

"Why?"

He rubbed a hand over his jaw, one shocking revelation coming after the next. I wasn't sure how much more I could take. I wasn't sure how much longer I could pretend to feel nothing as soon as the cameras stopped filming and the lights were off.

"You know..." He shook his head. "I think I realized she was the type of woman who wanted commitment."

"And you weren't ready to give that."

"Not at the time, no."

Man, he was good. He'd been right to suggest we stick to the truth as much as possible. But I wondered just how much of this was true. Sure, I'd been at the party. But had he been attracted to me as he'd said?

Bridget kept pushing. "Let me make sure I have this straight. You were attracted to Emerson, but you hired her anyway. Is that why you hired her?"

"No," Nate said in a firm tone that I assumed was meant both to reassure me and end that line of questioning. His attention was on me when he said, "I hired Em because she was the best person for the job. The best person for my daughter."

"Mm." I didn't like the way Bridget appraised us. "I'm sure it wasn't easy—deciding not to pursue her when she was sleeping just a few doors down."

"I tried to avoid her as much as possible."

I snorted then quickly lifted my hand to cover my mouth.

"What's that, Emerson?" Bridget asked.

"Oh, um, I just…sneezed." I snorted again for good measure. "Excuse me."

Nate's mouth twitched as if he was fighting back a laugh.

Bridget evaluated me then finally returned to questioning Nate. "What changed?"

"Everything." He turned to me with a smile, leaning in for another kiss on the cheek. Did he have to lay it on so thick?

Bridget crossed her legs. "Emerson, when did things change for you?"

"I think—" I glanced at Nate. *Stick as close to the truth as possible.* "Things changed slowly for me. I'd see what a good dad he was. Or I'd be reminded of how fun he could be when he'd let go. He'd do something thoughtful. All those small moments added up over time."

"It wasn't love at first sight, then?"

I barked out a laugh. "Definitely not."

Bridget inclined her head. "At least she's honest."

"It's one of the reasons I love her," Nate said, giving my hand a squeeze. "Her authenticity and her willingness to put me in my place."

"I thought that was what drove you crazy," I teased before I could stop myself.

"That too."

"So you were going to keep your engagement a secret, but the news came out," Bridget said. "Tell us about that."

I told her about Nate coming to the hospital, tweaking the details obviously to fit the narrative Nate and I were trying to sell. Carefully omitting the part about losing my job and avoiding any mention of the Hartwell Agency. But most of it was true—the fact that he'd never left my side. His insistence on paying my hospital bill despite my protests. His concern. Even now, when he spoke of his reaction to my hospitalization, the worry lines were still etched into his skin.

I knew he cared about me. I knew that wasn't an act, but just as my heart softened toward him, it was quickly replaced by the sting of his rejection this morning. My feelings were too mixed up where Nate was concerned, and the less physical contact we had, the better.

CHAPTER EIGHTEEN

Emerson

Nate was already in bed when I entered the room. He was propped up against the headboard, the covers pulled to his waist. We'd survived the interview, and I'd spent the rest of the day avoiding him. But now, it was late. I was tired. And his chest was gloriously bare.

One year. I'd locked myself into a year of this torture.

God, why did my fake fiancé have to be so freaking sexy?

Especially with those glasses perched on his nose, his brow furrowed in concentration. He glanced up at me and then scowled. "What the fuck are you wearing?"

I frowned then followed his eyes down the length of my body. I had on an oversized T-shirt that stopped high on my thighs, the spot where Nate's eyes lingered.

"It's a T-shirt," I said in a flippant tone.

I'd picked it up in the gift shop after the interview so I wouldn't have to wear another set of the sexy lingerie Jay had sent. Barely there lace and sheer designs were only asking for trouble. I plugged in my phone and busied myself with getting things just right on my nightstand.

"Yeah. I know." He let out a heavy sigh, and I bit the inside of my cheek so I wouldn't laugh at his discomfort. "But where are your pants?"

"It's not like I'm naked beneath my shirt," I said, lifting the hem to reveal my boy shorts.

"Emerson," he growled.

"What?" I paused. "Oh, are you concerned you won't be able to keep your hands off me?" I hadn't meant to say that.

But now that I had, I was curious. Did he regret this morning? Regret waking up together—or regret stopping us?

Hell, I didn't know how we'd ended up tangled together. I just knew that it felt good. More than good—amazing. But he'd been right to stop us, even if I'd never been hornier or more embarrassed.

Pretending to be engaged in public was one thing, but this was... Well, it felt as if the lines were blurring between real and pretend. My heart and my head were getting confused, and we were playing a dangerous game.

"I shouldn't have..." He cleared his throat. "I'm sorry."

Sorry? He was actually apologizing?

I wasn't sure whether to be happy or not, considering the context. Instead of responding, I went over to the pile of pillows on the floor and started gathering them up.

"What are you doing?" he asked.

"Making sure you stay on your side of the bed, mister," I said in a playful tone as I laid the pillows in a line down the middle. I didn't want to fight with Nate. He'd apologized, and he was sincere. Besides, I had enough drama in my life, and I needed us to be a team.

"Seems a bit juvenile if you ask me," he said.

"Well, I *didn't* ask you." I stood back to admire my handi-work. "There." I dusted off my hands.

"This is—" He started kicking at the pillows. "Ridiculous." He took one and tossed it on the floor.

"*You're* ridiculous," I said in a huff. Why couldn't he just leave it? I was trying to make peace with him.

"We're not sleeping with a wall of pillows," he said, taking another and chucking it across the room.

I scrambled to retrieve it, growing more and more annoyed. I put it back on the bed, back in place. Only for him to throw it again. When I bent forward to seize it, another pillow hit my ass.

I scowled and turned to face him, but when I did, he was biting back the sexiest grin.

"Oh. You're going to pay for that." I lobbed a pillow at his gorgeous face, but he caught it.

"Am I?" he taunted.

I grabbed another pillow just as he threw the first, hitting me in the side. *Motherfucker.* I jogged over to him and kept my pillow in hand, using it to swipe at him. But he was quicker than I'd expected, and he was already on his knees, moving across the bed.

"We'll see who's going to pay," he said.

He stood on the other side of the enormous mattress, pillow in hand. Ready to battle. I debated my next move, but when he lunged to get me, I jumped onto the mattress to give myself a higher vantage point.

I swung my pillow and clipped his face. But my satisfaction was short-lived. He chuckled darkly, and it ignited my core in the most delicious of ways. "You're going down, Thorne."

"Am I, *Crawford?*" I shifted from one foot to the other, ready to leap from the mattress.

I loved a good challenge. And Nate was definitely giving me one.

When he lunged at me, I jumped to the floor and scrambled away, laughing. I was fast, but he was cunning. And before I knew it, I'd taken two hits from the pillow.

Bastard. He was fast.

I was laughing so hard, I bent over to catch my breath. I held up my hand, but he didn't take any mercy on me, instead coming at me again and again with the pillow. Sensing that he wasn't going to relent, I dug deep, donning my alter ego as he had suggested. I'd tried it during my workout earlier, and it had been surprisingly powerful.

My alter ego was still taking shape, but with her in mind, I straightened. With renewed vigor, I backed Nate toward the bed, pummeling him with my pillow. Getting out all my frustration and pent-up desire with every swipe.

Damn. My alter ego was kinda awesome.

He fell back on the mattress with an oomph, and I climbed on top of him, pillow in hand, vengeance in my heart. I wasn't thinking about anything but winning. At least not until I felt his erection dig into my underwear.

I gasped, planting my hands on his chest, our pelvises kissing. Nate gripped my hips and peered up at me. And I was afraid to move.

I sucked in a breath and stilled as his hands steadied on my waist. For a minute, we just stared at each other, suspended in time.

Ever so slowly, he slid his hands up my sides, up my rib cage. His thumbs brushed the undersides of my breasts, and my skin broke out in goose bumps. I wanted him to touch me. I *needed* him to touch me.

But then I remembered how quickly he could switch off his feelings, shift his desire, and I climbed off him. I wasn't going to wait for him to reject me again.

"We should…" I glanced around the room, only then realizing what a mess we'd made. "We should clean up and go to sleep before we do something we'll regret."

I started picking up the pillows but stilled when Nate came to stand behind me. His front was to my back, our reflection staring at us from the full-length mirror. His chest rose and fell, our breath the only sound in the room as he stared at me, perhaps debating what to say, if anything.

"The only thing I regret is stopping this morning. Because I want you." His eyes were hooded, breathing shaky. "I shouldn't, but I do." He swallowed hard, meeting my eyes as his mouth dipped to my ear. "And I'm tired of holding back."

"Nate," I whispered, feeling as if we were on some precipice. I wanted to tell him that I wanted him too, but I was scared. Scared to let myself be vulnerable, especially with the sting of this morning's rejection still fresh. So, I resorted to humor, deflection. "I thought you said no more naked nannies."

"You aren't the nanny anymore." He slid his hand over my stomach, pulling me to him. Letting me feel his arousal. "You're my fiancée."

My core ignited at the sound of those words from his lips, even as I tried to tell myself this was a terrible idea.

"Fake fiancée," I corrected, trying to maintain the distinction as the lines blurred even more.

His eyes met mine in our reflection. He lifted my left hand, my engagement ring sparkling like a promise.

"The ring on your finger is mine." He brought the back of it to his mouth for a kiss. Then he turned my hand and slid it down my stomach, down farther until I was cupping myself with his hand resting over mine. "This pussy should be mine too."

I moaned both at his words and his touch. Not to mention what he was suggesting. But then I swallowed hard and shook my head as if to clear it. "I— We—"

What if we had sex, and it was terrible? That seemed impossible. Laughable, considering our chemistry. But what if it made everything awkward? What if…

"I know." His expression was solemn and heated and as

conflicted as I felt. "I know you said this was just business, but I want more."

"Since when?" I asked.

"Always." His eyes were locked on mine. "What I said earlier, about wanting you that night on Knox's yacht, was true."

I gasped. "But—but—" I sputtered. "When I started working for you, you couldn't stand me."

"No." He dipped his head, running his nose along my neck. "I couldn't stand the fact that you were my daughter's nanny and I wanted you."

"You…" I swallowed hard. "What?"

"I wanted you," Nate rasped. "I *want* you, Em."

Was I dreaming?

"You did? I mean…you *do?*"

He nodded. "Why do you think I made up those asinine rules? Why do you think I kept my distance?" He grasped my chin. "It was to avoid being tempted."

I nearly pinched myself, but I knew I was awake. And this was real. But as much as I wanted to lean into this, into everything he was offering, I hesitated.

This morning… I swallowed hard, remembering how that had felt. How it had felt to give in to something I'd wanted for so long, only for Nate to rip it away at the last second.

"And now?" I asked.

"I'm done with rules. I'm done with distance and denial and everything else I've tried. I want you."

I wanted him too. I'd always wanted him, even when he'd driven me crazy.

But I knew myself. And I knew Nate. We wanted different things.

Having sex with him would be a mistake.

He peered down at me with those gorgeous blue eyes, and

I remembered how many times I'd dreamed of this exact scenario. Of him wanting me.

Hell, I'd crushed on the man for years. What he was suggesting, offering, it was the chance of a lifetime. And while I knew I might come to regret it, part of me also wanted to say fuck it. I'd wanted Nate for so long, too long, to even consider saying no.

I turned to face him, toying with the hair at the nape of his neck. He watched me, his gaze ping-ponging between my eyes and my lips. His hands were resting on my hips, his fingers gripping me as if to restrain himself.

"Let's make a deal," I said, needing to maintain some semblance of control over the situation.

"We already made a deal," he teased.

"An amendment to our deal, then," I said then took a breath, steeling myself. "What if what happens in Abu Dhabi stays in Abu Dhabi?"

"Like a vacation fling," he said.

"Exactly." I'd had a vacation fling once, years ago. It had been fun. Easy. There had been no expectations. No... complications.

Something that looked like disappointment flashed through Nate's eyes. But then he studied my expression, his gaze more neutral. "Except it's not a vacation fling because we'll be going home together."

This was infinitely more complicated, and we both knew it. But as ridiculous as it might sound, putting a deadline on the physical aspects of our relationship felt like a way to protect myself. To stop things before they could get too out of hand. Before I was in over my head.

Oh, who was I kidding? I was already in way over my head.

I huffed, pushing away that thought. Regardless of the consequences, I wasn't sure I had the strength to turn him down.

"You know what I mean," I said.

"I do." His expression was solemn. "Are you sure that's what you want?"

My mind was racing. *Yes. No. I don't know.*

"It's what I need," I said honestly.

"Okay," he said. "Then there's something I need in return."

"What's that?" I asked, afraid to know the answer.

"I need you to promise me that, no matter what happens between us, Brooklyn will always come first."

"Of course," I said without thinking. *Of course* I would always put Brooklyn first. But right now, all I could think about was his lips.

"Thank you." He nodded, and my breathing grew shallow as he cupped my cheek.

Oh my god. We were really doing this. We were—he was…

He caressed my lips with his, his touch gentle. There was no hesitation in his kiss, more that he seemed to be taking his time to savor this moment. Or maybe I was reading into the situation, wanting it to mean more than it did, despite everything I'd tried to tell myself.

But damn, what a kiss.

I groaned at the feel of his lips on mine. His mouth exploring mine.

The kiss was a dance, our mouths gliding and grazing. Grinding and claiming. As with everything else when it came to Nate and me, there was a push and pull. Entice; retreat. Sample; spar.

"I have dreamed of little else but these lips—" He traced my bottom lip with the pad of his thumb. "For months."

I smiled, loving this insight. "Is that so?"

"Yes. And these legs." He reached down and picked me up, wrapping my legs around him. "God, Em," he groaned. "You have the most gorgeous fucking legs."

He carried me over to the bed, kicking aside one of the pillows from our fight with a huff. He placed me gently on the bed, standing back and rubbing a hand over his chin. "Fuck me, you are something."

His cock tented his boxer briefs, and I swallowed hard at the sight. If I hadn't already been aroused, I would be now. Aroused and impatient. I crooked my finger. I was tired of looking; I wanted to touch. To play. To feel. To kiss. To suck.

"What's that look?" he asked, prowling closer.

"I want you naked," I said, figuring it was the quickest route to getting what I wanted.

He pushed his boxer briefs over his hips, his cock springing toward his stomach. My mouth went dry at the sight, and I was so focused on him—the beauty of his chest, the deep V that led to his cock, which stood proud and at attention.

"If you keep looking at me that way, this is going to be over before it even gets started."

I laughed, but his expression was downright serious. "Clothes. Off," he ordered, and I was more than happy to comply.

I stripped off my shirt then my underwear. Nate's eyes tracked all that bare skin, searing me with the heat in his gaze, sheer want nearly overpowering me. I slid my hand down my stomach as if to touch myself, but Nate shook his head.

"Don't you dare touch that greedy little clit." He kneeled between my legs. "Your orgasms are *mine*."

It was almost as if he was taunting me to do just that. To defy him.

I squirmed beneath his attention, impatient for his touch. But then he placed his hands on my thighs and gently pried them apart like it was his goddamn right. And I forgot about anything else but letting him devour me. Own me.

And did he ever. The man was possessed. Licking and sucking and teasing me… Oh, how he teased me, holding my orgasm just out of reach. Not just once. Again and again, he brought me to the edge, my body aching for release until I was writhing on the sheets close to begging him to let me come. And I *never* begged.

"Something wrong, Em?" he taunted. The bastard damn well knew what was wrong.

I narrowed my eyes at him, sweat dotting my forehead. "I swear to god, Nate. If you don't let me come—"

The corner of his mouth tilted upward, his lips slick with my desire. "Beg."

"Nate," I gritted out, so keyed up I wanted to explode. I was close…*so* close. It was almost painful.

"Yes?" His tone was sweet, but his smile was downright wicked.

I huffed, fighting the urge to capitulate when all I could think about was coming. But I knew he wouldn't give me what I wanted until I did as he asked. I took a few deep breaths. Smiled. "Please."

"Please, what?" He resumed circling my clit with his finger, the pleasure building despite his lazy strokes.

Oh, I was going to make him pay for this.

"Please, Nate," I moaned. Obscenely. Loudly. Clearly overacting. "*Please* let me come on your cock." But by the time the words came from my mouth, I meant them. I wanted that.

He let out a garbled sound. I smirked, pleased to have thrown him off his game, at least momentarily. "Since you asked nicely," he said, stroking himself. *Holy shit,* that was hot. "I'll let you come on my tongue. *And* on my cock."

"You're so magnanimous," I said, unable to hide my sass.

He cupped the back of my neck, his touch possessive as

he claimed my mouth. I could taste my desire on his tongue. "Shut up, Em, and sit on my face."

I didn't need to be told twice. He lay on the bed, and I straddled his head, my pleasure rising quickly from the change in position and the fact that I was confident he wasn't going to withhold my pleasure again. If he did, I *would* take matters into my own hands this time, regardless of his earlier edict.

He grasped my hips, pulling me down to his mouth. Lavishing me with attention. I glanced down to see him looking up at me, watching me. And he kept one hand on my hip while reaching up with the other to tweak my nipples.

"Yes." The pleasure built, like a runner careening toward the finish line. "Yes." I leaned back, resting my hands on his thighs as I reached the pinnacle.

My orgasm would not, *could* not, wait any longer. My body had been primed over and over again by this man, and I was more than ready to come. Nate kept flicking that spot, and I was met with a rush of satisfaction, my toes curling as my orgasm blazed through me.

It was all-encompassing. Overpowering. Destructive. Like a wildfire that tore through anything in its path.

I flopped on the bed beside Nate, unable to move or even think. He'd owned my body. And I was fully prepared to beg again if it would lead to another orgasm of that magnitude.

I mean...*damn*.

Nate chuckled, clearly pleased with himself as he grabbed a condom from the intimacy kit in the nightstand. I was on birth control, but I was grateful he'd taken the lead without being asked. He rolled it on, and I was transfixed by the sight. He was... Fuck, he was sexy.

He crawled up my body, grabbing my wrists and forcing them above my head. Why was that so hot?

He traced the line of my jaw. "You're stunning."

My eyes tracked his face. The chiseled lines I knew so well. Those full lips. His broad shoulders and narrow waist. I tried to memorize the feel of his skin on mine. The sight of his body—full of desire for me.

His cock was wedged between my thighs, and I moaned when he ground into me. The friction was almost enough, but not quite.

"Why do you love to torture me?" I asked, arching my hips. Seeking more.

"Me?" he asked, rolling us so I was on top. "You're the one who prances around *my* house in those barely there workout shorts."

"I—" I smoothed my hands down his chest, distracted by all the bare, glorious skin beneath my hands. "I'm an athlete."

"I know," he said. "And I love that about you. But do you have to wear so little clothing?"

I laughed, sliding along his length. "I didn't realize it bothered you. I didn't realize you even noticed."

His breathing was erratic, the grip on my hips tightening. "Fuck me, Em."

"I thought you'd never ask." I sank down on his cock.

He gasped, squeezing his eyes shut in pleasure when he was buried deep inside me. And when he opened them again, his gaze was intense as he cupped my cheek. "I notice every-thing about you. I always have."

He wasn't supposed to say things like that. Not when we'd agreed this was temporary. But I couldn't bring myself to remind him of that. Not when he was so deep inside me that I didn't know where I ended and he began. Not when he was looking at me as if I was his entire world. And not when he began to thrust, stealing the air from my lungs.

"Holy…" I shuddered, overwhelmed by the riot of sensations.

"That's it." He rested his hand at the base of my throat. "God, you feel so good, Em. Just like I knew you would."

I still couldn't get over the fact that he'd wanted me. All this time, *Nate* had wanted *me*. I shuddered.

He used his other hand to play with my clit, driving up into me with slow yet forceful movements. Despite his seeming control, I knew he was close to snapping. It was clear in the way he clenched his teeth, a bead of sweat forming on his forehead.

I smoothed my hands over his chest then leaned back to fondle his balls. He froze, and when I looked back at his face, his eyes were closed. His mouth pinched shut.

"Did I—"

He grabbed my wrist and pulled it around to place it on his chest over his heart. "Your pussy is gripping me so tight. And if you keep doing that, I'm going to come."

"Good." I smirked.

"No." He shook his head, grabbing my hips and pulling me down onto him harder. Faster. "Not until I make you come at least one more time. If not two." The determined set to his jaw told me not to argue. And it wasn't like I was going to anyway. If the man wanted to give me three orgasms, who was I to complain?

I basked in his attention. In the way his eyes locked on mine. Our bodies connected and in sync. My own racing toward my next orgasm with every swivel of my hips.

"That's it, Em," he rasped. "Ride my cock."

Oh god. Those words. From his mouth.

This was better than any of the fantasies I'd had about Nate. He was so...engaged. So in tune with my needs even now, using his thumb to circle my clit.

There was a rush of sensation, and I convulsed with pleasure. His stomach tightened, as did his grip on my hips, almost to the point of pain. But then his face contorted, and he shattered.

Of all the looks I'd seen on Nate's face, this one was my favorite. I wasn't sure I'd ever seen anything more beautiful than the sated, dazed expression he currently wore. Especially since I knew I was responsible for it.

He held me close, running his hand down my spine. It felt so normal. So right. He kissed the top of my head then went to dispose of the condom.

When he returned to the bed, he immediately pulled me into his arms. And as I lay there, listening to his heartbeat, I didn't know how I'd ever be the same. How I'd ever walk away when this inevitably ended.

CHAPTER NINETEEN

Emerson

"That meal was delicious," I said as Nate slid his hand into mine. The hallway was empty. No one was around to watch. But he'd taken my hand all the same. "Thank you."

Nate and I had gone to dinner to make a public appearance. It had been…strange. To feel like I was on display while eating dinner. People gawked, whispered, tried to sneak photos. That had been the point, but still…it was invasive.

Nate held the door to the suite open for me. Brooklyn was already asleep. The temp nanny from the Hartwell Agency gave us a quick rundown of their evening, and we thanked her before she headed off to her room.

"I liked her," I said about the nanny.

"I like *you*," Nate said. His hands were on my hips, rushing me toward our bedroom. "Fuck. You're sexy."

I kissed him, tugging on his lapels, needing him closer. The nanny forgotten, for now at least. At some point, we'd have to find my replacement. But I didn't want to think about that. Not right now.

"So are you." I tugged on his jacket, needing him naked. Now. "Everyone in the restaurant was staring at you."

"No." He dipped his head and kissed the skin where my neck met my shoulder. "They were staring at you."

My skin heated at his praise, and I stripped off his jacket, tossing it on the chair. He gripped my hip, then he was sliding my dress up my leg, but the material made it difficult to get very far.

He groaned in frustration and moved to his knees. "This dress is sexy as hell, but if you don't show me how to get it off in the next two seconds, I'm going to tear it." He searched the material.

"Don't you dare." I glared at him, knowing it wasn't an idle threat. "Jay would have a fit."

"I don't fucking care." He grunted, trying to get it off.

I laughed and stood. "Well, I do."

I slid the zipper down my side, tugging the dress over my head and laying it gently on the desk chair. When I came face-to-face with Nate again, he growled, his desire evident in his eyes and the hard-on tenting his pants. "You were naked under there the whole time?"

I bit back a smile. I couldn't help it. Sometimes it was just too fun to provoke him. "Yep."

He growled, narrowing his eyes at me.

"Relax, caveman." I patted his chest. "Jackson was with us."

That seemed to incense him even more. His nostrils flared. "I'm having him reassigned."

I laughed. "No. You're not."

He looked downright murderous. "Thorne," he chided.

"Ooh." I smirked. "I haven't heard that nickname in a while. I must really be in trouble."

He slid his hands into his pockets, the picture of calm, cool elegance. "On your knees."

"Why?" I cocked my hip, loving the way his eyes tracked my every move. "Are you going to punish me?"

"I'm going to fuck that feisty mouth. And then I'm going to remind you who that pussy belongs to."

Heat gushed to my core. *Yes, please.* But I didn't say that. Instead, I held his gaze, defiant to the very end.

Nate said nothing, but his look said everything. *Obey or suffer the consequences.*

Slowly, ever so slowly, I lowered myself to my knees, determined to suck him off until *he* was the one begging for mercy.

"Crawl to me," he rasped.

"What?" My eyes darted to him, my breath catching.

He was fully clothed, and I was completely naked. Completely at his mercy. And I realized that I trusted him implicitly. Maybe not with my heart. But I trusted him to make me feel good. To take care of me.

"You heard me," he said.

I debated telling him no solely to see what he'd do, but the idea of prowling over to him had a fresh wave of arousal washing over me. With painstaking slowness, I started moving in his direction. The tile was cold and hard beneath my hands and knees. But the entire time, he lavished me with compliments and praise.

"You're so beautiful," he rasped.

I inched closer, and he issued another. "Look at that lithe, strong body."

Instead of making me feel demeaned, Nate made the act feel powerful. Regal, even. I was a queen, even if I was the one on my knees for him.

"Yes," he encouraged. "That's it."

It wasn't even that big a distance, but I'd taken my time getting to him. Giving him the show he so clearly wanted.

And when I brushed against his legs, he reached down to caress my hair.

"Good girl," he cooed, smoothing his hand down my cheek until he was cupping my chin and guiding me to look at him. "Pull out my cock."

I unzipped his pants with painstaking slowness. When I pushed them down over his hips, his cock bobbed toward his stomach. I peered up at him, waiting for his next demand.

"See how hard I am for you." He sounded almost…angry. "How hard I am for you all the damn time."

He cupped my cheek, his caress both possessive and gentle. The look in his eyes spoke of adoration and told me that I was completely in control, despite his commanding language.

As soon as my tongue hit his skin, he hissed. I licked him from root to tip, and my name came out as a strangled sigh.

I peered up at him, loving the array of expressions that flitted across his face as I took my time licking and sucking and pleasuring him. Taking him in my mouth as deep as I could go. Surprise. Desire. Agony. Anticipation.

I gripped the backs of his legs, urging him on. Begging for more. He cradled the back of my head, gently thrusting into my mouth. I could sense him losing control. He was getting close; it was clear from the way he hissed with nearly every breath to the tightening of his grip on my hair.

"That's enough," he said abruptly and pulled out.

"Hate to tell you this," I said, wiping my mouth as he stripped off the rest of his clothes. "But you'll *never* be able to fuck the feisty out of me."

His dark chuckle made my core quiver with need. "Maybe not, but I'll certainly have fun trying."

He picked me up and tossed me onto the mattress. I blinked a few times then laughed, loving how physical and playful he could be when it came to sex. As an athlete, I craved movement and play, and I appreciated his strength.

He yanked on my legs, pulling me closer to the edge. He grabbed something from the pocket of his pants, and I assumed it was a condom. I propped myself up on my elbows, curious when he removed the cap from one of Brooklyn's temporary tattoo markers.

"What are you doing?"

He held down my thigh with one hand and started writing on the skin near my bikini line with the other. I kept trying to get a good look at what he was doing, but he wouldn't let me.

Finally, he stood back, immensely pleased with himself. "There."

On my thigh, in Nate's scrawl, was (Nate's Version).

I couldn't help myself; I laughed. Nate was claiming his ownership in a way a Swiftie like me would love. Taylor Swift had fought a very public battle to regain the rights to her songs, designating the ones she rerecorded and owned with (Taylor's Version). So Nate was saying that I belonged to him, and the idea that he'd want to proclaim that we belonged together made me giddy.

And then he knelt to the floor and pushed my thighs apart, baring me to him. My breath caught when I realized what he had planned next.

"Mm," I said, eagerly awaiting his mouth on my clit. His hands on my body. God, I loved when he touched me. Kissed me.

If only this were more than just physical for him. Because it was definitely becoming more for me.

He licked my clit, and I shuddered, wishing it were true but knowing it was impossible. He roamed my body with his hands, touching, grabbing, caressing, pinching as he sucked my clit. It was sensory overload, and I was here for it.

He slid a finger inside me, driving me higher and higher. I clenched the sheets, my toes curling from pleasure and anticipation. *This* was exactly what I'd needed.

My body wound tighter and tighter like my muscles when I was preparing to launch the shot put. I was so close to release. I was about to come when he slowed. Stopped.

I clenched and unclenched the sheets, lifted my head and glared at him. "Nate."

"Yes?" His tone was sweet, but his expression was wicked.

I narrowed my eyes at him, gritting out, "Why'd you stop?"

He slowly, gently, started rubbing my clit again. "Who does this pussy belong to?" He dipped his finger inside, then swiped the juices over my already slick nerve endings.

"Me," I said, feeling extra defiant.

He slapped my pussy. I was so shocked, I just blinked at him. But if he'd intended it as a punishment, it had backfired. Because all the blood came rushing back, along with an overwhelming wave of arousal.

"Try again," he said, giving my new tattoo a pointed look.

I was tempted to defy him again, if only to see if he'd slap my pussy another time. God, it felt so good. How had I lived all my life without experiencing that before?

"Emerson." His voice rumbled over me like thunder from an approaching storm. Nate pushed me right up to the edge again, until I was begging for him to fill me. To let me come.

"Answer me." His eyes were wild, his body taut with tension.

"You," I said. "Only you."

"Damn right." He settled himself against the headboard, sliding a condom down his length. "Now, come ride my cock."

I'd had no idea Nate would have such a filthy mouth, but I was here for it. I loved it. Loved hearing his barely restrained control. Loved the way he seemed ready to snap—because of me. *Me!*

Part of me had worried that it would be a mistake to sleep with him, and not because he was my boss or because I'd agreed to be his fake fiancée for a year. But because he'd been at the top of my celebrity fuck-it list for so long, I was afraid I'd built up an unrealistic image of him in my mind.

I tried to push those thoughts away. They weren't fair to him. I'd long since realized that he was so much more than I'd ever hoped for. And when it came to sex with Nate, he'd definitely met and far exceeded anything I'd imagined in my fantasies.

I braced myself on the headboard, sinking down onto him slowly. He groaned but didn't rush me, our eyes locked on each other as our bodies became one.

When I was fully seated, he growled. "Yes, Em. That's it. You feel so good. Like you were made for me."

I started rocking, and he explored my body with his hands. Touching me everywhere—my shoulders, my back, my hips, my stomach, my breasts. It was as if he was mapping me, memorizing my every freckle and scar.

"You are…" He shook his head, his eyes pinging between mine and where we were joined. I rotated my hips, swiveling and changing the tempo. His eyes glazed over, and whatever he'd been going to say was forgotten.

"I am…" I smirked.

But then he started rubbing circles on my clit, and I forgot about anything else. "Oh god. I'm going to—" I gripped his shoulders, my orgasm barreling into me.

He slid his free hand up my chest, coming to rest on my neck. His touch was gentle, his gaze reverent. And I'd never felt more cherished.

"That's it," he groaned, thrusting up into me. Both of our movements becoming more frantic. Our breathing erratic.

Until I squeezed my eyes and threw back my head, letting the release overpower me.

"Fuck." He grunted, following me over the edge. "Yes, Em. *Yes.*"

I wanted to rest my head against his chest, but then I remembered that this was temporary. With time, his lust or infatuation or whatever Nate felt for me would fade just like the tattoo he'd drawn on my skin.

My phone rang, Kendall's name flashing on the screen with a request to FaceTime. She'd tried calling a few times the past few days, but I'd either been busy or avoiding her. But the longer I put off this conversation, the more suspicious it would seem.

And I honestly missed talking to my best friend, even if I loathed the idea of lying to her. It was one thing not to tell her about my training or my anxiety over competing, though I'd had some success with Nate's alter ego idea lately. It was another to lie to her face about being engaged to her fiancé's brother.

I straightened and took a deep breath, smiling before I pressed the button to connect the call. Fortunately, Brooklyn was already asleep. I'd checked on her earlier, and she'd been in a deep sleep.

Nate was still on set, and I wasn't sure when he'd be back. They'd started filming this afternoon, and I knew it could involve long days—twelve hours wasn't outside the norm. But selfishly, I hoped he'd return soon.

"Hey!" I said as soon as she appeared on the screen.

"Emmy! Hey!" She looked so happy. So relaxed. *Like*

someone newly engaged would. I needed to channel that energy. "I'm so glad I finally caught you!"

"Yeah. Sorry." I cringed. "Things have been crazy here."

"I bet. Well…" She smiled. "I just wanted to call and wish my best friend congratulations."

I tried to ignore my own image and hoped I looked equally as overjoyed. The orgasms certainly helped. "Thank you." I didn't feel like much of a best friend at the moment.

"How's Paris?" I asked, eager to focus her attention away from me and my surprise engagement.

"Good. We decided to stay another week and then head home. How's Abu Dhabi?"

"Beautiful," I said. "And the Huxley Grand here is unreal." I panned the camera around so she could see my room and the scenery, even if it was nighttime.

"Looks nice." She leaned forward. "So…you and Nate, huh?"

"Me and Nate," I said, not sure what else *to* say.

She rolled her bottom lip between her teeth then asked, "Why didn't you tell me?"

"Honestly…" I said, knowing I should've anticipated this. Her tone wasn't accusatory or hurt. Just…confused. We were best friends. We'd always told each other everything. Or almost everything. "At first, I wasn't even sure it would last. And then I didn't tell you because I was embarrassed."

"What?" She jerked her head back. "Why?"

"Because I went on and on about how I couldn't stand him. And he was my boss."

She frowned. "You know I'd never judge you."

"I know. I just—" I huffed. "You had a lot going on with your mom and Knox. And by the time I was finally ready to tell you about Nate, things had fallen apart with Knox."

"I'm sorry I wasn't a better friend," she said, and I hated myself for ever making her think that.

"Kendall." I frowned. "No. That's not what—"

"I know." She waved a hand through the air. "I know that's not what you were trying to say, but I still wish I'd been there for you. Not so wrapped up in my own life."

"You've always been there for me."

"Well, I'm going to be more aware of it. Starting now. Gah. I have so many questions," she said. "Like when it started. And how it happened." She gasped. "Wait. The Birkin. Were you together then?"

I nodded, sticking to the timeline Nate and I had agreed to. Letting Kendall fill in the blanks.

I was so tempted to tell her the truth. To just blurt it all out and be done with it. But I couldn't. Even though I knew Kendall would never judge me for what I'd done, I just... She'd always been such a rule-follower that I wasn't sure she'd understand my decision. Or, worse still, be disappointed in me. But it was more than that. I couldn't break my promise to Nate. I couldn't risk jeopardizing Brooklyn's future.

She smirked. "I should've known. I mean, who buys their nanny a $20,000 purse for her birthday?"

"Right?" I laughed, trying to play off my discomfort.

"And now your anxiety about attending Brooklyn's play makes more sense," she said, and I merely nodded. "I'm glad he's spoiling you. You deserve it. Especially after the last douchenozzle you dated."

"You're one to talk," I joked.

"Hey! Jude has come a long way," she said, referring to Knox's son and her ex.

"I'm glad to hear it, but he's no Knox."

"No." She smiled dreamily, glancing down at her engagement ring. "He's not. No one is."

"So have you guys made any plans for your wedding?" I asked, latching on to a safer topic. A better topic than my relationship with Nate. "Do you think you'll have a big wedding?"

"Knox wants to elope. He offered to get married while we're in Paris."

My jaw dropped. "Seriously?" She nodded. "I guess you told him no since you asked me to be your maid of honor." She'd sent me a video a few days ago with the prettiest maid of honor proposal. I'd immediately accepted, of course.

"Maid or *matron*," she said with a knowing look. "Depending on when you and Nate decide to get married."

I laughed, though it sounded nervous to my ears. "We're not in any rush. For now, we're just enjoying being engaged."

"That's good. And I'm so excited that we can enjoy being engaged together. I was hoping you'd help me pick a dress when we're back in town."

"That sounds like fun," I said, but then I sighed. "But I'm guessing dress shopping would turn into a circus with me there, and that's not fair to you."

"Please. When you're engaged to a billionaire, the designers come to you." She laughed. "But I don't blame you for not wanting to be mobbed by photographers."

"It's just…surreal, you know. I'm used to doing whatever I want. Going where I want. Sure, I used to get recognized sometimes. But this is a whole nother level."

It was a little better in Abu Dhabi, but I kept wondering when the fervor from our engagement announcement would die down. I wondered if I'd ever be able to live a normal life again. When I'd agreed to this charade, I'd known that my life would change. But I'd underestimated just how much.

She frowned. "I'm sure that's difficult. It sounds like it's wearing on you."

"Thanks," I said. "But it's not all bad. Nate had Jay send a whole new wardrobe for me to Abu Dhabi, and it's all fabulous."

Kendall grinned, shaking her head. "Sometimes this life is crazy."

"No joke," I said, holding up my ring. "I cannot get over how much this diamond is worth or the fact that it came from his mother's collection. A *collection!*"

"Have you seen it?" she asked.

I shook my head. "Has Knox showed you the family jewels?"

And then we both burst out laughing. We were laughing so hard, tears were streaming down my cheeks, and I had to clutch my stomach.

"Sorry," I said between fits of laughter. "Sorry."

We finally calmed down, and she said, "Knox has given me a few pieces, but it's my impression the bulk of it was left to Nate."

"Really?" I asked.

"Yeah. When it came to the money, all the kids got equal shares of the hotel fortune. But the personal items were designated in their parents' wills. Nate got the majority of their mom's jewelry collection, and Knox got the sports memorabilia."

"Interesting," I said.

"Let me see the ring again."

I held up my hand, allowing her to inspect it through the screen. "Nate chose well for you. The ring is gorgeous, and you've always wanted a red diamond."

"I know. And the crazy thing is, I never told him."

"Seriously?" she asked.

I nodded. I would've asked Kendall if Nate had reached out to her for help selecting my engagement ring, but I knew that wasn't possible, considering the circumstances of our engagement. Still, it was the only thing that made sense.

"I guess he really does know you." She grinned.

"Guess so," I said, still stuck on the fact that he'd picked my dream ring. All by himself. What were the chances?

"Emmy," she said in a softer voice. "How are you, really? I was terrified when I heard you'd been hospitalized."

I'd forgotten that I hadn't talked to Kendall on the phone since then. We'd only texted, and it had been brief. The whole incident felt like so long ago, and yet it had barely been a week. A week ago, and a world away.

"I'm okay," I said, hoping to reassure her.

She'd been worried about me—the concern was written across her face. Her mom's cancer was now in remission, but even minor health concerns still put Kendall on edge.

"What happened?"

I told her what I could, which wasn't much because we still didn't know. Hell, the tabloids and bloggers seemed to report with more certainty than my medical team. I'd Googled myself once briefly the other day, and I'd immediately regretted it. It was strange to read theories about myself and my hospital stay. They had some of the most outlandish ideas—everything from plastic surgery to a secret pregnancy. All bullshit, of course.

"And how's Nate? I'm so glad he could be there with you."

I nearly laughed because, of course, that's what had started all of this. But then I remembered how he'd spent the night at my bedside. How he'd argued with the doctor, advocating for me. How concerned he'd been then and since.

"He's been very…protective."

"Like, sweet? Or overbearing?"

I gave her a look that said, "What do you think?" And then told her, "He took away my phone."

She rolled her eyes. "At least he seems to have given it back. And he hasn't had your car towed."

"No. He just has his bodyguard drive me everywhere."

Kendall smiled, dragging a hand through her hair. "Oh lord. These Crawford men…"

We both started laughing.

"But seriously," she said, resting her elbow on the table, which had the effect of flashing her engagement ring at me. "Can you believe it? We're going to marry brothers."

"Yep," I chirped, popping open my water bottle and taking a large gulp. I might be having fun with Nate now, but we were never going to walk down the aisle together.

"I mean, I'm still trying to wrap my head around the fact that you're engaged. And to Nate, of all people." Her expression turned more contemplative. "Though, I guess it does make sense."

"Oh yeah?" I asked, trying not to give too much away. Trying to play it cool.

"I could always tell there was something there."

"Yeah." I laughed. "You mean, like we couldn't stand each other."

"No." She shook her head. "There were definitely…sparks. Electricity."

I had a feeling she was reading more into the situation than there'd been, but whatever. If that's what she believed, all the better. It would make our relationship seem more authentic.

"How's Knox?" I asked, desperate for a change of subject.

After that, we talked about the upcoming MLS Super-Draft and my qualifiers. Kendall said she and Knox were planning to come. Considering the frenzy since the announcement of our engagement, I imagined there'd be increased media attention at the event as well.

Fuck. Just what I didn't need. More attention when I was already feeling the pressure to compete.

At least my dad had backed off a little the past few days. Either he was too busy enjoying Aspen, or he realized I needed a more gentle hand. But whatever was responsible for it, I was grateful.

"Hang on for a sec," Kendall said, putting the call on mute briefly before returning her attention to the screen. "Sorry, Emmy. I've gotta go. Knox is taking me out for a surprise."

I smiled. "Have fun."

"You too. Love you, Em."

"Love you too," I said before disconnecting the call. Well, that had gone better and worse than I'd expected.

I caught up on my emails, perusing Brooklyn's lesson plan for tomorrow and my dad's workout. I washed my face and climbed into bed, planning to read some of my book. But I could barely keep my eyes open, and I soon fell asleep.

The mattress dipped behind me, Nate's warm body coming to cradle mine. I sighed and snuggled into his arms.

"Hey," I said with my eyes still closed. "How was filming?"

"Shh," he hushed. "Go back to sleep."

Now that he was here, I didn't want to sleep. I backed into him, wiggling my ass.

"Em," he growled. "Don't start something you can't finish."

"Who said I can't finish it?" I asked, his hand already moving over my stomach. My breasts. My neck. "Unless you're too tired."

"Fuck no," he rasped, and then he flipped me over and showed me just how much energy he had as we competed to outdo each other with pleasure.

CHAPTER TWENTY

Nate

I pressed my lips to the hollow of Emerson's throat. I was due on set in a few hours, but all I wanted was to spend the day in bed with her. This was quickly becoming a problem. My addiction to her. My *need* for her. And not just in my bed. In my life.

"Fuck. You smell so good." I inhaled her scent. Was it her skin, her hair, or just…her?

Whatever the cause, her scent drove me crazy. Like a field of flowers on a summer day. It was fresh and full and lush, just like her presence in my life.

"Did you just sniff me?" she asked.

"Yes." I did it again, this time closer to her nape. She giggled. "What is that smell? It drives me crazy." *You drive me crazy.*

"My perfume?" she asked as I continued kissing her skin. Using my lips to shower her with affection.

"No." I continued my descent, kissing the tops of her breasts. Over the silk of her sleep camisole. It was so tempting to peel the fabric aside, but I wanted to draw this out as long as possible.

She arched her back, thrusting her breasts toward me. "Oh god," she moaned. "That feels so good."

I kissed her stomach over the shirt. I was happier than I'd been in a long time, and I couldn't imagine giving this up. Giving *her* up. Especially not when it felt as if I'd finally just gotten to be with her.

"My soap?" she asked as I kissed the sliver of stomach between the bottom of her shirt and the waistband of those fucking shorts.

"No." I reveled in the feel of her skin beneath my hands. "It's unique to you."

"Why—ahh…" She bucked her hips when I peeled her shorts down and kissed near her hip bone. "Why do you say that?"

Because I'd smelled her shampoo, body soap, and perfume. And while they each reminded me of her, they weren't *her* scent. It was like the sum of them was greater than the parts, and it required her unique body chemistry to bring them to life.

"Dad!" Brooklyn called. "Emmy!"

I groaned and dropped my head to Emerson's stomach. I thought for sure she'd sleep another hour. Or at least long enough for Emerson and me to finish what we'd started. Apparently, I was wrong.

"To be continued," I said, wishing we didn't have to get up.

Emerson laughed and pushed out of bed, grabbing a robe and pulling it on. "Coming," she called to Brooklyn.

"I should probably get up," I said, knowing I had an inbox full of emails to review. Contracts waiting for my signature.

I pushed out of bed, my cock tenting my boxer briefs. Emerson gave me a pointed look. "You should *probably* do something about that."

"I was about to, if we hadn't been interrupted." I wrapped

my arms around her waist, pulling her to me and letting her feel my arousal.

"Don't tease me, Nate." But she was the one rocking her hips against me.

"I wouldn't dream of it."

"Later." Her voice was husky and full of want.

"Yes." I gave her another kiss, not wanting to let her go. "Later."

After a quick shower, I joined Emerson and Brooklyn for breakfast then caught up on emails and reviewed the section of the script we'd be working on today. The rest of my day was spent on set, and by the time I got back to the Huxley Grand, I was more than ready to relax with Brooklyn and Emerson after a long day. I was hoping for a quiet dinner. A chill evening with my two favorite girls.

I opened the door and set down my bag in the foyer, pausing when I heard a familiar voice. *Sloan?* I frowned. What was she doing here?

I continued through to the living room where Sloan, Emerson, and Brooklyn were making friendship bracelets while listening to music. I watched the three of them as they threaded their beads with great concentration. And for a moment, I could imagine this was our life. Our *real* life and not just an act.

The song "End Game" came on, and as I listened to the lyrics, I realized that I wanted to be Emerson's end game. Because she was certainly mine.

I loved her. I had for a while now. I just had been too scared to admit it.

Brooklyn said something that made Sloan and Emerson laugh. And as I watched Emerson—smiling and laughing with two of my favorite women—I felt a pang in my chest. I'd roped her into this. I'd convinced her to lie to everyone. But the biggest lie I'd been telling was to myself. Because this might be a fake engagement, but I had developed some very real feelings toward my fiancée.

"Dad!" Brooklyn jumped up, startling me. "Look who came to visit!"

Emerson smiled, and it seemed genuine. I wondered how long she'd been entertaining my cousin. I wondered if Sloan had pushed for details about our relationship or our plans for the wedding. *Shit.*

I leaned down to kiss Emerson's forehead, whispering, "Missed you," before I could think better of it.

To her, this might be a business agreement. A vacation fling. A fake engagement. Whatever the hell you wanted to call it. But to me, it was so much more. I'd never really let anyone in, not like I had Emerson.

And the idea of returning home and pretending as if none of this had ever happened seemed…impossible. Laughable, even. Surely she no longer wanted that. Right?

"Hey," I said, giving Sloan a hug when she stood to greet me. "I didn't realize you were going to be in Abu Dhabi."

"Just thought I'd pop over on my way to Singapore."

Just pop over, my ass. Sloan's unexpected visit had a purpose, and I didn't think it was solely motivated by seeing Brooklyn.

"Singapore?" I asked.

"Visiting some of our hotels there," she said.

I nodded. "Did Graham come too?"

She laughed. "He's too preoccupied with the Mexico launch."

"Ah. Right."

"Enough boring talk about hotels," Brooklyn said.

"It's not boring," Sloan insisted, wrapping her arm around Brooklyn's shoulder. "And one day, it may be your job to run the Huxley empire."

Brooklyn groaned, and I interjected. "*Only* if that's what Brooklyn wants." I gave Sloan a pointed look.

I wasn't going to coerce my daughter into taking over the family business. Hell, I didn't want her to turn out like Graham. My cousin might love running the hotel empire, but it was his life. It consumed him.

"Someday, she may not have the choice," Sloan said in an ominous tone. "Unless you're planning to have more children." She gave Emerson and me a pointed look.

"I think you're forgetting about Jude," I said quickly, though we all knew that Jude's passion was in working with Knox and the LA Leatherbacks.

"Right." Sloan blew a raspberry—as if to say, that's not happening.

"Knox and Kendall," I suggested.

Sloan barked out a laugh. "He's even older than you. Do you really think he wants to have another kid at his age?"

"What about you?" I asked, annoyed that she kept acting like this was somehow solely my problem or my fault. "Or Jasper. Or Graham. Any one of you could have your own children instead of relying on Knox and me."

"I'm sorry—" Emerson interjected. "But I don't understand. Can't you just sell the company if there's no one left in the family who's able or willing to run it?"

"We—"

Sloan cut me off. "That's a family secret."

"And *Emerson's* family," I insisted.

Sloan shook her head, glaring at me as if to silence me. Before I could protest Sloan's statement or answer Emerson's question, there was a knock at the door. Jackson peeked his head in.

"Hey, Queen B," Jackson said to Brooklyn. "The car's ready."

I turned to Brooklyn. "Where are you going?"

"*We—*" she grinned "—are going on a kayaking tour."

I groaned. Seriously? I was exhausted from our filming schedule. And the idea of kayaking in the hot sun after a long day of work sounded awful.

But my attention snagged on Sloan. Her eyes were wide, and she was looking at Jackson as if she'd seen a ghost. When I turned back to Jackson, he was stiff, his expression shuttered.

"Come on, Dad." Brooklyn tugged on my hand, distracting me from whatever the hell was going on between Jackson and Sloan. I wasn't sure I wanted to know. "It's going to be so cool. Emmy researched it, and it looks amazing. We'll learn all about biodiversity and the mangroves. And we'll get to watch the sun set from the water."

She was so excited, I found it impossible to say no.

"Fine," I sighed. "Let me get changed."

"Yay!" Brooklyn jumped up from the couch and ran off to her room.

"My room's just down the hall," Sloan said, hooking her thumb over her shoulder. "I'll be back in ten."

"Sounds good," I said, knowing I needed to get up. Get moving. Before I fell asleep on the couch.

Once everyone had left, Emerson straddled my lap. "You okay?"

"I'm exhausted," I admitted, unable to pretend any longer. My role was emotionally demanding, and I was still running the studio while acting in the film. The work never stopped.

Emerson started massaging my temples, my scalp. I groaned, dropping my head forward, resting it against her chest. "God, that feels amazing."

"Good." I could hear the smile in her voice. She kept massaging my scalp and neck, and little by little, my body relaxed.

"What's up with Sloan and Jackson?" Emerson eventually

asked, careful to keep her voice low as she kissed her way down my neck.

"I don't know." I glanced toward Brooklyn's room, confirming the door was still closed. "But I was wondering the same thing."

"Do you think your family sent her to check up on us?" she whispered.

"I doubt it," I said. "Knowing Sloan, she took it upon herself. She's very protective of Brooklyn."

"I know. I can respect that."

"Did she give any indication of how long she's staying?" I asked, knowing we didn't have much time before Sloan or Brooklyn returned.

She shook her head. "Not a clue. I mean, she did say she 'popped over' on her way to Singapore. But she doesn't seem to be in any rush to leave."

I nodded. I didn't say it, but we both knew Sloan's visit could complicate things. Hell, I already resented the intrusion on my time with Emerson. We only had a week left until we went home—went back to being friends or whatever we were. And the last thing I wanted was to share our precious alone time.

"How did it go today?" Emerson asked.

"Fine." I could barely form words.

"Just fine?" she asked. "Did Meghan Hart finally show up?"

"No." I laughed.

It had become a bit of a running joke with Emerson. Meghan Hart had yet to show up, and I was beginning to think she never would. I couldn't imagine being able to maintain such privacy despite being such a well-known author. It must be nice.

"You should come visit the set," I said, knowing Emerson had read the book the movie was based on.

"Seriously?" she asked. But then she shook her head, her excitement fading. "I don't want to be a distraction."

"Are you kidding?" I pulled back to look at her. "I'd love to have you there." I should've thought to invite her sooner, but I knew she was busy with her training and taking care of Brooklyn.

"I suppose people would expect your fiancée to visit you on set."

"Exactly," I said, hating that she felt the need to mention our fake engagement to validate her visit, instead of just wanting to come see me.

Brooklyn bounded into the room, and Emerson slid off my lap to sit at my side. "Where's Auntie Sloan?" She frowned at us. "And why haven't you changed?"

Emerson stood, patting my thigh as she did so. "Your dad's going to stay here."

I peered up at her, furrowing my brow. *I am?*

"He needs his rest after filming, and I think it would be fun to have a girls' adventure."

Brooklyn perked up at that. "Okay. Can we go shopping too? And get mani-pedis?" She turned to me and batted her eyes. "Please, Dad?"

"Fine," I sighed, pulling my wallet out of my pocket and handing her my black Amex.

"You dropped something," Emerson said, picking it up and staring at it.

It was a picture of Emerson and Brooklyn, one I'd discovered in the daily calendar she'd made for me for Christmas. Every other photo had been of Brooklyn on her own, except this one. As soon as I'd seen the photo, I'd torn it out and stuck it in my wallet.

"You keep this with you?" Emerson asked.

"Since Christmas," Brooklyn said as if the answer was obvious.

As in, before *we were fake-engaged.*

Emerson's eyes remained on mine. Questioning. She handed it back without saying a word. Did she know how I felt about her? That it wasn't pretend for me?

Part of me thought my feelings for her were obvious—they had to be. But another part feared she believed they were all part of the ruse. I didn't know what to do. I was afraid if I told her, it would make things awkward, especially if she didn't feel the same way. But I couldn't stand the thought of giving her up—not now, not in a year, not ever.

"Get some rest," Emerson said, brushing my hair away from my face and kissing my temple.

"Thanks," I said, lying down and trying to ignore my tumultuous thoughts. "Have fun."

"Oh, we will." She grinned, fanning herself with my black Amex card.

I narrowed my eyes at her, though I trusted Emerson not to go overboard. "I'm sure." My eyes slid closed, and I waved at them over the back of the couch.

When I woke again, it was to an empty suite. It was quiet, and I assumed everyone was still out enjoying their adventure. It made me happy to think of Brooklyn getting to spend time with her two favorite women. Two women who were strong and independent and... Well, I only hoped things were going well between Sloan and Emerson.

I pushed myself off the couch, glancing at the time on my phone. I had a missed call from Pierce. I changed into my workout clothes and headed to the gym for a run.

I placed my phone on the treadmill and hit the button to connect the call. "Pierce. Hey. What's up?"

"Just checking in on how things were going."

Checking in? Pierce never called just to "check in."

"Fine," I said, furrowing my brow. "Why?"

"I was just wondering if there was a reason you've only

made one public appearance as a couple since landing in Abu Dhabi."

I frowned, increasing the speed on the treadmill. "We've been busy. I'm filming. She's training. We both want to spend time with Brooklyn."

"Those all sound like excuses. You just announced your engagement. You need to get your ass out there and sell this relationship, not…hole up in your hotel room."

Ha! What a joke.

"Emerson and I did that *Vogue* interview. We went out to dinner. We've posted on social media. Besides, we're busy. And don't you think that our absence only adds to the allure?"

"No. I think it has people questioning what you're trying to hide. Is she giving you pushback or something?"

"No." Not at all. Quite the opposite. I was the one who didn't want to be so public about our relationship. "You know that I like to keep my private life private."

"Nate," he sighed. "I get that. I do." I honestly wasn't sure he did. "And I was fine with your decision to sneak out of the hospital."

I put him on mute and ratcheted up the speed on the treadmill. He was really starting to piss me off.

"Sneaking out of the hospital," as he'd put it, hadn't been part of any strategy other than protecting Emerson.

"But, Nate," he continued, "you need to think big picture here."

I was thinking big picture. Big picture was that I loved Emerson, and I'd do anything to protect her. *Damn*, it felt good to admit that. Scary but good.

I was still concerned about Emerson's health and mental state. She seemed a lot more relaxed since coming to Abu Dhabi, and I wanted to keep it that way. I wanted to shield her from the publicity storm and backlash that could come with being engaged to me. I refused to ask her for more than she'd already given me. And she'd given me a lot.

"What's really going on?" Pierce asked. "Is the chemistry just not there or something?"

I took him off mute and answered. "Actually, the opposite."

He was silent, which was never good. And then he said, "Oh shit. You're fucking her."

"I'm not…" I was going to use a different word. Something less crass. But all I could come up with was, "I'm in love with her."

"Have you told her?"

I sighed. "No."

I was afraid to. I didn't know how she felt. I was waiting for the right moment.

Yeah. Those all sound like excuses.

"Good. Don't," Pierce said.

I jerked my head back. "Excuse me?"

"You can fuck her all you want, but don't fuck this up. There's too much at stake."

"Jesus, Pierce," I spat. I used a towel to wipe my forehead. "I know that. And I'm not going to fuck it up."

At least, I hoped I wasn't. I didn't *want* to fuck it up. Emerson was important to me.

"Good. Because I think you're forgetting something very important."

"What's that?" I huffed, feeling the burn of my muscles.

"You're paying her to pretend to be in love with you."

"Yes." I held a hand to my chest, hating the reminder. Wishing I could ease the ache building there. "I know. But it's real. At least, it is for me."

I understood that Pierce was looking out for my best interests, or at least he thought he was. But he didn't know what Emerson's and my relationship was really like.

"Look, Nate," he sighed. "I know you don't want to hear this, but you need her help. You've been together, what? A month?"

Yes, but I'd known Emerson for much longer. Still, I said nothing.

"If you want to tell her after the custody battle is settled, fine. But not now."

I wanted to protest. I wanted to tell him to mind his own business, but deep down, I knew Pierce was right, even if I didn't want to admit it. I sighed.

"Nate," he said. "Promise me."

"Fine," I said, knowing that if Emerson didn't feel the same way or our relationship imploded, it would be awkward at best. There was too much at stake, especially Brooklyn's custody. So, I pushed my wants to the side and focused—again—on what was best for my daughter. If Emerson was still intent on ending our physical relationship when we went home, then I'd find a way to live with her decision, impossible as it seemed. "Anything else?"

"No."

"Good." I ended the call without saying goodbye and pushed myself to run as hard and as fast as I could.

Pierce was right. I needed to remember that this was a business agreement. Nothing more. In a year, this arrangement would end. And Emerson would leave. Everyone always did.

CHAPTER TWENTY-ONE

Emerson

"Just a little farther," Cat said, whipping the golf cart around various trailers. She was a PA for Nate's film, and she was ferrying Jackson and me to the location where filming was currently taking place so I could visit my fiancé.

Since Sloan had left for Singapore, Brooklyn had stayed behind at the hotel with one of the local nannies from the Hartwell Agency. The nanny had seemed nice enough, but it was difficult to think of letting anyone take my place in Brooklyn's life.

Yesterday had been fun, more than fun, if I was being honest. I liked Nate's family, and I liked Sloan. She adored Brooklyn, and I was so happy that I got to spend time with someone who was so important to Brooklyn, even if I did feel bad for lying to both of them.

"They might be in the middle of filming," Cat said. "So we'll need to stay quiet on the set."

"No problem." I looked at the little city that had sprung up out of nothing to accommodate the cast and crew. It was impressive and wild.

"Here we are," she said, throwing it into park.

We crossed a street that was cordoned off, and then I heard some people screaming my name. Calling for me. At first, I assumed it was more paparazzi. But then I realized it was a bunch of women. Fans of the book, the movie, Nate, or whatever.

While I'd assumed my engagement to Nate would cause a stir, I didn't think either of us had expected quite the response we'd received. Overwhelmingly positive. But also just overwhelming. People were talking about us, speculating about our relationship. Offering their congratulations. Making predictions and betting on the details of our wedding. It was...a lot.

I was dreading returning home to LA and not just because of the lack of privacy. I didn't want to go back to how things had been. I didn't know if I could.

This was supposed to be a business arrangement, nothing more.

No feelings.

No complications.

No...

I tried to focus on something—anything—else.

Like the fact that I was on a movie set for one of the hottest films. A film that was an adaptation of a Meghan Hart novel I'd read and loved. Part of me secretly hoped I'd get to meet the elusive romance author, but I knew it was unlikely. Even Nate hadn't met her in person, and he was producing and starring in the film.

That said, I'd never imagined I'd be fake-engaged to Nate Crawford. *Sleeping* with Nate Crawford. Falling for Nate Crawford. I supposed if all that could happen, anything was possible.

Cat held her finger up to her lips, and I followed her, stepping over cords and other filming gear. I wasn't sure what to expect. I knew I wasn't going to watch Nate and his costar film a sex scene, which was a relief.

I had no real claim to Nate. And even if I had, pretending to have sex with a costar was part of his job. Yet it pained me to imagine Nate with anyone else.

I watched as Nate strode toward his costar, emanating charisma. He was magnetic, and everyone on set was attuned to him. Glued to his every move as if under a spell.

I could see why. He'd always captivated me, and he definitely did the character of Brock Ransom justice. Then again, Nate had always been the star of my every romantic fantasy. I thought of all the times I'd watched a movie with Nate starring in it. All the times I'd fantasized about him. All the other countless fans who had done or would do the same thing.

But it was different now that I was with Nate. Now that I... I shook my head. Sex scenes. Fans. It all hit differently.

This was exactly why I'd wanted to avoid sleeping with him in the first place. I told myself I'd gotten caught up in the moment. In the idea of being his fiancée. In the way he looked at me, treated me. Hell, maybe the sex had turned my brain to mush.

Nate cupped his costar's cheek, and I felt a twinge of jealousy. I'd known this was a possibility. The film was based on a steamy romance after all. The characters were going to have to be intimate.

It's his job, I reminded myself.

He's just playing a part.

I didn't want to distract Nate or any of the performers from their work. Even if I did want to smash something.

Jackson nudged me and mouthed, "You okay?"

I smiled brightly and nodded, giving him a thumbs-up in return. *God. Could I be more obvious?*

But it was difficult to ignore that hum of jealousy. Watching

Nate and his costar, Mila, I could see how easy it would be to fall for your costar. Nate had even dated a few of his in the past, and I could understand why. You spent a lot of time together on set. You were going through an intensely emotional experience. And it would be difficult to separate truth from fiction.

But when he leaned in, resting his forehead against hers, my jealousy was replaced by something more painful. *Recognition*. Because he was looking at her the same way he looked at me.

Was that all I was to him? Another costar? Another actress in his ongoing performance?

I clutched myself as if to stem the pain that accompanied this crushing realization. I'd fallen for it. *Him.*

Oh my god. I loved him.

I froze, feeling as if my biggest secret had not just been revealed but broadcast to the world. I glanced around to confirm I'd only uttered the words in my head, and everyone else was looking at the actors.

Shit. This wasn't supposed to happen.

They continued filming, and I clenched my fists so hard, my nails were going to leave a mark. I was fine. I could do this.

Nate might be the award-winning actor, but I was beginning to think I could be too, with the performance I was giving. It wasn't even about lying to friends, family, strangers, the whole world. That was becoming almost second nature, scarily enough.

It was the fact that I loved him, and I had to act like it was pretend…while we were both simultaneously pretending it was real. What a mess.

And I wasn't fine. Watching Nate pretend to fall in love with his costar merely reminded me that his "feelings" for me were just as believable. *Oh god.* My heart lurched painfully in my chest. And here I'd convinced myself that I was different. That what we had…

The urge to run became nearly overwhelming. To ground myself, I tried to visualize my favorite running route. Something. *Anything.*

God. How long was this scene?

And why had I ever thought I could handle this?

What happens in Abu Dhabi stays in Abu Dhabi. Ha! Talk about wanting to have your cake and eat it too.

I'd been a fool to suggest that. A bigger fool to think I could separate emotions from sex when it came to Nate. Real from pretend.

What the hell am I supposed to do now?

"And cut," the director finally called.

The entire crew seemed to release the collective breath they'd been holding. Nate shook his head as if awakening from a trance. I couldn't imagine how emotionally taxing it was to perform his role, though I had some idea, considering the fact that I'd been pretending to be his fiancée.

When the crew sprang into action, Cat leaned over. "That was amazing. They got it on the first take, though we'll still have to do a safety take."

Oh god. Another round?

I wasn't sure I could put myself through that *again*. Once had been torture enough.

"What'd you think?" Cat asked.

Nate's performance had definitely provoked a reaction in me, even if I wasn't happy about it. I smiled, trying not to betray just how flustered I was. "Impressive."

I mean, I *was* impressed. I'd been on commercial sets and photo shoots myself, and getting the shot in one take was incredible. And with how demanding this scene was, I could understand why the actors might be motivated to complete it in one take even if they'd still have to shoot a safety.

But I was too preoccupied with my own feelings to process anything else. I unclenched my fists. Told myself to get it together. I was supposed to be happy to see Nate. He was my fiancé, for fuck's sake.

"Em." Nate smiled, coming over to give me a hug. All eyes were suddenly focused on us. "Hey."

When he leaned in to give me a kiss, I turned my head at the last second, giving him my cheek instead. It was an unconscious move, but his expression betrayed surprise. He quickly covered it.

I made a show of looking around. "The location and everything look amazing," I said, trying to recover before I did something totally stupid like tell him how great his chemistry with his costar was. How *believable*.

He leaned in, and it probably looked like he was kissing my cheek as he whispered, "What's wrong?"

I shook my head. Nothing. Not a damn thing was wrong except for the fact that I'd allowed my feelings to get mixed up. How could I not when he did things like tattoo my skin with his name. When he claimed my body with power and passion. When…

"Good," he gritted out. "Because people are watching."

"Then we better put on one hell of a show." I forced a smile, hating his unspoken reminder that this was all an act.

It was part of the job, right?

This entire trip, I'd been preoccupied with thoughts of waking up in bed with Nate. With the words he'd said. With the things we'd done. But coming to the set had been a wake-up call.

Nate was a good actor. He had the awards and accolades to prove it. And I'd been kidding myself that whatever we were could be something more.

Wanting more was foolish and destructive. He'd asked me

to be his fake fiancée for a reason—Brooklyn. And falling for Nate had never been part of the plan.

Nate introduced me to some of his costars and the crew, and while my body moved on autopilot, my mind had checked out. This was his world, and I was merely visiting. One day, in the not-too-distant future, I'd have to return to reality.

A reality where I wasn't Nate's fiancée. Where I'd fallen for someone who would never love me back. And where I'd invested my heart and soul into a family that would never be mine.

With filming done for the day, everyone headed back to their trailers to clean up and rest. Cat ferried Jackson, Nate, and me back to Nate's trailer. If I weren't so upset about my realizations, I probably would've been flipping out about the fact that *I*, Emerson Thorne, was about to enter a swanky-looking trailer with "Nate Crawford" on the door and the man himself at my heels.

Jackson assumed his post at the bottom of the stairs. Nate held the door open for me, waiting until I climbed the stairs to the trailer. The interior looked like something from a design magazine, though I didn't know why I'd expected anything else. It had a small kitchen and dining area and what looked to be a bed at the back. The windows were tinted. The blinds drawn.

Nate closed the door and then rounded on me. "What's wrong?"

"Nothing," I said, wishing he'd leave it alone. My emotions felt too raw. I was too vulnerable. And this conversation had the potential to be too explosive.

"Em," he growled.

"Look," I sighed. "I'm sorry about earlier. I didn't mean to embarrass you in front of your costars and crew."

He scoffed, backing me up until he was caging me against

the wall. My heart was pounding. He bracketed me with his arms, and it was intense. Sexy.

I was such a goner for this man.

Why did he have to look at me that way? Why did he have to make me believe he could possibly feel the same for me?

"You think I give a fuck about their opinion?" He waited for me to respond, react, something. But then he shook his head and dropped his arms, disappointment radiating off him.

I stood there, wrapping my arms around myself, not knowing what to do or say. It was one thing to have sex with my fake fiancée; it was another entirely to tell him how I felt. And knowing what was at stake, realizing how invested I already was, I decided the best course of action was to keep my mouth shut.

"Come on, Em," he pleaded. "I know something's bothering you. Why won't you talk to me?"

"Because it's not important." The words were barely audible.

I wanted to tell him. I did. But…it was a bad idea.

This would blow over. I just needed to wait him out instead of blurting out my feelings and making a huge mistake.

"The fuck it isn't." He grasped my chin, lifting until our eyes met. His were angry and confused and a tumultuous swirl of emotions I couldn't name. "Don't you get it? *You're* important to me. And if something's bothering you, I want you to tell me about it."

"I—" I glanced away. Tried to steady my breathing and failed. "I can't."

"Why?"

"Because our situation is already complicated enough. And seeing you with your costar—" I clamped my mouth shut. I'd said more than I'd intended to.

"Wait. Are you jealous?"

"I—" I closed my mouth then opened it. Closed my mouth once more. He wasn't going to give up, was he? Not until I told him something. "I'm not jealous. Not exactly."

"Then what are you?" he asked, but he sounded almost disappointed, defeated, and it made me want to confide in him.

"I…" I turned away, embarrassed to admit this but knowing I couldn't hold back anymore. "When I saw you looking at Mila, I realized it was the same way you look at me."

"And that bothered you." It wasn't a question, not exactly.

I pressed my lips together as if to stop the word from even forming. I didn't want to admit it, but Nate's unguarded expression had me saying, "Yes."

"Why?"

"I think the answer should be obvious." I couldn't look at him. I looked anywhere but at him, inspecting the inside of the trailer as if I'd never seen one before.

My chest felt tight, and I wished I'd never said anything. God, why was he making this so difficult?

"I want to hear you say the words."

He looked at me with such intensity that I turned away. I couldn't. Wouldn't.

It was too big a risk. Nothing good could come from admitting my true feelings to Nate. There was too much on the line.

"Do you want to know why you saw the same expression on my face when I looked at my costar as when I look at you?" he finally asked.

Yes. No. I don't know.

When I didn't answer, he continued, "Because I was imagining you. And when I'm with you, I'm not acting. I haven't been for a long time."

"Wh-what?" I gasped, spinning to face him once more.

He nodded, cupping my cheek. "I'm falling for you, Em."

I sucked in a sharp breath. *He...what?*

I could scarcely believe my ears. Some of the tightness in my chest eased, replaced by a tingling. A warmth.

"I've been burned so many times. And I know this isn't what you wanted," he continued. "But I can't fight this anymore."

I wanted so badly to believe the words were true. I ran through our interactions. I tried to filter them through this new lens, but I kept getting stuck. I was hung up on the fact that he might've been saying one thing but feeling another. He might still be, even now.

"But, but—" I shook my head. No. No way. He didn't mean that. "You're such a good actor, you convinced yourself this was real." Convinced me his feelings were real.

He leaned his forehead to mine, his gaze intense and unwavering. "You're wrong."

"But this is all pretend."

"It isn't," he said. "At least not for me. And I don't think it is for you either."

I closed my eyes, trying to calm my racing heart. I wanted to believe him. I wanted his words to be true so badly.

"You once asked me why I spent the night in the hospital chair," he said. "The truth is, I was terrified of losing you. And whether I realized it or not, I was falling for you even then. Before then, if I'm being honest."

"You...were?" I asked, scarcely believing my ears.

He nodded, his expression solemn. "And the rose tattoo." I couldn't do anything but stare at him, mouth agape. "Do you know why I selected that?"

"Because I'm the thorn in your side," I said, thinking of the play on my last name—Thorne.

He shook his head, his expression solemn. "Have you

heard the quote by Rumi that 'a rose's rarest essence lives in the thorn'?"

"No. What does it mean?"

"Basically, just as a rose isn't complete without its thorn, a human isn't complete without trials and tribulations."

I lifted my head. "To appreciate beauty, you have to understand pain."

"Exactly." He smiled softly. "And you, Emerson—" he cupped my cheek "—are the beauty. The rose."

And all this time, I'd thought... Well, I'd been wrong. So very wrong. About him. Me. Us. All of it.

"I don't think you realize just how much you mean to me," he said with a sincerity that stole the breath from my lungs. And just when I didn't think I could possibly handle any more, he said, "I love you, Em. I love you." He smiled then, and it was filled with hesitancy and hope. "So damn much."

I blinked a few times then pinched myself for good measure.

He furrowed his brow. "What are you doing?"

"I, uh—" My cheeks flamed with heat. "Just trying to reassure myself this is real."

He chuckled, tucking my hair behind my ear. "It's real. What I feel for you is very real. And it was never an act, except when I pretended not to like you."

I rolled my eyes, but I couldn't hide the smile forming on my face. Relief and euphoria nearly overwhelmed me. I wasn't a fool. I wasn't alone in my feelings. Nate loved me, and I loved him.

"Nate," I said.

"Yeah?" he asked.

I draped my arms around his neck, smiling up at him. "I love you too."

He smiled back. Genuine. Dazzling. Earth-shattering.

"Say it again," he rasped, claiming my mouth.

"I love you," I gasped as he pulled my skirt up over my hips. He smoothed his hands over my thighs and groaned when he came to my ass.

He spun me around, and I glanced over my shoulder, loving the crazed look in his eyes.

"Fuck, Em. This ass." He gave it a slap—just enough to sting but not enough to leave a mark. And then he ran a hand lovingly over the material of my silk thong, smoothing his hand down my ass.

He pressed gently on my upper back, forcing me to grip the back of the banquette. He knelt to the floor and kissed his way up my leg. First one, then the other. "Your legs are my favorite part of you, besides your heart." He slid his finger over the silk, making it even wetter if that was possible. Then he followed the same path with his tongue. He was the perfect blend of sweet and dirty.

"Don't you—" I closed my eyes as my core clenched on air; I needed more "—have somewhere to be?" What about the safety shot? And I vaguely remembered Cat saying something about the cast having dinner together.

"This is the only place I want to be."

He kept licking and sucking, making it his mission to make me come. I loved how thorough he was. How determined. I'd never been with someone so obsessed with my pleasure. So determined to make sure I came first and often. As if my orgasm was a coveted prize.

"Look how wet you are for me," he said. "You're dripping. Your pussy wants my cock."

"Yes," I moaned. "Please." He didn't even have to make me beg; I was doing it all on my own.

"Come for me, and then I'll let you have my cock."

I shuddered with pleasure at his words. At his dark promise. His mouth met my sensitive skin once more, and I rocked against him, clutching the back of the banquette until the pleasure overpowered me.

"Good girl." Nate gave my ass a playful slap. I wanted to be offended by the term, but he didn't give me much time to think about it, the sound of his zipper hissing in the air.

"Do you want to see how many more times I can make you come?"

"Yes." My voice came out throaty, almost…needy.

"Yes…" he said in an expectant tone, sliding on a condom.

"Yes." I swallowed. "Please?"

"Tell me what you want."

"I want you to bend me over this bench and fuck me."

"Good girl." He slapped my ass again.

I glared at him. "Stop calling me that."

"I would," he said, sliding his fingers through my arousal. "But you seem to like it."

I growled at him, but he merely nudged me forward, a sexy smirk in place. "Now, be a good girl and hold on tight."

He lined himself up with my center. My legs were still shaking from the first orgasm when he plunged inside me. His strokes were hard and fast…ruthless.

I caught sight of our reflection in the window, and my breath caught. He looked like a man possessed, his hair tousled in the sexiest way, eyes unfocused. And I was bent forward, my mouth open as if on a scream. My skirt rucked up over my hips.

We looked…wild. Uninhibited. Out of control.

"Look at us," he said, holding me to him. "Look at your pussy taking my cock." He rubbed my clit with one hand, the other cupping my breast beneath my shirt. If he kept doing that, I was going to fucking explode.

This was what I'd always wanted. Connection. Playfulness. Devotion. Love.

"So good." I turned back to kiss him.

"I love you," he panted, our kiss sloppy and my heart full.

I moaned both from his words and what he was doing to my body. "I love you."

With those words, it was as if something was unlocked. Or perhaps unleashed. Nate must have felt it too because his movements became erratic, and he thrust deeper and harder. I gasped at the intensity of it, and then I screamed his name, riding out my release as he unloaded inside me.

Nate stumbled a little, and I flopped forward on the bench, unable to stand. He sank to the floor, sitting beside me with his head resting against the edge of the seat. My body kept shaking, letting out these little aftershocks of pleasure.

"That was…" He panted.

"Wild." I laughed.

"Come 'ere," he said, tugging me down onto him. Holding me in his arms.

In that moment, I knew I was exactly where I was meant to be. And that all the trials I'd faced, all the struggles, had led me to this man.

CHAPTER TWENTY-TWO

Nate

I finished my coffee and placed the mug in the dishwasher. My body was still adjusting back to LA time now that we'd returned from Abu Dhabi, and I needed the extra caffeine, especially with how busy Emerson and I were at night. My body wanted more sleep, but all I wanted was her.

Emerson was curling her hair when I walked into the bathroom. Her dress dipped low on her chest and showed off a big swath of her toned stomach and back. She was so fucking gorgeous. So fucking mine.

Pierce would've told me this was a mistake, but I didn't care what anyone else thought. He didn't know Emerson. Regardless of what happened between us, I trusted that she'd always put Brooklyn first.

And with the court date set for the custody hearing, hopefully we wouldn't have to have that hanging over us much longer.

I leaned against the counter, watching her get ready.

"Keep looking at me that way, and we won't make it to dinner," she said.

I laughed. But when she set down the curling iron, I slid my hands over her ass, pulling her into me.

"I have something to tell you."

"Oh yeah?" she asked, her eyebrow arching. Her breath catching.

"My agent has an opportunity for us. Well, it's more for you." I felt bad about the fact that I'd ruined her nannying career, even if I still thought she'd been using it as a crutch.

"What is it?" she asked.

"Peloton wants you to teach a class."

"They do?" She seemed surprised, though I didn't know why. She'd be a natural. "That could be fun."

"I think you'd be great at it," I said, and I meant it. It was right up her alley. She had great energy. She was captivating. And she was good at motivating people and pushing them out of their comfort zone. She certainly had me.

"Would you join me?"

Her question surprised me. "Would you want me to?"

"I think it could be fun. I mean, I'm guessing that's what people would tune in to see. To watch our relationship dynamic."

"You mean to watch you punish me," I joked.

"That too." She smirked.

I chuckled, releasing her so she could continue getting ready.

She gnawed on her bottom lip. "I should probably talk to my dad about it first."

I appreciated her loyalty, but I knew he'd most likely say no. That said, I didn't want to argue with her about it, not when we were about to leave for dinner at her parents'. She was already stressed enough, and I refused to add to it.

So, I simply nodded.

"Also, these are for you," I said, removing a small velvet box from my pocket. "A gift."

She arched one eyebrow. I opened the lid to reveal a pair of earrings in the shape of roses, and she gasped. "Those are stunning." She reached out but didn't touch them, almost as if she was afraid to.

"They were custom-designed by a viscount for his wife in the late nineteenth century."

"Wow. They're so intricate and detailed."

I nodded. "They're Burmese rubies and diamonds. My mother loved how unique they were. They seem as if they're made for you." I held them out to her.

"I-I—" She shook her head and backed away. "They're beautiful, but I wouldn't feel right about accepting her jewelry."

I could tell Emerson loved the earrings, and I couldn't imagine anyone else wearing them. "You wear her ring."

"Yeah, but it's one thing to borrow a piece. It's another entirely to keep it."

"I want you to have them." I held them out to her, all but begging her to accept my present.

"Are you…" She tilted her head, evaluating me. "You're sure?"

"Yes," I said with confidence.

"It's just…" She shook her head. "I know how much your mother's collection means to you."

I was touched by her hesitation and her words. Trinity would've never done such a thing.

"I was hoping my gift would show you how much you mean to me," I said, dipping my head to meet her eyes.

She nodded, finally accepting the earrings from me. She put them on with shaky hands, pinning her hair back to showcase the gift.

I slid my arms around her waist, loving the sight of us together. She was my match in every way that mattered. Committed to family, especially my daughter. Able to withstand the pressure of public life, while preferring privacy. Polished, refined, and sexy as hell. "You look beautiful."

"Thank you." She met my gaze, and she looked as if she was going to say something but stopped herself.

"Jackson and Brooklyn are ready whenever you are," I said.

"Great." She smiled at herself in the mirror as she applied her lipstick, but it seemed forced.

"Come on, Em." I dropped a kiss to her shoulder, then her neck. "I know your dad's not my biggest fan." I rested my chin on her shoulder. "But I promise I'll do my best to charm him. And having Brooklyn there will help."

She nodded, though she didn't seem convinced.

I wasn't going to admit it, but I was surprisingly nervous about meeting Emerson's family. Maybe because I felt bad for lying about our engagement. Maybe because I knew it weighed on Emerson.

Or maybe because I was afraid it might blow up. *I* might blow up.

Her dad's attitude pissed me off. Not just the way he'd handled her hospital visit but everything about her career and her training. What kind of father pushed his daughter when she'd just gotten out of the hospital? I clenched my fists.

"Hey," she said. "What's that look for?"

I inhaled and released my fists along with an exhale. "Nothing." *Not a damn thing.* I slid my hand over her stomach. "Let's get this over with. The sooner we leave, the sooner we can come home."

During the drive, Emerson fiddled with her engagement ring and cast nervous glances out the window. Fortunately, Brooklyn didn't seem to notice, filling us in on everything she'd missed at school while we'd been in Abu Dhabi.

A few paparazzi tried to follow us but couldn't get past

the front gate to Emerson's dads' community. Some of my security team had gone ahead to provide additional support. When we arrived, I followed Emerson and Brooklyn up the stairs to their front door, wiping my hands on my slacks. Emerson rang the bell, and the door swung open a moment later.

"Hi, Papa J." She gave him a hug and then turned to us. "Nate." His smile was warm as he shook my hand. "And Brooklyn. This is my dad James."

He smiled down at Brooklyn. "It's nice to finally meet you in person."

Brooklyn preened. "I've never had a grandpa before." And then she threw her arms around him.

He looked stunned at first but quickly hugged her back. "I've never had a granddaughter before. And I'm so glad it's you."

Emerson glanced at me over her shoulder—panicked. I placed my hand on the small of her back, trying to reassure her. I had to have faith that this would all work out somehow.

I didn't know how. But I had to hope that it would.

"Declan is inside," James said, leading us through the house. "And Astrid."

We were introduced, and while Declan was friendly to Brooklyn, I got the feeling I had my work cut out for me. Since he was her coach and her father, I already knew we weren't going to agree on a number of things. He viewed me as an obstacle. And I didn't like how hard he pushed Emerson.

"It's so nice out," James said. "We thought we might eat outside."

We'd barely made it through the back door when a chorus of voices shouted, "Surprise!"

I took a few steps back, and Emerson tensed. All eyes

were on us, and there were a lot of them. I spotted my brother and cousins in the crowd, along with friends and colleagues. Emerson's fellow athletes and other family members. *Shit.*

Emerson turned back to me and smiled. Barely moving her lips, she asked, "Did you know about this?"

"No." I maintained my smile as a server handed us each a glass of champagne. "Did you?"

She shook her head and turned to me, placing her palm on my chest. James, or Papa J as Emerson referred to him, gave a speech about love and family and commitment. And with every word, I imagined having that with the woman at my side. I might not be ready to marry again, but the idea no longer seemed as abhorrent as it once had. I was still processing that when everyone lifted their glasses to toast the happy couple. Us.

Emerson's red diamond sparkled, reminding me of the passion we shared and the depth of my trust and love for her. A wave of calm washed over me, a sense of peace.

I turned to her and smiled, brushing her hair away from her face, knowing that everyone would expect us to kiss. And I didn't really care what they expected, but in this instance, I was happy to deliver.

Everyone else faded into the background. They were still there, but I only had eyes for Emerson. Her breathing was shaky and her smile bright.

"What are you doing?" she whispered.

"Kissing you," I said, and then I cupped her cheek, using my other hand to pull her even closer.

When I pressed my lips to hers, my world exploded with colors and sensations. I lost myself in her, only pulling back when the whistles and cheers became too loud to ignore.

Emerson smiled up at me, our foreheads still kissing. Knox and Kendall approached to offer their congratulations.

It was the first time we'd seen them since our engagement and theirs. *Crazy to think...*

"Congrats. I'm happy for you," Knox said while Kendall and Emerson hugged. "Surprised—" He winced, and I wondered if Kendall had pinched him before he could finish his thought. "But happy."

Kendall smiled at me with tears in her eyes. "Congratulations."

"Same to you," I said, genuinely pleased for my brother.

"I mean..." Knox rubbed a hand over his beard. "What are the chances?"

Was he asking for real or just making idle conversation? I wasn't going to answer.

Declan glared at me from across the yard. He'd stayed in the background. His displeasure was clear, even if he was a gracious host to everyone else.

"Thanks," I said, shaking my brother's hand and then embracing him.

Apart from Sloan's unexpected visit, I'd only had short phone conversations with my family since the engagement. I'd blamed it on my hectic filming schedule. And I assumed they all had questions—especially Knox.

Even if they were surprised, surely they could see how perfectly Emerson fit into my life. From her relationship with my daughter to her interactions with the rest of my family. The way she supported me and challenged me and...

On and on, the evening went, everyone wanting to talk to us. To admire Emerson's ring. To hear about my proposal. To wish us congratulations. It was exhausting when all I wanted was to be with Emerson.

"Finally," I sighed, careful to keep my voice low as I kissed Emerson's neck. "A moment alone."

She laughed. She was much more relaxed now that she'd had a few glasses of champagne.

"Oh no," she murmured, her lips against my jaw. "Papa J looks like he's on a mission."

I arched an eyebrow and turned in the direction of her gaze. James was approaching, a familiar blonde in tow.

"Nate," James said. "I'd like to introduce you to Juliana Wright. She's an—"

"Event planner, yes," I said, shaking her hand with a smile. "Nice to see you again."

Juliana and Emerson hugged. I gestured at the flowers. "I should've realized you were behind this."

Juliana smiled. "Surprise! And congratulations."

"Thank you," I said to both her and James. "It's beautiful."

"I guess I shouldn't be surprised you two know each other," James said. "Since you both seem to know everyone."

"Juliana has planned several of Brooklyn's birthday parties." I peered over at Brooklyn, who was sitting with Knox and Kendall, grinning from ear to ear. "As well as a number of events for my studio."

"Oh good," James said. "Then hopefully you won't mind that I reached out to her about the wedding. With how busy we all are, I thought it might be good to get the ball rolling. I hope I didn't overstep."

"Not at all," I said, because what else could I possibly say? Meanwhile, Emerson clenched my hand in warning. "And, of course, we'd love to work with Juliana."

"Do you have a date in mind?" she asked. "Or a venue? Then I can start seeing what's available."

I opened my mouth to feed Juliana our standard line about enjoying our engagement and not being in any rush to the altar. I loved Emerson, but our relationship was still new. I wasn't sure when, or even if, I'd want to get married. And I didn't know what that would mean for our future.

Emerson wanted marriage. Children. And while I wanted

to give her everything her heart desired, I didn't know if I could.

I hoped I'd have a clearer head about the situation *after* everything was resolved with Trinity. But the fact that I was still dealing with her bullshit nearly a decade after our divorce definitely made me hesitant to walk down the aisle again.

James said, "Emerson's always wanted a spring wedding."

"I, uh—" Emerson's mouth gaped open and closed. She tilted her head. "Yeah."

"Now is the perfect time to start planning for next spring," Juliana said. "I can have my assistant reach out to schedule a meeting."

"Great," I said, not really sure what else to do.

I hadn't expected James to put us on the spot like this. But if I were getting married, Juliana would've been my first choice to plan the wedding. So, for now, I went along with it.

"You should enjoy tonight." Juliana smiled. "My office will be in touch. Congratulations again."

"Thank you."

Declan and Astrid joined us as Emerson took another glass from a passing server.

"Are you sure that's a good idea, Emmy?" Declan asked.

"Don't be a buzzkill, Dad," Astrid said as Emerson downed it in one gulp. "I mean, can't we just take a minute to revel in the fact that Emmy is engaged to her celebrity crush?"

I turned to Emerson, brow raised. "Is that so?"

Emerson glared at Astrid, and I tried not to laugh. I liked Astrid.

"Oh yeah," Astrid said with a smug grin. "She used to have a poster of you on her wall. And one year for Christmas—"

"Okay." Emerson covered her sister's mouth with her

hand, dragging her away from the group. "I think that's enough. Thank you very much."

Oh, I was definitely holding on to that information for later.

James was pulled into another conversation, leaving me alone with Declan. *Great.*

"Walk with me," he said, clapping a hand on my shoulder and giving it a squeeze.

I forced a smile and walked with him to the house. He led me inside, closing his office door behind us.

"Take a seat." His tone was commanding. This wasn't a request. And I wasn't going to cower.

He wanted to talk to me man-to-man? *Fine.*

I slid my hands into my pockets and remained standing. Cool. Calm. Unaffected.

Declan leaned against his desk, crossing his arms over his chest. "Why do you want to marry my daughter?"

"Because I love her," I said. I might not be interested in marriage, but I did love Emerson.

He scoffed. "Cut the shit. You may be able to fool everyone out there—" he gestured to the backyard "—but I know something else is going on."

Oh shit. What did he know? I tried not to let my panic show.

"Nothing is going on except for the fact that we want to spend our lives together."

"No." He shook his head, wagging his finger at me. "No. She's different since she met you. She pushes back about doing her training. And she was never this stressed."

He was right; Emerson was stressed. And while I understood where he was coming from as a father myself, it felt like he was looking for someone to blame, when he should be shouldering part of the responsibility. Still, I didn't want to antagonize him. I didn't want to cause even more tension for Emerson.

I needed to disarm the situation. Ideally, I'd charm him and disengage before he tried to delve too deeply into our relationship.

"I know that being engaged to me comes with a certain level of…attention," I said. "I've tried to shield Emerson from it as best I can. And when I can't, I've given her tools."

"Did you know the paparazzi and your *fans* have been harassing her at training?"

Whatever expression I made must have shown my surprise. Emerson hadn't mentioned anything about it.

"I had to kick one of them out of her locker room."

I jerked my head back. "What?"

Why hadn't she told me?

He nodded. "She's putting up with a lot of shit just to be with you."

"I know," I said, thinking it was even more true than he realized. The invasion of privacy. The lies…

"But that was true even before you were engaged. I mean…" He smoothed a hand over his hair. "She used to despise you."

I cringed but tried not to let it show.

"For months," he continued, "she was miserable. *You—*" he pointed at me "—made her miserable."

I knew it was true, but it was even worse hearing it from Emerson's dad. I hadn't realized just how unhappy I'd made her.

"And then—out of the blue, a mere six months later—we find out you're engaged." He shook his head. "It doesn't add up. Why would an infamous billionaire bachelor suddenly change his ways and decide to get married again? And why her? Why, of all the women in the world, did you choose my daughter?"

I wasn't sure whether he was questioning me or merely

lamenting the situation. He'd almost said the words as an accusation, as if I were trying to punish him or something.

"We chose each other," I said. "Because we love each other. And you, of all people, should realize that love isn't always convenient or easy or simple. But when you find the right person—the person who you're meant to be with—it's worth it."

He nodded, contemplating my words. And then he started clapping, slowly, the sound echoing throughout the room and mocking me.

"You know—" he sneered "—I have to hand it to you. You put on a good performance. And for a minute, I almost believed you. But everyone knows your reputation."

"You can believe me or not. Regardless of what you think, Emerson and I *are* getting married."

Shit. Shut up. You're only digging a deeper hole for yourself.

"So, why hide that? Why hide your relationship from her family? I mean, do you know how it feels to find out that your daughter is engaged from a reporter? A fucking member of the paparazzi?"

"Emerson wanted to tell you," I said, improvising. Trying to spin this to protect Emerson and make sure it sounded believable. "But I asked her not to."

"Mm." His gaze was piercing, and I was afraid he'd see right through me and the stack of lies I was telling. "I spend more time with her than almost anyone. I know her better than anyone. And she never mentioned anything. Not about the fact that you were dating. Not about her feelings for you. Nothing."

"I'm sorry we kept it a secret from you," I said, knowing I'd let this conversation get more out of control than I should've. "We didn't want to. But she was worried you wouldn't approve. And clearly, she was right to be concerned."

"If only she'd—"

"Would you have listened even if she had?" I asked, thinking of all the things Emerson had told me about wanting to retire and Declan pushing back. Pushing her to keep going.

"I *do* listen to her, but I also know what she's capable of." The look he gave me screamed *she's worth so much more than you.*

"Do you want to know the real reason she's been stressed?" I asked, unable to hold back. Without waiting for his response, I said, "It's because you push her too hard."

He slammed his fist down on the desk. "What do you know about hard work? You probably had a billion dollars in your bank account before you could walk. I'm her father." He jabbed his chest with his finger. "And I know how hard to push her."

I ignored his comment about my wealth and asked, "Do you?"

"Yes. I've been her coach—"

"Maybe that's the problem," I interrupted. "You're thinking more like her coach than her dad. And if she's stressed," I said, clenching my fist in my pocket, "it's because she doesn't want to compete anymore, and you *aren't* listening."

A muscle jumped in his neck. "You've known her all of, what—six minutes? And you think you can make her happy. You think you can give her what she wants?"

I didn't balk. Hell, part of me had been bracing for this conversation from the moment our engagement had been announced. And yet, I was still unprepared.

So, I adopted the persona everyone would expect of me, especially someone like Declan. "I'm a fucking billionaire," I scoffed. "Of course I can give her what she wants."

He shook his head. "I'm not talking about money, and you know it."

No, he wasn't. But I wasn't going to let him know he'd rattled me. Because whether I wanted to admit it or not, his comments rankled. I didn't deserve her, but I wasn't going to confess that to him.

"So what is it you don't like, Declan? The timeline? The fact that I'm rich? That I love your daughter?"

"Everything!" he roared. "Because I know Emerson. And from what little I know about you, I'm afraid you're going to hurt her."

"Or maybe," I said, angry and beyond giving a shit, "you're afraid you're no longer the most important man in her life."

It was a low blow, but I knew it had struck home when I saw his expression. I told myself he deserved it. I told myself I was standing up for Emerson, but even so, I knew I'd crossed a line.

He lifted his head, palms pressed to his desk. "Get out."

So much for smoothing things over.

CHAPTER TWENTY-THREE

Emerson

I plopped down on the bed with a giggle. "That was…"

"Intense?" Nate asked, untucking his shirt.

When my dads had invited us over for dinner, I'd never expected that they'd throw a surprise engagement party. And —apart from Papa J's pestering to get on the schedule with Juliana—it had been fun.

"I don't know why you're so grumpy. We pulled it off." I flopped back on the bed with a contented sigh. "*I* had fun."

"*You* had alcohol," Nate said in a wry tone.

"Yeah. So?" I propped myself up on my elbows, watching him undress.

Brooklyn was staying with Knox and Kendall for the night, and I'd spent most of the evening looking forward to being alone with Nate. Ever since we'd returned to LA, it was as if life had gone into warp speed. Brooklyn was back at school. I'd buckled down on my training as we neared the homestretch before my competition. And Nate was back at the office.

All of that was mostly manageable. But it was the frenzy that still surrounded our relationship that was the most exhausting. I hadn't fully appreciated the bubble of privacy we'd enjoyed while visiting Abu Dhabi until we'd come home.

"So…nothing," Nate said.

Now that I'd thought about it, he'd been quiet on the ride home. Distracted. Sullen, even.

He chuckled and shook his head.

"What?"

"You're cute when you're buzzed."

"Cute?" I scoffed. I did *not* like being called "cute," especially by the sexiest man alive. Literally. He'd been awarded that at least two times. *Three?*

He smirked. "Three what?"

"The number of orgasms you're going to give me." I stood, smoothing down my dress. Determined to show him just how *not* cute I was.

Hooded eyes met mine, electricity surging between us. "I think I can make it four."

"Is that so?" I challenged.

He stepped closer, his clothes brushing against my back. I shivered. I stood there, almost frozen. Waiting to see what he'd do next.

He trailed his fingers down my back, tracing the column of my spine. His touch was electrifying, and I'd been waiting all evening to be alone with him.

All week, really. He'd been so busy with his film and everything else. And I'd been either training or recovering or taking care of Brooklyn. By the end of the day, we were both exhausted. Time alone together felt like a rare occurrence.

He came to face me, gripping my chin and tilting my head back to place a kiss on my lips. He led the kiss, his touch demanding and insistent, yet controlled. Nate was always in control. At least, until I made him relinquish it.

But this time, he wasn't giving anything up. He was taking. My lips. My mouth. My body. My heart.

He pulled back and asked, "Is this what you imagined?"

I tilted my head to the side, too distracted by his touch to follow. "Huh?"

He kissed my jaw, behind my ear. "When you stared at my poster at night and touched yourself."

I stiffened. I was going to kill my sister for mentioning that to him.

"Oh, come on, Em." He leaned in, his breath a whisper against my ear. "We both know that's what you were doing. So..." He trailed a finger over my shoulder, down my arm. "Tell me what you imagined."

"No," I said, crossing my arms over my chest and trying to ignore the way my body reacted to his touch. His proximity. "Because you're making fun of me."

"I'm not making fun of you," he rasped. "In fact, I'll tell you one of mine if you tell me one of yours."

"One of your *what*?" I asked.

"One of the fantasies I had about you." He dragged a finger down my sternum.

"Huh?" I asked. Either the alcohol was affecting me even more than I'd realized, or my brain simply could not believe what I was hearing.

"That night I saw you on Knox's yacht..." He brushed my hair over my shoulder and kissed my neck.

"Mm." I hummed. "What about it?"

"I watched your poker game."

"What?" My eyes widened. How had I not seen him? And how much had *he* seen?

He chuckled darkly. "You were so sexy in that white bikini. And then you schooled those jokers in poker."

I barked out a laugh. I hadn't expected him to say that.

"I imagined pulling up a seat and joining the game.

Betting such obscene amounts, forcing them to leave so I could have you all to myself."

"Y-you did?" I asked, breathless as he slid my dress from my shoulders. It pooled on the floor, and my skin broke out in goose bumps from his words.

"I did," he said, standing behind me. "But I would've won."

I scoffed. "No way."

"Yes," he said with a confidence that bordered on arrogance. "I would've taken all your chips and all your clothes. And then I would've set you on the table and eaten you like the feast you are."

I gulped, incredibly turned on by his words. By the scene he'd described. "I wish you had."

"So do I," he said. "But then you might never have agreed to be Brooklyn's nanny, and she needs you just as much as I do."

I melted at his words and the way he was looking at me. But then his expression turned darker.

"Hey," I said, smoothing my hand over his cheek. "What's that look for?"

"I'm sorry for how I treated you the first few months you were working for me."

I placed my hand over his heart. "You've already told me that."

"I know," he said, his expression solemn. "But I regret it. Just like I regret roping you into this whole mess." He gestured with his hands.

Where was this coming from? Was this because of the engagement party? Something else?

"Nate, look at me." When he finally did, his expression was one of regret. "I agreed to this."

"Yeah, but only after I'd already made it impossible to refuse."

"What's going on?" I asked, draping my arms around his neck.

"I feel bad about lying to everyone. I feel bad that you have to lie to your family and friends, and that our relationship might cause friction with them."

I didn't want to think about that right now. Just like I didn't want to think about the fact that Nate and I weren't on the same page when it came to marriage and children. Hell, we were on opposite ends of the spectrum.

Instead, I unbuttoned his pants. "If it'll make you feel better, you can tell me about another one of your fantasies," I joked.

His dark chuckle reverberated in my chest. God, I loved the sound of his laugh. It was sexy, especially when I knew I'd been the cause of it.

"Well, there was this one time…"

BROOKLYN SKIPPED UP TO KNOX AND KENDALL'S FRONT DOOR, her dress fluttering around her. "This is so exciting!"

I laughed, thinking of how nice it was of Kendall to include Brooklyn in her search for her dream wedding gown. Kendall had asked Brooklyn to be her flower girl, and she was beyond excited.

Before we could even knock, the front door opened and Kendall's mom beckoned us in. She gave us both big hugs, and I was glad to see her looking so well after everything she'd been through.

"Congratulations, Emerson."

"Thank you." I smiled, and we followed her to the living room.

I hugged Kendall then surveyed the space. It had been turned into a private showroom. There were racks and racks of designer gowns, gorgeous shoes, veils, all waiting for Kendall to try them on. And in the middle of the room stood Jay, a huge grin on his face. I'd seen him twice since I'd returned from Abu Dhabi—once to help with my overall wardrobe and another time to finalize my looks for the awards shows Nate and I would be attending. He was fun and stylish and elegant.

"Wow." I shook my head. "That's a lot of gowns."

"Not all these dresses are for me," Kendall said, flashing me a secretive smile as Papa J and Astrid entered the room.

Brooklyn ran over to Astrid and gave her a big hug. Then she turned to Papa J and did the same, tugging them both over to join her on a sofa. Dad wasn't here, and I tried not to dwell on the potential reasons for his absence.

He didn't support my relationship with Nate, which stung, even if it had started out as a lie. Dad was pissed that I'd flown to New York last week to teach a Peloton class when I should've been focusing on my training. Hell, he was probably mad that I was going to potentially blow my calorie budget with this party, even though I was the maid of honor.

"That's right," Jay said. "These—" he gestured to the racks on the left side of the room "—are for you."

"What?" I jerked my head back, hoping my panic didn't show. "But this is Kendall's special day. I'm the maid of honor, not the bride."

"You *are* a bride. And—" she took my hands in hers "—I can think of nothing better than trying on wedding gowns with my best friend."

"I-I—" I scrambled for an excuse. A way out of this. Nate and I might be in love, but we weren't getting married. Not now. And maybe not ever.

I tried not to let that fact bother me. But then something

like this happened, slamming the truth of my situation in my face.

"Our girl is so shocked, she's speechless," Jay said, clapping his hands together, clearly pleased.

What was I supposed to say? Kendall's surprise was so sweet. And I didn't want to disappoint her or draw unnecessary attention on a day that was supposed to be fun.

Knox's chef handed out champagne to everyone. Sparkling water for Brooklyn and me.

Kendall raised her glass. "To playing dress-up with my best friend."

Everyone drank to her toast, and then Jay rubbed his hands together. "Let's try on some dresses."

"Yes!" everyone said in unison, their excitement definitely outpacing my own. Astrid shot me a concerned look, and I knew I better start acting like the blushing bride everyone believed me to be.

I smiled, pulling Kendall into a tight hug. "Thank you for being so thoughtful."

Jay guided me toward my rack of dresses. "Come. Gaze upon these beauties."

This should've been a dream come true. Trying on designer wedding gowns with my best friend. A room full of dresses handpicked for me by my favorite stylist. And yet…I was overwhelmed. I could already feel the anxiety creeping in.

For any other bride, wedding dress shopping was supposed to be fun. And maybe if my engagement—my whole relationship—weren't based on a lie, it would be. But at the moment, I was filled with nothing but dread.

Dresses would only lead to more questions. More lies. About our plans for the wedding. The season. The venue. The…

I sighed as I perused the gowns, carefully admiring their

delicate lace and hand-sewn beading. Lying to everyone important in my life was exhausting, especially my best friend.

"Kendall was sparse with the details about your wedding," Jay said. "So I brought a range of styles."

"Thank you, Jay. You have…exquisite taste, as ever."

He smiled, clearly pleased by my compliment. "If you could tell me more about the venue or time of day, it would help narrow down some of the styles. Though, really, you can wear whatever you want. It's your day!"

I laughed, hoping to hide my discomfort. "Nate and I have been so busy, we haven't had much time to discuss it."

"Not at all?" Papa J asked with a frown.

I lifted a shoulder, at a loss for words.

"Just a general idea, then," Jay said with an encouraging smile, and it felt as if everyone else was listening in. "Where do you envision yourself getting married? Beach? Backyard? Hotel?"

Brooklyn laughed at something Astrid said, and I glanced over at her. The sight of Brooklyn made me remember why I was doing this. Hell, I was being paid ten million dollars to play the role of Nate's fiancée. And it was time to sell it.

"Outside somewhere. Maybe at one of the Huxley Grand hotels, but not the LA one," I said, seeing it all come together in my mind. Nate standing at the end of the aisle. His eyes on me as I walked toward him. "Somewhere warm but not hot. Luxurious and elegant but still…welcoming. Like Morocco," I blurted the first place that had come to me. It was never going to happen, so what did it even matter?

"Would you want two dresses? One for the ceremony and another for the reception?"

"Yes," Kendall said, nudging me with her shoulder.

I laughed. "Yeah. She's right."

"Okay. Let's focus on the ceremony one first," Jay said,

and Kendall returned to her rack just as the house alarm chimed.

Knox shuffled in, covering his eyes with his hand. "Hey, everyone. Just pretend I'm not here."

"Knox," Kendall chided. "You're not supposed to be here."

"I know. I'm sorry, *mi cielo*." I melted at the way he called her "my heaven" in Spanish. He adored my best friend. "I forgot my laptop."

"I'll get it, Uncle Knox!" Brooklyn said, jumping up from her seat and running down the hall to his office.

Kendall turned Knox so his back was to the living room and all the dresses. Knox wrapped his arms around her waist and kissed her. They were perfect together—partners in every sense of the term. Unlike Nate's and my relationship, nothing about their love was fake. And I was so happy for them, even if it was another painful reminder that nothing about my future was settled.

The bridge of my nose stung, so I turned away and made a show of looking at the dresses. All the while, I tried to ignore the doubts plaguing me. Nate and I had never discussed the future. We'd been so focused on getting through my competition and the custody hearing and everything else. But I kept wondering what would happen after the hearing? After we'd satisfied the terms of our contract. What, then?

I was too afraid to ask.

Knox soon left. Papa J and Astrid joined me, while Kendall's mom and Brooklyn stood with her.

"Dad couldn't make it?" I asked, wanting to know if Dad's disapproval of my engagement was as obvious to everyone else.

Papa J's and Astrid's faces flashed with concern before they quickly smoothed their features into smiles. My stomach clenched.

"You know fashion is my thing, not Dad's," Papa J said.

"Can you even imagine?" Astrid laughed, though it sounded strained. "Dad would hate sitting through this."

I had a feeling that had more to do with the groom than anything else. Dad might have attended the engagement party, but I doubted he'd changed his mind about my relationship with Nate.

"These are stunning," Papa J said, and I got the impression he was trying to distract me. "You should try this one."

I nodded. It was a beautiful gown, but every time I looked at the beaded designs, my eyes grew watery and my chest tight. Nate might love me, but he didn't want to get married. Was I really willing to give up what I wanted most to be with him?

It wasn't like I expected him to propose for real—it was a little premature for that. But I wanted to know if it was even a possibility. If he would even consider the idea of marriage and a baby. I had a feeling I already knew the answer. And since that answer was no, I didn't know how I was going to make it through this without crying.

"Hey," Papa J said in a quiet tone, placing his hand on my shoulder. "Are you okay?"

"Yeah. I'm just—" I forced myself to smile. "I can't believe I'm trying on wedding gowns."

"I'm so happy for you," Papa J said, pulling me into his arms. "And I'm happy to share in this special day."

My heart thudded painfully, and I was filled with an overwhelming sense of guilt. My family was getting invested in this relationship. Hell, Papa J had already been talking about plans for next Christmas. And Brooklyn kept calling him Grandpa, and Astrid Auntie. And he loved it. They all did.

Suddenly, everything felt like both too much and not enough. I mean, how would they feel if they knew that we were only pretending to be engaged? That the ring on my finger was a lie. Nate said he loved me, but our relationship was still defined—*bound*—by a contract.

"I think this is a good start," Jay said while one of his assistants carried the gowns to the first-floor guest room.

While Kendall and I changed, Jay waited in the hall in case we needed any assistance. I put on the first one, and it was beautiful. But I couldn't breathe. It was too tight; not just the dress—that feeling in my chest.

Oh my god. What am I doing?

It was one thing to pretend to be engaged. It was another to fall in love with my fake fiancé. And yet another to *want* to follow through with the wedding, when I was pretty sure Nate never wanted to marry again.

I started clawing at the zipper, desperately trying to get out of the dress.

"Em, what's wrong?" Kendall asked.

"I can't—" I tugged on the fabric, my skin growing hot and tight and itchy. "I need to. Get this off. I can't get..." I grunted, afraid I was going to have another reaction like the one that had landed me in the hospital. "Breathe."

"Hey." She placed her hand on my arm. "Try to stay calm. We *will* get you out, even if I have to cut the dress myself."

That only drove my anxiety higher, and none of my mental exercises were working.

Kendall finally had to call Jay in. The two of them got me out of the dress. Jay asked if something like this had ever happened before. And then he'd whispered something about a panic attack after Kendall had suggested calling for a doctor.

I sank to the floor in a puddle of tulle and sequins. I was still panting as I clutched the dress to my chest.

"Breathe," Kendall said in a calm tone. "Just breathe, Emmy."

I took deep, slow breaths, trying to harness the strength

of my alter ego. She was a badass—calm, cool, in control. She always wore the perfect red lipstick and a sleeve of tattoos that looked like a maze of thorns with roses woven throughout.

I kept imagining her, channeling her, until my vision was no longer spotty. Until my heart wasn't racing. But I was exhausted—emotionally and physically wrung out.

The lies, the media attention, my upcoming competition, the custody battle, all of it was wearing on me. It was wearing me out.

Jay returned with some water and then shut the door after he'd left.

Kendall sat next to me and took my hand in hers. "Emmy," she said, and I could feel her watching me with concern. "What's wrong?"

"I'm just…" I sighed, so damn tempted to tell her everything. But I couldn't. Not when the hearing was so close and the risk was too high. Hell, part of me worried that my meltdown would lead to even more speculation about my relationship with Nate. And that was the last thing we needed right now. "I'm overwhelmed."

"You want to talk about it?" she asked.

"I wouldn't even know where to start," I admitted.

"That's understandable. You've had a lot going on."

She had no idea. But only because I hadn't told her. I *couldn't* tell her.

"But I hope you know," she continued, "that no matter what happens, I'm always here for you."

"Thanks, Kendall," I said, appreciating it more than she could know. I sensed she was waiting for me to tell her something more. To explain my freak-out.

I settled for something that was true. "I never realized how exhausting it would be to live in the spotlight."

Her smile was sympathetic. "I'm sure it is. That's why,

when Jay offered to bring the dresses here, I asked him to bring some for you. I'm sorry if this wasn't how you wanted to try on wedding gowns. I just thought it would be something fun and relaxing to do together."

At those words, I started to cry. My best friend had done something so thoughtful, and I was ruining everything. Not just her surprise, but her *day*.

"Hey." She rubbed circles on my back. "It's going to be okay."

"Is it?" I asked, my voice cracking. "I'm a terrible maid of honor."

"Em." She placed her hand on my shoulder. "You're a great maid of honor, and an even better friend."

"Thanks," I sniffled. "But I'm worried. It's just..." My exhale was shaky. "Everything's changing. You're getting married."

"*You're* getting married and becoming a bonus mom," she said with a kind smile, but I tried to gloss over that.

"*You're* becoming a bonus mom," I teased.

"Ugh." She shuddered. "I don't want to think about the fact that my ex will technically be my stepson."

I laughed despite myself. "At least he's supportive of your relationship."

She nodded, her expression thoughtful. "True. And I know Brooklyn's ecstatic that you'll be her bonus mom. She adores you, and I know how much you love her."

I nodded, thinking of how incredible Brooklyn was. And how lucky I was to have her in my life. "I do. I just wish everyone I love was as supportive of my relationship with Nate."

"What are you talking about? Papa J and Astrid seem thrilled."

I hunched my shoulders, curling in on myself. "My dad isn't."

She held my hands in hers. "What did he say?"

"He doesn't approve of Nate. But he's also pissed because I told him my next race would be my last."

She blinked a few times. "You're retiring?"

"It's long overdue," I said, still feeling immense relief at the idea.

She smiled. "I'm sure retiring feels very bittersweet, but now you'll have more time to focus on the wedding and your athleisure line and everything else you've always wanted to do but never had time for."

"Exactly," I said, relieved that she automatically understood.

"Or you could become a regular Peloton instructor. I took your class," she said. "It was so much fun!"

"Thanks." I grinned, knowing that my alter ego had supported me then just as she had today. "I had a blast."

Kendall laughed. "You sound surprised."

"Yeah, I mean, I guess I didn't expect to like it so much."

"Why not?" Kendall furrowed her brow. "It seems right up your alley. And—" she nudged me "—it broke the record for most people streaming a single live class."

"Crazy, right?" I still couldn't quite believe it myself.

"Yes. But so, *so* awesome. And totally deserved."

I waved a hand through the air. "I'm sure most people tuned in for Nate."

"What?" Kendall shook her head. "No way. Em." She grasped my shoulder, forcing me to stop and look at her. "They tuned in for you. He was just an added bonus."

I laughed so hard I snorted. "Not sure Nate Crawford would ever be considered anything but a star."

"Maybe not, but in that class, you shone brighter than anyone. Even—" she leaned in "—him."

I rolled my eyes. "I love you, but you're clearly biased."

She shook her head. "It's not just me. Knox agrees."

I sucked in air through my teeth. "Ouch. Don't let Nate hear that," I joked.

"I'm serious, Em. Knox was impressed, and that's no small feat."

"True," I said.

"So, do you think you'll do more of them?"

I knew she was trying to distract me, but I appreciated it all the same. Technically, I never had to work again. Thanks to my endorsements and the ten million from Nate, I was set. But I had yet to touch the money from him. And I still wasn't sure I would.

It didn't sit right with me. If anything, keeping the money for myself felt like something Trinity would do. And the last person I ever wanted to be compared to was her, especially if it made Nate question my reasons for being with him.

Everyone kept asking about the plans for the wedding. My plans for my future. I knew they only asked because they cared about me, loved me. But until I knew what was going to happen between Nate and me, it was difficult to make any decisions. And I hated that it felt like I was putting my life on hold for a man.

CHAPTER TWENTY-FOUR

Nate

"We have a problem," Pierce said when I answered his call.

I was headed to Graham's for a game of poker with him, Knox, and Jasper when Pierce's name had flashed on the screen of my car.

I braced myself. "What kind of problem?"

I prayed it was something with the studio. Something that could be fixed quickly and easily. And preferably without much added expense. But judging from his tone, I didn't have much faith that would be the case.

"Trinity's lawyer is going to bring up your engagement at the hearing."

"So?" I asked. We'd known all along that was a possibility. Hell, we'd been counting on it since my relationship with Emerson definitely improved my reputation.

"*So*," Pierce sighed. "I'm concerned the judge will ask if it's a publicity stunt. If it's fake."

"Maybe it started out that way, but I can honestly say my feelings for her are real."

"Right. And that's great," he said. It had become something of a "don't ask, don't tell" topic since our conversation a few weeks ago. "And I'm happy for you. But if they ask if it was ever fake under oath, you can't lie."

I squeezed the wheel so hard, my knuckles turned white. "Fuck."

The hearing was being conducted in open court, despite our request for it to be a closed proceeding. I had a feeling the judge was looking forward to his fifteen minutes of fame or however long he thought he could string this out. Pierce continued talking, but all I could focus on was the fact that everything I'd worked so hard for was unraveling.

"I thought we were only submitting written testimony," I finally said, trying to think back through our last custody hearing. It had been years ago, and I'd wanted to block it out. But Trinity had reopened that old wound, and the memories were flooding in.

"We are, but the judge will swear you and Trinity in and then ask any questions he feels are necessary."

Well, shit. I really was screwed.

"Are you sure we can trust Emerson to stay quiet?"

I practically growled. "Yes."

Did he seriously just ask me that? After everything she'd done?

"But I will not ask her to lie under oath," I said, cutting him off before he could even consider it. "Nor will I."

"It wasn't a strategy I was going to propose," Pierce said.

"Good. Now instead of questioning my fiancée's integrity, why don't you find a solution." I would not let Trinity drag Emerson through the mud. I would not let her take Brooklyn away.

"I'm working on it." Pierce's tone was terse. "But, Nate…" He paused, and I pulled into the parking garage at the Huxley Grand. "You need to seriously consider what you're willing to do, because we're running out of time."

"I know." I slammed my hand on the wheel. *Fuck.*

We ended the call, and I considered turning the car around and going anywhere but here. My fingers were poised over my phone, ready to text Graham that I wasn't coming when I got a message from Knox asking where I was. I took it as a sign and shot back a quick reply that I was on my way.

I rode the elevator to the penthouse in silence, still seething from Pierce's remarks. Maybe this wouldn't be so bad. Besides, where else was I going to go?

My family had always been my safe place, my home. I could be myself with them. At least, that had always been the case until my fake engagement. Now, I was lying to them. I was putting on an act. And I was just...so tired from it all.

After my call with Pierce, I wondered what it was all for. What was even the point?

I stared at the doors, giving myself a moment. Just *one* moment. To feel pity, anger, worry, and all the emotions swirling within me. Just one, and then... The elevator chimed, signaling my arrival at the penthouse. I straightened and smoothed back my hair before stepping out of the elevator.

Graham was sitting at the table, shuffling cards. But he glanced up when I walked in, lifting his chin in greeting. "Nate."

"Graham," I said, taking a seat across from him.

"You look like shit," he said.

"Nice to see you too."

"What's wrong?" he asked, not even bothering with pleasantries. He'd never had time for small talk, even as a child.

"Pierce called while I was on the way here. He wanted to talk about the custody hearing."

He took a sip of his whiskey. "I already submitted my written testimony."

"Thank you."

"Do you want me to come to the hearing with you?"

I appreciated that more than he could know. Graham rarely took time away from work, from the hotel empire he oversaw. So, for him to offer to attend the hearing meant a lot to me.

Even so, I knew I couldn't let it come to that. Not if I was going to keep my fake engagement a secret. Not if I was going to protect my daughter and the woman I loved.

"Thanks. I'll let you know," I said, eager to end the conversation as Knox and Jasper joined us, each with a drink in hand.

"You want one?" Knox asked, holding up his glass of whiskey.

I shook my head. "I'm good, thanks."

Jasper dealt us in. While we played, we caught up on life. Knox's soccer team was doing well. If they kept it up, they'd be on track to win another MLS Cup. Jasper was...well, technically he worked in marketing for Huxley Hotels, but I was convinced he was a professional flirt. Most of the time he seemed to be sitting around doing nothing of real substance. Wasting his life.

"How was Mexico?" I asked Graham. He'd just returned from inspecting the new Huxley Grand development in Ixtapa.

He glowered. "Progress is slower than I'd like."

"Of course it is," Jasper said with an annoyed huff.

Sometimes I wondered if Graham and Sloan had gotten all the work ethic between them and Jasper none.

Graham ignored Jasper's dig and kept his attention on me. "It's going to be a beautiful property, and we're planning a soft opening for influencers and travel bloggers."

Knox and I weren't involved in the day-to-day operations of the Huxley Hotel empire anymore. Besides, Graham and Sloan were better suited to running the family business. And to a lesser extent, Jasper. I was more than happy to take more of a behind-the-scenes role.

"Even Lily?" Knox asked, referring to a popular luxury-travel blogger who had a site named Gilded Lily. After she'd given a negative review to one of the Huxley Grand locations months ago, Graham had been on the warpath.

Graham gnashed his teeth. "Jasper insisted on putting her on the invite list."

"Yes," Jasper said, dealing another round of cards. "But I didn't think you'd agree."

"Is that wise?" I asked.

Graham straightened. "Maybe it will be a chance to show her how wrong she is about the Huxley brand."

When they started arguing, Knox turned to me. "Is Emerson okay?"

"Yeah." I frowned. "Why wouldn't she be?"

"Oh, uh—" He cleared his throat. "Never mind. Perhaps I misunderstood."

"Misunderstood what exactly?" I asked.

I checked my cards then glanced at everyone else to get a reading of what had been dealt. Jasper frowned, though I wasn't sure whether it was about his hand or what Knox had said. Graham arched an eyebrow and took a swig of his whiskey.

"Kendall mentioned something about a panic attack," Knox said.

"A what?" I gaped at him. "When?" And why the fuck had no one told me about it?

"The other day, when she was at our house looking at wedding dresses."

"For Kendall," I said.

"For both of them," Knox said. "Kendall thought it would be a fun surprise."

"What?"

I'd been out of town, but still…Emerson had never mentioned anything. Neither had Brooklyn, for that matter —at least not about a panic attack. The dresses, yes. Brooklyn had gushed about them, but I didn't realize Emerson had been trying them on too.

"Yeah. You know—" Jasper gave me a pointed look "— wedding dresses. For when she walks down the aisle to *marry* you."

Great. Papa J was already making plans for Christmas, and now Emerson was trying on wedding gowns. Next thing I knew, I'd be walking down the aisle to maintain this charade.

Though, the thought of marrying again no longer terrified me as much as it once had. But it was too soon, right? Besides, there was too much going on with Trinity's custody claim to think about the future.

"Yes. Yes." I rolled my eyes, trying to ignore his tone and the insinuation that flowed from it. "I know."

Graham leaned back, resting his arm on the empty chair next to him. "Is she pregnant?"

"What?" I jerked my head back. "No." At least, I didn't think so. *Shit.* Was that yet another thing she was keeping from me, like this panic attack? "Why would you think that?"

"Because I don't know what to think," he said, surprising me with his unexpected outburst. "None of us does."

"Graham," Knox said in a warning tone. I got the feeling this wasn't the first time they'd talked about this. Talked about *me. Fuck.*

I glanced between these men—my brothers. "If you have something to say, say it."

"Your engagement came out of the blue. None of us even knew you were dating Emerson," Knox said. "I mean, even Kendall was surprised."

"Dating." Jasper chortled. "Is that what we're calling it?"

I stood so quickly, my chair nearly fell over. "Tread very carefully," I seethed. "That's my future wife you're talking about."

He arched an eyebrow. "Not if the rumors are to be believed."

"I didn't think you paid attention to rumors."

"Kind of hard not to when everyone's asking me if they're true." Jasper's gaze was questioning. Assessing.

Fuck. First Pierce, and now this?

I'd come here hoping to relax and catch up with my family, and now I was dealing with a fucking inquisition. I was so tempted to tell them everything—the truth about my engagement, the bullshit with Trinity, how I'd fallen for Emerson. But…my shoulders slumped. I couldn't.

If I couldn't before, I definitely couldn't now. Not after everything Pierce had told me. But I hated lying to them.

They'd always kept me grounded. Kept me sane. We'd always been there for one another, whether it was after our parents had all perished in that plane crash, when Brooklyn was born, during my divorce, our grandparents' deaths, my Oscar win. Big or small, good or bad, they'd always been there for me.

I fumbled for something to say, finally settling on, "I didn't want to tell anyone we were together," as I sat back down.

"Because you were ashamed?" Knox asked, and I wondered if he'd been channeling his own feelings about his relationship with Kendall. She was twenty years younger than him. She'd been his employee at the time. And she used to date his son.

I knew he didn't feel that way anymore. They were getting married, and I was happy for him. But it wasn't hard to see why he might jump to that conclusion.

"Because I didn't want to put that kind of pressure on our relationship. And I didn't want to get Brooklyn's hopes up."

Graham nodded, considering. They were all quiet, and it was unnerving.

I felt myself growing hotter and madder. At my family for pushing. At Emerson for hiding her panic attack. At the entire fucking situation. This was all Trinity's fault.

"Knox dated Jude's ex for months, and none of us knew about it. You didn't get butthurt at him for keeping that secret. Nor do I see any of you questioning his decision, even though it had a bigger impact on our family dynamics."

"We're just worried about you," Knox said, taking my ire in stride. "That's all."

I glanced around the table at each of them, absorbing their various expressions. Talk about being ganged up on. I scoffed. "Why can't you just be happy for me?"

"You've had a lot going on," Knox continued, ever the protective older brother.

"I *always* have a lot going on."

And so did Emerson. Fuck. I dragged my hand through my hair. I was supposed to be minimizing her stress, especially with her upcoming competition. Not exacerbating it. To hear that she'd suffered a panic attack and I hadn't been there for her...

That she hadn't even told me... I held a hand to my chest, pain lancing through me. It hurt.

And to know that this was my fault—I was the one who'd put us in this position in the first place.

Knox shook his head. "This is different. A tell-all, a new film that's generating tons of attention, Trinity's bullshit, *and* an engagement."

"That doesn't mean you should jump to conclusions. I mean, how would you feel if I insinuated that you were marrying Kendall because she was pregnant?" I asked, knowing Knox didn't want more kids.

He lifted a shoulder. "I'd be fucking thrilled if she were."

"What?" Jasper and I blurted at the same time. Even stoic Graham raised an eyebrow in question.

"She's *not* pregnant," Knox continued. "But if I have my way, that won't be the case for long."

I gaped at him, repeating, "What?" because I couldn't think of anything else.

He nodded, a wistful smile forming on his face. "We want to have children."

"You do?" I nearly choked. He was forty-seven. He had a son who was almost thirty. Was he seriously considering starting over again?

"Yeah. I do." He smoothed his hand down his beard.

I didn't know what to say. I sure as hell hadn't been expecting that.

"You don't?" Graham asked me.

"I…" I sighed. "I don't honestly know." It was difficult to focus on the future when I was still dealing with Trinity's manipulative bullshit.

"What about Emerson?" Jasper asked. "Surely she wants children of her own. She's only twenty-nine. And she loves kids enough to be a nanny." He shuddered.

Jasper was right. Emerson *did* want kids. *Did I?* And how would Brooklyn feel about becoming an older sister?

"Well?" Jasper asked, and I realized everyone was staring at me.

Shit.

"We only just got engaged. And Emerson is still training." They didn't need to know that she planned to retire soon. "Now is not the time to discuss having kids. And why do you care so much?" I asked, growing agitated. I was just trying to survive the custody battle and Emerson's competition. I couldn't deal with these types of questions right now—and from my family, of all people.

"Jesus." Jasper threw his hands in the air. "What the hell is your problem, Nate?"

I sighed, resting my head in my hands. I was overwhelmed. Exhausted. And afraid. Afraid I was going to lose Brooklyn. Lose Emerson.

"I'm afraid I'm going to lose everything," I said into my palms.

"What are you talking about?" Knox asked. "Did something happen with the movie? Is the studio in trouble?"

"No." *Thank god.* I sat up and faced them. "I'm worried about Emerson—she's pushing herself too hard. And Pierce's concerned that Trinity could win this time."

"What?" Graham jerked his head back. "How? She never calls. She never visits. Rarely sends birthday or Christmas gifts. I could go on and on about what a shitty mother she is."

What was I supposed to say? He was right, but, "I just...I can't let this hearing happen." When I saw the questioning glances they shared, I rushed to add, "I don't want to put Brooklyn through that."

That was true—for so many reasons.

"Pay Trinity off. We all know that's what she wants anyway," Jasper said with disgust.

I shook my head. "No. She wants Mom's Marie Antoinette necklace."

They gave a collective gasp. Knox shook his head, stricken. Jasper was up and out of his chair. Graham banged his fist on the table. "No fucking way."

"That's exactly what I told her."

"So what are we going to do?" Jasper asked, and I appreciated the show of solidarity.

"Look," I sighed, afraid they'd see right through my bullshit, as always. "Pierce is handling it. I appreciate your concern, but I don't want to talk about this anymore."

After a pause, Knox placed his hand on my shoulder. "You know we're always here for you. And we'd do anything to help you."

I nodded. They dropped the matter, and I figured that was the end of it.

It wasn't until after Knox and Jasper left that Graham broached the topic again. "What aren't you telling us?"

I opened my mouth to say something, but I found myself admitting the truth. Graham was like a vault when it came to secrets. He would never tell. And while talking to Knox was tempting, I didn't want to put him in the awkward position of lying to Kendall.

Even so, I hadn't intended to tell Graham anything. But now that I'd started, I couldn't seem to stop. It felt so freeing to finally confide in someone. To unload about the engagement and my agreement with Emerson. About how I'd fallen for her. About my fears for the hearing.

"I don't get it," he finally said.

"Get what?" I asked.

"You say that you and Emerson love each other, but you're literally paying her—rather handsomely, I might add —to be your fake fiancée."

"I know, but things changed. For both of us."

"Okay." He scoffed. "I hope you're right. But you've always hated that relationships were transactional to Trinity. How is this any different?"

It *was* different. Or at least I wanted to believe it was.

EMERSON'S COMPETITION WAS TOMORROW, AND I'D BEEN contemplating what to say to her for days. I hadn't mentioned her panic attack and neither had she, but she'd seemed off lately, distant. I didn't know if that was part of her mental prep for the competition, but judging from the worried glances Papa J and Astrid had cast Emerson all day, I didn't think so.

The last thing I wanted to do was upset her before her race, but I knew I wouldn't be able to live with myself if I stayed silent and she got hurt. So, I waited until Brooklyn was hanging out with Papa J and Astrid in the suite I'd reserved for her family to broach the subject with Emerson.

I'd given them the suite as a peace offering. And Declan had begrudgingly accepted the accommodations despite the fact that it was the closest—and by far the nicest—hotel to the venue.

"How are you feeling about tomorrow?" I asked as she stretched on the floor. Damn, she was sexy. It was difficult to focus on what needed to be said instead of what I wanted to do to her.

She exhaled slowly, deepening the stretch even more. "Good."

"And practice went well?" I asked, just trying to get a feel for whatever was going on in her head.

"Yeah."

I sensed hesitation, even if she wouldn't admit it. And I'd seen the look on her face on the track today—fear, anxiety, and so much more. I didn't want to make things worse for Emerson, but if I didn't say something, who would? Her dad sure as shit wasn't going to. And I had a feeling Papa J and Astrid weren't willing to risk getting in the middle of them.

"Look, I hate to ask, but are you sure about this?"

She jerked her head back. "I haven't worked this hard for this long to pull out at the last minute."

"But you heard the doctor, and stress and…" We still didn't have any answers. She'd seen an allergist and another specialist, and no one could tell us anything.

She scoffed. "You're kidding me, right?"

"No. I'm not kidding. I'm worried about you, and it feels as if I'm the only one willing to say what needs to be said."

"Nate." She held up a hand. "I'm not having this conversation with you. Not right now."

"If not now, then when?" I asked. Tomorrow, it might be too late. "What is it going to take for you to stop? You landed in the hospital. You had a panic attack at Knox's."

Her gaze whipped to me. "You know about that?"

"Seriously?" I glared at her. "That's what you're upset about right now?"

"No. I'm upset that you're questioning my ability to compete the night before the race. I'm pissed that you have the audacity to try to tell me what to do." She hurled the words with such force, they might as well have been the shot put.

"I'm not…" I huffed.

"Yes, you are. And if you care about me, you'll drop this," she said through gritted teeth.

"Drop this? You look two seconds away from passing out. Em." I sighed, trying to get my emotions under control. "Am I supposed to stand by and watch while you self-destruct?"

Emerson's body had been sending her messages for months—telling her to stop. To reduce her stress. And yet, she'd continued to ignore those signs. I worried that if she kept pushing, she'd hurt herself even worse. I worried the competition would finally push her over the edge and I'd lose her for good.

"You don't know what I'm capable of. I've competed with broken bones. And I never let it stop me before."

"This isn't about what you're capable of," I said, softening my tone. Wishing I could get through to her. Wishing I could make her understand. "Because I know you're strong. You're one of the strongest people I know. But you've told me time and again that you don't want to do this. Yet your dad keeps pushing and pushing and pushing."

She shook her head, disappointment written across her face. "And you're no different."

"That's not fair." I crossed my arms over my chest. "I'm worried about you. I don't want to see you get hurt."

Perhaps it wasn't the best timing, but she could still pull out. And why did she even care? We both knew she was ready to retire. Why risk it?

She grabbed her suitcase and started throwing stuff into it. It wasn't long before she zipped it up.

"Where are you going?" I asked.

"I can't deal with this right now." She headed for the door. "I need to focus. Tomorrow's my last race, and I can't afford to have any distractions right now."

I wanted to blame her outburst on a case of pre-race nerves, but it felt like more than that. It felt as if she was slipping away.

"Em," I pleaded, rushing to catch up to her. To stop her. "I wasn't trying to upset you."

"Really? Because right now, it feels like you're more concerned with proving my father wrong than caring about what I want."

It wasn't the first time we'd argued about her dad. But I'd tried to keep my opinions to myself. He was her coach, but not for much longer.

I gnashed my teeth. *Seriously?* "How am *I* the bad guy here? *He's* the one pushing you to do something you don't even want."

"It's my last event," she said. "I made a promise. And regardless of the outcome, I'm going to give it my all. This is my decision, and if you can't accept that, don't bother coming tomorrow."

"What?" I choked on the word. "Emerson, wait." I grabbed her wrist. "I'm sorry, okay? I just…" I huffed, pulling her to me. I held her close once more. Wishing I could change her mind. Protect her. Wishing I could *know* that she'd never leave me.

I hated feeling like this—so…out of control.

I sighed and kissed the top of her head. "Don't go. *Please*. I love you, and I'm worried about you."

"Then say *that*." She pulled back to peer up at me. "Instead of trying to tell me what to do. And trust me to know what's best for me. To decide what's best for me, even when you may not agree. Because I want a partner, not another parent."

I nodded, hating that I'd made her feel that way. "I want to be the kind of partner you deserve. And of course, I'll be there. Supporting you. Cheering you on." And not because she was my fake fiancée or because it was part of our contract, but because I loved her.

CHAPTER TWENTY-FIVE

Emerson

"Tell me what you need from me," Nate said after Brooklyn had gone to bed.

We'd spent a quiet evening in our suite, opting for room service. There were too many paparazzi lurking around. Too many fans desperate for a glimpse of Nate or our family. Nate was determined not to let his presence at my side interfere with my performance tomorrow.

I draped my arms around his neck. "All I need is you."

I appreciated his support, especially considering his earlier concern. Deep down, I knew he loved me and was there for me. He'd shown me that again and again. And while I didn't like what he'd said, I respected him for sharing his concerns with me.

Nate wrapped his arms around me. "You have me, Em."

I leaned into his touch. "I'm not sure I ever thanked you for suggesting the idea of an alter ego to me."

"Yeah?" He kissed the end of my nose.

"Yeah. Whenever I start to feel out of control, my alter ego helps me calm down more quickly. And I've been channeling her in practice."

"That's great, Em." He smiled. "I'm so glad you've found it useful."

He kissed me. But when he tried to pull back, I held on, dragging us deeper into the kiss. Into his touch. Our mouths and tongues and hands eager and seeking. But when I tugged on his waistline, he placed his hand over mine. I frowned, but he shook his head.

"You need your rest," he said, bringing our joined hands to his heart. "And I don't want to do anything to jeopardize your success."

I considered pushing him, but he was right. I did need my rest. There would be time for sex after the competition, even if it might take the edge off now.

"I'm going to check my stuff again for tomorrow and get ready for bed." That usually helped calm me the night before a competition and put me in the right frame of mind.

I verified our timing for the morning with Jackson and my dad. Nate had insisted that I take Jackson with us, and my dad had agreed. I double-checked my backpack. Laid out my outfit for the race. Took a shower and did some light yoga. And by the time I'd washed my face and brushed my teeth, I still wasn't tired.

Even so, I told myself to lie down. To get in bed and stick to the routine. Nate kissed me goodnight and then turned off the light.

"I'm glad you stayed," Nate said in the darkness, his body wrapped around mine.

"Me too," I said, snuggling into his arms. I couldn't imagine sleeping alone tonight, even if I had been upset earlier. "I'm sorry if I overreacted earlier. I'm just…" I blew out a breath. "Stressed."

"I know, Em." He kissed my neck. "But you've got this. You've trained for this. And no matter what happens tomorrow, you should be proud of yourself."

The bridge of my nose stung. I hadn't realized how much I'd needed to hear that. I appreciated Nate's words of encouragement more than he could ever know.

I sniffled at his kindness, his support, the sound magnified in the darkness.

"Hey." His voice was gentle. Reassuring. "What's wrong?"

"I just really appreciate you." I sniffled again, warm, fat tears falling down my cheeks as everything caught up to me. "I can't believe this is my last race."

He handed me a tissue then stroked his hand up and down my arm. He didn't say anything, just waited. Giving me the space to sort through my feelings.

I dried my eyes. "I've been looking forward to this for a long time, and now that it's here…"

I trailed off, not even sure what to say. I felt too much. And I hadn't realized how hard it would hit me to say goodbye to the sport I'd dedicated so many years to.

I mean, yes, I'd known it would be emotional. But for so long, I'd been so focused on the future—what would come after retirement—that I hadn't really stopped to consider what it would be like to cross that finish line knowing it was the last time.

"You don't have to retire," Nate finally said. "And you also don't have to make any decisions tomorrow."

"I know," I sighed. At this point in my career, I had more options than I would've ever dared dream of. And many of them were thanks to the man beside me.

"But…" he prompted.

"But I have decided. And I *want* to retire."

"I know it's not the same, but this reminds me of the process of watching Brooklyn grow up. And how sometimes it just creeps up on me and then hits me out of the blue with a big wave of emotions."

"Yeah?" I asked, turning in his arms.

"Yeah." He smiled at me, his face shadowed in darkness. "There's that mix of excitement about the future, joy in the present, and grief over the past. Over the stages you've already lived and will likely never experience again."

I loved hearing his insight as a dad. His relationship with Brooklyn, his love and devotion for his daughter, was one of the things I loved most about Nate. Because no matter what else was going on or how busy he was, his first thought was always of her. And now, well, me.

"I get that," I said. "That's been one of the hardest parts of being a nanny. Taking joy and pride in seeing the kids mature, but also knowing that they don't need me as much anymore. Or that when I leave a job, I won't get to continue to watch them grow."

"I can't imagine pouring so much love and care into a child, while knowing the entire time that you'll eventually have to walk away."

"It's hard," I said, praying I would never have to walk away from Brooklyn.

"And you know who's probably struggling with some of these same feelings you are?"

I tucked in closer to his side. "My dad," I grumbled.

Nate stroked my hair, and my body relaxed even further beneath his touch. "Yep. I mean, if Brooklyn told me she was making a major life change, and it meant I'd have less time with her, I'd probably be putting up a fight too."

"I didn't consider that." I pulled back momentarily, attempting in vain to read his expression. "Though I am surprised to hear you take his side."

Nate had never shied away from sharing his opinion about my dad in the past. And the two of them always seemed to clash when it came to me. I hoped they'd eventually be able to move past that, especially now that I was retiring. But I worried that my dad would never fully accept

Nate. And while I knew I wouldn't let that stop me from being with the man I loved, it would certainly affect some of the most important relationships in my life.

Nate chuckled, holding me even closer. His chest was warm beneath my cheek, and his heart was steady and reassuring. "He's not a bad guy. And he *does* love you, even if he's not always the best at showing it."

"I know. And honestly, that's a big part of why I want to retire. Because while I'm scared of how it will impact our relationship, I also know that it's time. It's time for him to stop being my coach and start being my dad."

He cleared his throat, and I laughed.

"I know. I know," I sighed. "You were right."

"What was that?" His voice rasped against my ear.

"You heard me." I was tempted to give his chest a playful slap, but I was too damn comfortable.

"I know." He pressed a kiss to my hair. "But it's just so rare that you say those words to me."

"Right?" I teased. "Because they're never true."

He tickled me, and I wriggled in his arms. But he only held me tighter.

"Hey!" I grunted, trying to escape his hold. I loved that he was so strong. I loved that we could mess around like this and have fun. "I'm supposed to be relaxing here."

"Okay. Okay." He settled back into position, and I got comfy in the crook of his arm. "You're right."

We talked for a while longer, but I was soon drifting off to sleep.

I woke in the morning to an empty bed. I turned for the nightstand and found a large bouquet of red roses, along with a note and was that...a friendship bracelet?

Em,

Good luck today, not that you need it. I love you.

Love,
Nate

AND BROOKLYN

I LAUGHED WHEN I REALIZED THAT SHE MUST HAVE ADDED HER name after he'd already signed the card. It was crammed in there, but I was touched she'd done that. I continued reading.

PS: We left early to let you focus. We'll be waiting at the finish line.

I PICKED UP THE BRACELET. IT WAS ALL RED APART FROM THE white disks with gold letters on them that spelled "Fearless." A reference to one of our favorite songs and my mantra for the day. I wiped away a tear, feeling so very fortunate to have Nate and Brooklyn in my life.

I slipped on the bracelet with a smile, feeling stronger and more powerful already. I listened to my race-day playlist while I was getting ready. When the song, "You're on Your Own, Kid," came on, I paused to really listen to the lyrics. They just hit different that morning. And I smiled at my reflection as I applied red lipstick in honor of my badass alter ego. I was just refilling my water bottle when there was a knock at the door. My dad stood in the hall, Jackson behind him.

"Morning," Dad said, frowning at my red lips. I often wore makeup to practice, but a red lip was bold for a race.

I nodded but said nothing as we walked toward the entrance to the parking garage.

Some of the other members of Jackson's team from Hudson Security would protect Nate and Brooklyn, as well as the rest of our family. I inhaled deeply, trying not to think of how many people would be watching me compete.

"Did you eat?" Dad asked.

I nodded. I'd eaten, but I was so nervous about my race, I felt like I was going to throw up. The mere idea of opening my mouth had me staying quiet for fear that I'd do just that. Instead, I kept my focus on what lay ahead. I channeled my alter ego and took calming breaths.

Jackson drove us to the field, closemouthed the entire time, though his eyes kept darting back to me. I tried to ignore his concern, just as I'd tried to ignore Nate's last night. But he was right to be worried—they both were. I wasn't sure I could do this, though I'd never admit that aloud.

Dad was quiet during the drive, giving me a chance to go through my race-day routine. I appreciated the continuity of the ritual, even if it felt as if an extra layer of tension covered us like a weighted blanket. I was convinced this was my last race. And Dad remained optimistic I'd change my mind.

I pushed away thoughts of failure. Of my retirement. Of everything but the race. This was my last competition, and I wanted to make it count. I wanted to go out on a high.

When we reached the stadium, the crowd was larger than it had ever been. Most of them probably hoping for a glimpse of Nate. I took a deep breath and tried to ignore the circus that came with being his fake fiancée. Today was about me. It was about doing the best that I could.

"You're ready for this, Em," Dad said. "It's what we've trained for day after day. It's what you were born to do."

I nodded and inserted my earbuds, trying to tune everything else out. The pressure. The anxiety. The stress.

My alter ego wouldn't give a shit about any of that, so neither did I.

Even though we'd parked in a gated lot, paparazzi were staked out at the gate. I tried to ignore them too. Today wasn't about Nate or our relationship, though his support—and Brooklyn's—had bolstered me. This was about me and my accomplishments.

Despite all the drama leading up to this, I felt strong. Clearheaded. I wanted to race. And I wanted to end my career on my own terms.

Dad and I signed in and then went to the warm-up area, running through some basic drills. My fellow competitors proceeded through their own warm-ups, and I tried to ignore the curious looks sent my way.

They didn't matter. Nothing mattered but doing the best I could. Giving it my all. Leaving the track with nothing left in my tank. This was my last shot, and I wasn't going to blow it.

The following afternoon, I lay on the track, staring at the ceiling in disbelief. My chest was still heaving from finishing the 800 meter, but I'd done it. I'd won.

And I'd *killed* almost every event I'd competed in, starting with the 100-meter hurdles yesterday, the high jump, the shot put, and the 200-meter sprint. And then I'd carried that momentum through to today, hitting personal records on the long jump and javelin before finishing first overall.

And yet, as the tears fell—relief and joy and every other emotion—I knew this was it. My last race. It was bittersweet, but I was grateful to go out on a high.

As soon as I stepped off the track, Nate swept me up in his arms despite the fact that I was a sweaty, teary-eyed mess. A million cameras went off as he held me close and whispered, "You did it, Em."

When he set me down, Brooklyn was smiling at me. "Way to go, Emmy!"

"Thanks!" I wrapped my arm around her shoulder. "And thanks for my good luck bracelet." I held it up, and she preened.

Dad was next to join me, his smile watery and full of pride. "I knew you had it in you."

Reporters converged on us, and I could feel my chest tighten from his words, his expression. But I was exhausted after finishing the final three events, including the 800 meter. And I wasn't in the right frame of mind to give a proper retort. Not on the heels of my victory. Not with so many people watching our every move.

I sucked down a recovery drink and did a few quick interviews while we waited for the medals ceremony. As I stood on that podium and looked out over the crowd, seeing the faces of the people I loved, I was filled with a sense of peace. Of rightness.

This was my last race, and I had dominated. I mean, *damn.* My alter ego sure had come through for me. She'd been at my side during every event, every doubt, and every success. And so had Nate.

Dad draped his arm over my shoulder as we walked off the field together. He didn't say anything about the future, and neither did I. And for that, I was grateful.

It wasn't until we met for dinner that he broached the topic. Nate had reserved a private room at the restaurant at the Huxley Grand, where everyone was staying. Kendall was chatting with Astrid about her residency. Brooklyn and Nate were discussing what she wanted to order. Papa J and Knox were debating men's fashion, of all things, especially that of the LA Leatherbacks players. I had to laugh, and I was happy to relax and revel in my achievement with all the people I loved most in the world.

Dad came to stand next to me. "I'm proud of you, Emmy. I know you wanted to quit, but I hope you're glad you didn't give up."

"I am," I sighed. It had been a long road to get here, and I couldn't have done it without his support. "Thank you for believing in me. For pushing me, even when I wasn't happy about it."

He hugged me to his side. "Always."

"That said, I haven't changed my mind about retiring," I said, wanting to get it out of the way. "It feels good to go out on a high." I felt as if a weight had released from my shoulders. "I have nothing left to prove."

"You don't need to make any decisions tonight. Not when you're still coming down from the race. These are big decisions—retiring, getting married. I just want to make sure you think things through. That you're making the decision that's best for *you* and for the right reasons."

I shook my head. "It doesn't matter whether it's tonight or in a week or even a month, I'll still want to retire. I know you might not want to believe this, but I'm doing this for me. This is what I want. What I *need.*"

He nodded, considering, and I braced myself for a fight. Finally, he said, "I'm not happy about your decision, but I will respect it."

"You will?" I blurted, surprised he wasn't trying to stall for more time for me to reconsider or talk me out of it.

"Don't you remember what I always said about quitting?"

I furrowed my brow, trying to recall his words. "Whenever I'd tell you I wanted to quit, you'd say, 'Okay. You can quit, but only on a good day.'"

"Exactly. And today was a good day." He smiled.

"It was, but I still want to quit."

He nodded, his expression solemn. "What about Nate?"

"What about Nate?" I asked.

"Oh, Emmy," Papa J interrupted in a chipper voice. "You did amazing today." He hugged me to him.

A muscle in Dad's jaw twitched, and I sensed there was more he wanted to say. He opened his mouth, but Papa J cut him off.

"Declan," Papa J chided with a shake of his head as he released me. "Not tonight."

"If not tonight, then when? At the wedding?"

"What's going on?" I asked, glancing between them just as Nate joined us, placing his hand on my lower back.

"You okay?" Nate asked.

Dad turned to me, ignoring Nate's warning glare and Papa J's plea to let it go. "Is this really the life you want?"

"Declan," Papa J hissed, clearly horrified.

I shook my head, close to tears. I was physically and emotionally exhausted from two days of intense competition. Not to mention wrung out from the sense of finality that had come with crossing the finish line and deciding to retire.

Nate didn't speak; he deferred to me. And for that, I would be forever grateful. Because even though I knew his instinct was to jump in, to protect me, he'd given me the space and the support to stand my ground. To fight my own battles with him at my side.

I straightened. "I appreciate your concern," I said to Dad. "But I love Nate, and I want to be with him." Whatever that looked like for us.

"He's—"

"Declan," Papa J said, resting a hand on his shoulder and giving it a firm squeeze. "You need to drop this. You said what you wanted to say. Emerson assured you that she's happy. Let. It. Go," he gritted out.

Dad's face turned red. And for a moment, I thought he was going to punch someone—namely Nate. But then he turned into Papa J's chest and burst into sobs. Papa J spoke to him in a low tone, rubbing his back. Comforting him.

I stood there, rooted to the spot. Staring with my mouth agape. I wasn't sure I'd ever seen my dad cry. And I didn't know what to do.

I heard Dad say something that sounded like, "I'm losing her." And that snapped me out of whatever trance I'd been in. I went over to him, placing my hand on his shoulder.

"You're not losing me."

"I know, but...you're retiring and getting married. And everything that has always been *ours* will no longer exist."

"You don't think I worry about that too?" I asked. "You don't think I worry that everything is changing. Or that I'll miss seeing you every day at training even though you drive me crazy sometimes?"

Papa J rubbed Dad's back in support, silently urging him on. Urging us to mend this rift once and for all.

Dad stepped closer, his eyes watery. "I'm your dad, and I feel so privileged to have experienced all of this with you. To have watched you accomplish all that you did and to know that I had a hand in it. And even if you hadn't won all those medals or placed first—" he settled his hands on my shoulders "—I still would've been proud of you. I know I didn't say that enough, but I am. And I will always love you. I will always want to protect you."

I was blown away. Maybe this had nothing to do with Nate and everything to do with my dad's fears about the changes coming to our future. I found myself saying, "I love you, Dad. And I'm so grateful for you. You helped me achieve everything I ever dreamed of and so much more, and I'm so happy that I got to share this with you." I smiled, barely holding back tears. "I appreciate you wanting to protect me, but I'm not a little girl anymore. And I love Nate."

"I know." He dropped his head. "I do. I see the way you

two look at each other." He lifted his head, his attention on Nate. "I'm sorry I've been such an ass."

Nate's expression was thoughtful. "I get it. If someone were trying to marry Brooklyn, I'd probably be acting the same way."

I gaped at the two of them. They'd finally gotten past their egos. They'd finally found common ground—as fathers.

Everyone seemed to breathe a sigh of relief. I grasped Dad's bicep. "I know these changes feel big and scary right now, but this could be a good thing for us. I love you, and that's never going to change."

He nodded, opening his arms for a hug. "You're right. *That* will never change."

We embraced, and I felt lighter despite the heavy conversation. It had been necessary. Cathartic.

"And maybe now we can find new things to bond over," I said, pulling back. Nate gave my shoulder a squeeze and then excused himself to check on Brooklyn.

"Like hockey," Dad said, seeming lighter too. His suggestion was laughable—I'd never particularly enjoyed watching the sport, much to Dad's great disappointment.

"Or planning my wedding," I teased.

"Har. Har." He rolled his eyes.

"What?" I smirked. "Too soon?"

"Wedding planning is more of Papa J's thing," he said. "You and I both know that."

"True," I said. "But we've always loved skiing together, and I'm sure we will find ways to spend time together even if we aren't training."

He nodded. "You're right."

"And—" I twirled my ring on my finger, using it to ground me. "I know you and Nate haven't always seen eye to eye, but I really want you two to get along. I don't know if you realize this, but Nate was the one who gave me a tip that helped me overcome my anxiety about competing."

"He did?" He jerked his head back, turning to watch Nate with something that looked like surprise and appreciation.

"Yes," I said. "Please, Dad?" I hooked my arm in his and leaned my head on his shoulder. "This is important to me. You're *both* important to me."

"I—"

Papa J whispered something in his ear that sounded a lot like "grandkids," and Dad smiled.

Dad nodded, his expression solemn. "I'll try."

That was all I could ask for. It was a start. I might not know what the future held for Nate and me, but I loved him. He and Brooklyn were my family. And if Nate and I never got married, never had more children, this was enough. *We* were enough.

CHAPTER TWENTY-SIX

Nate

"Dad, what's going to happen at the hearing?" Brooklyn asked, climbing into her bed.

I'd tried to shield her from the custody hearing as much as I could, but it was damn near impossible when it was plastered all over the internet. Even if my daughter hadn't had a phone of her own, people talked. Other kids at her school were likely gossiping about it. I felt powerless in so many ways.

"What do you hope will happen?" I asked. I didn't want to assume I knew Brooklyn's answer, even if I was fairly confident what she'd say.

She burst into tears, and I hated seeing her so upset. "Please don't make me live with *her*. I only want to live with you."

"I know." I wrapped my arms around her. "I know. And while I don't know what the outcome will be, I promise I will do everything in my power to keep you with me."

"I just..." She sniffled. "I just want you to promise that we're going to be a family forever. You and Emerson and me."

Even if Emerson and I were actually engaged, there was nothing I could do to assure Brooklyn we'd always be a family. Hell, my parents' sudden and tragic deaths were proof of that. And it would be an even bigger lie to promise something so beyond my control.

"We will *always* love you," I said, knowing that no matter what happened between Emerson and me, she would always love my daughter. She would always put Brooklyn first.

Brooklyn started crying harder, burying her face in my chest as sobs racked her body. *Damn Trinity.* I rubbed Brooklyn's back, my heart aching at the sight of her distress.

"Sweetheart," I said gently. "It will all work out." And I vowed that it would, even if I had to give Trinity my mom's necklace.

All along, I'd hoped it wouldn't come to that. But at this point, I wasn't sure I had another option—at least not if I wanted to prevent the hearing from happening. And I did—desperately.

If it had been about money, I would've just paid Trinity off. But she wanted something that didn't belong to her. Something she had no right to demand.

Brooklyn said something, but her words were muffled by my chest.

"What was that?" I asked.

She sat back a little but wouldn't meet my gaze. She focused on the tassels of her blanket. She kept twirling them around her fingers. "How can I know that Emerson won't leave like Mom did?"

"You can't," I said, hating the words as they left my mouth. Yet knowing they were true all the same. "But we have to trust that Emerson loves us and isn't going anywhere."

"I do trust her," Brooklyn said, frowning. "But…I'm scared."

If her biological mother had ditched her, how could

Brooklyn trust anyone? It had always been a concern of mine, and I knew she'd talked to her therapist about it on multiple occasions. But clearly this custody hearing was stirring up more feelings regarding that issue—understandably.

Perhaps her therapist was right, and the only way to reassure Brooklyn was to show up for her—to be there for her again and again. And to model the behavior myself. I couldn't guarantee that my trust wouldn't be broken again—by Emerson or anyone else—but I could try. I could continue to give her the benefit of the doubt. And I would continue to hope she'd never betray me when so many others had.

I only hoped I was right. Because even though our engagement might be fake, I loved Emerson. And I couldn't imagine our lives without her.

"You know what?" I asked, squeezing Brooklyn tight. "Sometimes, I'm scared too. Trusting someone is a leap of faith. There are no guarantees. But Emerson has shown us time and time again that she wants to be here. That she loves us." I wished I could promise more, but that was the best I could offer.

"Think of all the times Emerson has been there for you," I said. "Whether it was showing up at your play—"

"Or helping me learn the lines or prepare my song for Christmas," Brooklyn finished for me.

"Exactly," I said, and we continued to list other instances, my heart swelling with love for Emerson with every example Brooklyn shared.

Not only had Emerson been there for both my daughter and me. Emerson had consistently shown that she didn't care about my money or fame. I thought back to Brooklyn's birthday party, when she'd tackled the paparazzo. And even more recently, to the way she'd defended me to her dad. Plus, so many other instances, large and small.

She might love designer clothes and luxury handbags.

And I'd seen the way her eyes gleamed anytime she looked at her engagement ring. But she didn't *need* those things to be happy. And I knew well enough that if she wanted a Birkin or anything else, she was determined and hardworking enough to buy it for herself or to find a way to pay for it.

She was nothing like Trinity.

I stayed with Brooklyn a while longer, talking and reading books. Hoping my presence would calm and reassure her. Eventually, she fell asleep, and I watched her for a minute, marveling at how grown-up and yet how young she still seemed.

After a long while, I forced myself to leave, pressing a kiss to her forehead before tiptoeing to the door. I found Emerson in the kitchen, busying herself with Brooklyn's backpack.

"You don't have to do that," I said, our shoulders brushing as I took the folder from her and signed it.

"I like to," she said. "I like taking care of Brooklyn. And it feels normal, when everything else in my life is anything but."

I nodded, placing the folder back in the backpack. I knew exactly what Emerson meant. My daughter grounded me, kept me focused. Brooklyn didn't care whether I was famous or rich. She loved me because I was her dad. And lately, it felt as if I was failing her.

I was failing Brooklyn, and I was failing Emerson. And I was so *sick* of letting Trinity run our lives. I was done with watching Brooklyn and Emerson suffer.

So, I went to my office and called Pierce to explain my plan. When I finished, he asked, "You're sure about this?"

I nodded. "I'm sure."

I loved Emerson, and I was determined to show her that, regardless of the cost. And there was nothing I wouldn't do to protect my daughter.

If Trinity didn't take my offer to have the piece appraised

and pay the equivalent value, then I'd surrender Marie Antoinette's necklace to her. I would be sad to relinquish a piece of my mom's collection, especially to someone as undeserving as Trinity. But letting go of something that had belonged to my mom didn't mean letting go of my memories of her.

Over the past few weeks, I'd come to realize that I didn't care about the money or even the principle of it. If buying Trinity off meant I was able to move on with my life once and for all, I'd do it. Because by holding on, I was never going to be able to let go.

Ironically enough, it was Emerson's dad Declan who'd made me realize that.

He kept pushing and pushing Emerson to do what he thought was best, without regard for what she wanted or needed. And I'd been doing the same with this fake engagement. Asking Emerson to lie for me. To help me instead of pursuing her own goals. To... I sighed, dragging a hand through my hair. I was done.

I was done with Trinity's bullshit. I was done hurting the woman I loved.

When Pierce eventually called to say that Trinity would only accept the necklace, I'd made my peace with the idea of parting with it. It was a one-of-a-kind piece that was worth a fortune. But nothing was as priceless to me as Brooklyn and Emerson.

I didn't tell Emerson what had happened—at least not immediately. Instead, I mentioned that the hearing had been postponed by a few days because the judge had had a family emergency. I felt bad for making her believe the custody hearing was still moving forward, merely postponed, but I hoped it would all be worth it in the end.

I called Alexis to see if Brooklyn could spend the night. She immediately agreed. Then, I roped Kendall into helping me by getting Emerson out of the house. I told her I was planning a surprise, and she was more than happy to concoct some excuse about Emerson's maid of honor duties than to push for more information.

With Emerson preoccupied and the rest of my plan coming together, I packed an overnight bag for Brooklyn. Jackson drove me to pick up Brooklyn from school. She was surprised and happy to see me, though her face quickly fell.

"What happened? Did we lose?" she asked, a panicked look in her eyes.

"No, sweetheart. I would never let anyone keep you from me. From now on, you never have to worry about going to live with her. And it's up to you to decide what kind of relationship, if any, you want to have with her."

She jumped into my arms, her sense of relief palpable. It matched my own. And it only made me wish I'd just given Trinity the damn necklace sooner. I could've avoided a lot of stress and heartache.

"Where's Emmy?" she asked.

"She's with Kendall working on some stuff for the wedding," I said as Jackson pulled away from the school.

"Hers or yours?" Brooklyn asked.

"Kendall's," I said.

Brooklyn huffed. "Ugh."

"What?" I asked.

"Uncle Knox and Kendall are getting married in a few months, and you and Emerson haven't even set a date."

I tried, and failed, to hide my smirk. "I didn't realize it bothered you so much."

She crossed her arms over her chest with a huff. "Well, it does."

"Okay." I chuckled, pulling her into my side. "I'm glad you're excited. And I planned to talk to Emerson about the wedding once everything had calmed down."

"It's calmed down now," Brooklyn said. "So let's make some plans."

I would hardly claim that things were back to normal, but I was thrilled she was so excited about the idea of me marrying Emerson.

"Speaking of plans," I said. "Would you like to spend the night at Sophia's tonight?"

She perked right up. "Would I ever!"

I laughed and asked Jackson to head for Sophia's house. Even though I felt bad about sending Brooklyn to a friend's house so soon after dropping the news that the custody hearing was over, I just wanted her to have fun with her best friend. To do something normal. And I needed some time alone with Emerson to enact the next phase of my plan.

When Emerson got home, she dropped her keys on the counter with a sigh.

"Hey," I said, leaning in for a kiss.

"Hey." She smiled.

"I have something I need to tell you," we said, almost at the same time, though in slightly different terms.

"You go first," I said, even though I was bursting to tell her about everything. I'd been sitting on so much big news for days, and Emerson was always the first person I wanted to tell.

"I'm still figuring out what retirement looks like for me. But I've always wanted to give back, and I finally found an organization I'm excited to partner with—Girls RUN the World. Their mission is to empower girls and their communities by building their confidence, kindness, and decision-making skills through running. And it's aimed at promoting both the individual and the team at any ability level."

"That's great." I smiled. "I'm proud of you. And I'm sure Brooklyn would love to be involved. I'd be happy to help too."

"That's the thing." She inhaled. "You sort of already did, albeit anonymously." She slid a piece of paper across the counter to me, and I read the letter. The organization thanked Emerson for her donation of five million dollars and expressed their gratitude and excitement for her support.

I jerked my gaze to hers. "But that's…"

"The exact amount you paid me," she said. "I never spent it because I never felt right about accepting it in the first place. And you can keep the other five million."

If there'd ever been any question in my mind that Emerson was with me for the money, that would've dispelled it. She'd given up five million dollars that she'd earned. Because she hadn't felt right about it.

"That's incredible," I said, still trying to process the fact that she'd donated the five million dollars I'd given her. Not part of it; all of it. "And I have a confession."

"What's that?"

"Graham knows about us."

Her eyes widened. "What? How?"

"I admitted it to him one night in a moment of weakness."

"Why are you telling me this now?" she asked, brow furrowed.

"Because it means that I breached the contract, and I owe you ten million dollars."

She blinked a few times then shook her head. "Nate." She placed her hand on my arm. "You don't owe me anything. That's not how love works."

I smiled, her words merely confirming what I already knew. That Emerson loved me for me. And while trust would never come easily to me, I wanted to try again. Because Emerson was unlike any other woman I'd been with, and I would never take that for granted.

And now for the next part of my plan—telling her about Trinity.

"I have something else I need to tell you," I said.

"Okay," she said, stretching out the word. She fiddled with her ring, her nerves showing.

"There will be no custody hearing. Trinity dropped her custody claim. It's over."

She stared at me in shock. "It's...*what?*"

I nodded, a smile spreading across my face. "It's over."

"But..." she sputtered. "But that doesn't make any sense. Why would she suddenly decide to let it go after all these months? Unless..." She held a hand to her mouth. "Nate, you didn't."

"I did, and it was worth it. Because she gave me something priceless in return. She not only dropped this claim, but her right to any future ones. She signed away her parental rights."

Emerson gasped. "She's a fool."

I nodded. "That she is."

I'd never pushed for Trinity to sign away her parental rights in the past; it had never felt like the right thing to do to me. But I'd given her numerous chances to connect with Brooklyn, and it was painfully clear that she didn't care. It was clear that it was harming Brooklyn more than helping. So when Pierce had suggested pushing for that as a condition for giving Trinity the necklace, I'd agreed.

"How do you feel about it all?" she finally asked.

"Mostly...relieved. My mom never met Brooklyn, but I think she'd say I did the right thing."

"I'm sure it wasn't easy to part with a piece of her collection, but I think you're right." Her shoulders slumped. "I can't believe it's over."

"Yeah." I chuckled. "I can't quite believe it either."

"What about Brooklyn?" she asked. "I know she's spending the night at Sophia's, but have you told her?"

"I already talked to her, and she was relieved."

"What did you tell her?" she asked.

"That going forward, she would always live with me. And that she'd only have to see Trinity if *she* wanted to."

She smiled. "I bet she was happy about that."

I nodded. "She was. She also keeps pestering me about when we're going to set a date for the wedding."

Emerson laughed. "Yeah. Same."

Which meant there was only one thing left to do. I removed our engagement contract from a drawer in the kitchen where I'd hidden it earlier. And then I held it up for her to see.

"We satisfied the terms of our agreement. We don't have to lie anymore." And then I tore it straight down the middle.

CHAPTER TWENTY-SEVEN

Emerson

I gaped at Nate, the pieces of paper fluttering to the floor. Had he really just done that? Had he torn up our contract?

After all these months, all the fighting, the worrying, and the lies…it was difficult to believe it was really over. It was oddly anticlimactic, even if I was beyond grateful.

The custody battle was won, though Nate's victory hadn't come without considerable cost. I mean…his mom's necklace?

Despite the sacrifice, I wasn't sure I'd ever seen him more at ease. I was happy for him, truly. Relieved for Brooklyn. But also…sad for her. I mean, how dare anyone—especially her own mother—ever make her feel like she wasn't enough.

I was still trying to process all of that and what would come next. Selfishly, I wondered what this would mean for us. I'd always known this day would come. It had just come sooner than I'd expected.

If Nate had torn up our contract, then…we were no longer going to be fake-engaged. I stared down at my engagement ring, knowing what needed to be done. I tried to ignore the tightness in my chest and the way the bridge of my nose stung. I slid my engagement ring off my finger even though I loathed to see it go. It wasn't about giving up the ring, though it was a stunning piece of jewelry. It was about what it represented. Because even though our engagement had been fake, my feelings for Nate were very real.

"I suppose you'll be wanting this back now," I said, holding it out to him.

Please say no. Please say no.

"Yes," he said in a strong, clear voice that made my heart drop. But then he added, "But only so I can propose properly this time."

"Wh-what?" I whispered, afraid I'd misheard. Misunderstood.

"Come with me," he said, but I merely stood there in shocked silence. He took my hand and gave it a tug. "Come on." He led me toward the door to the backyard.

I furrowed my brow, trying not to get my hopes up. I knew Nate loved me, but...he didn't want to get married. Right?

"Wh-what is all this?" I asked, trying to take it all in.

Fairy lights gently illuminated the backyard. An acoustic version of "Paper Rings" played softly in the background, the piano giving a playful and romantic feel to the love song. Candles and red rose petals floated on top of the pool. And on the grass were what looked like thousands of red roses and more candles in various heights, all forming a U shape.

Nate grinned and guided me to the roses, stopping once we were in the center of them. "Emerson." His voice was thick with emotion. "The first time I saw you, I was **enchanted**." He paused to meet my eyes as he said "enchanted."

"There was an **invisible string** pulling me to you. And yet, I was scared because I knew **all too well**," he said, pausing

343

again to look me in the eye, "what it felt like to be **haunted** by the past.

"Then you became Brooklyn's nanny, and you were *fearless* and *happiness* personified and completely **untouchable**. *Don't blame me* for staying away when all I wanted was to be your **lover**. Because even though *I knew you were trouble*, I also knew you were meant to be **mine**."

Oh my god. I gasped. Could this man be any more perfect? He was pouring out his love and referencing so many titles of Taylor Swift songs, I couldn't keep up.

Nate smiled, as if he knew I'd just connected the dots. Nodding, he took a shaky breath then continued.

"Every day with you is **the best day**. Every day, **sparks fly**, and I fall a little more in love with you. With your kindness and generosity. With your perseverance and your strength. With your beauty and your independence. You are an incredible partner, and I know that I'm **the lucky one** in this relationship."

By this point, tears were streaming down my face. I couldn't believe how much effort he'd put into his speech, and I was barely holding it together.

A camera flashed nearby. I jolted, my eyes darting to the source. Afraid of who I might find—a paparazzo?

Instead, the woman taking photos smiled and wiped away tears of her own. Nate gave my hand a squeeze, pulling my attention back to him. I relaxed, knowing that whoever she was, Nate trusted her.

"So, **long story short**, **this is me trying** to convince you to **stay**. Because I love you, and you're **the 1** that I want to spend **forever & always** with. Emerson, **you belong with me**. And Brooklyn and I belong with you."

My smile must have split my face, both from his words and the way he was looking at me. I'd never felt more loved or desired than I did when I was with Nate.

"I just have one *question?*" He knelt to the ground and opened the little red box to reveal my red diamond engagement ring. "Will you stay with me *evermore?* Will you marry me?"

I sank to my knees, completely overwhelmed with love for this incredible man. "Yes." I kissed him. "Yes. I love you, Nate. Forever and always." I cupped his cheeks. "And I'm the lucky one."

He smiled, sliding the ring back on to my finger. Back where it belonged. "Thank fuck."

He pulled me into his arms, claiming me with a sweet kiss filled with emotion. After all that we'd been through, after all that we'd overcome, I couldn't believe where we'd ended up. And yet, it made perfect sense.

He pulled back and wiped away my tears, his blue eyes searing in their intensity. "You're so beautiful."

I smiled and ducked my head. He stood and then offered me his hand, pulling me up with him. He tucked me into his side. We couldn't stop touching or kissing or smiling.

He leaned in, whispering, "I can't wait to have sex with my fiancée."

"Mm." I grinned. "I like the sound of that. This is incredible, by the way." I glanced around, trying to take it all in. To freeze this memory in my mind forever, just as I'd done every time I'd stepped on the medal stand to accept my Olympic gold medals. "When did you have time to do all this?"

"I had a little help." He winked.

"Juliana?" I guessed.

"Yep."

"If tonight was any indication, I can't wait to see what she does for our wedding."

"About that…" He tangled his fingers with mine. "I was thinking maybe the Huxley Grand in Marrakesh."

I stilled. "You were?"

He lifted a shoulder. "Why not?"

"I thought you'd want something smaller and more intimate."

"I want whatever you want. And I have a feeling the Huxley Grand Marrakesh is what you want. It's grand yet warm. Luxurious without feeling stuffy. Sumptuous…"

"Mm." I narrowed my eyes at him. "And this feeling wouldn't happen to come from a tip from a little Jay bird, would it?" I teased.

He smirked. "Maybe."

I laughed. "I don't know whether to be touched or disturbed."

"Disturbed?" He jerked his head back. "Why?"

"Because it's not the first time you've used your little network of spies to find out what I want. Kendall and the Birkin, and now Jay."

He muttered something that sounded a lot like, "You have no idea."

"Who was the photographer tonight?" I asked, only then noticing that she'd slipped out discreetly.

"Harper. She does some consulting work as a film location scout for Rain Shadow Productions."

"Ah." I tilted my head back. "So that's how you know her."

"She also happens to be best friends with Juliana. And her husband, Enzo, used to play for the Leatherbacks."

"Holy shit. She's married to Lorenzo Mancini?"

That gave me a whole new appreciation for Harper. If anyone could respect the need for privacy, it was the wife of an international soccer superstar. Plus, I assumed Nate had made her sign an NDA.

Nate frowned. "Yes. You know Enzo?"

"I know *of* him. He's a legend. Kendall was obsessed with him when he played."

Nate flashed me a wry grin as he tucked my hair behind my ear. "I can't wait to mention that to Knox."

I laughed. "Nah. Kendall only has eyes for him."

And then it hit me. Kendall and I were marrying brothers. For real. I started crying again, happy tears.

"What is it?" Nate asked, using his thumbs to swipe away my tears.

"Gah! I wish I could call Kendall and tell her we're engaged, but she already thinks we are, so it takes the fun out of it. Wait…" I stilled. "Was she in on this?"

Nate chuckled, tucking my hair behind my ear. "Only the fact that I wanted to surprise you, not that I was proposing. I'm sorry I ruined your telling her for real." He kissed my neck, peeling aside my dress to kiss my shoulder. "And yes, she helped."

"Mm." I hummed as he continued his assault on my senses.

"If it were up to me, I would've done something lavish and elaborate. But since the world already believes we're engaged, I had to be careful."

"Are you kidding?" I faced him. "Nate, this is exactly what I would've wanted. It's romantic and intimate, and the way you incorporated the song titles into your speech…" I scanned his face, wondering how I'd gotten so lucky. "It was better than my *wildest dreams*."

He smiled, perhaps appreciating my own nod to his speech. "Good." He swept me into his arms, carrying me toward the house.

"What are you doing?" I laughed, looping my arms around his neck.

"Taking my fiancée to bed."

"What about all the candles?" I asked, peering over his shoulder. They were beautiful, but I was afraid they'd start a fire.

"Juliana's team will take care of it."

He carried me to the bedroom then tossed me on the bed. I bounced a little, laughing as I did so. But instead of joining me, he dragged a hand through his hair, closing his eyes briefly and inhaling slowly.

"Hey," I asked. "You okay?"

When he turned to me, his smile was watery. "I'm just so fucking happy. So fucking relieved."

"About the custody hearing?"

"That, and the fact that I worried you might say no."

"Seriously?" I furrowed my brow. "I would never say no to us."

He crawled over the bed to me, bracing himself on his arms above me. His gaze was so intense, in that moment, it felt as if I could see to his very soul. "I don't know what I would've done if you had. I can't imagine a life without you."

I grabbed his shirt and pulled him down to me for a kiss. "Luckily, you don't have to."

He chuckled. "True. Because it would suck to have my new tattoo removed so soon after getting it."

"Tattoo?" I asked. "What tattoo?" What the hell was he talking about?

He claimed my mouth, his hands roaming my body. I stripped off his shirt, eager to feel his skin. To have nothing between us.

And then I saw it. Right there on the inside of Nate's forearm in a small handwritten font was a tattoo.

(EM'S VERSION)

I GASPED, RUNNING MY FINGERS OVER HIS SKIN. "YOU *DIDN'T*."

"I *did*." He grinned. "You like?"

"I love it. I can't believe… I can't believe you did this." He'd proclaimed his love where anyone could see it. And he'd done it by showing everyone that I owned him. Owned his heart.

"Good." He kissed me like I was his everything, and I kissed him back just as passionately. Nate was everything I'd ever wanted—him and Brooklyn. He was a partner in every sense of the word, and I couldn't imagine spending my life with anyone else.

He flipped us so that I was lying on my back, and I watched as he lined himself up with my entrance. He paused, silently checking in with me. We'd never had sex without a condom, and I loved that he wanted my explicit consent.

I nodded, more than eager to feel him inside me. To become one.

"I love you," he said, thrusting into me.

I couldn't form a response, the sensation of being filled by him was so intense. The way our bodies joined. The love we had for each other.

"I love you." He kissed my temple. My cheek.

I pulled him closer, wrapping my legs around his waist, needing as much of his skin touching me as humanly possible.

"I love you." He rested his forehead against mine, our noses brushing.

"I love you." I peered into his eyes, knowing that he was meant for me. Just as I was meant for him and Brooklyn. We were a family. "Forever and always," I said, echoing his proposal.

"Forever and always," he said, claiming my lips as he claimed my body.

I was filled with relief, joy, exaltation. It was the end of one chapter and the beginning of another.

His thrusts came harder and faster as he reached between

us to rub my clit. I cried out from the intensity of it. The flood of sensations.

"Oh god," he moaned. "Emerson."

Our movements were more frantic. Our breathing ragged. All our feelings laid bare. There were no more lies. No more doubts. There was only us.

I felt...liberated.

My toes curled, my muscles tensing. And then my body took over, riding my pleasure higher and higher until it exploded. Until I called his name in ecstasy and stars burst behind my eyes. It felt like the high of a good workout. A race won. All the best things in the world.

Nate followed behind, grunting out his release until we were both sweating and spent.

After we'd showered and climbed back into bed together, he held up my left hand, and together, we admired my ring. "Do you know why I selected a red diamond for your engagement ring?"

"I always figured it was because it was rare and expensive —a statement. But I secretly told myself it was because you know I love the color red."

"That's part of it. Red diamonds are so rare, there're less than thirty true red diamonds in existence."

My jaw dropped, and I stared at my engagement ring with even greater appreciation.

"And as you know, this diamond was part of my mother's collection." His voice rumbled over me, his chest warm beneath my skin. "She always said to find a woman who was like a red diamond. Incredibly rare and able to withstand intense pressure." He took a deep breath. "You're the woman she envisioned for me. You're the only woman worthy of this ring."

"She...what?" I asked, propping myself up on his chest to look at him. His eyes were full of such love and devotion that it overwhelmed me. Oh my god. I was going to start crying all over again.

He nodded, a smile on his face as he tucked my hair behind my ear. "She would've loved you, and she would've loved for you to wear this ring."

"Well, I love her jewelry, and I'm honored that you've shared that part of her with me."

He flashed me a mischievous smile. "Wait until you see the vault."

I jerked my head back. "What the hell is 'the vault'? Nate Crawford, have you been holding out on me?" I teased.

He stood, pulling on some boxer briefs before holding out his hand. "Come 'ere." He grabbed my wrist and gave a gentle tug. "Come on."

I wrapped his shirt around me and followed him to his closet. He pressed a button, and it revealed a keypad that had been so seamlessly integrated into the wall, I would've never noticed it. He typed in a code, and then I could hear the barrels clicking into place like a vault in an old bank-robbery movie. The door opened, and the lights in the room automatically turned on.

I followed him inside. "What *is* this place?"

"There's a panic room that way." He indicated to a door. Inside was a mini kitchen, couches, and a TV.

"I thought…" I tilted my head. "I thought the panic room was in the gym."

"It is, but that's mostly for staff or as a backup to this one," he said.

"Wow." I nodded slowly. "Two panic rooms." That was concerning. "Have you ever had to use them?"

"Only once," he said. "It was a false alarm. But Jackson doesn't like to leave anything to chance."

I nodded. I'd seen how thorough Jackson and the team from Hudson Security were. They guarded this place like

Fort Knox, even if they were excellent at keeping a low profile.

"And this—" Nate opened the second door "—is the vault."

The shelves were covered in black velvet, necklaces and bracelets and rings and even tiaras on display. All glittering beneath the spotlights that illuminated them. It was like an art gallery for rare gems. A treasure trove. It had been here all this time, and I'd never had a clue.

I walked over to one of the necklaces, afraid to even touch it. Rows and rows of diamonds. And that was just *one* necklace. One of many. Beneath them were even more drawers of jewels and gems. All of the highest quality.

And... *Holy shit.* I couldn't even fathom how much this was worth. Assuming there were other pieces like the Marie Antoinette necklace—priceless seemed like such an inadequate term.

"Knox has a few pieces, but I got the bulk of her collection. I'm saving some of them for Brooklyn." He smiled. "But my mom would've wanted these pieces to be enjoyed. *I* want them to be enjoyed by someone who appreciates them. By you."

I stopped when I came to a framed picture. It was of a woman and a little boy, who had to be Nate. He was sitting on her lap, and she had her arms draped around him. Her wrist was covered in diamond bracelets, and they both wore the biggest smiles.

Nate came up behind me, pulling me into his chest. "I wish she could've met you and Brooklyn."

"So do I," I said, setting the frame back down and turning in his arms. I wrapped my arms around his neck, playing with the hair at his nape. "Any other hidden passages or secrets you need to tell me about?" I teased.

He considered it a moment then said, "I love you."

I laughed. "That's not a secret." I kissed him. "And I love you too."

"Mm?" He swayed us from side to side. "I can't wait to marry you."

I pressed my lips to his. "Neither can I. But…"

"But what?" he asked.

"I guess I'm just surprised. I had resigned myself to the fact that you might never want to marry, and I'm still trying to wrap my head around this change of heart."

"Em—" He clasped my hands and placed them over his heart. "Haven't you realized by now that I would give you anything?"

"I—" I shook my head, stunned. "Yeah. I mean, yes. But I don't want you to marry me because you think it's what I want. I want it to be something we agree to. Something we both desire."

"I wouldn't have proposed if I didn't want you to be my wife."

I was afraid to ask, but I couldn't hold back. Not now. Not after all we'd been through. "And kids?"

He lifted a shoulder. "If you want to grow our family someday, I'm open to it."

Open to it? I'd never expected him to say those words.

I was still stuck on that when he backed away, looking through the drawers until he found whatever he'd been searching for. "Face the mirror," he said. I turned, and he draped a large, multistrand diamond-and-sapphire necklace over my chest.

My nipples immediately pebbled, and he dragged the stones up my chest in such an erotic way. Goose bumps broke out along my skin, and he pressed his hips into me, letting me feel his desire. He secured the clasp, then smoothed his hands over my shoulders.

"It suits you."

"It's beautiful," I said, delicately fingering the necklace. The setting was an older style. Something that looked like it had once belonged to a monarch.

"And this," he said, adding a few bracelets. A ring to my right hand. A tiara. A *real* tiara.

"What a set," I breathed. "Incredible."

"It's called a *parure*. A matched set of pieces intended to be worn together. The word comes from the French verb *parer*, which means 'to adorn.' And it once belonged to the Queen of Sweden."

Holy...

I would've felt like a girl playing dress-up, but it was all real. And his touch was so tantalizing.

He slid the shirt from my shoulders, leaving me naked, apart from all the gems adorning my skin. The weight of them was heavy, but it was nothing compared to the way Nate was looking at me.

He met my gaze in the mirror as he slid his hand down my stomach, teasing my clit. "You are exquisite. Everything about you is."

I was already so aroused, I thought I might come from that alone. I released a shaky exhale, wanting to touch him. Kiss him. But he kept me locked in place, his touch making it impossible to move.

I moaned, my legs starting to wobble.

"That's it, Em." He kissed my shoulder, and it sent sparks dancing over my skin.

We were electric. And Nate made me feel as if I was *everything* to him.

I was so close to coming that when he pulled away, I whimpered. He smirked, inciting my ire. At least until he kneeled before me, lifting my thigh and draping it over his shoulder.

Oh thank god. I let out the breath I'd been holding. As

much as I loved the way Nate edged me, I wasn't in the mood to be teased tonight.

Fortunately, he didn't seem to be either. He licked and sucked my clit with intensity and focus, adding one finger and then two, until my legs were shaking and I was panting his name.

I grasped his shoulders, feeling as if I'd float away otherwise. My ring sparkled from its position, my heart racing at the reality that he was mine. I was his. And nothing would tear us apart.

"You are the most beautiful thing in here. And you are more priceless than all of these gems." And if my knees hadn't already been weak from what he'd just done, they were now.

He kept teasing me, his eyes intent on mine. Our hearts connected. His ministrations driving me higher and higher, until I couldn't take it anymore.

My body exploded, all my muscles tightening as my mind went to that hazy place where time and space ceased to exist. Where there was only sensation and feeling. *Love.* And bliss.

I smiled down at him, feeling dazed. He peered up at me, my arousal still painting his chin. Only then did he loosen his hold on me, gently setting my foot back on the floor. But it was going to take longer for me to come back down to earth.

CHAPTER TWENTY-EIGHT

Nate

Six months later

"Hey," Emerson said, rushing in the door. Pierce had just left, and I was still reeling from our conversation. "Sorry I'm late. I know we have a meeting with Juliana."

"It's fine." I stood and went to greet her, wrapping my arms around her. "She called to say she was running behind because of traffic."

"Oh good." She smiled, relaxing. "Hi."

"Hi." I grinned, kissing her.

Brooklyn was at Sophia's house, soaking up the last rays of summer vacation. They'd be starting back to school soon, and I couldn't believe my baby was going to be a teenager in a few months. *Teenager!*

"What's that look for?" Emerson asked.

"Just thinking about how Brooklyn is almost thirteen. And we'll be planning her party before we know it."

Emerson smiled—a smile filled with both pride and sadness. "Our baby's growing."

"We could have another one," I suggested. It wasn't the

first time. And while I knew Emerson wanted to have children, she'd been putting me off. What I didn't understand was why.

"We could," she said. "But I want to wait until after the wedding."

I groaned. At the rate our wedding planning was going, there was never going to be a wedding. The guest list was complicated. Security for an A-list party required elaborate planning. And I was over it. I got the feeling Emerson was too.

"I know," she sighed, resting her head on my chest. "Next spring feels so far away."

I inhaled her scent, filled with a sense of contentedness. "I know it's your dream to get married in the spring, but we could move it up."

"When?" she asked. "Our schedule is so hectic. Even just coordinating with our immediate family has been a nightmare. Everyone is so busy."

She was right. Knox and Kendall were running the Leatherbacks. And so was Jude, who was just as passionate about the team. Graham and Astrid were workaholics. Sloan was in London. Jasper was…well…Jasper. And Emerson's dads were just as busy. James oversaw a plastic surgery practice that was in high demand. And Declan had taken on some promising new athletes to coach. Sometimes, it felt impossible to get everyone together all at once.

"What about Christmas?" I asked.

She pulled back to look at me. "What about it?"

"We could have a surprise Christmas wedding. Invite everyone to the cabin at Bear Creek. Not tell them it was for our wedding, but have them bring dressy clothes for a holiday party."

Emerson seemed to be considering it, but then she shook her head. "I don't know. A surprise wedding? I mean, how is

Juliana going to feel? She's put in so much hard work already."

"We'll pay her more." The fuck if I cared about the money. This was Emerson we were talking about. "This is whatever *we* want. She knows that, Em. She wants us to be happy, and we are paying well for her services."

"I know," she said. "I do. But…it's just not what I'd envisioned. And changing everything at the last minute seems like even more work. I mean, you've got the movie premiere and awards shows. And I've got," she sighed. Paused. "I've got a new product rollout for my athleisure line."

She'd accomplished her dream of designing an inclusive and adaptive athleisure line. Enzo Mancini, the retired soccer superstar from the LA Leatherbacks, and Harrison Hayes, Juliana's husband and a retired NFL player, had both invested in her vision. And all of Emerson's hard work was paying off.

In addition to her clothing line, she continued to volunteer with Girls RUN the World. Brooklyn often went with her, and I loved that my daughter had gotten so involved with such a worthy organization.

Emerson had taught two more Peloton classes. And she'd been hired as a mental strength coach by three of LA's biggest pro sports teams—the Hollywood Heatwaves football team, the Hollywood Hawks hockey team, and the LA Leatherbacks soccer team.

"Plus, December is one of the most important times of the season for the Heatwaves and the Leatherbacks," she said.

I couldn't be prouder of her, and I knew that she felt fulfilled in her new role. The only drawback was the fact that she was constantly surrounded by athletic, attractive men. I tried not to get jealous; I really did.

"Yeah, but the Leatherbacks would be done with the MLS Cup by then."

"Still…" she hedged.

"I know," I said, gliding my hands up and down her arms. "I do. But sometimes it feels as if we're letting everything else come first."

She frowned. "I didn't realize our wedding was that important to you."

I lifted her chin. "It's important to *you*." By default, it was important to me.

I slid my hand down Emerson's arms. "Just think about it. Okay?" I gave her hands a squeeze.

"Okay," she said, but I could tell she wasn't convinced.

"Did your meeting with Pierce go okay?" Emerson asked, heading for the kitchen. "I saw him on the way out."

I nodded. "Yeah. Well, it was…surprising."

"Surprising?" She tilted her head. "How so?"

"He— Well… Come see."

She refilled her water bottle and then came to the table.

"Is that…" Emerson stepped closer to inspect the piece. Frowned.

I nodded, staring down at the glittering gems. Something I'd thought I'd never see again. "The Marie Antoinette necklace."

She shook her head. "I find it hard to believe that Trinity would just decide to give it back all of a sudden."

I barked out a laugh. "No. She didn't. Well I'm not entirely sure how it went down. But Pierce delivered it and said he was returning it to its rightful owner."

"He didn't…" She lowered her voice. "He didn't steal it from her, did he?"

"No. Pierce likes to skirt the rules, but he wouldn't do that."

"So then…" She lifted her hands. "Where did it come from?"

"I have a hunch, but I'm not sure," I said, thinking back

to my earlier conversation with Graham and his indignation at the injustice of the situation. Still…what had he done?

Trinity had always refused my offer to pay her the necklace's estimated value. So, if anything, I had to guess that Graham had offered her something else. Or perhaps threatened something.

"Well, I'm glad you got it back. Trinity was wrong to ask for it in the first place."

I didn't want to talk about Trinity. She was no longer part of our lives, and she wouldn't be again unless Brooklyn chose to have a relationship with her.

"Does this mean she wants her parental rights back?" she asked.

I shook my head. "No. The documents were signed and finalized. She can never have those back."

Emerson's shoulders relaxed. "Good."

I nodded. I couldn't agree more.

"I want to talk to you about something," I said, getting to the point of my meeting with Pierce.

"That sounds ominous. And if it's about signing a prenup, I already told you I'm fine with it."

"I know," I said. "And I appreciate that. But that's not what this is about."

"Okay." She furrowed her brow. "What is it about, then?"

"I wanted to ask if you'd consider adopting Brooklyn."

Her eyes widened, and then they filled with tears. "Oh my god. You're serious?"

I nodded, smiling. "Yes, Em. It's what I want. And I know it's what Brooklyn wants too."

"Yes," she said. "Of course I want to adopt her. I'm—" She was so choked up, she could barely speak. "I'm so incredibly honored."

I held her to me, filled with love for this amazing woman.

I couldn't wait to make her my wife. And Brooklyn was going to be overjoyed.

"So you see…" I rubbed Emerson's back. "The sooner we get married, the sooner we can make that happen."

Not that we had to be married for her to adopt Brooklyn. As Pierce had told me, California had allowed adoptions in situations like ours. But I *wanted* to marry Emerson. I wanted it to be official. And I wanted her to be my wife.

The alarm chimed, alerting us that someone had pulled through the gate. Emerson straightened, and I wiped away her tears. "That will be Juliana."

She nodded, seeming lighter somehow. Emerson offered to get the door while I returned Marie Antoinette's necklace to its rightful place in the vault.

"Juliana, hey." I greeted her before taking the chair next to Emerson.

Andre delivered a charcuterie platter and sparkling water, and I thanked him.

Juliana pulled out her tablet and started tapping on the screen. "Why don't we work on finalizing the guest list?"

"Sure," Emerson said. "My dad had a few more people he wanted to add."

"Just remember that the venue caps us at three hundred guests before we have to change the location for the vows."

"I'm sure the owner can help us out," I joked because Graham was the owner.

"Unfortunately, it's a fire code situation. So, I'm not sure even the formidable Graham Mackenzie can do something about it."

If Graham could convince Trinity to give back the Marie Antoinette necklace, I had faith that he could do anything. But I didn't tell Juliana that. I was still too shocked to fully comprehend the fact that it was mine once more.

I draped my arm over the back of Emerson's chair. Juliana

continued talking, detailing the wedding plans. Emerson was quiet, and I wondered what she was thinking. At least until she asked, "What if we changed venues entirely?"

"To accommodate a larger guest list?" Juliana asked.

Emerson shook her head. "Smaller, actually. I know this is a lot to ask, but we're wondering if we could move the wedding up and change the location."

I placed my hand on her thigh. "Em, are you sure?"

She turned to me and smiled, cupping my cheek. "Yes." She kissed me. "You were right. We were letting everything else come first, and nothing is more important to me than our relationship. Our family."

"Em, that's not what I—"

She shook her head. "I know that's not what you meant. But this wedding is turning into something that's less about us as a couple and more about everyone else."

I nodded. That was exactly what I'd been trying to say. And exactly what we'd been trying to avoid from the start.

"What are you thinking?" Juliana asked, her tone showing no signs of exasperation despite our big request. She truly was the consummate professional.

"I have a cabin up in Bear Creek."

Emerson laughed. "He calls it a cabin, but it's a mansion in the woods."

Juliana laughed. "Okay. Do you have pictures?"

I pulled out my phone and showed her the ones from the real estate listing when Alexis had found it for me a few years ago.

"Oh yeah," Juliana said. "I remember this property. Alexis showed it to Harrison and me when we were looking at vacation homes. It was gorgeous, but we decided to keep renting until we find the perfect vacation home."

She skimmed through the photos. "Okay. Good kitchen—big enough for the caterer. Beautiful deck if the weather's nice enough to hold the ceremony outside. Or—" She gasped when she came to the image of the living room. "This view is stunning. And then you wouldn't have to stress about the weather. But if it snows…"

Emerson looked at me and smiled. "We'd look like we were getting married in a snow globe."

"It's a great venue, but you'd have to significantly cut your guest list."

"What if we invited only immediate family?" Emerson said. "Fifteen, maybe twenty, people tops."

"That would…" Juliana shook her head and stared at the screen again. "That would be a big cut. And the wedding would have a very different feel from what we've been planning. But it would be easy enough to execute, and it would definitely be intimate and special."

"That sounds more like us," Emerson said, smiling at me. She seemed more relaxed as well. I definitely was. "But what about the deposits and everything?"

I waved away her concern, but Juliana spoke first. "Some of them, we can get part back since it's still early. And the venue is so popular, they won't have issues rebooking. The bigger question is what the new timeline looks like."

"Well…" Emerson glanced at me, and I took her hand in mine. "We were thinking a surprise Christmas wedding."

Juliana's eyes lit up. "Yes. That sounds beautiful. And we could continue to let everyone believe you're having the big spring wedding."

"Yes," Emerson said. "Exactly."

"If that's what you want," Juliana said with confidence, "I can make it happen."

Emerson turned to me, and for the first time in months, she seemed excited about the wedding. "What do you think?"

"It would be beautiful, but it's up to you, Em." I lifted her hand to my mouth, placing a kiss on her wrist.

Our eyes met, and when she nodded, I didn't sense any hesitation. Only joy. "Let's do this."

Four Months Later

It was Christmas Eve, and everyone was at our Bear Creek home for the holidays. Declan, James, and Knox were drinking whiskey and talking by the fire. Sloan was admiring the decorations while trying to ignore Jackson. Jasper, Astrid, and Jude were talking about all the skiing they wanted to do while we were here. Brooklyn and Graham were playing chess by the fire with Prince Albert and Queen V at their feet. And Emerson was upstairs getting ready with Kendall—the only person we'd let in on our secret.

Graham passed me to refill his whiskey, and I placed a hand on his arm. "I know what you did. And thank you. I owe you one."

I still didn't know exactly *how* he'd done it, but I was convinced he was behind Trinity's unexpected decision to return the Marie Antoinette necklace. Blackmail, leverage, whatever it was, it had worked. And I hadn't heard a peep from Trinity since.

"I don't know what you're talking about." Graham stared ahead, stone-faced. "But you're welcome. And I'll be sure to take you up on that favor sometime."

Of course he would. I smirked, letting him go and joining the group by the fireplace.

When Emerson texted me, I clapped a hand on Declan's

shoulder. "Can you go upstairs? Emerson wanted your help with something."

"Sure," he said, setting down his drink and heading for the stairs just as Kendall rejoined us, flashing me a watery smile.

After a few minutes had passed, I gave Brooklyn the same message. Emerson and I had suspected that Brooklyn would be too excited to keep our surprise wedding to herself, but we'd wanted to let her in on the secret before everyone else. So this was the best solution we could devise.

"If everyone could please join me in the living room," Juliana said, gliding down the stairs. Conversation jerked to a halt.

She pushed open the double doors to the living room, where all the furniture had been removed for the ceremony. She'd been here preparing all day. I'd paid her extra, of course, since it was Christmas Eve. But she'd assured me it was no big deal since the wedding was so small and she was staying just a few miles away with friends.

Everyone stopped talking, a variety of confused expressions playing on their faces. I heard people whisper, "What's going on?" and "Do you know what's happening?"

But as soon as they entered the room, there was a collective gasp as the answer became clear. An aisle lined with chairs led to a floral arch Emerson was absolutely going to love. It was covered with evergreens and red roses and other seasonal flowers. And so many candles. It was so romantic, and I couldn't wait for her to see it. I couldn't wait to see *her*.

A pianist started playing the baby grand piano—all acoustic versions of Taylor Swift songs. It was intimate and perfect.

Graham frowned at me, as did most of the guests. "What's going on?"

"Surprise!" I said, moving to the front of the room where

Pierce stood, waiting to officiate the ceremony. "Emerson and I are getting married."

"Wait," Knox said, pausing mid-stride with his hand on Kendall's back. "What?" He turned to her. "Did you know about this?"

She lifted a shoulder, suppressing a smile. *"Maybe?"*

"We didn't want to wait until the spring. And we wanted something more private and intimate."

"Well…" James peered around, dabbing at the corner of his eye with a handkerchief. "This certainly fits the bill. It's stunning."

"Thank you," I said, relieved that he didn't appear upset by the change of plans. Of everyone, he'd been the most excited—and invested—in the big wedding. "Sorry to have kept you all in the dark, but we wanted it to be a surprise."

"It certainly is," Astrid muttered, loud enough for me to hear.

"If everyone can please take their seats," Juliana said, appearing in the doorway. "We're ready to start the ceremony."

Everyone did as Juliana had asked, and a hush fell over the room. I looked around, feeling a sense of rightness. Of peace and contentment and home.

I smiled and took my place beside Pierce. The fragrance of roses and evergreens perfumed the air, and I took a deep breath to center myself in this moment. To cement it in my mind.

The song changed, shifting to an acoustic version of "Snow on the Beach," and Brooklyn walked in holding a small bouquet. She'd changed into the dress we'd chosen for the wedding—a champagne color covered in sequins. She was already crying, and she looked so beautiful. I smiled, ignoring the sting at the bridge of my nose while I waited at the altar for her to join me.

I pulled her into a hug, kissing the top of her head. "You look beautiful."

"Thanks, Dad. Wait till you see Emmy," she whispered.

I smiled and straightened as the song changed again to "Today was a Fairytale." So far, that certainly was turning out to be true.

Emerson and Declan appeared at the threshold of the living room, and everyone turned to look at her. She was radiant. Her lace gown sculpted to her athletic body, dipping low on her chest before flaring out at her knees.

She wore a gorgeous ruby necklace and earrings from my mother's collection. It complemented the style of her dress and her engagement ring. And I couldn't wait to slide her wedding band on her finger.

I drank in the sight of Emerson walking down the aisle toward me, a huge smile on her face. A tear snaked its way down her cheek, and she quickly wiped it away.

Declan stopped when they reached me. Pierce waited a beat before saying, "A marriage is nurtured by love, support, and mutual respect. And it is bolstered by the love and support of the couple's family and friends. With this in mind, do you give your blessing?"

My eyes widened. Pierce hadn't talked about this with Emerson and me, but I knew she hadn't wanted to be "given away" using the traditional terms. That said, I had no idea how Declan would respond.

Even though it had taken him some time to warm up to me, Declan's and my relationship had come a long way the past few months. Sometimes we even worked out together, though he about killed me with his drills. And he adored Brooklyn.

After a tense beat, Declan said, "On behalf of those here today, and those who have gone before, I give our blessing."

I was incredibly touched by his obvious intent to include

my family—my parents and grandparents, especially—in his blessing and acceptance of our marriage.

Declan swiped away a tear as he placed Emerson's hand in mine. I thanked him, hoping he would know how much his words meant to me.

And then I placed my full attention back on my bride. My future wife.

I leaned in and whispered, "You look beautiful," to Emerson.

She was my rose, and I would've gone through everything I had and more just to be with her.

I nearly kissed her when Pierce cleared his throat. "I think we're getting a little ahead of ourselves."

Everyone chuckled, including me. And I kept Emerson's hands in mine as Pierce started his speech. I wouldn't have expected him to be as sentimental as he was, but it was fitting for the occasion.

We recited our vows. The entire time, I couldn't take my eyes off Emerson. She was breathtaking. And she looked so happy. I couldn't wait to spend the rest of my life with her.

When I looked closer at the dress, I realized that the lace flowers were roses. I loved that she'd woven something so significant to us into the dress she was wearing to marry me. I also couldn't wait to strip it off her and shower my wife with affection.

"Dad," Brooklyn gasped. "It's snowing."

Emerson turned to look outside, but my eyes never left her. She delighted in the snow, the fat flakes falling softly to the ground outside.

Emerson took a breath and then held out her hand to Brooklyn, inviting her to join our circle. I held Brooklyn's other hand in mine, completing the link.

"Brooklyn." Emerson smiled at Brooklyn.

Brooklyn tilted her head. We hadn't told her about this

part of the ceremony. About the vows Emerson wanted to make to my daughter as well.

"I'm marrying your dad today, but I also want to make some promises to you."

Brooklyn nodded, peering up at Emerson with such adoration, it made my chest ache. I'd been so happy when the adoption paperwork had been finalized last month—we all had. We'd had a big celebration in honor of it.

"I promise to always love and support you," Emerson said. "To encourage you and listen to you. To be there for you. In my heart, you are my child, and I will *always* love you." Emerson swiped away a tear. "Always," she said emphatically and in a low tone.

Brooklyn threw her arms around Emerson. "I love you too, Emmy."

By this point, nearly everyone was crying. After everything we'd been through—losing my parents at such a young age, Trinity's betrayal, her abandonment of Brooklyn—this happy ending was long overdue. I hugged both of them, filled with so much love and happiness.

Pierce cleared his throat. "I now pronounce you husband and wife. You may kiss."

I wrapped my arms around Emerson, bending her back in a dramatic bow. And then I kissed her deeply, passionately. Trying to convey all the love I had for this woman and all the hopes I had for our future.

Everyone cheered, Brooklyn loudest of all.

I'd always loved Christmas, and this was one I'd never forget. What Emerson had given Brooklyn and me was better than any gift I'd ever received. Encouragement. Trust. Love. Hope.

I smiled and grabbed Brooklyn's hand, and the three of us walked back down the aisle as a family. Because that's what we were.

Acknowledgements

This story, well...it did not turn out how I expected. And I. AM. OKAY. WITH. IT.

Seriously, every book I write is an adventure, and *Reputation* was no exception.

Nate and Emerson were both so strong-willed. So...set in what they wanted. And I loved seeing them come together for Brooklyn.

It took them a while to get there, but when they finally admitted their desire for each other it was... FIRE!

I loved writing their story, even if I felt blocked for a while. As an intuitive writer, I can't move forward if something feels "wrong." And so I was stuck for a while. Stuck and dealing with a lot of stuff in my personal life—mostly good. But it was a lot. There was a wedding for a close family member, multiple book signings, and my husband travelled A LOT for work last year. Sometimes my writing is my escape and helps me stay sane. And other times—like when everything else is chaos—it only adds fuel to that fire.

Thank you for going on this journey with me. I've been blown away by the response to *Reputation* from the moment you met Nate and Emerson in *Temptation* to the release of *Reputation*. And I am so so happy that so many of you love these characters as much as I do!

A HUGE thank you to all the readers who share your love for my stories. I could not do this without you.

Nor could I do this without my incredible team. Thank you to Angela for always being encouraging and supportive.

For helping me with all the details, so I can focus on the big picture.

A huge thank you to my beta readers. Thank you for making me a stronger writer, for offering your unique insight and advice. You each bring something different to the table, and I'm always amazed and impressed by your suggestions. I'm so incredibly honored to have you on my team!

Thank you, Jade. You make me a stronger writer, and you challenge me on pacing. You are so clever and always provide great insight. I'm so grateful for your friendship, and our long chats! This story wouldn't be the same without you. Fingers crossed we FINALLY get to meet IRL this year!

A huge thank you to Kristen for being such an amazing friend. I value your judgment and honesty, and I so appreciate your support. We've been through so much together, and I treasure your friendship and advice. Seriously, I cannot thank you enough for all that you do. You are my "hype girl." You always pump me up and make me feel fabulous.

JudyAnnLovesBooks, you are so freaking awesome. I appreciate your honesty and your opinion. Your details always make the story sparkle.

Thank you to Ellen, as always. Thank you for being so supportive and positive, for being a friend. And thank you for sharing your incredible eye for detail. Your comments are always priceless, and this book was no exception! I couldn't do it without you.

Thank you to Brit! I love writing strong, badass female main characters, and you help ensure that they live up to their potential. And that the men who dare to love them do too. I love our two-author support group. LOL I love our voice mail chats, and I can't wait to meet in person.

To my editor, Lisa with Silently Correcting Your Grammar. I so appreciate your attention to detail, and your patience with my questions. You always go above and beyond and this time was no exception. I value your insight and your friendship. Thank you for being honest and kind in your comments and for helping me see what was missing at the very end.

A huge shout out to all my fellow authors. Sometimes this job can feel so solitary, but I know you're all out there. And we're all cheering each other on.

A big thank you to the Hartley's Hustlers and my Sweethearts. You rock! I cannot possibly tell you how much your support means to me! I appreciate everything you do to promote my books and to encourage me throughout my writing journey.

Thank you to my husband for always encouraging me. For always supporting my dreams and believing in me. You are better than any book boyfriend I could ever imagine. You constantly build me up, and I couldn't ask for a better partner.

And to my daughter, for always putting a smile on my face. You are spirited and independent, and I wouldn't have it any other way. Dream big, my darling.

Thank you to my parents for always being so encouraging. For reading my books. For being my biggest fans!

Dear reader, if this list of people shows you anything, it's that dreams are often the effort of many. I'm grateful to have such an awesome team. And I'm honored that you've taken the time to read my words.

About the Author

Jenna Hartley is *USA Today* bestselling author who writes feel-good forbidden romance, much like her own real-life love story. She's known for writing strong women and swoon-worthy men, as well as blending panty-melting and heart-warming moments.

When she's not reading or writing romance, Jenna can be found tending to her growing indoor plant collection (pun intended), organizing, and hiking. She lives in Texas with her family and loves nothing more than a good book and good chocolate, except a dance party with her daughter.

www.authorjennahartley.com

Also by Jenna Hartley

Love in LA Series
Inevitable
Unexpected
Irresistible
Undeniable
Unpredictable
Irreplaceable

Alondra Valley Series
Feels Like Love
Love Like No Other
A Love Like That

Tempt Series
Temptation
Reputation

For the most current list of Jenna's titles, please visit her website www.authorjennahartley.com.

Or scan the QR code on the following page to be taken to her author page on Amazon.com

SCAN ME

Made in the USA
Monee, IL
03 January 2025

75878882R00214